GW01605564

Technicians of Death

by the same author

THE CONNECTOR
COUNTERSTRIKE ENTEBBE
DOOMSDAY CONTRACT

Tony Williamson

Technicians of Death

COLLINS
St James's Place, London
1978

William Collins Sons & Co Ltd
London · Glasgow · Sydney · Auckland
Toronto · Johannesburg

First published 1978

ISBN 0 00 222483 6
Set in Times
Made and Printed in Great Britain by
William Collins Sons & Co Ltd Glasgow

I would like to acknowledge the valuable assistance provided by the United States Navy on various aspects of the Guppy Class submarine.

My gratitude also to many people in Thailand and Burma who provided so much information on the heroin industry in the 'Golden Triangle', and would wish to remain anonymous.

My thanks to Jacques Bes, who introduced me to the Mon people and provided such memorable hospitality in his 'Floating House' on the River Kwai, and to the managers of 'The Oriental' in Bangkok.

May their Thailand survive.

For
Pratwang Kolkhuntoed

Chapter 1

'I wish to purchase a country,' said the Chinaman with an affable expression. 'Nothing too ostentatious, you understand. A relatively compact nation which is prosperous and reasonably secure.'

'Is that possible?' asked the Arab, his dark features strained and not a little bewildered.

'It has been done in the past. I see no reason why it cannot be done in the future.'

'But a country? I mean, what about the people? The government? The rest of the world?'

'There is always a way. People die, governments fall, the world sits by and contemplates its own vulnerability.'

The Arab moved uneasily in the solid teak chair, carved and lacquered a thousand years ago. Around him the room stood in lofty silence, its rich reds and golds curling in and out of each other in a fresco of opulence. Gilded columns rose from a pink marble floor to a vaulted ceiling upon which vivid murals depicted scenes from the legend of Harumi, Thailand's Monkey God. These in turn gazed down upon the huge replica of the thirteenth-century Jinarat Buddha, considered only second in potency to the famed Green Buddha. It was the kind of room that humbled the proud and reassured the weak, regarding all with a timeless arrogance.

'I do not understand why you discuss this matter with me,' said the Arab, diffidently.

'You are here on a mission,' the Chinaman replied. 'You are also Palestinian, which means that you know a great deal about the difficulties of finding a country you can call your own.'

'We have our struggles,' the Arab admitted. 'But how can that be of interest to you?'

The Chinaman gazed at him with a disappointed expression, then rose and moved to one of the series of windows which extended along the length of the room. They were narrow, latticed in teak, and looked out across terraces and patios to the teeming traffic on the Chao Phya River, Bangkok's busiest waterway. The extensive grounds of the villa presented a sharp contrast to the bustling river, a wild profusion of colour in which rare orchids vied with lotus and jasmine against stately palms and eccentric cacti. The effect was impressive, set as it was against the untidy skyline of the city, but any illusion of tranquillity was destroyed by the regular patrols of blue-suited guards, each of them carrying blunt-nosed Skorpion machine-pistols on short slings. They moved in well-disciplined pairs along the terraces and around the high walls topped with serpents' tongues in gilded iron. Others stood silently at the corners of the villa's main pavilion, their eyes constantly sweeping the grounds that sloped down to the river. In the five acres that surrounded the gilded magnificence of the villa, nothing moved without their knowledge and approval.

Inside the lofty room Chung Li turned from contemplating the river. He was uncertain of the course he should take and the knowledge angered him, although none of this showed in his impassive features. He was a slim man with still, dark eyes which at times appeared to be lidless, like a lizard in the sun. His skin was dry, a pale yellow, stretched tight over small bones. He could have been a hundred years old, or twenty, it was impossible to tell. He spoke finally in a reflective tone, the words whispering across the room like dry leaves.

'My country is finished. A year, perhaps two, and then Thailand will fall to the Maoists and the old ways will be destroyed forever.'

The Arab facing him across the room, trying hard to look sympathetic, was Arif Bassad. He had appeared in Bangkok almost a week ago, haunting the sleazy bars of the city's New Petchburi district and showing little taste or discrimination in the women he took back to his cheap hotel. His presence in the city would have gone unnoticed had he not begun to leave word in various clubs and bars that he was in the market for Splits, the base morphine compound which was refined into heroin. The fact that he wanted Splits, rather than heroin, identified him as a dealer with processing facilities. This in turn meant that Chung Li was automatically informed.

Chung, in spite of his gentle manner and impassive smile, was one of the most powerful men in Thailand's flourishing narcotics industry. For the past decade, and particularly since Laos and Cambodia had fallen to the communist forces, he had controlled South-East Asia's 'Golden Triangle' – an area of Burma and Laos along the Thai border which was responsible for some eighty per cent of the world's opium. It was Chung who set the price and conditions of trade, and until the American forces withdrew from Thailand in the spring of 1976, he had controlled all major shipments of narcotics out of the 'Golden Triangle' with the assistance of key personnel in the US forces and the CIA. As a result of this his influence had extended throughout the western hemisphere, though not as Chung Li. The world's narcotics syndicates knew him by a far more sinister name. The Scorpion.

Arif Bassad knew nothing of this, only that he was clearly in a most dangerous situation. He was a short, thickset man with a stubble around his chin that looked as though it couldn't make up its mind whether or not to become a beard. He had been picked up in a coffee bar that afternoon by two politely distant Thais and, after a token protest, had accompanied them to their car. At first he had felt elation, convinced that carefully dropped hints had borne fruit and all that remained was the customary haggling over price. Instead of being taken to some small back room in the city's Chinatown, he found himself in a totally different world of opulence and power. From the start the Chinaman knew far too much about him, and the implications of this filled him with dread.

The only security Bassad had ever known was the kind found in the ranks of the Popular Front for the Liberation of Palestine; the loyalty of despair that commits mind and body out of desperation rather than courage. His early years had been spent in a refugee camp on the border of Syria and the Lebanon, an existence of such mindless deprivation that he still awoke in the night, sobbing with fear and flailing at restless images in the dark. In later years the images had become stronger, as though time was on their side, and the shroud of hatred which held them at bay grew tattered, revealing fragments of hell.

At the age of fifteen he had been raiding Israeli villages, able at last to focus his hate and finding solace in the carnage of war. After that there had always been violence. The Israeli wars and the private wars in Jordan, Syria, and finally the Lebanon. Suffering and death were such commonplace events that he had long since ceased to marvel at his own survival, adopting instead the pragmatic view that ultimately his time would come and, in a way, its coming would bring relief.

Yet the relentless erosion of the Palestinian cause, the senseless slaughter of women and children in a hundred camps across the Middle East, filled him with despair. The Cause was drowning in its own blood and the agony of his people was being squandered on an uncaring world. It was the remorseless tide of these events which were tearing down the barriers in Arif's mind, raising ghosts, eroding resolve, and when the Cause lay in mangled ruins along the streets of Beirut he fled to Kuwait.

The PFLP was in disarray, most of its key people in hiding following the abortive operation in Uganda when the Israelis killed every Palestinian they found at Entebbe and began a systematic hunt for all those who had a part in it – from Carlos and Bouvier to Waddi Haddad and George Habash, the founders of the movement. All that Bassad could learn in Kuwait was that the Front was no longer active in Libya and the bases in Uganda had been disbanded, or eliminated by Idi Amin. Syria was actively fighting Arafat, and the Arab nations which had supplied funds without question for thirty years were suddenly finding excuses, instead of dollars.

The aftermath of Entebbe and Beirut was a harsh reappraisal of the aims of the Front, the admission that the techniques of isolation they had employed against Israel were beginning to be used against them. The struggle must be stepped up before the Cause itself was forgotten, but to achieve this funds were needed. With most of the commando units destroyed or badly mauled in the Lebanon there was little hope of direct action against institutions or governments, and the world's airlines were alert for hijack attempts. The answer had to be more subtle, but equally damaging. And so Arif Bassad had been sent to Bangkok.

'You disappoint me, Arif Bassad,' said the impassive Chinaman, making the smallest of gestures before continuing. 'I was not surprised to find you here, only that your people should choose a man so sadly lacking in imagination.'

A narrow door had opened at the end of the room and a slim Thai woman was entering with a tray containing goblets of wine.

'There is nothing left to fight for in the Lebanon and Israel is a lost cause,' Arif explained. 'I decided that if I could buy the base for heroin I could make enough money to go to South America.'

Arif noticed that the girl was remarkably beautiful with pale skin and jet black eyes. She placed the tray on the table beside them, bowing formally with steepled hands before stepping back. On the tray, beside the goblets, was a chocolate brown bar which the Arab recognized as morphine base. The Chinaman picked it up, gazing at it as though its purpose was a mystery to him, then placing it before the Palestinian.

'You understand about Split, then?' he asked softly.

Arif swallowed and managed a nod. 'It can be processed without difficulty.'

'By you?'

'Of course.'

'Splendid. You may tell me how it is done?'

Arif's hands were sweating again and he resisted the impulse to wipe them on his trousers. Chung was waiting, gazing at the woman with a politely distant smile.

'It would not be done by me.'

'Ah,' said Chung, as though this changed everything. 'So you lied about your knowledge?'

'I only wanted to buy a little.'

'Again you lie. In the bars you have been saying that you would buy it by the kilo. Many kilos.'

'They misunderstood. I can afford two, perhaps three kilos.'

Chung studied his fingertips until the Arab began to squirm in his chair.

'Let us say three kilos, then. You might purchase it for six thousand dollars and then you would have to smuggle it out, process it in the right equipment at exactly eighty-five degrees centigrade. By adding acetic acid you would produce the alkaloid diacetymorphine, better known as heroin. You would then mix it with lactose, three parts to one of heroin, giving you some twelve kilos. These in turn would be divided into twelve milligram bags worth, on the streets of America, approximately one million dollars a kilo.'

The Chinaman beamed at him, then added as an afterthought, 'Of course you would never get that far. At the least you would be in prison, at the most you would be dead.'

'I did not intend to try,' stammered Arif. 'I have a friend in Baghdad. He will take it from there.'

'Baghdad?' Chung looked interested. 'It occurs to me that recently a man called Carlos Ramirez was known to be in Baghdad. I think they also call him The Jackal.'

The Arab's mouth went dry and he quickly shook his head. 'I know nothing of Carlos. I am not connected with Carlos.'

'But you must be. He is part of your movement.'

Again Arif shook his head, more violently this time. 'No. He is with another front, a terror group. I have no connection with that kind of thing.'

Chung nodded impassively and gestured at the goblet of wine. 'Please drink. It is a sweet Thai wine which I am sure you will find agreeable.'

Arif took the cold metal goblet and sipped the wine, trying to hide the shaking of his hands.

'Let us consider another possibility,' continued Chung. 'Your movement is desperately in need of funds and, at present, short of friends. At the same time you have an extensive organization with links in Germany, through the Baader Meinhof, Holland through the Red Aid, and South America through the Tupamara. If you could arrange for a steady supply of heroin through, say, a sympathetic Arab country, you would soon be in a position to distribute throughout the western hemisphere.

'In short you would have a most lucrative sideline whilst satisfying your vendetta against the societies of Europe and North America. It would give you a new lever with which to tilt governments, more subtle than the bomb, more deadly than the sword. It is a plan of great vision, worthy of such a man as . . . Carlos himself.'

The Arab wiped his face with the back of his hand wondering why he was perspiring so much and how it was that the room seemed suddenly brighter. Even Chung's voice had grown louder, more resonant. Arif took another drink of the wine, savouring the delicate flavours which seemed to explode against his palate. He smiled at the Chinaman, unaccountably exhilarated. He was keenly aware of his purpose and mentally chided himself for briefly losing confidence.

'I cannot comment on such a possibility, Mr Chung because I am here to buy only small quantities. The plan you describe would require large resources and much money.'

'Indeed,' Chung agreed, watching him shrewdly. 'So let us take it a step further. To control heroin traffic in the West you would need a list of every major distributor and the amounts they were able to handle. Only one organization has a complete list, and the family which is responsible for narcotics resides in San Francisco. It would be naïve of me not to believe that you have plans to obtain that list.'

The Arab laughed, only mildly astonished at his sudden assurance. The Chinaman was a fool to believe that he had the slightest intention of betraying his own people. With an effort he controlled the laughter, sensing that it had become shrill, almost hysterical. The room seemed incredibly bright, as if the day had just begun when, in fact, it should almost be sunset. He glanced at the woman, wondering if she had noticed, and found her staring at him intently. He let his glance move over her with deliberate boldness, imagining how she would be in bed and knowing instinctively that she would be fantastic. She smiled, as though aware of the thought, and stepped towards him.

'We need to know all about your plans,' Chung was saying. 'It is important for us both.'

Arif was only dimly aware of the words. The woman had placed her hands on his face, caressing him with delicate fingers. He was conscious of exquisite sensations flowing through his body in tingling waves of pleasure. The room had become so bright that he was forced to close his eyes, but the golden light persisted, heightening his senses. The beat of his heart was a distant thunder, the pressure of the woman's hips against him indescribably sensual. He put his arms around her, feeling the small, firm buttocks writhe against his hands. Hair that smelled of jasmine fell across his face, then her mouth searched out his own, her tongue slipping between his lips and coiling there, assaulting his senses until his body arched and he moaned with an intensity of feeling. He knew he was going to ejaculate, sitting there in front of Chung, but with the thought was the realization that he was completely powerless to prevent it.

A hand pressed down into his groin and he thrust against it, gasping. And then he screamed as the hand gripped hard and pain seared through him with sickening intensity. It was a full minute before he could sit upright and gaze at the Chinaman with horrified eyes.

'There is no more time for games, Mr Bassad,' Chung said with a thin contempt. 'You will tell me what your instructions were and how you plan to carry them out.'

The Arab tried to focus, but the room seemed to be expanding until the Chinaman was a small figure in the distance, then contracting until the face before him was huge and terrifying. One moment he was conscious only of the man, the next of every colour and sound in the room. Beside him the woman was waiting, eager to begin again.

'I know nothing,' he said hoarsely.

The hand seemed to move in slow motion, but he could only watch with a sob of fear as it crawled between his legs. When it stopped there was a blinding, searing pain and the taste of vomit in his mouth.

'It is better that you answer,' Chung said, with polite concern. 'The drug you have been given has not yet reached its peak. When it does the experience may prove too much for you.'

The Arab wiped at the perspiration running down his face, the breath still shuddering from him. 'I am here to make contacts,' he said miserably. 'We are interested in the trade.'

'How much can you handle?'

Arif shrugged, out of his depth. 'I don't know. We have the people, but not the experience.'

'And your route?'

'Air cargo to Baghdad, then to Kuwait for processing. After that I don't know.' The delicate hand hovered before his face and he shuddered. 'I don't know. I swear it.'

'And the list?'

The Arab hesitated, then spoke rapidly as the Chinaman's face tightened, gleaming like old ivory. 'It was discussed. I think there are plans, but I don't know what they are.'

Chung nodded, rising to his feet. He seemed to tower above him in a golden room. 'Then we must find out. In the meantime you will get word to Carlos that he is needed here. I will not deal with minions.'

'Carlos! Such a thing is impossible.'

'Nothing is impossible, Bassad. You have contacts, a network which can reach him. You will provide me with the names and recognition codes of all your key people.'

The Arab's eyes were small beads of fear. The room pulsed around him, objects changing into shimmering creatures that defied comprehension, and as the drug took him to new heights of sensitivity the light became shifting planes of colour that shook the mind. In another world he heard his voice replying to the Chinaman.

'You don't know what you ask. To do such a thing would be to betray the Fedayeen. I would be as nothing.'

Chung gazed at him with pity. 'But you are nothing, Arif Bassad. I ask only what is mine to have.'

The woman moved closer, stroking him gently with butterfly wings, and each place she touched became a thousand tingling chords. A fragment of himself stood by and watched in horror as his body responded, the arms clutching her to him, the mouth sucking greedily on hers. Even though the mind was aware of what must follow, the body paid no heed and thrust urgently at the hands which pulled clothes away, moved on burning skin, circled and caressed the centre of his need.

The Chinaman went across the room and through a door which opened on to the terrace. Two guards closed in beside him, but he ignored their presence. The sky hung over the city like melting wax, waiting for the night. It was a scene that normally soothed the mind, but this evening the humid atmosphere was reflecting the dying sun so that as he watched a crimson pall appeared, as though the city itself was in flames. It was a depressing reminder that one day the fire would no longer be an optical illusion, but reality as war scorched the earth the way it had in Laos and Vietnam.

It was an event that Chung had no intention of experiencing. Long before the tanks and rockets came he would have said his farewells to Thailand, taking with him the fortune he had amassed over the years and any other fortunes that happened to come his way. His thin mouth tightened into a contented smile. Pieces were beginning to fall into place, and there was yet time to achieve all his aims.

A gasping scream echoed along the terrace and he turned, cocking his head, listening to the sound like a man savouring the tone of a fragile bell. After a moment he nodded, satisfied with the degrees of pain and terror. It would not be long now.

Chapter 2

'So who do we hit?'

'The Dealer.'

'Dealer in what?'

'Shit.'

The American turned in the bed and gazed at the woman beside him for a moment before commenting dryly, 'You know, for a lady you've got a hell of a vocabulary.'

She laughed softly, then leaned over and teased him with her tongue. She was tall, dark and leggy with short hair she combed with her fingers. The tan of her body still gleamed with perspiration and her eyes were windows to nowhere.

'I'm talking about H, horse, snow, dream dust, shit, it's all the same. We're going to hit the man who calls the shots, Joe Farrazi.'

'You're out of your mind.' He rose from the bed and gazed down at her, no longer amused. 'He's got more muscle than King Kong. Nobody gets near Farrazi.'

'We do,' she said calmly. 'And all you have to worry about is driving the car.'

His name was Lee Corey and he had flown in from the East Coast a week ago with all the right credentials and the reputation of being one of the best wheel men around. He was tall, fair haired with a hard muscled frame and lean, alert features. He had an easy, uncomplicated smile, and clear blue eyes that had a disturbing habit of looking into, rather than at, those he observed. The FBI trace they had run on him had turned up an impressive list, from a diamond robbery in Copenhagen to a prison break in Utah, and he handled the powerful Dodge Charger as though he'd been driving the streets of San Francisco all his life. He also had an interesting way of livening up the afternoons.

Karen Brint smiled with the thought, her gaze moving over him with deliberate slowness. He ignored the look, crossing the motel room to stare out through venetian blinds at the river of traffic heading into the city. The light was fading and in the gathering gloom the glow of neon was beginning to rise in the sky.

'How many of us go in?' he asked finally.

'Six.'

'You mean those Arabs you've been meeting down the coast?'

'Questions make me nervous, Lee.'

She sat up and wrapped a sheet around her, lighting a cigarette and blowing smoke at the digital clock beside the bed. It blinked and became 6.20.

'We've got about an hour,' she said, making no attempt to conceal the hunger in her voice.

'It's the Arabs that bother me,' said Lee, as though he hadn't heard her. 'I was told this was big league stuff.'

'They're not just Arabs. They're Palestinians. Freedom fighters. The best.'

'But why?' he asked with a puzzled expression. 'You can put any team together in this part of the world. Any kind of team you want with guys even the fuzz don't want to play with.'

'It's not that kind of a hit,' she said sharply. 'You're in because we need a hot driver who knows how to cut up the traffic. Everyone else was picked a month ago.'

'If it's political I'm out!'

He turned on the words, his eyes no longer friendly. For the first time since she had met the American she was aware of the menace in him. The realization came as no surprise; some of the most charming and considerate men she had known had been proven killers. Carlos Ramirez had been such a man, a sensitive and passionate lover who never seemed far from laughter. Yet behind the mocking eyes was the mind of a predator, capable of killing without compunction. She smiled warily at Lee, her brief anger fading as she accepted the fact that he owed no allegiance to the Palestinian cause.

'You're impatient,' she said. 'Just relax, you'll know it all soon enough.'

'Soon enough is now. Either you lay it on me before your pals arrive, or you go find yourself another set of wheels.'

Her eyes took on an enamel sheen, reflecting everything she didn't want to see. 'Don't give me that shit, Corey. You pull out now and it won't be wheels you'll need, it'll be crutches!'

He reached over and took the cigarette from her fingers, blowing on the end until it glowed. When he reached across her to stub it out in the ashtray not a muscle moved in her face. He grinned and moved back to the window. Outside it had begun to rain with indifferent haste, like a leaking roof after a storm. Beside the bed the clock digitated and settled on 6.25.

'Farrazi has a book,' she said in a voice that grated with frustration. 'It lists the names of every major dealer and pusher in North America. We know it's in the house, locked in a safe that only Farrazi can open. If anyone else tries the contents will be incinerated.'

'And he's going to hand it over.'

She nodded. 'You don't know my people. They're technicians with a new set of rules and all the equipment. They'll have grenades and machine-pistols and by the time they get to Farrazi he'll think it's World War Three!'

'It won't make any difference. If he hands that book over he's a dead man.'

Karen nodded complacently. 'Sure he is. But this is Sunday. Family night. Sitting round his table will be his two sisters and their husbands. His mother and his brother. His wife and a fifteen-year-old daughter he'd cut off an arm and a leg for.'

Corey sighed and nodded. 'Maybe he will.'

'All you have to do is drive the car, Lee. Get us in and get us out.' She paused, her eyes searching him. 'And I wasn't joking about the crutches.'

'You did manage to get that point across.' He picked up his trousers and pulled them on, finding some satisfaction in the disappointment that turned down the corners of her mouth.

She glanced at the clock, then as he picked up his shirt gazed pointedly at the bed.

'It's not that late.'

'By the time you have a shower it will be.' He forced a smile. 'Maybe later we'll have something to celebrate.'

The irritation was still there, but she nodded and went into the bathroom. He waited until he heard the sound of water, then crossed to the bureau and tore a page from a notebook in his jacket. He wrote quickly, cramming words into cryptic sentences which began with: 'Blue Index, Code Four, Sight Only.'

Emptying a pack of Gauloises, he folded the sheet of paper and placed it inside together with one cigarette. He threw the others behind the bureau.

When Karen emerged from the bathroom she was brisk and efficient, pulling on dark slacks and a plaid shirt as she began to rattle off instructions.

'You checked the car out this morning?'

'It's in better condition than I am.'

'Gas?'

'Full tank.'

'Plates?'

He gave her a long cool look until she shrugged uncomfortably.

'I have to ask.'

'Sure you do. That's why you're paying me five grand. So you can go for a ride in a hot car with lousy brakes and freaky cylinders, then watch it run out of gas two blocks down the street.'

'Screw you, Corey,' she said emphatically.

'You just did.'

Her mouth relaxed and she touched his cheek lightly. 'This won't take long.'

'And then.'

She hesitated and made circles in the air. 'We go to ground. The others buy bus tickets and split.'

'And the list?'

Her eyes flicked at him, suddenly wary. 'You're making me nervous again, Lee.'

'So take a tranquillizer.'

She glanced at her watch, then picked up her handbag and moved to the door. He waited until she had it open and was beginning to tighten up, then strolled across to her.

'You said seven.'

'Bring the car, we'll have a drink on the way.'

He nodded and stepped out of the room to the pebbled courtyard that gave some semblance of style to the limp façade of the motel. The Dodge Charger was in the parking lot at the rear and he paused at the end of the line of faded pine cabins to take the crumpled pack of Gauloises from his pocket and fish out the last cigarette. Lighting it, he moved to the car, crumpling the pack casually in his hand and tossing it on the ground. The place appeared to be deserted and he knew it was a waste of time trying to locate his cover, but as he was pulling out of the parking lot a shadowy figure detached itself from the rear of the end cabin and began moving towards one of the cars.

Chapter 3

The blue phone bleeped in the tenth-floor office that looked out over Washington's Mall towards the brilliantly lit dome of the Capitol. It was 10.15 p.m. and the pastrami on rye had been cold for an hour beside the small, wiry figure of Max Weller.

He lifted the phone and grunted a monosyllable, continuing to read the overlong report from the office of the public prosecutor.

'We have a Code Four Blue Index,' said the voice.

The Director of FBI's C2 turned to the scramble box and considered the available channels. 'Scramble on Victor Nine,' he said crisply.

The phone squawked and he winced in annoyance, as he always did, then pressed the V9 selector.

'Origin?'

'Valley Lodge Motel, Frisco. It's sight only, agents Spencer and Dakin are the duty cover.'

'It's about time. Let's have it.'

'I hope you've got a sense of humour.'

Weller glared at the phone. 'I haven't had a good laugh since Richard Nixon's inaugural address! Talk!'

'Message reads: Target Farrazi. Hit team hot for shit list. Six Arabs plus one. Going for broke. ETA 20.00 hours. Leave window.'

Weller swivelled his chair and glowered at the city. So Corey had finally surfaced. After a week of silence they had the target. He closed his eyes and went over the message. Arabs meant it was political. Farrazi meant it was going to be heavy with no quarter from either side. He felt a brief glow of triumph. It was better than they'd hoped, and much bigger. If Corey could get hold of Farrazi's list they could hit every major centre from Aspen, Colorado to New York and Montreal.

'You got a make on that?' asked the voice, with barely concealed impatience.

'All I need,' replied Weller. 'Who is this?'

'Sneider. Bureau Chief, San Francisco east.'

'Okay, Sneider, you've got thirty minutes to pull in every available man. I want Farrazi's place sewn up tight. Use Q cars and move in after the raiders have entered the grounds. You got that?'

'Check. How about Farrazi? Do we tip him?'

'We don't owe Farrazi a thing, except maybe two hundred years in the pen. Let them play their string, then wind it up as they pull out.'

'What about your man?'

Weller smiled a thin smile. 'Don't get in his way. He'll be driving the car. Give him all the room he needs.'

After Sneider had rung off, the Director of C2 cancelled the scramble circuit and called the switchboard.

'Get me Purnell at the DEA,' he told the operator. 'If he's left, put a call in to his private number.'

He tried to get back into the case file, but the vacant prose that characterized the report finally defeated him. After five minutes the phone burped and he picked it up.

'Weller.'

'Hi, Max. What can I do for you that's cheap and legal?'

'How bad do you want Farrazi?'

Purnell whistled softly into the phone. 'I'm listening.'

'A group of politicals are about to hit him hard.'

'They'll need to. He goes to bed with two goons and a riot gun.'

'Any ideas why Palestinians might want his distribution list?'

The Director of Drug Enforcement Administration was silent for a moment. When he spoke his words were cautious. 'I might have. Our Paris bureau has been making noises. It's a hot potato, Max.'

'The big ones always are, Harry. What's the word?'

'A new connection. We're still running it down, but it's heavy traffic with politicals calling the shots: Baader Meinhof, Red Aid, PFLP, Black Panther. You name it and they're promising delivery.'

'How about the Triads in Amsterdam and London?'

'They're sitting on the fence waiting for the ball to bounce their way. Farrazi's network supplies them with horse in Frisco and coke on the Continent.'

'And Farrazi's list?'

Purnell paused briefly, then said with conviction. 'They can hit him as hard as they want, but that list is like the Holy Grail. Without it the families might as well go on relief. There's just no way Farrazi will hand it over.'

'But suppose he did? Where does that put them?'

'It puts them at the top of the league. They can supply every main dealer in the West, including the Triads. But that doesn't mean a thing unless they can deliver.'

'So somebody is pretty sure he can. Any names?'

'The only one I heard lately is Carlos Ramirez, but according to the Company boys he's locked up tight in Venezuela.'

'The CIA have been wrong before.'

'Sure they have. Look, Max, if there's some kamikaze squad going in for self-destruction the best we can hope for is that they take Farrazi along for the ride. The rest of it is fantasy time.'

'You fancy a side bet, Harry?'

'What have you got? A crystal ball?'

Weller smiled at the scepticism in Purnell's voice. 'Just a man on the inside. He's not given to exaggeration, and he's taking it all very seriously.'

'Who is it?'

'You know better than that, Harry,' he chided him gently. 'Just stay by that phone for an hour or so and think nice thoughts about Farrazi and his little black book.'

Weller put down the phone and swung his chair to face the window. In the street below a siren howled in the night, echoing along the Mall. For a moment at least the muggers would twitch and look over their shoulders, the hookers would lose their smiles and the pushers would mentally count their little plastic bags and wish they were some place else.

Chapter 4

'When the station-wagon hits the gate you start rolling. As soon as Faruq is through he'll get out of your way.'

'You're sure about that?' Lee asked cynically.

Karen gave him an irritable look. 'He knows exactly what to do.'

They were sitting in the Dodge Charger at the end of Tahoe Drive, an elegant tree-lined street where spacious villas sprawled discreetly behind Leylandii Firs and Blue Cedar. Half-way along the street a white stucco arch framed a wrought iron gate. Beyond it the drive wound through shrubs to a large, two-storey villa which was the home of Enrico Farrazi. A thin, cadaverous man in a blue pinstripe suit lounged by the gate picking his teeth with a broken match. His name was Felipe, The Ferret, Poletta and his only immediate concern was a piece of chicken which was stubbornly refusing to be dislodged from between his first and second bicuspids.

Felipe had a nose for trouble, hence his nickname 'the Ferret', and over the years he had survived through an instinctive awareness of imminent danger. On this occasion, however, his senses had been mellowed by his favourite meal of barbecue chicken and a bottle of wine. The night was warm and peaceful, and even the obstruction between his teeth was providing a mildly satisfying diversion. His sixth sense had failed to alert him to the shadowy presence of a powerful saloon at the end of the street, and the old delivery van which had rattled by a moment before did not merit anything more than a cursory glance.

He yawned contentedly, glancing at his watch and thinking of Lisa who would be waiting for him when he returned to the apartment. The thought produced a flood of erotic images which he savoured, turning them in his mind. It was a perfect relationship, satisfying as it did both his sexual appetite and his more mercenary nature. During the day Lisa carried out a lucrative trade as a hooker, immune from pimps and protection because of her formidable connections. Then at night she would titivate Felipe with accounts of her more kinky clients until passion transcended curiosity and he buried himself between her experienced thighs. The fact that there was rarely less than three hundred dollars on the table beside the bed never failed to make the experience all the more satisfying.

Felipe lit a black cheroot and blew smoke at the night. Along the street the delivery van was returning, its headlights sweeping across the gate. The Ferret watched it idly, secure in the knowledge that life was good and there would always be an endless supply of Lisas.

Whilst this was undoubtedly true, it was no longer of any consequence to Felipe Poletta. The headlights of the van were suddenly turning in, searing the eyes, and he didn't even hear the thud of the silencer before the nine-millimetre bullet smashed into his brain.

The group had met in a deserted parking lot in the city's commercial district, the Palestinians moving out of the shadows like a well-drilled team. Karen introduced them as they climbed into the car, a fact which they acknowledged with the briefest inclinations of the head.

The one who appeared to have some authority was called Haj Nasir, a man of medium height and build with a drooping moustache and small, unfriendly eyes. He arrived with a lean, swarthy man referred to simply as Hassan. He wore a badly fitting brown suit and was pure Palestinian, right down to his decayed teeth. Zaeed al-Hadja was tall, lethargic, with dark features and a v-shaped scar on his left cheek. The last one into the car was Kamal, a squat and surly character with nervous eyes and hands. He kept clicking the safety catch on and off the machine-pistol until Lee offered to hold it for him while he took a tranquillizer.

The clicking stopped as Kamal searched for a reply, but Zaeed was already leaning forward, his lips twisting into a mocking grin that did nothing to soften the edge of malice in his voice.

'We've got a clown. Karen tells us we've got a wheel, but he's a clown as well.'

Lee shrugged. 'So laugh a little.'

The Palestinian lifted the Mauser machine-pistol with its stubby silencer and tapped him gently on the shoulder. 'Take care, clown. Where we come from Americans are next in line to the Jews.'

'Well where you're going they shoot back!'

Zaeed's mouth became ugly and for a moment Lee thought that the menace which emanated from the group, as acrid and real as the smell of cordite, was going to erupt into violence. The German woman recognized the danger and slapped the Palestinian's gun aside.

'What the hell are you playing at!' she hissed. 'You think this is a game?'

Nasir spoke in Arabic from the shadows in the rear. She replied swiftly, her voice harsh and uncompromising.

Lee gave no indication that he could understand, aware that Zaeed was watching him intently. The conversation continued for some two minutes, during which time he managed to look bored, although he learned more about the operation than he had in the past week.

Nasir clearly resented the need to involve an American whose motives were mercenary, rather than political. Karen, with scathing contempt, reminded him that the entire operation was to enable the Black September movement to achieve a mercenary goal.

'My orders came from Kuwait,' she said savagely, 'and they are precise. We are to obtain Farrazi's list of distributors so that we can go into business. The shit business, Nasir. For money!'

'Funds,' he corrected her. 'The money is merely the means to an end. Without funds to buy weapons we are no more than straws on the back of the camel.'

'There are no camels here, and the reason I command is because I understand the American ways – including the ways of the police. Within minutes of hitting Farrazi this whole area will be sealed off – and it will take a man like Corey to get us out.'

Nasir sighed and made a small gesture to Zaeed. Reluctantly the Arab relaxed and Karen switched to English.

'Faruq and Ahmed will follow in the van?'

Nasir nodded. 'When we park in Tahoe Drive they will go to the far end, wait four minutes, then move on our signal.'

'My signal,' she said firmly. 'I will decide if the operation proceeds.'

Nasir's shrug was a study in contempt. He replied in Arabic, his eyes hooded, his voice a thin, dry whisper. 'We are all servants of the Cause, Fräulein, even though some of us seek power first and honour second.'

Karen's mouth had a glow of malice that cut a line across her face. 'I am here because I wish to be here,' she said sharply. 'You are here because there is nowhere else for you to go!'

They started to move slowly down the road as soon as the delivery van began to approach the entrance to Farrazi's villa. Lee kept the engine idling in third, teasing the clutch, rolling forward with only the sound of the wheels. Ahead of them the lights of the van suddenly swung inwards, illuminating the man beside the gate who immediately began to crumple to the ground, like an abandoned puppet, his arms and legs splaying out at impossible angles. It would have been curiously comical had it not been for the fact that he was so obviously dead.

The van went straight at the gate, hitting it squarely with engine roaring, smashing it open before lurching on up the drive towards the lights of the house. Corey was close behind, gunning the engine, swinging wide with squealing tyres as he went between the gates sagging now on shattered hinges. Ahead of them the van was slowing down, blowing clouds of steam from a fractured radiator.

'Get out of the way, you stupid bastard!' Karen said savagely, then with helpless anger: 'Why doesn't he pull over?'

Lee smiled mirthlessly. 'Some people are just natural road hogs.'

They swung round a bend in the drive, still behind the van, losing vital seconds that would soon be measured in bullets. The van finally stopped some five yards from the front door, hissing noisily. Even as Ahmed opened the cab door and lunged forward, two men were stepping out of the house. Light stabbed from their hands in stroboscopic flashes, stretching the Arab to his toes, turning him in a spasmodic pirouette until he was crashing into the side of the van before sliding slowly to the ground.

The images were sharp, but fleeting, as Corey braked and swung the car into a sliding turn, flicking off his lights. Cool air rushed in as three doors opened and the Palestinians lunged out into the night. He killed the engine and followed suit, hitting gravel and lifting his head in time to hear the steady thud of Nasir's machine-pistol.

There was movement to his left and he rose to one knee, the Walther PPK in his hand. It was Karen, her eyes fixed on the house. As he watched she rose and ran for the door. Lee followed more slowly, the conviction growing that Max Weller had failed to get his message, or even worse, had failed to act on it.

Beside the door two dark-suited men lay in widening pools of blood. Beyond them, in the lofty entrance hall, another man in a black tuxedo lay in a crumpled heap, his hand still bent inside his jacket, reaching for the gun he never found. Twin flights of stairs rose out of the hall to a gallery above, and as Lee entered Hassan was reaching the top of the stairs, swinging his Schmeisser to the right. He had guessed wrong. From his left there was the crack of a pistol and the Palestinian sprawled against the balustrade, trying desperately to turn even as the pistol cracked again. This time he slipped back, his weight taking him over the balustrade so that he fell with arms flailing weakly in space. As he hit the marble floor Faruq was reaching the top of the opposite stairs, stepping out and firing in one smooth motion. There was no answering shot from the pistol.

The dining-room had heavy oak doors with bronze handles. Nasir stood on one side, Zaeed on the other. Kamal, a Schmeisser in his hands, stepped forward and smashed his heel into the doors. They burst open, revealing a long dining table laid with crystal and silver. At the head of the table, facing the door, was a slim, grey-haired man who looked more like an accountant than the Mafia's chief narcotics distributor.

Beside him was a woman in her fifties with an ample figure and lined, tired features. She was trying to control the terror that was twisting the corner of her mouth, clutching the pretty young girl beside her. On the other side of the table sat a woman in her thirties, tall and dark, with eyes that gleamed arrogantly at the men in the doorway. Beside her was a man with black hair and frozen features, his hands placed carefully on the table before him, not a muscle moving. He looked fresh from the deep freeze, and when Farrazi spoke he gave no indication that he had even heard.

Watching him, almost with disbelief, was another woman in her thirties who bore such a strong resemblance to his wife that she could only be the sister. The man next to her was on his feet, fists clenched with impotent anger as Zaeed and Nasir stepped into the room, their weapons moving restlessly over the table. The final occupant was a grey, wrinkled woman in a black dress with a heavy diamond brooch at her throat. She was already unpinning this, and as Zaeed stepped towards Farrazi she threw it contemptuously along the table. It clattered among the crystal, drawing their gaze to its dazzling stones.

'Who you are is not important to me,' Farrazi said quietly, placing a white linen napkin on his plate. 'All that matters is that you listen, understand, and believe exactly what I say.'

He paused, his eyes moving from Zaeed to Nasir, then to Karen as she stepped into the room. The presence of a woman with a machine-pistol did not seem to surprise him at all.

'The fact that you have entered my home in the presence of my family can be forgotten. Everything that has happened will be forgotten the moment you leave this house, providing you leave now. If you refuse, if you make any further threat against us, then you are dead.'

He paused, his eyes burning at them. 'And not only you will die, but everyone who knows your names will die. Your mothers, sisters, brothers, wives and children. Do you understand me? We will spare no one.'

Karen laughed harshly and placed her pistol against the neck of the old woman. 'Then you will have to begin a war, Farrazi, because we are Palestinian and members of the Gaza Commandos. Maybe you should go to Israel and join the army.'

Farrazi's face went grey and the woman beside him began to sob. He patted her hand gently, then rose to his feet.

'Your business is with me, then. I suggest we leave my family and go to my study.'

'Sit down, you bastard,' Zaeed said. 'You move when you're told. You too,' he said to the man already standing.

'We have no time to play games, Farrazi,' Karen said. 'In thirty seconds we begin killing. The only way to stop us is by opening that special safe you have somewhere round here and giving us the book.'

Farrazi let the seconds tick by, then said quietly. 'What book?'

Karen swung her gun and pressed the trigger. The bullet hit the man who had been gazing her her with unconcealed fury. It smashed into his chest, jerking him back, then forward, so that he flopped across the table with bright, dead eyes.

The man facing him began to moan. His wife turned her head long enough to register contempt. At the head of the table Farrazi's wife was pulling the young girl against her, shielding her with her arms. Everyone else was very still except the old woman. She turned on Karen and stabbed a gnarled finger at the gun.

'If you're going to use that again, remember that you're closest to me.'

'Mama!' Farrazi said hoarsely. 'Please say nothing.'

'I want that book, Farrazi,' Karen said sharply. 'Don't make it worse.'

'You waste your bullets the way you waste your lives,' he said wearily. 'The book is not mine to give.'

Karen smiled a death's head smile and pulled the trigger. The terrified moaning of the man they had all stopped looking at became a horrified gasp, and then a sigh that expired before it crossed the room. The old woman considered the dead man with sad eyes, then reached across and placed her napkin over the head that now lolled limply to one side.

In the hall Corey watched the slaughter with revulsion. Faruq and Kamal had taken up positions on either side of the door, ready for any threat, and from their guarded glances they were clearly under orders to take no chances with him.

In the dining-room Farrazi's daughter had begun to cry hysterically. Karen had stepped up to the old woman and was holding the gun against her throat. She sat stiffly in her chair, gazing imperiously at her son, as though daring him to surrender because of her. Farrazi watched for a moment then shuddered and put his head in his hands.

'Enrico!' his mother said sharply. 'Don't look away from me now.'

He lifted gaunt features. The Mauser gave a soft thud, the impact making the woman twist to one side, then slide slowly to the floor.

'You are dead,' he whispered. 'You are a thousand times dead. All of you jackals will beg for oblivion. I swear it now!'

The gun fired again and the tall, elegant woman cried out in a bewildered voice, then slumped across the table. Farrazi stared at Karen, sickened by what he saw in her eyes.

'Kamal!' she said savagely. 'There is something you can do.'

Kamal stepped into the room, the gleam of perspiration giving his features an oily sheen, like a mask of somebody else's nightmare. He moved to the young girl as Karen, Zaeed and Nasir took up positions beside the remaining people at the table. Farrazi watched with horror in his eyes as the Palestinian swept crystal and china from the table, then threw the shivering girl across it. Her mother reached out, wailing in terror, but the gun at her throat stilled the protest.

With a single, savage movement Kamal ripped the dress from the girl's body, then dropped his hands to his trousers.

Farrazi moved. He rose like a dead man and began to walk towards the door. There were no words. None were needed. Karen signalled to Kamal and he stepped back, allowing the mother to pull the hysterical girl to her. Karen and Nasir followed Farrazi into the hall, across to a door which opened into the study. He moved to a bookcase and pressed a catch, swinging it aside. The safe was large with a digital combination panel. He tapped out a series of numbers, then placed his palm against a sensor screen. There was a hum of power, the clicking of circuits, then he stepped back and pulled the heavy steel door open. Inside, on the centre shelf, was a heavy ledger in a tray of magnesium. Wires led from the tray to a panel in the side of the safe.

Farrazi handed the book to Karen. She took it, then raised the gun in her hand. He waited, his face deathly pale but calm. After a moment she lowered the gun.

'Why should I save you the trouble, Farrazi? After today you're as dead as your mother.'

He nodded. 'Perhaps. But first I will find all of you.'

She shook her head, amused by his persistence. 'To get to me you have to kill a thousand Palestinians.'

She turned and left him in the study. In the hall Kamal and Zaeed were standing in the doorway to the dining-room. Zaeed looked at her, asking the question. She held up the book.

'Leave them. We have what we came for.'

Corey was waiting by the front door, controlling his revulsion with an effort as she came up to him, laughing exultantly.

'Let's go, wheel man. It's your turn now.'

They were stepping out of the door when the spotlights hit the house and the amplified voice shattered the night.

'This is the police. The house is surrounded. You have one minute to throw down your guns and come out with your hands behind your head.'

'The bastards!' Karen said. 'The fucking bastards!'

The vehicle closest to the door was the van, the body of Ahmed lying beside it. Kamal and Zaeed didn't waste a second. The voice was still echoing around the grounds when they were lunging out, firing towards the lights, then sprawling beneath it. The night exploded.

Faruq was crossing the hall, reloading the Schmeisser, when Farrazi stepped out of the study and shot him in the back. Before either Nasir or Karen could turn he was back under cover.

'You stupid cow,' Nasir said bitterly. 'You should have killed him.'

Karen turned to Corey who was pressed against the wall. Heavy calibre bullets were raking the doorway, splintering wood and exploding ragged holes in the elegant hall.

'Can we reach the car?'

'No way.'

She gave him a furious look, as though he was the one with the magic wand, then took a quick look out of the door. A dozen riot guns exploded in the shrubbery, cracking in the air above her head, blowing panels out of the door. She jerked back, her face white.

'We've got to reach it.'

'You want the keys, you can have them.'

She swung round, her mouth ugly with fear. 'Don't give me a hard time, Corey, or you'll be the first one out!'

From beneath the van Zaeed and Kamal were systematically shooting out the spotlights. The last one was in a tree near the bend in the drive, but even as the police raked the van with automatic fire it winked out.

'All right,' Karen said tersely. 'This is all that matters.' She waved the book. 'Nasir goes first, heading for the north side of the house. I go second running for the trees by the drive. As soon as we go you start for the car.'

She looked at them, waiting for an argument. Nasir's face was gaunt with the knowledge of his own impending death, but he nodded. Corey shrugged, wondering how long it would be before Farrazi took another shot at them from the study. In or out was no choice at all.

'Just as long as you know that once I'm in that car I don't wait for parking tickets!'

She nodded, her mouth tight. 'I'll be in the drive the minute you start the engine.'

There was a brief lull in the gunfire outside, then the click of the loudspeaker coming on.

'Now!' screamed Karen.

The voice that began to make some new proposal never got started. Gunfire erupted around the grounds as Nasir raced for the corner of the house, flicking bursts towards the shrubbery. He got half-way there before the figure stepped into view, the riot gun held steady. Nasir tried to swing his gun, knowing there was no more time. The Savage exploded and the Palestinian was picked up in mid-stride and flung against the side of the house. A Schmeisser chattered and bullets searched for the FBI man, but he was already back out of sight. Nasir coughed blood, cursing in Arabic, gazing back to the doorway as Corey lunged for the car.

The stake-out men were using Sharps and Savages, with at least two sub-machine-guns. Corey cursed under his breath as he ran. If Ferrazi had not been lurking in the hall with all the right motives for blowing a hole in him, he could have doubled back the moment Karen ran for the trees. As it was he could only run, hearing the bullets crack above his head, wondering if Weller had thought to tell the men that the tall, fair-haired guy with a friendly grin was on their side and should not be shot at under any circumstances.

A burst of nine millimetres exploded across the drive in front of him and he had the answer.

Dear old Max, always ready to put his last man on the firing line. Behind him a riot gun blasted open the petrol tank of the van and in seconds the vehicle was erupting into flames. The two Arabs beneath it scrambled out and began a suicidal run, emptying their guns at the shadowy figures in the darkness. A dozen weapons opened fire, cutting them down in a hail of bullets.

The diversion gave Corey the time he needed to reach the Dodge and get behind the wheel. He fumbled the key the first time, then it turned and the engine roared into life. The slim figure of Karen lurched out of the darkness, clutching her side. Somehow she managed to get the door open and fall into the seat beside him. The leather-bound book was still clutched in her hand, but her strength was running out of her in a glistening stream.

For a moment he debated switching off the engine and letting the men come for him, but the mood they were in tonight suggested they were more than likely to move in shooting. Karen made the decision for him, gesturing with the Mauser. She was weak, but dangerous, and with a squeal of tyres he spun the car and took off over the wide flat lawn.

Heading down the drive would be suicidal. They would have it blocked at the gate and at least one man posted with a riot gun. His only chance was to take them all by surprise and hope they hadn't blocked the street as well. The tyres had difficulty gripping the turf, but that was the least of his troubles. In the darkness ahead he was trying to gauge the thinnest point in the line of shrubbery. The trees stood out against the night sky and he could see a gap wide enough to take the car. At the last moment he switched on the lights, locked the wheel with his arms and slammed the accelerator down to the floor.

The Dodge leapt for the gap, smashing through shrubs, lunging over a rockery and hurtling at the wall. It seemed an age before they hit, and then bricks and plaster were flying in every direction as the impact smashed the decorative wall apart.

The car landed on the sidewalk with screaming tyres, going into a sliding skid on to the road. Lee corrected by instinct, using handbrake, clutch and accelerator with split-second timing. There were four cars grouped at the entrance to Farrazi's villa, but the road itself was clear. The relief washed through him as he went through the gears at full revs, flashing past the cars and the startled FBI man beside the driveway.

At the end of the street he turned south, reducing speed and cutting through side streets until he hit the access road to the skyway. He knew it would take the FBI team at least two minutes to sort themselves out, and if Weller was anywhere around he would know who was driving the Dodge and why. Traffic was light on the skyway and he quickly picked up speed, dropping down to the James Lich Freeway that carried him out of town on to Highway 101.

After fifteen minutes he was clear of the city and cruising through open country towards Redwood City. There had been no road blocks, not even as they passed the approaches to the airport. There was little doubt in his mind now that Max had called off his men, content to let him work it out his own way.

He pulled into a picnic area, parking behind a screen of bushes, then switched off the engine and considered Karen. She was barely conscious, her pulse so weak he had difficulty finding it. But the gun was still clutched grimly in her blood-stained hand, the heavy book beneath it on her lap.

Her eyes flickered open and she spoke in a husky whisper, like the sound of air from a spent balloon.

'You got us clear.'

'As far as Redwood.'

'You're fantastic. Head for Monterey, then use the phone.'

'I'll need a number.'

She nodded, her eyes closing as though sleep was only a breath away.

'I'll tell you when we're there.'

'Look, Karen,' he said carefully. 'Unless you get to hospital you won't be talking to anyone by the time I get to Monterey.'

'Drive, wheelman,' she said, the intensity returning briefly to her voice. 'I'm the only one who can make the call.'

He took the gun firmly from her hand and threw it in the back with the book. 'Not this time, Karen. If you want the book to get anywhere, you're going to have to tell me. Now.'

The anger put bright spots on her death-white features, but after a moment she nodded.

'All right. Two calls. One to Kuwait, the other to Bangkok.'

He waited, but she had drifted off again, her breath rustling like dead leaves in an empty room. He tried to staunch the flow of blood. The wound was a bad one, angling upwards from the lower left rib. The nearest hospital would be Redwood City, but in the battered car with a bloody passenger he would be arrested on sight.

'Who in Bangkok, Karen?' he said finally. 'What name?'

Her eyes flickered open, trying to focus on him. 'Scorpion.' she said weakly. 'Must speak to Scorpion.'

'And Kuwait?'

'Haj Falil Gadir. Only him. No one else.'

'What about Carlos? Where is he?'

Her eyes widened with astonishment, then anger put strength in her limbs and she clawed herself upright. 'What do you know about Carlos?'

Lee held her wrists as she struggled weakly. 'You're going to hospital, Karen. I need to know your contacts and your reasons.'

With blazing eyes she tried to strike at him and when that proved impossible she could only spit at his face, again and again. He let the rage burn out until she sagged limply against the seat.

'You bastard,' she whispered. 'You set us up. Oh you fucking bastard.'

The stillness came from within, relaxing her contorted features, dissolving the hatred in her eyes, the cruelty in her mouth. He checked her pulse, although he knew she was dead.

It was the first time since they met that he felt at ease beside her.

Chapter 5

'I've been doing some work on your obituary, Corey,' said Max Weller, his voice vibrating with pleasure. 'You could easily end up as the patron saint of Detroit. In fact, when you say "ten-four" they go on double time!'

'I didn't think we were allowed obituaries,' Lee replied. 'I assumed you just put us away in unmarked graves to preserve our cover . . . until you felt in the mood to resurrect us!'

Max allowed himself a ghost of a smile. 'For you it's more likely to be an unmarked car in a scrapyard somewhere. Have you any idea what our Q cars cost?'

Lee shook his head. 'I imagine we get a special rate.'

Max took on the intense expression of a man convinced he could levitate. 'Special! Corey, we pay a premium! Our cars go faster, break down less frequently and require fewer services than any ordinary car. They're supposed to last for years – not weeks!'

'Can I help it if they bend easily?'

Max choked on a handful of peanuts and Lee watched with thinly veiled enjoyment. They were cruising at 1300 miles per hour some 54,000 feet above the Atlantic. Around them the elegant cabin of the Air France Concorde hummed a supersonic song. The stewardesses, in their chic Air France uniforms, moved among the passengers with smiling efficiency. The one assigned to the forward section wore a small gold brooch which bore the name 'Yvette'. Although the name itself conjured up all the right images, it had the full back-up of slender legs, rounded hips and a derrière that had no right to be this high off the ground.

He watched it with a warm glow of appreciation until Max

had stopped spluttering and resumed the conversation in more normal tone, the one that always reminded Lee of chocolate-covered wasps.

'Automobiles are designed to be driven at reasonable speeds on strips of concrete built for that purpose. They're called highways!'

'You didn't like my detour?'

'Oh it was beautiful. You almost killed one man and put the fear of God into the bureau chief. He'd never seen anyone do sixty miles an hour through a rockery before, and when you hit the wall you ruined six months' work by his analyst. He had to walk home. Even this morning he can't talk about it.'

'Poor guy,' Lee said sympathetically, although he didn't believe a word of it. 'Next time I'm in Frisco I'll pay him a call.'

'He'd hit you,' Max assured him. 'I've never heard such venom in a man's voice when he asked me for your name.'

'He didn't mention in passing that his team were trying to kill me at the time. I mean, those guys were blasting away with elephant guns.'

Max gave him a look of contempt. 'We got your message, Corey. You asked for a window, right? We knew you were the wheelman, right? All you had to do was go down the drive and turn left.'

'Ah!' Lee winced. 'You mean it wasn't blocked?'

'You could have picked up coffee and sandwiches. Instead you turn a nice new automobile into something that would lower the tone of an east-side scrapyard. Every time I give you a car, Corey, I have sleepless nights. It's not the money.' He held up a beseeching hand. 'It's not even the tickets we have to fix, or all those hysterical citizens who see you driving on their roads as though it's the day before Doomsday. It's the department, Corey. It's the look on the face of the director when he gets the keys back. We have a budget, an allocation, but with you around the only way we can stay in business is to go out and steal some cars.'

Lee was admiring the stewardess again. She noticed and came over, looking like a woman who knew about all the things she liked, and was quite prepared to indulge herself from time to time.

'What would you like to drink, sir?' she asked.

'That's a good question. Normally I prefer a dry Martini, but at this speed and this height we could have separation problems.'

She took it very well. 'Perhaps shaken rather than stirred?'

'Not a bad idea. I don't suppose you're carrying any supersonic olives?'

'Just the normal sub-sonic variety, sir.'

Max stirred restlessly. 'Are you all through, Corey?'

Lee adopted a worried expression. 'It's my first Concorde. It's got to be right.'

'Maybe you'd rather have a beer?' Weller grated.

'Only if the specific gravity can stand Mach Two.' He looked hopefully at Yvette. 'You wouldn't be carrying a hydrometer by any chance?'

She shook her head, looking sad. 'I knew we'd forgotten something.'

Lee sighed regretfully, but it was drowned by Weller's snort of disgust.

'I'll have rye on the rocks,' he told her crisply, 'and he'll have Coke.'

'You should know better than that, Max,' Lee chided. 'They're not allowed to get the passengers *that* high!'

She tried to look disapproving, but her eyes were twinkling. 'Perhaps you ought to come to the bar and see if there's anything you'd like,' she said, allowing a perfectly sculptured eyebrow to underline all the right words. Lee beamed and started to rise from his seat.

'What a good idea.'

'Forget it, Corey,' said Max, tapping the briefcase beside him. 'We've got work to do.'

'In that case,' he said dejectedly, 'I'll settle for a Vodka Martini, shaken, with a twist of lime.'

She nodded, smiled, and flicked a resentful glance at Weller who was already opening the briefcase. Lee watched the derrière all the way to the bar – and she knew it.

He had caught the morning flight from San Francisco after a long telephone call to Washington. The in-flight movie was all about tough cops and twitchy crooks, so he unplugged his earphones and went to sleep. At Washington a VIP car was waiting to whisk him to the Concorde terminal, and fifteen minutes later they were lifting up over the capital and turning east. He passed the Farrazi ledger to Max as soon as he was on board. The Director of C2 held it reverently for a moment, then placed it in his briefcase.

It was still there as Max passed him three buff-coloured files in plastic pouches marked US Drug Enforcement Administration.

'You feel up to telling me why we're going to Paris,' Lee said, opening the first file and grimacing at the sheafs of closely typed pages. 'Or is it one of those proficiency tests where we have to work it out for ourselves?'

'I never over-rate my people. If you couldn't work out that we left the gate open at Farrazi's, you'll never come up with the answer to this one.'

'You're probably right,' Lee drawled, determined not to give him the satisfaction of working it out. 'Narcotics isn't my field, anyway.'

'We all know what your field is, Corey. But the Vice Squad's got all the men it needs!'

'You've got Farrazi's list, what more do you want?'

Max stabbed a finger at the files. 'Read. By the time we get to Paris I want you up to your eyeballs in . . .'

'Shit?' supplied Lee, dryly.

'Heroin will do,' Max said tersely. 'We've got a heavy session with the Narks, and there isn't that much time.'

He was still reading by the time the Concorde touched down at Charles-de Gaulle Airport. The files covered three areas, the processing, distribution and peddling of heroin. A good deal of the information was general and covered ground already familiar to Lee, but the analysis of current trends in Europe and America provided a fascinating insight into the motives behind the theft of Farrazi's list. Italy and France had been processing centres for morphine base for many years, but as Interpol isolated the traditional producers in Marseilles and Naples and began seizing large shipments worth millions of dollars, the factories were switched to Amsterdam. Chinese, controlling supplies in the Golden Triangle, began processing in Hong Kong or Taiwan and taking the initiative in Amsterdam. By the mid-seventies they controlled most of the production of pure heroin and virtually all the distribution of opium in the West.

The routes from Amsterdam were complex and hard to block. It was too easy to cross the Channel, or drive to Germany and Scandinavia. From there large consignments were shipped to Montreal and San Francisco. Intense diplomatic pressure on the Dutch began to yield results and in Amsterdam, a city noted for its liberal views on drugs, the police began to close in on the Chinese-dominated narcotics industry.

The Triads, as the Chinese thugs liked to be called, had emerged as a ruthless breed of criminal prepared to use extortion and murder as a base for their operations. In less than five years they had forged links with the close Chinese communities in a dozen major cities, and always the trail led back to Thailand. The dossier on this secret society made it clear that it was no more than a cover for a crooked Chinese syndicate, the leader of which was a man referred to as 'The Scorpion'. The name Triad was meant to invoke fear in the public at large, in particular the Chinese communities, and to cloak the criminal activities with more mysterious aims and motives.

The methods adopted by the Triads were crude and quickly attracted the attention of national police forces, and such international agencies as Interpol and the US Drug Enforcement Administration. By 1976 they were being forced out of Amsterdam, San Francisco and London's Soho, where a series of arrests and convictions had been executed by Britain's Scotland Yard.

In 1977 a vacuum had appeared to threaten the entire narcotics network. Production of heroin had retreated back to Hong Kong, apart from small mobile factories in Holland and Scandinavia. Even Aspen, Colorado, was under the magnifying glass as the trial of Claudine Longet exposed the less palatable vices of the jet set. Unless a new force could fill the gap, the drug pushers of the western world were going to find their lucrative trade dwindling, as more and more addicts found it impossible to obtain a fix and were forced to register themselves for government-controlled methadone programmes.

Lee finished the last file as the taxi turned off the Champs Elysées into Rue Boétie and stopped in front of a tall, grey building which was No. 58 and housed the US Drug Enforcement

Administration in Paris.

'You think you can hold your own now?' Max asked, putting the files into his briefcase and getting out of the taxi.

Lee paid the driver and followed him into the building. 'I know a bit more than I did this morning, but these guys are main liners . . . and I don't think they're going to fall about with enthusiasm if the bureau starts trespassing.'

'Perish the thought,' said Max with an innocent expression. 'In the first place we're holding the aces. And in the second, this meeting was their idea.'

'That's what I was afraid of,' Lee replied, convinced that Max had him set up for something very special. 'Just don't get too carried away with my expendability!'

Max's chuckle lasted all the way to the fifth floor.

Chapter 6

The Regional Director of the Drug Enforcement Administration was Maurice Gauthier, a short, dapper man in an impeccably tailored suit as grey as his carefully groomed hair. He had the kind of smile cultivated by diplomats and con men, capable of covering any occasion short of a funeral. Beside him in the large, air-conditioned office which looked across green and grey rooftops to the Arc de Triomphe, was a man in complete contrast. He was short, thickset with wrinkled features and hair. He was introduced as Uri Lasser and the darker pigmentation of his skin indicated that he began life somewhere in the Mediterranean, almost certainly Israel, although Lee resisted the temptation to inquire.

'We don't have a lot of time,' Gauthier announced as soon as they had taken seats, 'so I suggest that we go right into the briefing.'

'You're the second one to say that,' Lee murmured, giving them an encouraging smile. 'But I don't mind a recap.'

Gauthier shot Max an irritable look. The Director of C2 cracked a knuckle and made grating noises in his throat, as though his larynx was changing gear.

'There's a great deal to do,' said Gauthier. 'If we don't act quickly we could lose the initiative.'

'That would be a pity,' Lee agreed dryly. 'But all I've read so far is a lot of statistics about junk and a lot of ideas about where it's going to and coming from.'

'That aspect of our operations won't concern you, Corey,' Gauthier said testily. 'It's the plan your own department has come up with that brings you here. Naturally we're interested, we'd be fools not to be.'

Lee nodded and stretched out in his chair, his expression deceptively indolent as he turned to glance at his director. Weller was suddenly busy with his briefcase, taking out the leather-bound ledger. Lee waited until he had placed it on the desk, then said:

'Is this one of your special ideas, Max? One of those that shakes out all the bad guys and brings in the heavy mob?'

'We're here to find that out, Corey. It's too soon to say how far we'll get.'

'Or how deep? The last time I went along with your Svengali routine I ended up taking Windscale apart!'*

Weller made a show of controlling his anger, waving a contemptuous hand at the book. 'So what do you expect us to do with it? Hold a Press Conference and print the names in the Police Gazette?'

'It's a thought. If you weren't too busy you could even pick a few of them up for questioning.'

Gauthier considered him with the kind of patient smile he normally reserved for children and civil servants. 'We could also toss it out of the window. At the moment most of the key names in that book will know that Farrazi turned it over to someone. Who that someone is will be the sixty-four thousand dollar question they're all trying to answer, so if we pick up any of them they'll know, won't they?'

He beamed paternally and continued: 'We're talking about a network that handles at least seventy-five per cent of junk traffic in the West. If they even sniff a fed now they'll flush their stock down the nearest john and go into early retirement. In a month

* 'Doomsday Contract'

there'd be a new network, dealers and pushers we've never even heard of. All we can do is watch them, very carefully.'

The thickset man leaned forward, speaking for the first time with an accent that confirmed his Israeli origin. 'Or use it the way it was meant to be used.'

'And that's where I come in?'

They didn't need to answer. It was written on their faces.

'Max has come up with a rather interesting idea,' said Gauthier, in a silky voice. 'Your Palestinian friends needed the book to supply the network direct. That could only mean they can produce very large amounts of uncut heroin. Now if you were able to lay your hands on it . . .?'

'What's wrong with your own people? They all sick?'

Lee watched the smile go frosty round the edges, ignored Max's furious look. There was a tension in the three men that made him distinctly uneasy. They were walking around him on tiptoe and that could only mean they were all set to push him up the creek without the proverbial paddle.

'This is the big one, Corey,' said Max. 'I think you can pull it off.'

'How big?'

They looked at the Israeli. He breathed noisily through his nose, then shrugged to himself and said: 'With luck, the entire production of the Golden Triangle. In round figures, about nine and a half tonnes of heroin.'

Nobody laughed. Lee gazed at them for a moment, then rose and crossed to the coffee jug by the door. He poured some into a plastic cup, spooned in sugar and stirred. They waited, eyes hooded, mouths composed, hands folded submissively like three virgins at a Fellini party.

'You know what you are, don't you?' he said in a conversational tone. 'You're out of your tiny minds. You've been playing with the stuff for so long its got to the brain! Nine and a half tonnes! Jesus!'

'At street prices, in Europe and the States, it's worth ten billion dollars, give or take a hundred million!' supplied Lasser, quite unperturbed by Lee's reaction. 'And if we don't get hold of it fast we've got trouble.'

'Nobody gets hold of that amount. Not now. Not ever!'

'You could be right,' Gauthier conceded. 'But it won't do any harm to listen.'

'I second that,' said Max waspishly. 'Otherwise I might start doing irrational things – like writing nasty words on your file!'

Lee sat back with a disgusted expression. The Israeli got to his feet and began to move around the room, punctuating his words with sharp, aggressive gestures.

'The Palestinian group you tied into confirms reports our intelligence community has been getting for some months. They're ready to deal in junk, passing it down the line from one organization to another. Fringe groups, activists, people who believe that any means will justify the end, will start feeding the peddlers on their terms.

'In six months every junkie will be a potential terrorist. All you have to do is cut off their supply, start making conditions. Once the shakes begin they'll do anything for a fix . . . set fires, steal weapons, throw bombs. It's a whole new ball game, Corey, once they're calling the shots.'

Lee nodded grimly, beginning to understand why Farrazi's list had been so vital to Karen. To her way of thinking, it had been the Holy Grail. 'They'd make the Mafia look like the Salvation Army,' he said slowly.

'That's only part of it,' Lasser said. 'It's a double-edged sword, one that corrupts and produces a very useful by-product. Money. If they can pull it off they'll be able to pour billions of dollars into the PLO and the PFLP. I don't need to tell you what the money will be used for. Not food and clothing for their refugees. Arms. Enough to start another Arab-Israeli war.'

'All right,' acknowledged Lee, 'I can see the motive, but you're not going to tell me that Arafat and the PLO will risk dirtying their hands, or finding the money for that kind of trade. Their Arab friends wouldn't touch it with a ten-foot pole.'

'Nobody's suggesting that,' Lasser replied. 'The initiative came from a small group calling themselves the Gaza Commandos. They sent a man to Bangkok to sniff the wind and the Scorpion took it from there.

'Politically he's ripe for this kind of move. By making a deal with the Palestinians he gets the use of their organization, and their protection when he has to get out of Thailand.'

'That could be soon,' Gauthier added. 'Ever since the military coup in seventy-six the Chinese communists have been infiltrating the country from Cambodia and Laos. Something's going to blow, and when it does the Scorpion is top of everyone's list for target practice.'

'Even so,' Lee argued, 'they're not going to be crazy enough to take it out in one lump.'

Gauthier and the Israeli considered each other with poker faces, then turned to Max. He beamed. Lee knew then it had to be bad news.

'The Scorpion is running out of time and patience. You tell him how to get it out, and he'll play.'

'Just like that?'

'Not quite,' Max conceded, enjoying himself now. 'But if he thought you were someone else, someone who could guarantee delivery, then that would make all the difference.'

'Spit it out, Max.'

'Carlos Ramirez Sanchez. The Jackal.'

The air-conditioning breathed softly around them, the only sound in the room. Lee tried to come to terms with the idea, but it was too incredible to comprehend. Carlos was already a legend, a man hunted by every police force in the West. The list of his crimes against a dozen countries ranged from assassination to hijacking. Posing as Carlos was fractionally safer than playing Russian Roulette with a howitzer.

'You've really flipped, Max,' he said finally. 'If you put that in writing you'll get a one-way ticket to the funny farm.'

'It can be done, Corey,' said Lasser with disturbing conviction.

'Sure it can. And when I'm through with Carlos I can have a go at Idi Amin!'

'Corey,' Max grated in his most devastating tone. 'You're doing a pretty convincing job as a meat ball right now. We didn't come all this way without thinking it out.'

'How far?' Lee replied savagely. 'Did you get to the bit where I have my balls chopped off?'

'It's a heavy thought,' said Max, relishing the idea, 'but we can't have everything.'

'We have absolute proof that Carlos is hiding out in Venezuela,

Gauthier said in a soothing voice. 'He won't show his face for months, and if he does he'll never make the airports. He's run out of chances and he knows it.'

'We don't even look alike,' Lee exclaimed, exasperated by their stubbornness.

'Who can tell?' said Lasser. 'He's had plastic surgery so many times his own mother doesn't know him. You're about the same height, you've got the style, the build, and you speak Arabic. We can make your hair darker, let your sideburns grow a bit, put a few creases in your face to suggest a plastic job and you could pass. Maybe not here in Paris, certainly not in any Arab country. But we're talking about Thailand, six thousand miles from his hunting ground.'

'Word will get out the minute I start talking to this Scorpion character.'

'Wrong again,' said the Israeli. 'We intercepted a courier in Caracas. He was carrying a message for Carlos, telling him that it's vital he goes to Bangkok. The Scorpion has refused to deal with anyone else. That means they expect Carlos to go to Thailand. Only *he* doesn't know it.'

Lee made a bitter, exasperated gesture. They were putting him on the spot, ignoring a dozen chilling eventualities. 'Suppose I meet people who know him.'

Max gazed up at the ceiling whilst Gauthier studied the floor. After a moment the Israeli spoke in a flat, emotionless voice. 'The chances are remote. If it happens you kill, for they will surely attempt to kill you.'

'And that's the best you can offer?'

'Lee,' said Max, putting on his most paternal expression. 'I can't assign you to this one. It's for you to decide. All I can say is that by the time you leave Paris you'll know as much about Carlos as it is possible to know. Uri Lasser is one of Mossad's acknowledged experts. He's here to give you the ultimate briefing.'

Lee stared at them grimly. They stared back without remorse. He went to the window and looked out at the city. The sun was setting. There was blood in the sky.

'Nine and a half tonnes?' he asked, turning back.

'Ten billion dollars,' Max replied. 'In one single operation you could wipe out the junk traffic for six months. You'd force half a million junkies to take the cure.'

'You should have been a car salesman, Max,' he said bitterly. 'You'd have made a fortune.'

Max grinned wolfishly. 'Drive carefully, Corey. Our after-sales service doesn't operate in South-East Asia!'

Chapter 7

'Who are you?'

'Ilich Ramirez Sanchez.'

'Age?'

'Thirty.'

'Where were you born?'

'Caracas.'

'Your father?'

'Doctor Altagracia Ramirez.'

'Mother?'

'Dona Elba.'

'Brothers?'

'Vladimir, the youngest aged twenty, and Lenin, aged twenty-seven.'

'Where is your home?'

'San Cristobal.'

'College?'

'Fermin Toro, in Caracas.'

'University?'

'Patrice Lumumba, Moscow

'Who said "bullets make sense, words make nonsense"?'

'I did, in 1963.'

'Who is Adolfo Muller?'

'Carlos, The Jackal.'

'Glenn H. Gebhard?'

'Carlos, the Jackal.'

'Charles Clarke?'

'The same.'

'And *who* are you?'

'I am Carlos.'

'What are you?'

'A liberator.'

'What is your cell?'

'Commando Boudia.'

'Your allegiance?'

'The People's Front for the Liberation of Palestine.'

'Your Commander in Chief?'

'Waddi Haddad.'

'Your codename?'

'Eagle.'

'Your cover?'

'Lee Corey, an engineer selling auto spares. Born in New York, lived and worked in Detroit since 1971.'

'Married?'

'Divorced. No children.'

The short, wrinkled man leaned back in his chair and pinched the bridge of his nose. It was almost midnight and only a table lamp burned in the small flat located above a launderette in Rue Condorcet. They had been working for three days on the bulky files which bore the red and black emblem of Israel's Mossad. Occasionally Lasser would leave the flat to report to Gauthier, but Lee was confined to the dingy room until the fine incisions had healed along each side of his jaw, behind the ears and at the corners of his eyes. The process was almost complete, the scars little more than fine red lines. In a matter of days they would be almost invisible, but under close scrutiny would reveal the tell-tale signs of plastic surgery.

The Israeli stirred and spoke with his eyes closed. 'You will get by with your Arabic, he was never fluent himself, and your French is passable. The big problem is going to be Russian.

'I was wondering when we'd get round to that.'

Uri gave one of his rare grins and said: '*Esli dazhe eto tebe neponyatno, to po krainei mere staraisya kazatsya zainteresovannym.*'

Lee grinned. 'Why don't we speak English. It's a couple of years since I used Russian.'

'Not bad, but not good enough,' Lasser replied. 'You'd better invent a story. Some incident that turned you off the

Russians, maybe a KGB set-up that nearly got you chopped. You're so mad at them you refuse to speak their language.'

'It would have to be recent.'

Lasser nodded. 'After Entebbe. You were really on the run then. Yugoslavia, Iran, Kuwait, the Yemen. It can't be checked out, and you're noted for being a stubborn bastard.'

'The KGB could be operating in Thailand?'

'No way. That's China's little kibbutz and the country's crawling with Red Chinese agents. They'd as soon kill a Russian as an American.'

'Lovely people.'

'Salt of the earth.'

'So when do you give me the green light?'

Lasser steepled stubby fingers and considered the American across the dimly-lit room. It had begun to rain outside, drumming against the window. In the distance a siren wailed in the night.

'Tomorrow you have an engagement. You will meet a Miss Janine St Cere at the Café Lommard. If she likes you she will take you back to her apartment.'

'And?'

He grinned. 'Then we'll see about Thailand.'

The Israeli rose to his feet, stretched, picked up his creased raincoat and headed for the door. Lee let him reach it before saying in a disgusted voice. 'Did anyone ever tell you that you can be one hell of a pain!'

'My mother,' he replied. 'Shalom!'

Outside he put on the raincoat and walked along the street that glistened with reflected neon. There were three parked cars, two of them empty, one occupied by a couple who were oblivious to anything short of an earthquake registering plus five on the Richter scale. Uri paused beside the car and lit a cigarette, admiring the naked leg that was inching up the misted window. The muffled groans from within brought a gleam of amusement to his eyes, but as he shifted slightly to bring the wing mirror to a better angle, it gave way to a grim alertness. In the street behind him a dark-coated figure had paused, was now stepping into the doorway of a shop.

With a sigh of annoyance, the Israeli began to walk along the street, his right hand slipping inside his coat to click off the safety catch of the small 7·65 Beretta. At the intersection he turned right into Rue des Martyrs, then left almost immediately into Rue Lallier. He took his time, in spite of the rain which was falling steadily. Ahead the bright lights of Boulevard de Rochechouart held back the night, beyond it, rising up like a glittering tree, was Montmartre.

There was no need to look back, he could 'feel' the man following. The boulevard was still busy with traffic, hooting and jostling at the lights. He waited until they were about to change, then dashed across the wide street and took the first steep road up the hill. A clock in his head was ticking off the seconds. Exactly one hundred and twenty seconds later, he stopped and glanced back towards the boulevard below. A tall, loose-limbed figure was running across the road. Uri smiled contemptuously. An experienced tail would have crossed lower down, out of view, but this one was close to panic. He waited until the man had begun to climb the hill, then stepped away from the collection of pop jewellery he appeared to be admiring, and moved on up the winding street. A narrow alley appeared on his left and he turned into it, walking briskly between the cracked and faded buildings that leaned in towards each other, closing out the sky. Lights glowed through shuttered windows, latticed with sounds and moving shadows. Ahead the alley opened into a small square. He stopped, losing himself in the shadows, the Beretta cold in his hand.

The footsteps echoed between the walls, hurrying, then pausing uncertainly at the entrance to the square. There was silence, then the shuffling of feet followed by a tall, ungainly shadow that edged forward, searching the darkness. Uri let him take two steps beyond the buttress he was leaning against, then slammed a stiffened hand into the man's kidney. Even as he gasped in pain and began to lurch away, the gun was slapping across the neck, staying there. The ice-cold presence of the barrel froze the man in his tracks.

'Shalom,' he said softly.

'What is this? Are you crazy? You want my money, take it?'

Uri laughed softly, patting the tall, bony figure until he found the gun. He took it from the side pocket, noting that it was a 9-mm Luger. He put it in his raincoat, then swung the man against the wall. He stared back at him with sharp, thin features, his lanky form leaning in odd angles, as though parts of it wanted to take off in different directions. The eyes were small, black, the skin greasy and dark. With a sigh of resignation Uri realized he was an Arab, probably Palestinian. He raised the gun and tightened his finger on the trigger.

'You picked a bad night for it, friend.'

'Wait.' The word was shrill, vibrating with terror. 'I will talk.'

'Then we better find something interesting to tell me. Why were you watching the flat?'

'Orders. I just follow orders.' He swallowed, staring at the gun. 'We know who you are, that is enough.'

'Not for me, friend. What's your cell?'

'Cell?'

'Oh come on!'

'Raschid.'

'So you're Black September.'

The man nodded, a mixture of sweat and rain running off his face in rivulets.

'How long have you been watching?'

'Two days.'

'Who do you report to?'

'Haj Kalil.'

'That piece of shit! He couldn't run a brothel in an open prison. What orders do you get?'

'Just to watch. The – ah . . . the food is too much. Too much for one.'

'You reported that?'

He nodded trying to produce an ingratiating smile. The result was grotesque. 'Kalil thinks it is a woman.'

'He would. Tell him that if I find him on a quiet day I'll chop his balls off and solve all his problems.'

The Arab stared at him in astonishment, then gave a small sigh of relief. 'You mean I can go?'

'Sure you can,' said Uri, and put his gun away.

The tall, ungainly man lifted a hand, then glanced towards the alley as though unable to believe it was still there. Lasser waited, hands loosely at his side, and as the Arab turned to walk away his right hand lifted, a blade of bone and muscle, and slashed at the nape of his neck. The blow smashed vertebrae into the cortex, killing him instantly. Uri gazed down at the body, feeling some satisfaction that the kill had been clean and efficient. In all likelihood the Arab had not even felt the blow.

He walked back through the alley, down the hill to Boulevard de Rochechouart where he found a telephone kiosk. He dialled the number, let it ring three times, then hung up and dialled the number again. Lee answered immediately.

'You dressed?'

'Just about.'

'Okay, burn what you can't carry and run.'

'How long have I got?'

'An hour, maybe. But count on five minutes.'

'How do I get in touch?'

'You don't. Just keep the date with Janine tomorrow.'

'You okay?'

'You sound like my mother. Lose yourself, and watch out for a tail.'

'Now you sound like *my* mother.'

The phone clicked down and Uri replaced the receiver, stepping out of the booth. A taxi came into view, pulling into the kerb on his signal. He climbed in and settled back in the seat. The driver waited patiently, watching him in the mirror.

'Where to?' finally.

Uri breathed through his nose and thought about it. 'You ever been to Tel Aviv?'

The Café Lommard was a small bistro off Rue Lafayette, the tables cramped together beneath faded posters from the Lido and Moulin Rouge. Two waitresses seemed to do everything at the run, answering all questions with '*un moment*'. The smell of cooking from the kitchen filled the room, assaulting the senses with garlic, tarragon, rosemary and basil. The *patrons* could only wait, with mounting appetites, consuming fresh rolls like starving waifs, catching tantalizing glimpses of rich *bourguignonnes* flashing by with an army of *tournedos*, from *pompadour* to *jardinière*. At last, when iron control was beginning to break and mouths were thinning with fury, the culinary miracle would appear and all was forgiven. The fact that, frequently, the *tournedos* was *béarnaise* instead of *chasseur*, or *provençale* rather than *au poivre*, was of little consequence. After such a wait it was usually love at first sight and consummation took place immediately.

It took one hour and fifteen minutes for Lee and Janine to be served, but they both agreed that it was worth the wait just to watch the varying degrees of apoplexy among those diners who were unaware of the proprietor's reputation. It had been said that when you placed your order he went out and slaughtered the cow.

Janine St Cere was a tall, leggy girl with small features and long black hair. She wore well-tailored slacks and a fashionable fluffy sweater, and her hands were frequently still with the kind of repose that suggested she had a placid nature. Beyond that, after almost two hours, Lee knew very little. The conversation was animated, but inconsequential, ranging from the problems in Africa to the dangers of crossing a Parisian road. She never referred to Uri Lasser, so Lee made no mention of him, or the oddness of their meeting. As a person she was interesting enough, but more than once he detected a faint hesitation when replying to some innocuous question. On one occasion, after she had been telling him that she was thinking of changing her job from the export company she worked for, he asked casually if she preferred secretarial work. Her head began to shake, then she stopped and made an elaborate shrug.

'It is what I do best,' she answered vaguely.

It wasn't until they had reached the coffee stage that her mood changed and her questions suddenly took on a very different nature.

'I wonder if you know a friend of mine? He works in New York, but he's often in Detroit.'

'They're both pretty crowded cities.'

She smiled. 'True, but Glenn Gebhard seems to know everybody.'

Lee managed to look astounded. 'Glenn? That is surprising. I know him well.'

'Then you'll know his friend, also?'

'You mean Charles?'

She nodded, her dark eyes intent. 'I have the strangest feeling that I know you. I wonder if it's because Glenn may have mentioned you now and then. There was a nickname he used, for a very close friend.' She tried to recall the name. 'What was it . . . ? Ah, yes. "El Gordo." Would that be you?'

Lee drank some coffee, mentally cursing Lasser for not giving him more information about the girl. 'El Gordo' was a name given to Ramirez as a child, and if she knew that she was dangerous. He found it hard to believe that the Israeli would run any risks at this stage, but it was possible that the girl was for real.

'Odd you should say that,' he said casually. 'El Gordo means the "fat one", and that's what the kids used to call me at school.'

'Which school would that be?' she asked, then added quickly: 'No. Let me guess. You went to Fermin Toro in Caracas.'

Lee gazed at her without expression until she smiled and leaned over the table running her hand down his cheek, letting it rest along his chin. Her fingers lightly touched the fine scar.

'I almost didn't recognize you, Ili. Your voice is different, and your mouth.'

He shrugged, hiding his consternation by glancing at the near-by tables, as though wary of eavesdroppers. 'It's surprising what a good surgeon can do these days.'

'Even your voice?'

'They cauterized the larynx to alter the tone, just in case some official whiz-kid decides to make a voice print.'

'It's marvellous,' she said, with obvious sincerity. 'I'll bet even Sil wouldn't know you.'

Lee nodded, hoping that she meant Carlos's former girl-friend, Amparo Silva Masmela. 'Maybe. But the object of the exercise is not to be identified. That's why you worry me.'

'You don't need to. I'm not connected now, just a believer. The man who suggested we meet thought you might need a base in Paris.'

'I shan't be spending much time here.'

'But you'll be back now and then?'

Lee nodded cautiously. 'It's possible.'

'All right, use my place. It's not far from here, close to Rue Amélie. Bring back old memories.'

Her eyes gleamed as she let the words hang between them. He

knew she was again referring to Silva Masmela, the flat they had shared, but he had no way of knowing why. He gave a non-committal shrug, hoping she would enlarge on it. She did, and the words brought an icy shock of alarm.

'After all,' she said softly. 'That's where we met. Where you made love to me.'

Somehow he managed a mocking smile. 'I was beginning to think you'd forgotten.'

He beckoned to a waitress and paid for the meal, using the diversion to assess a situation that was rapidly getting out of hand. Although he had given no indication that he knew her when they met, she would assume this was all part of his cover. The problems were going to come thick and fast when they were in the privacy of her flat. If she started chatting about old times he would last about as long as an elephant in a minefield, which was fractionally longer than the Israeli would last when they next met, Lee promised himself fervently.

The invitation came as soon as they left the restaurant. With bitter resignation he accepted and waved down a cruising taxi. The journey was short, Janine chatting about weather and prices. Lee kept his part of the conversation down to monosyllables, hoping that she might take the hint and despatch him after a quick cup of coffee. The steady pressure of a slim thigh, together with the hand that clasped his arm, did little to strengthen that belief.

The taxi delivered them to a three-storey block of flats close to Les Invalides, and with mounting apprehension Lee followed the girl up to the second floor. He had no way of knowing whether he was supposed to have been here, so when she opened the door he walked into a small, comfortable lounge and looked around without expression. She dropped her handbag beside the sofa, gazing at him with disappointed eyes.

'Don't you like it?'

'Great,' he said with relief. 'I was just wondering how serious you were about my staying here.'

She stood up and put her arms around his neck, standing on her toes to kiss him, then leaning back with a contented smile. 'You can have a key in the morning, Ili. How often you use it is entirely up to you.'

'Okay,' he said. 'But you forget all about Ilich Ramirez Sanchez. From now on I'm Lee Corey. Especially here,' he added firmly, as she opened her mouth to protest. 'I'm still getting used to this cover.'

'All right, *chéri*,' she replied, kissing him lightly. 'But there are certain situations where I might forget.'

The eyes twinkled mischievously, leaving no doubt in his mind as to the kind of situation she was referring to.

After asking him to mix the drinks, she went into the bedroom and closed the door. He poured himself a large scotch and topped it up with soda, wondering what the hell Uri Lasser was trying to prove. The girl was behaving exactly the way she would if she had known Carlos. At no time had there been the slightest indication that she was working with the Israeli, or that she suspected the American was not Carlos. Any attempt to find out would almost certainly arouse suspicions if she were genuine. It was an exasperating situation, and he had an uncomfortable feeling that the moment of truth was only minutes away.

He was prowling around the apartment, looking for clues on the bookshelves and magazine racks, when she called from the bedroom. He swallowed a large measure of scotch, then went into the room, mentally cursing Max Weller every step of the way. The anger died the moment he stepped through the door. She was lying on the bed, wearing simple white briefs and an expression that could only be described as wanton. Her body was slender and darkly tanned, including the small, firm breasts that looked as though they had never seen a bra. The hips were round and full, disturbingly attractive, and her long legs moved invitingly as he reached the foot of the bed.

'I want you to take me the way you did that first time,' she said huskily. 'I've never forgotten that.'

Lee wished fervently that he could remember.

'I'd hate you to get into a rut,' he said, unbuttoning his shirt. 'You might be missing something sensational.'

She laughed and shook her head, watching avidly as he stripped off his shirt. Carlos normally carried more weight than he did, but she didn't seem to notice. He sat on the bed, removing shoes and socks, taking his time and hoping that she might give him some clue as to the particular style the Venezuelan favoured. She ran her hands over his shoulders and contentedly nuzzled his back, remarking in a casual tone that his skin seemed fairer.

'There's not been much chance to get out in the open for the past six months,' he informed her. 'But now I've got a new identity things are going to change.'

'Not everything,' she murmured, kissing the base of his spine. 'Promise?'

He turned towards her, forcing a smile, wondering just how different he was supposed to be. The absence of any unusual equipment ruled out deviations, and her position seemed straightforward enough. That meant the odds were about 64–1, he told himself wryly, providing Carlos had not made a study of Eastern sexuality. He started to reach for her, but she pushed him away, then turned on to her stomach and knelt on the bed.

'Now,' she said urgently. 'I want you to do it now.'

Lee breathed a sigh of relief and moved behind her. The invitation was unmistakable, so he slipped off her briefs and gripped the rounded hips. It was only as he entered her that he realized there had been another alternative, even as he moved inside her it might be all the proof she needed that he was not the Jackal. The thought died as she gasped with pleasure and murmured:

'Carlos. Oh, Carlos!'

He awoke to the sound of the shower in the bathroom and the appetizing aroma of coffee. Getting out of the bed he strolled into the lounge, heading towards the bathroom. The kitchen was separated from the rest of the room by a breakfast bar, and leering over it was the familiar face of Uri Lasser.

'Didn't you forget something?' he said pointedly.

Before Lee could think of a suitable expletive, the bathroom door had opened and Janine was stepping out in a towelling robe, gurgling with laughter at the scene.

'Lee, you look hysterical.'

'What's he doing here?'

'Uri?' she started to laugh again at his baffled expression. 'He's making coffee.'

'I can see he's making coffee, I mean *what* is he doing here?'

She stifled her laughter and glanced at the Israeli. 'I suppose he wants to ask me how you made out.'

'So you knew?' Lee asked tightly.

She nodded. 'Of course.'

He stalked past her into the bathroom and stood under the shower until his anger had been washed away. It took ten minutes. When he returned to the lounge with a towel knotted round his waist, Uri was in deep conversation with the girl. He helped himself to coffee and joined them.

'Okay, wise guy, what's the verdict?'

'It could be worse,' Uri said, lighting one of his slim cheroots and gazing thoughtfully at the smoke. 'You need to build up the arrogance, he's an intense man with a lot of self-confidence. Janine reckons that you were explaining too much, and he wouldn't do that. Not his style.'

'You knew him then?' Lee asked her.

'Oh, yes. For three months, until I began to suspect what he was. It was just as well I got out. Both his steady girl-friends were deported.'

'The chances are you'll never get into a similar situation in Thailand,' said Uri, 'and maybe that's just as well.'

'He did well to screw under the circumstances,' Janine said in a matter of fact tone of voice. 'Very well indeed.'

'One tries to please,' Lee commented dryly.

Uri chuckled. 'How close was he?'

'He might get by.' She turned to Lee, apologetic and amused at the same time. 'You won't convince one of Carlos's ex's, but you'll satisfy everyone else's curiosity.'

He acknowledged the dubious compliment with a cool look. 'Maybe you'd like to be more precise?'

She laughed and touched his cheek with lingering fingers. 'It wouldn't make any difference. You can't fake that sort of thing. You were just different. *Magnifique*, but different.'

Uri gazed at the ceiling with a pained expression. 'You two want me to take a walk?'

'Preferably out of the window!' Lee said with feeling.

The Israeli grinned and took an envelope from his pocket, tossing it on the table. 'Relax, American, you're just about through with me. You leave for Bangkok on tonight's flight.'

They both gazed at him with grim faces, the levity gone now as the reality of the game intruded upon them. Lee checked the contents of the envelope, glancing at the terse list of instructions Uri had included. It began with the words: From this moment you are The Jackal, a man hunted by some of the toughest hit men in the world. We cannot involve them in your deception, so if they find you – KILL.

It was a sobering thought and Uri's grim expression underlined the dangers he would be facing. Also on the list was the name of a Palestinian he could refer to as his Paris contact, a man connected with Haj Kalil.

'Suppose they check back to Paris?'

'No matter,' Uri said coolly. 'I found it necessary to terminate his existence last night.'

Lee nodded, not surprised. 'Before you phoned me?'

'Just about.'

'Then they'll be after you.'

Uri smiled grimly. 'They'll have to go a long way to find me. I leave for Caracas in three hours.'

'Carlos?'

'Of course. If he leaves Venezuela I will know, even if it proves impossible to stop him.'

'So what happens then?' Lee asked.

'It will create difficulties for us all,' the Israeli conceded. 'Especially you. Remember, if you ever see me in Thailand. In the street, drinking in a bar. Anywhere. It will mean one thing only, that Carlos is also there.'

'In that case,' Lee told him dryly. 'I hope we never lay eyes on each other again.'

Uri chuckled and rose to his feet, holding out his hand. 'A sad wish, but one which I also share. Shalom, my friend. May you prove to be as lucky and elusive as The Jackal himself.'

After the Israeli had left the room seemed smaller. Janine sat and sipped cold coffee, trying to conceal the fears that were mirrored in her eyes. Lee considered her for a moment, then said in a casual tone:

'I leave in six hours. Maybe we should go through that Carlos routine again. Just in case you missed something the last time.'

Her laughter gurgled all the way to the bedroom.

Chapter 8

The girl was olive skinned with slender legs and a narrow waist. The hair was long, a raven's wing, the face powdered paler than the rest of her body. Her hands and feet were surprisingly small, the nails perfectly tapered and painted an iridescent green. She moved with a simple, uncomplicated rhythm to the heavy beat of the hard rock music, her face languid and composed, as though it was all part of her favourite dream. The fact that she was quite naked didn't seem to concern her at all.

Lee Corey was doing his best to look equally unconcerned, but as the hips swayed an arm's length away he had the distinct feeling he wasn't fooling anyone. At the bar, which ran along one side of the small dance floor, a line of smiling Thai girls were dividing their attention between the dancer and the lone American. The girl finished her number and knelt before him to collect the flimsy gown and silver bikini which had taken her less than a minute to discard.

'Big Pappasan like the show,' she whispered.

'Sensational,' Lee drawled.

She regarded him intently for a moment, then rose to her feet, her expression becoming distant as she acknowledged the lack of vibrations. The lights above the floor glowed perceptibly brighter and the invisible disc jockey began to play a slow-tempo number. A waitress drifted over in a red bikini, smiling at the American before looking pointedly at his empty glass.

'Just a beer,' he said.

She nodded, turned and flicked her hips, then glanced back over her shoulder. 'For one?'

'That's how many of us there are.'

'It doesn't have to be that way.'

'Tonight it does.'

She shrugged, her disappointment mirrored along the row of faces at the bar. '*Mai pen rai*,' she said, giving the fatalistic answer that had been the Thai philosophy for a thousand years –

'That's the way it goes.'

The Lockheed Tristar had touched down at Bangkok's Don Muang Airport at 1600 hours local time, depositing a tired and dishevelled Corey into a hot, humid world that teemed with colourful people. After struggling through a jostling mass of bodies to collect his cases, he struggled back to the main concourse and made his way to a taxi rank where a dozen uniformed drivers immediately began to fight each other for the privilege of carrying him. He got into the car at the head of the queue and waited, eyes closed, face dripping with perspiration.

The driver who finally knocked at the window beamed and bowed, then pointed at another car. Lee beamed back, and closed his eyes. After a short interval, in which voices were heard to utter sharp words of reproach, the engine started and the taxi pulled away from the terminal, turning on to the main highway for Bangkok. The drive lasted forty minutes during which time Lee took only brief glances at the lush green countryside interlaced with its mosaic of canals, punctuated by rough concrete buildings with corrugated roofs that seemed to grow at each crossroad, thrown up in haste to be repented at leisure.

The taxi took him to a small hotel sandwiched between a massage parlour and a Chinese restaurant. The kindest description would be that it was singularly unimpressive, but it served his purpose. The heat inside was overpowering, but after haggling with an implacable Chinaman for five minutes, he managed to get the only room with a workable air-conditioner. It was almost seven by the time he had showered, changed into fresh linen slacks and a short-sleeved shirt, and ventured out into the teeming street.

Corey had been in cities he would have called crowded, but Bangkok made them look like ghost towns. The sidewalks were a constant stream of jostling people, forever moving to and from the network of rivers and canals that had earned the city the title of the 'Venice of the Orient'. The streets were kerb-to-kerb chaos. Trucks and limousines nudged battered vans and buses that bulged with humanity. The night air hung over them with suffocating humidity, muffling the endless chorus of strident horns. In spite of the turmoil around them, the faces were blandly patient. People jolted and bumped each other, but found the will to bow, murmuring apologies. Along the streets vendors of spiced chicken and crab meat on tiny sugar sticks plied their wares, oblivious to the human tide that threatened to engulf them. And everywhere the motorized rickshaws snorted fumes and played tag in the lumbering stream of traffic.

Corey made his way to the area around New Petchburi Road, visiting half a dozen sleazy bars crowded with bland young men and avid-eyed young women. At each place he stayed only long enough to drink a glass of the local beer and casually mention the fact that he was looking for a certain Chinaman with a sting in his tail. On each occasion the question was met with a blank stare and a disinterested shrug, but long before he arrived at one of the city's more notorious night-spots he knew that the message would be on its way to the Scorpion.

He was ordering his third bottle of Amarit, and getting an icy line of smiles from the bar, when the woman stepped out of nowhere and sat at his table. It was the behaviour of the waitress that prevented Lee from voicing his objection. The girl went very still, her eyes wary, her mouth nervous as though suddenly afraid to smile. The woman at his table gave her the briefest of glances. It was enough. With a nod she turned and went back to the bar. Lee watched the woman with an indifferent expression, noting the expensive ruby and sapphire rings, the quiet assurance.

'You are American?' she asked.

He nodded, as though the question barely deserved an answer.

'You are looking for someone?'

'If I am, it's my business.'

Her teeth gleamed in a mirthless smile and she opened a handbag, taking out a plain white card which she slid across the table. He turned it over to find a quite passable drawing of an eagle. He pushed it back to her, waiting. The waitress returned with his glass of beer. He gave her a twenty baht note and she left.

'The eagle has no meaning for you?' the woman asked finally, his silence making her uncertain.

'Who told you to find out?'

Her mouth went thin and ugly. She leaned across the table, making no attempt to conceal her anger. In spite of her slim figure and finely moulded features, there was a surprising strength in the woman. She wore well-tapered slacks and a blouse of

Thai silk, cut low enough to emphasize small, firm breasts.

'You will answer me.'

He sipped his beer, wondering if she would stamp her foot. Instead she gripped his wrist with fingers of steel, her voice suddenly harsh when it should have been shrill. A suspicion began to grow into certainty as she increased the pressure on his wrist. Around her neck muscles had begun to cord, and now he began to notice the set of the shoulders, the finely pencilled eyebrows and heavy make-up around the chin.

'If you don't let go of my wrist,' he said in a casual voice, 'I'm going to kick you right in the balls!' He smiled. 'That's assuming you haven't already lost them!'

Anger came and went in the transvestite, whose orders left no room for personal feelings. If the American was the man they were expecting any harm that came to him would be multiplied a hundred times on her own body.

'You were asking about a certain person,' she said carefully. 'That person wishes to know if the eagle has any significance in your life.'

'It might have. How about a Scorpion? Does that have any significance in yours?'

She nodded and rose to her feet. 'I have a car waiting.'

'I'll bet you have,' Lee said coldly. 'With a couple more garukis in the back.'

She hesitated, glancing towards the bar where the girls watched, their hostility carefully concealed behind inscrutable faces. 'My name is Dani,' she said. 'If you are Eagle, then your safety is more important than my own.'

'Well from where I'm sitting,' Lee said dryly, 'you don't look capable of protecting a bowl of rice in a Chinese restaurant!'

The transvestite's eyes glittered, then her hands moved to the hips and reappeared with a gleam of steel. The movement was smooth and fast, hardly pausing against the skin-tight slacks, yet each hand now held a knife. Lee was impressed. From the look of the weapons they were balanced for throwing, and he had no doubt that Dani knew how to use them. They were returned as swiftly as they appeared, each knife into hidden scabbards on the hips. Lee rose to his feet, dropped a note on the table, and followed her out of the club.

A large black Mercedes was waiting at the kerb, an attractive girl in jeans and shirt leaning casually against it. She was slim, feminine, with black hair coiled on the top of her head, but her eyes were cool and alert, constantly checking the street. Another girl was in the driving seat and as they approached she started the engine. The girl beside the Mercedes opened the rear door for them, then slid into the front seat beside the driver.

Lee gazed at the back of the girl's head, then looked at Dani with a grimace. 'Life could get complicated in this town.'

Dani glanced at him, shrugged and returned to watching the street.

'We all do our own thing.'

'That must be the understatement of the year,' he said dryly, deciding that there was no point in trying to think of them as men. The garuki was a quite acceptable part of Thai society, men who chose to dress and behave as women at an early age, often shortly after puberty. By using hormone creams and injections they lost facial hair and even developed breasts. The result, though confusing for tourists, was not regarded with disfavour by the Thais.

The car took them down Soi Nassa to Vithayu Road where it turned right on to Rama IV, crossing the busy canal where sampans, laden with fruit, moved along the waterway from the floating market. After five minutes they turned in towards the Chao Phya River, cutting through narrow streets of tall, gloomy buildings where the air was heavy with the odours of spices and opium. The character of the people had changed, most of them Chinese in dark blue p'u-fus, standing motionlessly in shadowed doorways as the Mercedes purred softly by. They turned again at the river, passing narrow jetties crowded with bales of bamboo and sacks of rice, the gaunt silhouettes of junks sharp against the night sky. On the water the ceaseless traffic moved behind brilliant spotlights, hooting at the strings of rice barges that chugged in sluggish procession in and out of the city.

The Mercedes stopped at tall iron gates topped with ornate dragons' tongues. A spotlight flashed briefly at the car, then the gates opened with a hum of electric motors. They entered along a drive that wound up through extensive grounds to the imposing villa. Lanterns shone at intervals along the terraces and on the walls of the main pavilion with its pagoda-style roof and gilded dragons on either side of the entrance. Other lanterns, flickering in the light breeze, hung in the branches of trees where they glowed like fireflies in the night.

It would have been a picturesque scene of Oriental charm and elegance had it not been for the guards who stepped from the shadows as Lee got out of the Mercedes. There were four of them, the leader a squat, hard-muscled man with small eyes and the kind of face that should never have been started. He held a Skorpion machine-pistol, its stubby barrel aimed steadily at the American.

'Against the car, legs spread, arms wide,' he grated.

Lee sighed and leaned against the car. With a face like that he had enough problems. One of the guards stepped forward and searched him thoroughly, removing his passport and wallet before allowing him to turn back. Dani was watching with an irritable expression, clearly annoyed by the guard's caution. She spoke rapidly in Thai, receiving a hard look and a menacing grunt for her pains.

Dani raised impeccable eyebrows and opened her handbag, taking out a compact. She checked her hair and lipstick, then glanced over the mirror at Corey.

'We have a slight problem. This gorilla we call Benny Dang is convinced we've got the wrong man. It happens at least once a week, but it helps to compensate for his enormous inferiority complex.'

'Maybe he should be humoured.'

'You're cool,' said Dani, giving him a dazzling smile. 'For a long nose you're very cool.'

'Why don't you piss off,' grated Benny. 'You ran the errand, now go play with yourself.'

Dani considered him with narrowed eyes, then glanced pointedly towards the house. 'I wouldn't keep him waiting, Benny honey. Not once he knows I'm back.'

With a smile that came straight from the deep freeze, she beckoned to her two companions and they strolled away. Lee looked after them, amused at the exaggerated sway of hips. He turned back to Benny who was watching him shrewdly. He tapped the passport with the machine-pistol.

'What's your name? Your real name?'

'Mickey Mouse.'

'Who sent you?'

'Donald Duck.'

There was a guard on either side of him, their faces masks of indifference. Benny Dang twisted his ugly mouth into a grotesque smile, nodding as though the idea amused him.

'That's very funny. Now let me try to make you laugh.'

Then he kicked him in the jaw.

It wasn't so much the force of the blow, which knocked the American flat on his back; or the speed of the kick which seemed to flash out of nowhere as though he was using somebody else's foot. It was the completely unsuspected nature of the attack; the incongruous sight of the squat, lumpy little man rising up on his toes like Nureyev and delivering a kick a good six inches above shoulder height.

Lee took his time getting to his feet, keeping a wary eye on the other two guards who looked bored enough to have seen it all before.

'That's very amusing. Who do you work out with? Margot Fonteyn?'

'Thai boxing is the most superior of the martial arts,' Dang told him. 'Now I ask you one more question. What is your father's name?'

Lee rubbed his jaw and thought about it. Dang's attitude could be genuine, but on the other hand it might be a test of his ability to cope with the situation. By answering the question he could settle the matter, but it would not be consistent with Carlos's natural caution, or his stubborn aggression.

'Well?' grated the Thai.

Lee stepped away from the two guards and dropped into a crouch, his hands extended, palms up, fingers slightly bent. 'I don't deal with the hired help. Let's try that kick again.'

Dang tossed the machine-pistol to one of his men and settled his squat frame into a wide-legged stance. He began to move, shuffling from side to side, each sequence of steps a rhythmic pattern, the ritualistic dance of Thai boxing that would normally, in the ring, be accompanied by pipes, cymbals and drums. They were also meant to be graceful, but in this respect Benny was a miserable failure. He moved, Lee decided, like an elephant with a particularly embarrassing complaint.

The first kick was low, tentative, followed by a left and right to the body. Lee side-stepped the kick, chopped at the left tricep, blocked the right and slammed his foot into the Thai's instep. He staggered back, favouring his left foot, his small eyes gleaming malevolently as he realized that his opponent had been here before. He began to pivot to the right for a 'teh' to the head when his communicator bleeped. He stopped, taking it from his tunic pocket and speaking briefly into it. The reply was sharp and authoritative. He switched it off and bowed formally to the American.

'Mr Chung is ready for you now.'

'What a pity,' Lee drawled. 'I was just getting interested.'

'There will be another time,' said Dang with quiet conviction. 'When Mr Chung has no more use for you.'

'Is that his real name?' Lee asked mockingly.

Dang's chuckle grated on everyone's nerves. 'If you wish you can call him the Scorpion.'

Chapter 9

Chung Li sipped a glass of wine and regarded the American with mild curiosity. They were sitting in heavy teak chairs beside the long low table inlaid with ivory and silver. The exquisite woman who had served them stood beside Lee, watching as he tasted the wine.

'So you are The Jackal,' observed Chung. 'It is difficult to put a face to a legend even more difficult to ensure that it is the right face.' He made a small, apologetic gesture. 'You will forgive me if I seek to reassure myself that the image before me is the genuine one.'

'Images can be deceptive,' Lee agreed smoothly. 'Especially mine which tends to change from time to time.'

The Chinaman's dry laughter whispered between them in the lofty room. 'Of necessity no doubt. I trust you will permit Sioo to examine you?'

Lee shrugged glancing up at her as she moved to face him. 'Whatever turns her on.'

The woman bent forward and began to study his face intently. Occasionally she would trace her fingers along a cheek, the line of his jaw, the mouth. Her probing stare was disconcerting, but Lee steeled himself to gaze back calmly. Her features were pale, flawless, with high cheek bones that enhanced the lotus eyes and full mouth. The almost white skin and perfectly sculptured face suggested that she had been born in the northern province of Chiengmai, noted for the beauty of its women. She was taller than average, her waist slender and flaring into full hips. There was grace and elegance about her, an almost hypnotic perfection of movement, like a gazelle in slow motion. She stepped away, measuring him with her eyes before turning to Chung and speaking softly in Cantonese. Chung nodded, sipped his wine and considered Corey until his mouth dried out and nerve ends began to jangle.

'You are somewhat different from the description I have,' he said, musingly. 'But that could be explained by the plastic surgery. To ask you questions would be an infinite waste of time, for if you are not Carlos you will most certainly know as much about him as I.'

'You mean I've memorized all those places and names for nothing?' Lee asked wryly.

Chung smiled and nodded. 'Indeed. All the proof of your identity is in your head and your hands. If you are not Carlos I will know soon enough, and then of course you will die in a particularly ugly fashion.'

Lee considered him without rancour, not a trace of his inner tension showing. The woman beside him touched his neck with gentle fingers, a smile curving her mouth, an echo of inner laughter. Her feline grace was at once sensual and sinister, and he felt instinctively that she was absorbing every beat of his heart, conscious of the slightest intonation, the movement of muscles, the steadiness of his hands. When her fingers stroked his skin it was like the touch of a blind woman reading braille, only she was interpreting the language of the body, intercepting messages from the brain. He rose from his chair and crossed to the Chinaman, looking down at him with amused contempt.

'I'm getting static, Chung. I've been getting it ever since your gay guys picked me up at the club. This may be your game, but when I play we get a new set of rules. The first is that as far as anyone else is concerned, my name is Lee Corey from Detroit. The second is that I decide on the team, not you or anyone connected with you.'

He paused, leaning forward until his face was only inches away from the inscrutable Chinaman. 'And the third one is a real, heavy thought, Chung. It goes like this – if anything happens to me while I'm in Thailand there'll be a hundred thousand hard-nosed Arabs with your name on their lips. You got that?'

'A long cool beer for Mr Corey, Sioo,' Chung said pleasantly, as though they had been discussing the time of day.

Lee returned to his seat. Chung waited until Sioo had crossed the wide expanse of marble floor, lightly, without a sound, then opened his hands, spreading an invisible pack of cards upon the table.

'You have the list which names the distributors.' It was a statement which the American acknowledged with a brief inclination of the head. 'Obviously you would not carry it with you, but a page perhaps? A name or two?'

'The first name from the first four pages.'

'Splendid. I will digest them later. Now you will tell me how you could use those names?'

'They'd get one offer. No haggling, no chat. If they accept they have as much horse as they can handle. If they refuse they get nothing – ever.'

'And the offer.'

'All supplies will be distributed through movements affiliated to the Refusal Front. We control the street price and the dealer's cut. Any aggro and our people take care of it.'

'The Mafia will not take that with serenity,' murmured Chung.

'They're motivated by money. As long as we control supplies, they'll have to do business.'

'And you, my friend? What motivates you?'

Lee gazed at him coolly. 'Power. In one year we can wreck the system, threaten social order, hit at the roots of Western complacency. In one year we can prove to the Arab world that we have the strength to strike the state of Israel from the map.'

'Ah yes, Israel,' said Chung, as though it was a rare disease. 'We do have this obsession with Israel.'

'Not an obsession,' Lee corrected him. 'A cause. The Fedayeen are sworn to return the State of Palestine to its people.'

'A most worthy aim, I agree,' said Chung. 'But we are men of the world, politically and emotionally. We both know that a war with Israel means economic ruin for us all, with only a wisp of a chance of winning. Which brings us to the mundane question of my own unworthy place in these events. Let us take first the unsavoury matter of monetary reward. In other words, how much for how little?'

Sioo appeared like a beautiful ghost, flowing across the golden room to place a tall, crystal glass of lager beside him. Lee acknowledged her smile, took a drink, then considered the Chinaman. He was waiting patiently, features composed, his frail body in sharp contrast to the gleaming Buddha at the end of the room.

'We want it all,' Lee said calmly. 'The total production of morphine base from the Golden Triangle.'

The ceramic features split, the mouth opening wide, the translucent skin shaping new angles as the laughter poured out in short, gasping explosions of contempt. Lee waited with a thin smile until the paroxysm had died.

'I came at your invitation, Chung. I came a very long way because I realized that you needed us as much as we need you. Thailand is hanging on the edge of the precipice. Around you are borders you cannot hold, inside are more Chinese-orientated communists than you could control. Your government is doing nothing to defuse the bomb, therefore it will explode. This year, next year, it doesn't matter. When it does yours will be the corpse they wave over the heads of the people.'

Chung nodded, unperturbed by the images. 'I would not attempt to disagree with your wisdom, only with your interpretation of my reactions to the events you prophesy.' His eyes grew dark, glittering in the amber light. 'There are many roads to travel, many havens to find. Hong Kong, Taiwan, Singapore, even your own homeland or any of the South American countries where money is its own passport.'

'You've still got to get that money out, and if it's a choice between gold and heroin, I think you'll choose to carry heroin.'

'It does require less effort,' Chung acknowledged, 'but it carries with it certain dangers.'

'Which I can remove,' said Lee. 'I get your heroin out, you get the money in any bank you name.'

'We are talking about nine and a half tonnes of crude heroin. Its street value, after processing and cutting, will be a million dollars a kilo. Nine and a half billion dollars.'

'Nobody's talking about street value,' Lee told him. 'You get five thousand a kilo maximum here.'

'If you have that amount available I will accept it,' Chung answered softly. 'But if you are suggesting something else – a partnership perhaps – then we are talking about billions of dollars.'

Lee finished the beer and gazed at the floor, wondering how far he could push the Chinaman. Cool hands moved on his shoulders, gently massaging muscles corded with tension. It was an enjoyable sensation and he allowed himself to relax. Chung waited, content to watch.

'You know, of course, we cannot raise that kind of money,' Lee said finally. 'But we can get the stuff out of Thailand. We can deliver and market your entire production, and that's something that no one else can do.'

'By what route?'

'Our business. All you need to know is that it's secure.'

'No route is secure for long. Destinations become known, connections become directions, signposts to disaster.'

'I'm talking about one shipment,' Lee said quietly. 'The entire production.'

A muscle jumped in the Chinaman's cheek and he frowned, as though irritated by his lack of control. As if to make up for it he raised his glass and considered the ruby wine, turning it slowly, then lowering it with a mild distaste.

'You amuse me, Signor Sanchez. But you also interest me. To take so much heroin anywhere at all is either an act of incredible folly, or the most audacious enterprise of our time.'

'That's why it must be done. The only problem is, can you

persuade your producers to go along?'

'Such a thing is not without difficulty, but those who do not wish to recover their profits outside our country can be persuaded to sell directly to me.' He paused, his gaze boring into the American. 'It would involve many millions of dollars. More than I would wish to lose.'

'I'm talking about winning. If you can put the shipment together, I can get it out.'

The Chinaman sighed and rose to his feet, moving slowly to one of the narrow, teak-latticed windows, where he stood immobile, looking out at the lanterns in the garden. Lee glanced up at Sioo, wondering at the girl's relationship with Chung. She was clearly more than a servant, yet her submissive attitude belied any position of power. She smiled, her eyes deep, her hand reaching out to brush his cheek, like a warm snowflake.

'I would need to know every detail, including the route,' Chung said at last. 'I will not give my decision until then.'

'Okay, but we have to agree on the split.'

Chung came back to his chair and sat down. 'The conditions of any agreement between us depends entirely on your vision for Palestine. If it consists only of that area of land bounded by Syria, Jordan, the Lebanon and the Mediterranean, then we may part now as incompatible friends. If, on the other hand, it can be extended to embrace another area of land, then we may well pursue this matter.'

Lee gazed at him blankly. 'We live on a pretty crowded planet, Chung. Apart from Israel, there just isn't anywhere else the Palestinians could go.'

'You are quite wrong. The Palestinians have endeavoured over the years to seize parts of Jordan, Syria and the Lebanon. Now let us suppose there was another Arab country, rich, yet vulnerable. How much would it cost to execute a coup d'état? One billion dollars? Two? Certainly not three.'

Lee swallowed, astounded by his audacity. One man, in a house in Thailand, was calmly suggesting that he could finance the seizure of an entire nation. That same man was smiling patiently, waiting for an answer.

'Three billion could buy enough arms to outfit an army,' Corey agreed. 'Guns, missiles, planes and tanks. But you'd still have to get the army there and pull it off before the rest of the world hit you with both feet.'

'Not necessarily,' Chung murmured, studying translucent fingers. 'The country I have in mind already has the potential army. All it lacks are the weapons and the will.'

Lee studied the Chinaman, on the point of asking the name of the country, then sensing a slight tension in Chung. It was as though he had expected a response, but finding none was now regarding the American with growing unease. The features remained the same, but the eyes and the hands were suddenly still. Each second would increase his suspicion, yet the wrong answer would confirm it.

With a dry mouth Lee allowed his instincts to take over. Chung could be referring to any one of three Arab countries, but Carlos would know which was the automatic choice. 'That's a tall order, Chung. Maybe too tall.' He paused, looking for signals in the Chinaman. There were none. He flipped a mental coin and said: 'Kuwait has some pretty powerful friends.'

The tension left Chung in a benign smile. He nodded, his eyes alive once more. 'It will require careful planning, but in this respect I may offer my own unworthy assistance. Providing the operation is carried out swiftly, and the oil fields seized, the coup could be accomplished with little bloodshed. Any retaliation by Arab neighbours would result in the destruction of the oil fields, and world opinion would be against this. Negotiation would replace retaliation and long before these were concluded every single person of authority could be dealt with, from princes to peasants.'

Chung paused, relishing the thought. 'In nineteen seventy-six there were six hundred thousand Palestinians in Kuwait, but with the débâcle in the Lebanon many more have entered the country, either as refugees or casual labour. I estimate that there are now some three-quarters of a million in a small country where the Kuwaitis themselves number less than half a million. You can see, I am sure, the enormous advantages of such a situation.'

Lee could see and was astounded at the simplicity of the plan. 'The Kuwaitis would still fight, and the Saudis would join with them.'

'We are talking about people who have grown soft with affluence. The country is now being used as a base by the PLO and the PFLP. A coup could be carried out on the basis of a civil war, the kind which decimates a population, terrifies a government, annihilates opposition. For half the proceeds of my heroin, I can offer you a nation.'

'And what do you get?' Lee asked quietly.

'Half of everything,' Chung replied. 'A position of great power in the country, cloaked with some respectable advisory role. Land, property, institutions, preferably in the oil city of Ahmadi. Many of my own people will join me, but they will be absorbed into my personal security force.' He beamed across the table, displaying a rare satisfaction. 'There is one other thing. I will require the mansion which occupies the centre of Ahmadi, called I believe "The White House". A bauble of decadence, but sufficient to indulge my unworthy desires.'

'I'm glad about that,' Lee said dryly. 'You seem to be pretty sure that I'll agree.'

Chung allowed the vestige of a smile to turn the corners of his thin mouth. 'There was never any doubt about that. The reason you are here is because you are a realist, a man who can persuade the dreamers in your movement. That part of it will be your own triumph. But before we can even begin to plan the future, you must convince me that you can live up to your reputation as "The Jackal". In other words, how do you propose to transport nine and a half tonnes of heroin into the United States of America?'

The question hung between them like a conjurer's sword, defying law and logic, a drunkard's dream. For Lee it represented a dilemma of conscience he had never envisaged. The assignment had begun with the rare chance to seize a massive quantity of heroin made possible by a unique combination of events. The prize was a crushing blow against the world's dope pedlars, the cost at worst a mistake which could still be remedied by acting on Farrazi's list. But the price had just gone up.

If he revealed his plan to smuggle the heroin half-way across the world, and then failed to confiscate it, the consequences could be catastrophic. Chung's plan was no idle dream. An armed uprising within a country had always placed world governments in a quandary, and with a major oil field at stake it was unlikely that any counter-measures would be taken. It had happened too often before, Lee reminded himself bitterly, in Africa and South America. No one protested for long. It was the age of capitulation.

Chung stirred, a flicker of impatience pursing his lips. The silence towered between them; an exclamation mark in time. The American furrowed his brow, as though searching for inspiration, which he was. To suggest an unworkable plan would destroy Chung's growing faith in his pose as Carlos, but to reveal more would be to court disaster.

'Uncertainty is the mother of confusion,' murmured Chung, as though reading his mind. 'It breeds trouble the way vermin breed lice.'

Lee sighed and nodded. 'Maybe you're right. I agree to your terms, providing you accept that my people control distribution.'

'Of course. But these are minor matters. You will please answer my question.'

'The route will be through the South China Sea and across the Pacific to San Francisco.'

'Impossible,' snapped the Chinaman, his voice sharp with disappointment. 'Your ship would be vulnerable for weeks.'

'I didn't say a ship,' Lee replied coolly. 'I intend to use a submarine, surfacing only at night.'

Chung was inscrutable again, his voice a whisper of hope. 'An intriguing thought were it not for the fact that submarines are not easy to acquire, or to operate.'

'I can find a crew,' Lee said tersely, 'and you can find a sub. The Americans left three at Vung Tau in Vietnam. They should have been scuttled, but someone fouled up. According to our information the Vietnamese have got two of them operational.'

'That can be verified,' Chung said, with barely suppressed excitement. 'What then?'

'We hijack one. A small team of your best men. We go in at night, get as far out as we can in darkness then submerge at dawn. We'll be back in less than forty-eight hours. If the Vietnamese blame anyone, it'll be the CIA.'

Chung rose to his feet, his pale hands steepled in a formal obeisance. 'You must forgive an old man's diffidence. It is clear that you have the cunning of your namesake. Sioo will see you to your room. Your things have already been brought from your hotel.' He made a small gesture of apology. 'I trust that you will forgive any presumption on my part.'

Lee shook his head. 'Saves me a trip.'

'Splendid,' murmured the Chinaman. 'We will talk again tomorrow.'

He turned and moved slowly to the gleaming Buddha, where he bowed and sank slowly to the floor, kneeling with lowered head. Against the golden bulk of the statue he was a small, dark, insignificant figure. Like a scorpion, Lee decided. As small and as deadly as a scorpion.

Chapter 10

The room was located in the east wing, a long two-storey structure that extended at a ninety degree angle from the ornate pavilion. The ground floor consisted of a large dining-room, kitchen and a modern American style study with panelled walls, hi-fi and video, and a valuable collection of ancient Oriental porcelain. There were four bedroom suites above, the one furthest from the stairs being allocated to Corey.

Sioo took him as far as the door, then left him with her Gioconda smile, touching his cheek once, almost with regret, before moving silently away. He entered an airy room, dominated by a low, elegant bed with a gilded canopy above. Standing beside the bed was the kind of girl you never wrote home to mother about. She was dark, slender, with eyes large enough to swallow any kind of story. She wore tight, well-cut jeans which did everything they were supposed to do for her hips. Above them a white silk blouse enhanced the golden glow of healthy skin, the thrust of small breasts.

She stood submissively by the bed with a nervous mouth and hands that looked as though they belonged some place else. 'My name is Tim,' she said simply. 'I am your girl if you like me.'

He crossed to a bureau that was topped with an array of bottles, poured himself a drink and offered one to her. She shook her head, watching everything he did with barely concealed anxiety. She looked like a bride who wished she had gone to somebody else's wedding.

He sat on the bed and gave her his most reassuring smile. 'Relax, Tim. I've spent the past twenty-four hours flying through God-knows how many time zones, fighting my way out of your airport, showing my face in too many bars and finally getting a foot in it from a very unpleasant character who calls himself Benny Dang. According to my watch it's ten-thirty tomorrow morning, so right now the only plan in mind is to crawl into that bed and go immediately to sleep.'

Her mouth trembled. He hated it when women's mouths trembled. 'You don't want me to stay?'

'I snore. It's something to do with my adenoids. You'd hate it.'

She shook her head firmly. 'No. Men who snore are men of strength. It is a pleasant sound.'

'I am an unpleasant snorer. Even the mosquitos pack up and leave.'

'I stay, if you want me?'

Lee sighed. If he didn't get her out in the next few minutes he would lose tomorrow as well as today.

'Tell you what,' he said persuasively. 'You come back in eight hours and we can talk about it over breakfast.'

She gazed at him with huge, despondent eyes, then turned towards the door. 'I will go.'

'Look,' he said, noting the sag to her shoulders. 'What's wrong with tomorrow?'

'The same that is wrong with today. It's okay. I will go. Mister Chung will choose someone else for you.'

Lee gazed at her with exasperation. 'You make it sound like a birthday treat. If there's any choosing to be done, I'll do it.'

'Then he will be angry. With me, with Sioo, with everyone. Girl you choose may be bad for here, for you.' She grinned wickedly. 'She may be garuki.'

He glared at her, then sat on the bed and took off his shoes and socks. 'Okay, you do the choosing. Tomorrow!'

She smiled and came back, collecting his shoes and socks. He watched her make a production out of putting them away, feeling the numbing waves of tiredness dulling his mind. She returned and waited. Without a word he gave her the shirt, then went into the bathroom. He cleaned his teeth, stripped and stood under the shower. When he stepped out she was there to wrap him in a towel that would have taken both of them.

He yawned, nodded his thanks and returned to the bed. She followed, folding the trousers neatly and placing them in the wardrobe. He rolled into bed and closed his eyes, wondering if she would take the hint. She didn't. After a moment she went into the bathroom and ran the shower. When it stopped he pried open an eye. She was coming out in a voluminous towel, looking very pleased with herself. He closed the eye and tried to go over his conversation with the Scorpion. It wasn't easy. Chung kept smiling at him with big brown eyes, and someone was stroking his back again.

'Go to sleep, Tim,' he said drowsily.

A slim, warm body moulded itself against his back and her mouth brushed his shoulder as she murmured: 'Goodnight, Lee.'

He thought about Max Weller updating obituaries in Washington; about Uri Lasser playing hide and seek in Caracas; about Harry Purnell dreaming of ten tonnes of Chinese pure. Then he thought about Tim and sleep went away.

With a sigh he rolled on to his back and looked into a pair of mischievous eyes. 'You don't believe in taking no for an answer, do you?'

She giggled and slid a slender thigh over him. 'When the head says yes and the body says no, I go away. But when the head says no and the body says . . .' A small hand encircled him, making further explanation superfluous.

'Are you trying to tell me that I don't know my own mind?'

She slid down on to him, her hips moving with an easy rhythm, the laughter tinkling in her voice as she said: 'I only do what your body tell me to, pappasan. So maybe you should talk to him.'

Lee tried to think of a suitable retort, but her movements were already heightening his senses, building waves of pleasure into a solitary need.

'I'll say one thing for you, Tim,' he murmured finally. 'You've got one hell of a way of winning an argument.'

Breakfast was served on a terrace which looked across the gardens to the busy river below. The air was hot, humid, heavy with the scents of jasmine and lotus. Above a coppery sky glowed with the morning sun, occasionally reflecting the dull rumble of the steady stream of aircraft flying low over the Gulf of Thailand into the airport at Pathum Thani. The meal consisted of fresh pineapple, melon, lychees in furry skins and small rolls of crisp, flaky pastry served with white butter and peach preserve.

Chung drank tea and studied a file of correspondence, occasionally passing a letter to Sioo with instructions in Chinese. Tim sat beside Lee, peeling and slicing fruit, passing it to him in silence on a small silver platter. Dani and her companions lounged in a group beside one of the many pools in the garden which fed each other through a series of rock-lined streams and waterfalls. The presence of the garukis, and Chung's preoccupation, gave Lee the uneasy feeling that he was still on trial, but there was little he could do about it except eat the pineapple and drink the coffee.

After half an hour the Chinaman handed the file to Sioo and turned to Corey with an apologetic bow. 'Forgive me. The matters are mundane, but nevertheless they must be dealt with. You slept well?'

His eyes flicked at Tim, as though she would answer for him. Lee nodded, smiling dryly. 'Eventually.'

Chung beamed approvingly at the girl. 'Splendid. I trust you are sufficiently recovered to discuss our proposition?'

'The sooner the better.'

The Chinaman rose to his feet and indicated the steps which led down into the grounds. 'Then let us enjoy the morning.'

Lee fell into step beside him, noting the two blue-smocked guards who began to follow, keeping some ten yards behind them. The garukis also began to get to their feet, but Chung made a small gesture to Dani and they relaxed. After circling one of the pools they decended to a sloping lawn in the centre of which was a tall, smooth-barked tree covered in white blossom which gave off a sweet scent. Chung stopped beneath it, indicating the tubular blossom.

'We call them the frangipani, the sad flower. It is our favourite tree.'

'Why sad?'

'The Thais associate it with love. In love there is always sadness.'

Lee nodded politely and wondered where the conversation was going. A tug hooted on the river and he glanced towards it, watching it pull a string of rice barges through a shoal of sampans. A long-tailed boat arced around the tug, throwing a curtain of spray, the boatman levering the trailing propeller shaft to change direction. He turned back as the Chinaman spoke.

'Perhaps you have never been in love, Carlos?'

'Lee,' he corrected him, avoiding the question. 'I prefer you to always respect my cover.'

'I stand rebuked.'

They walked on across the lawn, past a line of palm trees. A waterfall fell through rocks to a deep pool where golden carp browsed. Chung paused beside it, watching the fish move indolently in the clear water.

'You are pleased with our house girl, Tim?' he asked finally.

'I could do worse.'

'There are many beautiful women in Bangkok. A temptation for one such as you.'

'I'll let you know when I get bored.'

Chung was serious, his words slow and measured. 'It is important that you do. What we are embarking upon is very dangerous, and women have tongues that never know when to be still. I would be honoured if you allowed me to choose your companions as long as you are here.'

Lee shrugged. 'That's fine with me.'

'Excellent.' He seemed genuinely pleased. 'Now let us talk of submarines. I have established that there are indeed three Guppy class vessels at Vung Tau, two of them in service although the Vietnamese have not a fully trained crew so far. Within the next few days I will have details of the military strength at the port and the precise location of the submarines.'

'You don't waste any time.'

'In this country there is none to waste.'

'Okay, I'll contact my people in Paris and get a crew out here.'

Chung gazed at him with inscrutable features, then moved away towards an ornate spirit house surrounded by a variety of colourful flowers. He paused beside it, contemplating the miniature temple. After a moment he plucked a red flower growing near by and placed it in a vase at the foot of the pedestal supporting the spirit house. He stepped away, turning to the American with a formal obeisance, his hands together, pleading for indulgence.

'It will not be necessary to involve people outside this country.'

Lee allowed his mouth to tighten angrily. This had always been the weakest part of the plan. Neither Uri Lasser or Max Weller had believed that Chung would allow him to bring in a foreign crew, yet if he refused it meant that he would have to work on his own. The seven men waiting in Paris were trained submariners, all of them drawn from Naval Intelligence. They were the kind of insurance he could not afford to be without.

'No dice, Chung,' he said sharply. 'I pick my own men.'

'Not when your cargo belongs to me, my friend. We will use those who have no allegiance to either organization, who worship money rather than power.'

'Who can be bought by others?'

Chung smiled with humour. 'You are a stranger here, so I will excuse your ignorance. No man, woman or child in South-East Asia would dare to deal in treachery against me. It would mean death not just for them, but for their families, their parents, wives and children. None would survive. It would be as though their ancestors had never been.'

He spoke quietly, with a chilling finality, leaving no doubt in Corey's mind that he was capable of carrying out his threat. For the first time since he had arrived in Bangkok he could appreciate the sinister power of the Scorpion.

'My people are above treachery,' he said tersely. 'And they can also operate a submarine.'

The Chinaman's eyes glittered like a lizard in the sun, but the anger that burned there left no mark on his features. Instead he turned and started back towards the house, gesturing imperatively for him to follow.

Chung led him along the terrace, through the main pavilion

into the rear courtyard which was paved and shaded by a loggia cloaked with hanging vines. The east wing was more austere than the west, the windows smaller and some of them covered by metal grilles. Lee had assumed it served as living quarters for the guards and staff, and this was borne out by the long corridors from which doors opened into narrow, bleakly furnished rooms. The air was thick with the odours of spices and cooking oils, the clammy heat of unventilated kitchens and overcrowded rooms.

Chung led him up a flight of stone stairs to a room at the rear of the wing, outside of which stood a Thai guard with a stubby Skorpion machine-pistol. He snapped to attention as the Chinaman approached, bowing formally before opening the door. Corey stepped inside, his nose wrinkling with the acrid odours in the small room which contained a single stool and a low wooden bed. Curled up in the shadows, his emaciated frame in a protective foetal position, was an Arab, almost certainly a Palestinian.

'This is Arif Bassad,' said Chung, as though he was introducing a friend of the family. 'He came to Thailand last month on a secret mission for your people. Perhaps they mentioned him to you?'

Lee nodded, hiding his tension as the pathetic figure turned towards them. If he was a senior member of the PFLP, then the chances were that he had met Carlos. Casually the American stepped back against the wall, weighing up his chances. Chung was vulnerable, so he could use that as a threat to disarm the guard outside. After that the odds diminished. The chances of getting out of the grounds were slim, of getting out of Thailand virtually non-existent.

The Arab pushed himself upright, his features contorted with the effort. His eyes were black hollows in his head, his mouth a twisted gash that bubbled saliva. When he spoke it was a thin, whining plea for drink. Corey began to relax. The man was no threat. Whatever had been done to him had broken his mind as well as his body.

'This was one of your trusted agents,' said Chung. 'He is now desperately anxious to become one of mine. The drink he begs for is a special concoction to which he is now totally addicted. In exchange for it, he will give me anything I ask. That includes every secret with which he was ever entrusted.

'Why do you keep him?'

'He will die soon enough. Now and then he remembers something which is of interest to me.' Chung leaned down towards the Arab. 'Do you know who this is, Arif Bassad?'

The man swung his head towards Corey, trying to focus with vacant eyes. After a moment he shook his head, muttering unintelligibly.

'There's no reason why he should know me,' Lee said casually. 'I've never met him before.'

Chung nodded, then prodded the man with a finger. 'I asked you a question, my friend. You must answer, or I will call our other friend. She always gets an answer, doesn't she?'

Bassad began to shake, his thin legs and arms twitching uncontrollably. His grimy features twisted into a mask of terror, the words tumbling from him in an incomprehensible stream. It was a pathetic display made all the more horrifying by the Chinaman's calm satisfaction at the response. The Arab was repeating every name he ever knew, each one uttered with hope and terror. Lee turned towards the door, sickened by the sight.

Chung joined him in the corridor and spoke briefly to the guard, then led the way back down the stairs and out into the garden. Lee breathed deeply, trying to rid himself of all the wrong odours and images.

'You see how simple it is,' Chung commented. 'Loyalty cannot be bought by ideals. It must be purchased with the one currency that everyone understands. Fear.'

'That depends on the kind of people you're dealing with,' Lee replied, speaking with a callous indifference. 'That fool was telling you nothing of any value. It was just the ravings of a freaked out screwball.'

'You are quite right.' Chung agreed, showing him to chairs on the terrace. 'That is why I have just instructed the guard to cut his throat.'

He sat down, smiling pleasantly at Corey. 'I'm sure you agree that his existence was pointless.'

Lee could only nod, the Chinaman's indifference to death a chilling reminder of his own fate if his deception was uncovered. 'I still don't agree to the change. Running a sub is a risky business. I want people who know what they're doing.'

'Precisely,' said Chung, unperturbed by his stubborness. 'That is why we should recruit the very man who left those submarines at Vung Tau.'

Lee looked at him in astonishment. 'Are you out of your mind? Even if we could find him, he's a US Navy Commander.'

'My friend, you must learn to temper your arrogance with humility. When Vietnam fell it was an opportunity for numerous American servicemen to drop out of sight. Some of them had made fortunes in the black market, others were deeply involved in narcotic distribution. Others, like Commander Samuel Kitson, had discovered a taste for opium which was unlikely to be satisfied at home. After failing to scuttle the submarines he fled to Cambodia, and from there to Thailand. For the past two years he has been existing in the twilight world of the opium eater.'

'Where?' Lee asked incredulously.

Chung allowed himself the vestige of a smile. 'In Bangkok. My men are already searching for him. If he is still alive he will be here before nightfall.'

Lee sat back in his chair and surveyed the Chinaman with reluctant admiration. 'That's not bad. I apologize for my . . . lack of respect. But one man, even the Commander, isn't enough to operate a Guppy.'

'How many would you say?' Chung asked politely.

'I'm not sure. A skeleton crew of ten against a full crew of eighty-six. I planned on bringing in a dozen.'

Chung smiled and shook his head. 'We need no more than five trained men, the rest can be made up with members of my house. Commander Kitson can instruct my men. We are tracking down six possibilities, men who know the equipment, if not with actual service on submarines.'

'What kind of men?'

'The only kind worth using in a situation such as this. Men without a cause, without morals or ties. Men I can trust.'

Lee acknowledged the Chinaman's victory with a grimace, holding up his hands in mock surrender. 'Okay, Chung, you win. I go with your crew.'

He nodded, his small hands composed and still, but the eyes gleamed with satisfaction. 'It is as I had hoped,' he murmured.

'But now there is work to do. My people can locate those we need, in some cases speak to them, but one man needs special handling and I suggest you deal with it yourself.'

'Which man?'

'His name is Jack Masters, an ex-navy engineer who settled in Thailand six years ago. When the Americans were here he made a substantial living running a small coastal freighter between Thailand and Vietnam. Unfortunately, during the evacuation, his vessel was sunk by the Vietcong. Since then he has worked occasionally in the repair yards, but for most of the time he admires the lotus.'

'You think he could run the sub's engines?'

'My information is that he has a rare gift with engines. We will need him, but he will not be easy to persuade.'

'So I'll twist his arm a little.'

Chung shook his head. 'He is a difficult man, and alas one who has influential friends. He has no liking for my organization, or its methods, so any contact should be made on some other level.'

'I thought you had everyone in your pocket around here,' Lee said dryly.

The Chinaman made an eloquent gesture. 'He is a mosquito on the hide of an elephant. We need his co-operation, therefore we must be generous. Masters has two weaknesses. The sea and women. I'm sure we can satisfy them both.'

'Any idea where I find him?'

'He can usually be found in a massage parlour after dark. Sioo will let you know which establishment he favours at present. I suggest you make contact with him there.'

Chung rose to his feet and bowed politely, then beckoned to Dani who was sitting with the other garukis by the pool. She came over, wearing tight jeans and a blouse that clung to full breasts, hips swaying provocatively as though defying them to doubt her feminity.

'Dani and her girls are responsible for your safety,' Chung informed him. 'If anything happens to you she understands that there will no longer be a place for her in my house.' He paused and gazed at the garuki with a gentle smile. 'Or any other house.'

After he had gone Dani lit a cigarette and sat beside the

American. 'I'm told you can kill,' she said in a conversational voice.

'When it helps.'

'With your hands?'

'It's easier with a gun.'

She glanced at him with a disappointed expression. 'Hands are best, with or without a knife in them. What kind of gun do you want?'

He shrugged. 'Small calibre, good action. A Beretta or a Mauser.'

She nodded. 'I'll have a Mauser for tonight. You stay with us all the time. If we start flirting with you it means trouble. Got that?'

'I'll try to remember.'

She leaned forward, her flawless features intent. 'If I ever kiss you, get your gun out fast.'

'If you ever kiss me, sweetie, you better get yours out faster!'

Dani laughed softly and stood up, running her fingers down his cheek. 'Don't worry, honey, you're not my type.'

Corey watched her go, amused by the blend of mockery and menace that was so much a part of the garuki's nature. In spite of the slender figure, he suspected that they would give a devastating account of themselves.

A squat shadow fell across him and he glanced round to find Benny Dang.

'God but you're ugly,' he said cheerfully.

Broken teeth gaped at him. 'Not like Dani, eh?'

'I wondered if you'd noticed. Have you ever considered taking the hormone treatment yourself?' He gazed at the guard thoughtfully, as though visualizing the result. 'Could be dangerous, though. If you met a kinky hippopotamus you could be in real trouble.'

Benny's gnarled features contorted angrily and he bent down to the American, his rancid breath almost bringing tears to his eyes. He smelled like something that should have been buried weeks ago.

'You take care, American. Bangkok can be a dangerous place.'

'That's a heavy thought, Benny. Why don't you go downtown

and frighten all the bogey men away?'

The guard managed a grating chuckle, then glanced towards the house. When he turned back his small eyes shone with malice. 'You like Tim?'

Lee didn't bother to reply, letting him get it out of his system. After a moment Benny laughed again and made a lewd gesture with his hand.

'Tonight I'll get her ready for you, eh. Give her something to remember while she's taking care of you.'

'You're such a thoughtful, guy,' Lee said, rising casually to his feet and leaning towards the guard. 'But I really wouldn't want you to go to all that trouble.'

'No trouble,' grinned Benny, his corrugated features glowing with spite.

Lee nodded pleasantly, his hand reaching casually for the Skorpion machine-pistol that hung from Dang's shoulder. Before the Thai guard had begun to realize what he was doing, Lee had his finger on the trigger, his other hand swinging the short barrel into Benny's stomach. Even as he began to react, Lee was shaking his head and clicking off the safety catch.

'Move a muscle, Benny, and there's going to be a very messy accident.'

'You crazy bastard. I'll kill you for this.'

'Don't talk, shit-face, listen! You get in my way once more and I'm going to put you out of your misery.' He nudged him with the barrel. 'Nothing obvious, you understand. Just a knife or a bullet in the middle of the night. I'll cut you down before you even know it, then tell Chung that you made a try for me.'

'He'd never believe that,' said Benny, but there was doubt in his voice.

'You better believe it, Benny. I've taken care of people that make you look like the Sugar Plum Fairy. Now if you want to stay alive – stay out of my hair.'

He left him then, feeling his venomous gaze all the way into the house. What with one thing and another, he decided, it had been a pretty unpleasant morning.

Chapter 11

Jack Masters stretched out on the massage table and regarded the girl with a nonchalant grin. Her name was Lana and the number she wore on the simple white halter dress, cut short enough to show the full length of her slender legs, was seven, considered by the majority of the girls to be the most valuable number. In a land heavily influenced by superstition and horoscopes, the magic number was most frequently chosen by clients, although in the case of Lana the firm breasts and tiny waist undoubtedly assisted the mystical forces of destiny.

She moved around the dimly lit cubicle, folding his clothes neatly on a chair, placing the oil and talc beside the table, smiling shyly each time she glanced at the naked Englishman, as though she liked what she saw but wasn't quite sure what to do with it. After folding everything in sight she came over and put oil on her hands, sliding them over his chest and shoulders, watching his mouth relax.

'You want to pay me three hundred baht,' she said softly.

He forced his eyes open and managed to convey surprise. 'Not especially.'

The hands grew more insistent, sliding down to his waist, pausing there. 'It is three hundred for the special treatment.'

He smiled, then closed his eyes. 'Just the massage, please.'

The girl's mouth compressed into a thin line and she moved her hands back to his shoulders, using quick, sharp movements that dug the nails in deep. When he winced and opened his eyes she stepped away, indicating the white dress.

'You want me to take this off?'

He shrugged. 'Might as well. I wouldn't want you to get oil on it.'

She reached behind her neck and unfastened the halter, stepping out of the dress in a single, fluid movement. She wore the smallest pair of briefs he had ever seen. A white V of silk that only just served its purpose.

'You think I have a good body?'

He turned on his side, studying the slender legs, flaring hips, the pouting breasts that were only slightly lighter than the rest of her darkly tanned body. She waited, her eyes glowing. After a moment he nodded, then lay back.

'It's all right, I suppose. Are you sure you're up to this kind of work?'

Her mouth tightened angrily, an icy glitter frosting the eyes, but as he waited with bland indifference the anger melted and with a *mai pen rai* shrug she climbed up on to the table.

Jack Masters was tall, an inch over six feet, and at forty-three the muscles of his lean body were only just beginning to show a slackness around the waist and shoulders. His dark, wavy hair was flecked with grey, prominent at the temples so that his narrow features had a distinguished quality enhanced by the cool grey eyes and thin, austere lips. He looked more like a diplomat than a marine engineer, and his clipped Home Counties English would have been more at home in the first-class lounge of a luxury liner than the stinking hole of a tramp steamer, yet much of his life had been spent in just such surroundings.

He had arrived in Singapore at the age of twenty-five, bored with the discipline of a modern engine room where each watch was an exercise in drudgery and his need to get oil on his hands, to relate to the throbbing steel giant beneath his feet, went largely unsatisfied. The bustle and energy of Malaysia appealed, as did the lumpy coastal freighters with their eccentric masters and indolent crews. There was colour and madness in every port, and the China Seas were the strangest he had ever known; one moment so still that ocean and sky seemed as one, the next a seething cauldron of lightning and gigantic waves which hurled themselves at the heavens. Winds came out of nowhere, howling like demented dragons, and in their wake were indigo seas and skies dripping with colours so vivid the mind ached.

For Jack Masters it was like finding his way home. Every sound, smell and colour found an echo in his heart. He spent five years learning the ropes, tramping from the Bay of Bengal to the Sea of Japan, building a reputation on engines that should have been scrapped around the time he was born. Eventually he settled for

Thailand, largely because of the endless supply of beautiful women who seemed to want nothing more than to satisfy his very frequent urges. Unlike the Japanese or Filipinos, the Thais were reconciled to the fact that men were polygamous and felt this quality should be cultivated, rather than curtailed.

By the early seventies he was operating his own ship, a ten thousand tonner called *Leonora* that wheezed its way in and out of every port from Hong Kong to Rangoon. With a mixed crew of Thais and Filipinos he did all right, making a modest profit that paid the bills and the rent of his apartment in Bangkok. He also managed to feed and clothe three Thai girls who happily vied for his attentions whenever he was ashore, a sublimely satisfying state of affairs which he encouraged by periodically replacing one of them. He also did the occasional favour for people in high places, smuggling currency, precious stones and the odd bar of gold to Hong Kong, from where it could be legitimately transferred to Switzerland or the United States. He never charged for this service, accepting it as a small price to pay for the widening sphere of influence operating in his favour. He was one of the few people who could be trusted, not only to deliver a package, but to keep his mouth shut afterwards.

Masters had only one rule. No dope. He had a deep-rooted belief that heroin corrupted the minds and bodies of the user, not the producer, and to make a profit from this end was far worse than the vilest of violent crime. In the early seventies there was considerable pressure on him to run heroin and opium up the coast to Vietnam, where American servicemen provided a vast and lucrative market. One of the opium bosses who believed he could be persuaded by force was Chung Li, but after his thugs had beaten up half the *Leonora*'s crew the Englishman broke another of his rules. He tipped off the police and the Cong guerrillas operating in Vietnam, giving them the names and operating schedules of junks carrying the Scorpion's supplies. He also called on friends in the government to exert pressure on Chung. The result was a massive police operation which seized more than a million dollars' worth of heroin and arrested half the Scorpion's couriers. The following day he called on the Chinaman and advised him to drop the idea before things really got expensive. The only alternative was to have Masters killed, but Chung was enough of a realist to appreciate the repercussions of such an act. Instead he smiled an inscrutable smile and swallowed his losses, but two years later he made no secret of the pleasure he derived from watching the *Leonora* sink beneath a pillar of smoke in the Gulf of Siam, raked from stem to stern by a Vietcong gunboat.

With the withdrawal of the Americans from Thailand, and the increased activity by Chinese communists off the coasts of Cambodia and Laos, trade dwindled and there was little chance of raising capital to purchase another vessel. The days of the off-shore freighter in the South China Seas were numbered, and for the first time in his life Jack Masters was without a ship. He had only the circle of wealthy friends built up over the years to sustain him, and this they gladly did for a while. But time was running out for everyone. The Englishman found himself depending more and more on alcohol and the blissful distractions of the massage parlours, although even these were beginning to pall. As they said in his favourite commercial, he was smoking more but enjoying it less.

Corey found him sitting in a towel, drinking pink gin and staring glumly at a blank wall.

'You all through?'

Masters turned and considered him with a mildly irritated expression. 'Unless I'm very much mistaken, there's a line of empty cubicles along the corridor. Take your pick.'

Corey came in and sat on the massage table. 'I thought we'd have a chat.'

The Englishman gave him a suspicious look. 'Not gay are you?'

'Straight as they come. I'm interested in finding an engineer who likes to play with engines.'

'Any particular kind?'

'Oh, diesel and electric.'

Masters frowned. 'Electric? What kind of ship are you talking about?'

'The kind that uses diesel and electric.'

'You mean a sub?'

Corey shrugged and lit a cigarette. Masters sipped his gin, watching him with a wary expression. 'You're not a spook, are you?'

'No. I'm not gay and I'm not a spook.'

He pursed his lips thoughtfully. After a moment his face cleared and he nodded. 'In that case you're mad. It makes a change. I'm bored out of my skull with queers and spooks.'

Lee grinned, beginning to like the laconic Englishman. 'Could you operate the engines of a sub?'

'I could operate the engines of a municipal sewer. The question is: Would I want to?'

'It could be hairy,' Lee said softly.

Masters shrugged. 'Subs are hairy at the best of times. I gather this one is going to do something naughty.'

'Eventually it's going to cross the Pacific.'

'Fancy.'

They considered each other for a moment, then the Englishman ticked off five fingers. 'Before we go on, I want the make of sub, number of crew, the qualifications of the commander, the bossman and the nature of the crime we are intending to commit.'

'You planning to write the book?' Lee asked dryly.

'Not unless I have to.'

'Okay. It's a Class III Guppy. We'll run on a skeleton crew of five, but there'll be plenty of unskilled help around. The commander is ex-US Navy, submarines. His last command was a Guppy. I'll be calling the shots.'

'And the crime?'

'Non-lethal. We're just delivering cargo. That's all you need to know.'

'I don't play with H.'

'You're being paid to play with a submarine.'

Masters swallowed the rest of his gin and walked around the room, staring at each of the four walls before finally confronting Corey.

'You're obviously taking it all very seriously. I know the nearest sub is in Singapore, and that's Navy. Where's yours?'

'Vietnam.'

The Englishman gave a short, explosive laugh and went to his clothes, speaking to Corey as he dressed. 'You're absolutely mad. Bonkers. Round the fucking twist!'

'Which is where you'll be if you stay ashore much longer,' Lee replied quietly. 'You're the kind of insurance I need. And I'm the only one who can come up with something to replace the *Leonora*.'

Masters stopped half-way into his trousers. 'A ship? A coaster?'

Lee nodded. 'That's the deal. One trip, then you go shopping.'

The Englishman sat down and glared at the floor. His lean features grew gaunt, lined, like a man contemplating doom. 'You certainly don't screw around, do you.'

'There isn't time. Can you handle the Guppy for us?'

He nodded slowly. 'When?'

'Couple of days. You appreciate that we have one or two delivery problems.'

Masters laughed harshly. 'Stealing a sub from the Vietnamese is only slightly less dangerous than screwing an orang-utan.'

'That's a snip,' Lee said calmly. 'The trick is to pick the pretty one!'

The night air was warm and humid when they stepped out into the narrow street off Larn Luang Road. The glowing sign of the Fantasy Parlour beckoned with coloured curves, the reclining nude gazing down with blind, neon eyes. A few cars were parked in the street, a group of young men idling outside a bar. Dani stepped out of the shadows with Silva, slipping her arm through Lee's and pouting up at him.

'Lee, honey, I thought you'd never come out. What *were* you doing in there?'

Even as Dani spoke she was moving Lee briskly along the street. Silva had taken Masters by the arm, smiling at his bewildered expression. He gazed at Corey in consternation.

'Are these friends of yours?'

'Yeah. I was getting round to them.'

The Englishman made frantic signals with his eyes, as though he'd just got hold of something too embarrassing to put down. Lee glanced over his shoulder, seeing the other two garukis strolling arm in arm about ten yards behind. It was obvious from Dani's manner that something was up, but the street seemed to be peaceful enough. The thought had barely settled when the lights of two parked cars came on simultaneously. The engines started and they began moving slowly down the street towards them.

'Look, old chap, I think there's something you ought to know about your companions,' Masters was saying in a strangled voice.

Lee grinned at him and slid his arm round Dani's waist. 'She's gorgeous isn't she?' He leaned down and whispered in Dani's ear. 'How bad is it?'

'If we can get to the next corner there's an alley that gives us a run to the canal.'

Jack Masters was still trying to find the right words, his eyes rolling from side-to-side, like a vicar at a topless wedding. Lee let him struggle, dropping his left hand into his jacket pocket and flicking the catch off the Mauser. The cars were almost level with them, the end of the street still some twenty yards away.

'Lee,' said Jack, 'do you think I could just have a quiet word?'

'What is it, honey?' Silva asked him sweetly. 'Don't you fancy me?'

'It's not a question of fancying you,' Jack said politely. 'It's more a question of knowing what to do with you when I get you home.'

Silva gurgled with laughter. One of the cars suddenly accelerated in front of them and swung wide, blocking the end of the street.

'Now!' said Dani in a voice suddenly shrill.

Lee lunged against the wall, pulling Masters with him, the Mauser held low, searching for targets. The second car had stopped just behind them, the doors opening as Lee turned. Four darkly clothed men jumped out, a knife gleaming in at least one hand as they moved towards them in a tight group. Behind them, strolling innocuously arm in arm, were Dani's back-up girls. With perfect timing they separated and launched themselves at the unsuspecting group. A small, iron-hard foot slammed into the back of one man, then as his companion turned in alarm a high kick took him in the jaw. The garukis ran amok.

With palms turned down, fingers splayed, they slashed at

throats, stabbed elbows into kidneys, stamped on insteps, then with perfect balance pivoted and kicked for the head. The man with the knife slashed at the slender throat of Silva, face contorted with fury at the deception. She ducked, caught the wrist on the upswing and slammed stiff fingers into his eyes. He cried out, staggering blindly away, the knife falling from his hand.

Jack Masters watched with a shattered expression as Dani reached the car ahead and took on the first two men simultaneously. It was worth paying to watch. Her slim, graceful figure weaved left, then right, stiff hands slashing at the first man's throat even as she slammed a foot into the man behind her. The driver of the car was still getting out, totally bewildered by the chaos in the street. Dani kicked the door in his face, swayed away from a knife, then slammed a powerful knee into its owner's groin. He didn't like it and sat in the street trying to squeeze the pain away. A casual foot collided with a point just below the ear and he took no further interest in anything.

Silva and the back-up team had joined Dani, making it all look ridiculously easy in spite of knives wielded with considerable skill. Lee and the Englishman watched the display with astonishment, the gun forgotten as the garukis scattered groaning bodies over the street. After a particularly brutal assault that put the last man in line for major orthopaedic surgery, Masters said with a note of awe in his voice: 'I'll say one thing for you, Lee Corey. You do have the damndest friends!'

The last man on his feet tottered past on the way to the car. Lee caught him by the arm and swung him into the wall. He bounced off, standing glassy-eyed as the American tapped his nose with the Mauser. He was slim, sallow-faced with long greasy hair and eyes that would have looked better on a weasel. His mouth was bleeding and he clutched his stomach as though he'd forgotten where it was.

'Let's have a name,' Lee suggested in a conversational tone. 'One that makes sense to all of us.'

The man wheezed through battered lips, glancing around with fading hope. Dani arrived and whispered something in his ear, stroking his cheek and smiling sweetly as he sagged at the knees. He looked like a matador down to his last *cojone*.

'Do we get that name?'

'Boka,' he gasped. 'We got our orders from Boka.'

Lee looked inquiringly at Dani. She was grim, gesturing quickly to the other garukis. A car had entered the street, beginning to accelerate towards them.

'This way,' she said, turning into a narrow alley which was littered with garbage and heavy with odours of decay. They followed her between tall, darkened buildings, to open ground and a sagging jetty on the edge of a canal. Behind them headlights flashed briefly, a moment later footsteps echoed out to them.

Dani spoke in Thai to her three companions. They moved along the jetty, peering into the darkness, clearly hoping to find a boat.

'What about this Boka guy?' Lee asked.

'Bad news,' said Masters. 'He runs most of the city's brothels and sex clubs, not to mention the numbers racket, protection and murder.'

'He is big enemy of Chung,' said Dani.

'That's another bastard to watch for,' said the Englishman. 'They call him the Scorpion but it doesn't do him justice. If you can find a vulture with an oriental smile and fangs, we'll name it after him!'

'Didn't I mention that he's financing our little caper?' Lee murmured.

Masters gazed at him with bitter anger. 'No. No, you didn't!'

The footsteps had stopped in the alley. A pistol cracked and bullets began searching for them like hungry bees.

'They're shooting at us,' Lee announced helpfully.

'Not us,' Masters replied. 'You. I'm just an innocent bystander who should have stayed at home.'

There was a low whistle from the canal and a shadow glided forward. Another bullet split the air above their heads, then a heavier gun boomed in the alley. Lee glanced across the waste ground, the Mauser in his hand. There was movement, a deeper shadow flitting to one side. He fired without much hope of hitting the man, but the knowledge that they were armed would undoubtedly slow him down.

Dani was calling urgently from the jetty. Lee turned to Masters, nodding towards the alley. 'Somehow I don't think they're in a very sympathetic mood tonight. Even towards innocent bystanders.'

Masters moved towards the boat. 'I'm not exactly bubbling over with benevolence myself. In fact, if it wasn't for your vicious little fairies, I could quite cheerfully take a lump out of your head!'

The boat was a water-logged sampan with a tattered awning and a mound of rotting fruit in the bow. Masters managed to flounder into it, then gazed at Corey with an injured expression as though it was all his fault. Dani was the last in, two of the girls punting them away from the jetty into the centre of the canal whilst Silva manned the broken paddle that served as a rudder. A sluggish current swept them quickly out of sight beneath a low bridge. The air was still warm and heavy, muffling the sounds of the city as they glided along the canal between dark buildings and the occasional modern hotel. They passed within ten feet of a candle-lit terrace where late diners idled over their coffee. Music played from the bar and Masters looked hopefully towards it, as though a waiter would appear in time to take his order.

Dani crawled up to Lee and squatted beside him, her teeth gleaming in the dim light. 'They try to get ahead of us. The worst place will be Charoen Krung Road. We must go beneath it.'

'How soon?'

She gazed ahead, gauging their progress. 'Five minutes. No more. After that we go into Chao Phya River.'

'That sounds like fun. Why don't we get ashore now and grab a cab?'

'Everyone fear Boka, and this his district. Anyone see us, maybe even the taxi driver, they tell Boka's people.'

'Pity we didn't think of this before.'

Dani looked puzzled. 'It is strange how Boka find out about you.' She shrugged, adding the fatalistic '*mai pen rai*'.

A ribbon of traffic made a glowing arch in the sky ahead. Lee clicked on the Mauser, his eyes on the parapet of the bridge. There was no sign of waiting gunmen and a moment later the concrete highway closed over them. The sampan was moving faster as the current strengthened, sweeping them out of the canal into the sluggish waters of the Chao Phya River.

Silva steered the small craft out into the main current, turning downstream towards Chinatown. Behind them the Oriental Hotel stood out majestically against the city, its famous terrace a pool of light for the elegant diners. There was little traffic at this time of night, but the water was choppy, rocking the sampan so that at times it threatened to founder completely. A river bus hooted from the west bank, then began angling across the river towards the Mahachai Canal, spilling rivulets of light towards them.

'Keep low,' whispered Dani. 'They may be watching the river.'

'It would have made more sense to drop us at the Oriental,' Masters said irritably. 'There's no chance of Boka showing his face there.'

'And if I was Boka,' Lee replied, 'that's where I'd have a couple of guys waiting in a launch.'

Silva hissed a warning from the rear and they turned to see a brilliant spotlight moving slowly out from the east bank. The distant roar of a powerful engine echoed across the water, identifying it as one of the many long-tailed boats that plied the rivers and canals of Bangkok. It was the spotlight which made them uneasy. Instead of shining straight ahead, as would be expected, it was sweeping the river in regular arcs.

'Can you get the light?' Dani asked, in a tight voice.

'Not before they see us,' he answered.

The girls began working hard on the oars, pulling in towards the multi-coloured lights of Chinatown. Jack Masters sat grimly in the bow, feeling inadequate, having to remind himself that the slim figures toiling at the oars were not what they seemed, and in any event probably knew the currents of the river at least as well as he did. Chung Li's frontage was some five hundred yards beyond the Mahachai Canal, which was about five hundred yards too far. With a grimace he slipped off his shoes and wondered what all the sane people were doing that night.

The river bus hooted testily at them as it passed, sending a bow wave towards them that made the sampan wallow like a pregnant walrus. Dani spat at its wake, describing with lurid detail the habits, origins and ultimate destiny of the driver. Lee could have added a few of his own. The spotlight was no longer sweeping the river. The river bus had told it something was in mid-river. The powerful eight-cylinder engine roared, lifting the bow high, hurtling it towards them.

'If you go over the side,' Dani said in a matter of fact tone of voice, 'don't fight the current. Let it float you down to Buddha Yod Far Bridge.'

'You're such a comfort,' said Lee. 'But from the smell of this river I think I'd just as soon stay on board.'

He settled down on the wide wooden seat at the rear of the boat, gripping the Mauser in both hands and trying to counter the wallowing motion of the sampan. The spotlight was bearing down on them fast, finding and holding the sampan in stark relief against the water. A machine-gun began to chatter above the roar of the engine, cracking the air above them, erupting in murky fountains less than a foot from the bow. Lee concentrated on steadying the gun, finding the centre of the rushing beam of light. He squeezed the trigger, feeling the answering recoil, letting the rise and fall of the boat space the shots. It was the last one that found the target. The night went black, but the roar was still there, growing louder as the boat hurtled towards them.

Silva began to work the paddle furiously, trying to turn them aside. The men in the boat would be as blind as they were. Lee leaned over to help, gripping the wooden handle. But there was no more time. The long-tailed boat howled out of the night, striking them just above the stern, shattering the delapidated sampan like a fragile bowl.

Chapter 12

They were waiting for him in the shadows of Buddha Yod Far Bridge, a wide concrete structure that carried a six-lane highway across the river.

Corey had surfaced some fifty feet behind the boat, which had begun to turn in a wide arc. There was no sign of the sampan, or the rest of the occupants, and as the long-tailed boat circled slowly back Lee made the minimum of movement, letting the current carry him slowly down river. At one point he thought he would be swept into a maze of sagging jetties and sampans, where lanterns glowed through reed walls and the night air was redolent with the scent of charcoal from the small braziers on the boats. He could have reached them by striking out from the current, but this was Chinatown and Boka territory.

Instead he let the river carry him on to the squat, mud-encrusted centre pier of the bridge. He was clinging to it, debating whether to drift on a hundred yards or so before swimming for the shore, when a sampan glided noiselessly out of the darkness and a skilfully wielded oar smacked him hard on the back of the head.

He came round in a small concrete cell with a wooden bench against one wall and a foul smelling toilet against the other. A small grille close to the ceiling showed the grey light of dawn. His watch had gone, as had his wallet and clothes, but he guessed from the stillness outside it was not yet six a.m. His head ached abominably, and from the frequent waves of nausea his stomach was not too happy coping with the intake from the Chao Phya River.

The fact that he was alone could be taken as a good sign. If Boka's men had failed to get the rest of them, Chung would know by now and be planning some form of retaliation. He was assessing the possibilities of that situation, and finding it depressingly bleak, when the narrow wooden door was flung open and two grim-faced Thais entered. Without a word they dragged him to his feet and prodded him through the door with short lengths of bamboo that appeared to be filled with concrete.

He found himself in a long, barely furnished room with coco matting on the floor and wire mesh on the windows. A heavy teak chair occupied the centre of the room and his mouth dried out as he saw the leather straps hanging from the arms and legs. Beside the chair were two heavily muscled men with the kind of faces that encouraged euthanasia. Their eyes were small, bloodshot, beneath bony brows. Their lips were thick, purple with the excesses of opium, the skin of their faces ravaged by knives, alcohol and neglect. He knew, before they even slapped him into the chair and fastened the straps, that they were concerned with the more primitive part of the proceedings.

They let him sweat in the chair for ten minutes, enough time to imagine the worst, then the door at the end of the room opened and a man entered who could only be Boka. He walked over to the American and stared at him with contempt, then tapped a solid gold watch on his wrist.

'You have exactly one minute to convince me that you will co-operate. At the end of that time you will be beaten to the point of death.'

'You better be damn sure you don't pass that point, or Chung Li will take you apart with a blunt axe.'

Boka's smile made a hole in his stomach. It was the essence of cruelty, emanating such sadistic pleasure that the entire room seemed to reek with odours of evil. Corey swallowed the coppery taste of fear as he realized that the man enjoyed inflicting pain.

'You will tell me your name, your business, your age and occupation. You will give me three people in the United States who can verify that information. And then you will tell me precisely why you are in Bangkok and why you are important to Chung Li.'

Lee gazed at the ceiling, noting that it was solid concrete like the walls and floor. The first murmur of traffic was beginning to filter through the windows. In less than an hour it would be a steady roar.

'Shall we begin, Mr Corey?' Boka said.

'Lee Corey, aged thirty-four, employed by Van Tex Engineering of Detroit. I'm here to buy heroin, that's my only connection with Chung. I've got a route, using air cargo to the States in crates of machine tools which my company imports.'

Boka shook his head, eyes gleaming as he nodded to the men beside the chair. Lee locked his jaws and concentrated on a single image. It was a smiling face with blue eyes and blonde hair. The face of Paula Corey, frozen in memory at the age of twenty-four by the car bomb in Dallas meant for him. The intense emotion evoked by the image enabled him to blot out the fear and pain for a while at least.

The Thais used lengths of bamboo of varying thickness, but then they switched to those filled with concrete which smashed into shoulders, upper arms and ribs with sickening thuds. Lee managed to cling to the image until the corrosive pain broke down the barrier in his mind, but by then his body had taken enough and somewhere in the deep subconscious a synapse closed and he sank into oblivion.

Boka stepped forward and examined the welts on his body which slowly oozed blood. He signalled for the men to unfasten the straps, then moved arms and legs to ensure that the bones were intact. He checked the pupils, the pulse and the American's shallow breathing, before finally glancing at his watch with an irritable expression. He could be unconscious for an hour, and the longer the interrogation took the greater the chance of Chung finding out where he was being held.

Boka's contempt for the Scorpion's methods was tempered with considerable respect for the clandestine organization he controlled. It included people in very high places, not to mention CIA and insurgent agents, and if the American was of great importance the Chinaman would start a blood-bath that would curtail his operations for years. Yet the orders to find out the reason for Corey's visit to Chung had come direct from Taiwan, and that meant it was of great importance. If he failed to supply the information the masters he served in exile could well replace him. It was a chilling thought.

Boka was tall for a Thailander, with black shoulder-length hair and a ragged moustache that hung like a broken pelmet over stained yellow teeth. His eyes were slate grey, still and cruel, and his face bunched up around a wide, flat nose that looked as though it had frequently come into contact with blunt objects. The mangled ruins of the once serviceable nose suggested that Boka had either spent some time in the ring, or had cultivated more than his share of enemies.

In actual fact neither of these assumptions would be true. He spent his formative years as a novice at a Buddhist monastery in North Thailand outside the mountain village of Tha Wang Pha. After mastering the frugal disciplines of Buddha, he donned the saffron robes and went out along the mountain tracks with his begging bowl. The quantities of rice and fish donated by believers never seemed to compensate for the miles he tramped, and the endless nights on a solid wooden pallet was never his idea of fulfilment.

After the compulsory three months he left the confines of the monastery and headed for Chieng Mai, telling himself that the famed beauty of the women in that region would at least provide comfort, if not profit. Within a month they had provided both and Boka had burned his saffron robe and begun to let his hair grow again, vowing that it would hang to his shoulders.

The pale skins and almond eyes of the women in Chieng Mai province were almost as valuable a property as the opium gum that the Meo tribesmen brought out of the jungle-clad hills of Burma, two hundred kilometres to the east. At the age of seventeen girls could be bought from poor peasant families and sold to the brothels of Bangkok, Singapore and Rangoon. The girls themselves were invariably reconciled to the life, earning enough to live in comfort and send home money to support their families. Boka was persuasive and ruthless, realizing from the start that he could earn far more by exporting naïve virgins who believed they were going to work for wealthy families.

In his first month he delivered ten girls at $500 a head, and was rich enough to buy a house and rent a large villa in the centre of town. A year later he was supplying his own brothels and massage parlours in Bangkok, employing a small army of thugs to protect the establishments and the endless stream of American servicemen who frequented them. Boka, pimp and murderer, had become a man to be feared.

Gazing at the unconscious American, he cursed the blind stupidity of his own men for failing to recognize Corey's companions as garukis. This error alone was bad enough, but to compound it by allowing them to escape in the river was unforgiveable. The fact that the man responsible was one of his most promising lieutenants made it all the more infuriating. He would have to be dealt with, but for such a man the indignity of a beating would erode his loyalty whilst a reprimand would be taken as a sign of weakness. With bitter anger he knew that the man would have to be eliminated, probably before the day was out. The American groaned and opened his eyes, ending further conjecture on the precise manner of his lieutenant's death, although he made a mental note to make it macabre enough to be remembered for years to come.

Corey's eyes had begun to focus, hardening as memory returned. Boka felt a warm glow of pleasure that verged on gratitude. Here was the object of his anger, the custodian of the information he required, regarding him with scorn, even arrogance. Such a man deserved his personal attention.

'Hold up his feet,' he murmured, reaching for the bamboo.

The knock at the door froze them all. For a full minute no one spoke, every eye on Boka as he stared at the door. Those who knew they were here would have no reason to knock. His fingers flicked a command as he moved behind the chair, a gun gleaming in his hand with a dull sheen.

The man nearest the door produced a Walther P38 from his shirt, then unlatched it and stepped quickly aside. Dani entered, her clothes and hair showing the ravages of the river. She considered them all in turn, finishing with Boka, displaying no surprise at the weapons or the condition of Corey.

'It was good of you to join us,' Boka said thickly, his eyes signalling the man behind her. Before he had time to move Dani lifted empty hands and stepped into the centre of the room.

'I didn't need to come,' she said simply. 'But even a piece of shit such as you has the right to decide how long you live.'

Boka considered the garuki without expression. There was no sign of anyone outside the open door, the only sound the brief rattle of a truck passing on the main highway at the end of the narrow street. His own men were ready to fire the moment he gave the word, but he resisted the urge.

'You must be tired of living.' He shrugged and smiled. 'But I can understand that. You're a garuki. You can't fuck and you can't sing. What else is there?'

Dani flushed, but her gaze was steady. 'There is death, Boka. I thought you'd like to know the kind that Chung has arranged for you.'

The Thai's coarse features glistened as sweat erupted from its pitted surface, like brown paper that had begun to weep. He shook his head, but his voice lacked conviction. 'There hasn't been time. When there has, I'll know and be ready.'

Dani's mouth curled with scorn. 'You pimp! You think you

can compete with the Scorpion. He wants the American back, now, or in one hour his offer will be on every street in Bangkok. It's an offer no one can refuse, Boka. Even your own people.'

A barge moaned on the river and they glanced instinctively towards the window, as though the mournful sound was an echo of their own apprehension. Dani flashed a tight smile at Corey, then turned back to Boka who was trying to convince himself that the garuki was bluffing. The fact that he had been found so soon was a blow to his confidence. He had people on the street outside, people watching the river, yet the slim figure facing him seemed quite unconcerned. He tried not to lick lips that were suddenly dry, but failed. They both knew he had to ask the question.

'What offer?'

The garuki smiled her contempt. 'The first one to deliver your hands, your feet and your balls will receive one thousand dollars. Tomorrow the price will be two thousand. The day after, four. If you survive a week it will be over sixty thousand dollars. And the going rate for murder, set by you, is five hundred!'

The air in the room was suddenly stifling, as though someone had just shut all the doors and windows. He could feel the fear running down his face, like an army of invisible insects. His men watched and waited, their faces masks of indifference. But he knew that behind the opaque eyes they would be weighing the odds, assessing their chances. An hour from now they would no longer be concerned with how – only with when.

'If you have him back,' he said, 'what then?'

Dani's teeth gleamed. 'The matter is forgotten, unless you wish to remind Chung at some other time.'

Boka made an open-handed gesture, his mouth contorting into a placating grin as he desperately tried to recoup his shattered prestige. 'If I had known this man was so important to Chung I would have delivered him myself. You will tell him that?'

Dani nodded, then looked pointedly at the bloody, naked figure in the chair. 'You have his clothes?'

Boka swallowed, nodded, his eyes signalling the men beside the chair. They unfastened the straps, helped Corey to his feet and clumsily assisted him with shirt and trousers. When they had finished Dani stepped forward and took Lee's arm, supporting him as they turned towards the door.

'You understand, Mr Corey, that there was nothing personal in this,' Boka said awkwardly.

Lee paused, then stepped painfully away from Dani. He stooped and picked up one of the bamboo rods, testing its balance as though surprised by the weight.

'Nothing personal, Boka. Why should there be?'

Boka's granulated features glowed with relief. He was still smiling when the weighted length of bamboo hit him across the face, knocking him back over the chair to sprawl on the floor.

Dani's eyes went wide with shock, then very still as she glanced at Boka's men. They waited, uncertain. Corey moved slowly to the door, the bamboo still in his hand. He stopped and gazed around the room.

'Nothing personal. Tell him that.'

Outside they moved to a car where Silva sat tensely at the wheel. Dani bundled Corey inside, then jumped in beside him.

'Are you out of your fucking mind!' she screeched. 'He only had to lift his finger and we'd be dead.'

Lee gave her a crooked grin. 'One of us had to do something drastic. The minute he starts thinking straight he's going to know that you haven't been anywhere near Chung. Right?'

'Yes, but . . .' Dani looked at him in bewilderment. 'How could you know that?'

Lee grimaced and indicated the garuki's stained, wrinkled clothes and straggly hair.

'If you'd been back to the villa you'd have cleaned up and changed. Any idiot knows that a garuki wouldn't be seen dead looking the way you do!'

The car swerved erratically, missing a truck by inches as Silva exploded into laughter behind the wheel. A chorus of horns hooted at them along the street as drivers began to practise their first curses of the day. Pedestrians stopped and shook their heads, wondering sadly what the American could find to be amused about with two garukis at this hour of the morning. And then they, in turn, were amused by the thought that perhaps he had yet to discover his error.

Chapter 13

The full effects of the beating were beginning to tell by the time they reached the villa. Chung, his inscrutable features betraying only a mild relief at Corey's escape, took one look at his face and ordered him to bed. Dani had told him that the other two garukis had already returned with a resentful and waterlogged Jack Masters, so he took the advice and retired.

Tim was waiting with touching concern and a jar of cream which she worked gently into his battered shoulders and back. He slept fitfully for the remainder of the day and night, a fever gripping him in the early hours so that for a while he was delirious, one moment bathed in perspiration, the next shivering uncontrollably. In his lucid moments he was aware of Tim beside the bed, bathing his face and body with ice-cool towels that smelled of cucumber.

Chung came twice, questioning Tim, checking his pulse with concern. Sioo brought sedatives to lower his temperature, but there was little else they could do. The river and the beating had taken their toll and the fever had to run its course. By the end of the second day he was over the worst, stiff and weak, but able to reassure Chung when he called that evening.

'I'll be fine by morning,' he told him. 'All I need is something stronger than this strained chicken they've been feeding me.'

Chung beamed and steepled his hands. 'Please excuse my unworthy house for such lamentable neglect. It will be rectified in the time it takes to prepare whatever you desire.'

Lee indicated about an inch with thumb and forefinger. 'A steak that thick with a salad on the side.'

Chung bowed. 'I will instruct the kitchen myself.' He turned to leave, then paused and looked back. 'The Englishman tells me you promised a vessel in the region of five thousand tons for his services?'

Lee grinned. 'He was hard to please.'

'It is a considerable reward for such a menial task.'

'But worth every cent,' Lee said, his gaze direct, challenging. 'We've got to get that sub out of Vietnam in record time, then bring it here and train a full crew to cross the Pacific. Without a good skipper and a first-rate engineer we haven't got a prayer.'

Chung was silent for a moment, then nodded his head. 'Very well. It is agreed.'

He had reached the door when Lee spoke slowly from the bed. 'I gave Masters my word, Chung.'

The Chinaman considered him with mild reproof. 'I have given you mine. Treachery is a luxury not to be squandered lightly . . . or cheaply.'

The steak turned out to be two inches thick, so tender it could only be genuine Kobe beef from Japan. He ate it with crisp Chinese leaf, tomatoes and small white onions as fresh and sharp as chives. Tim sat and watched with a pleased expression, filling his glass with a dry white wine. When he finally put the tray aside she lay on the bed beside him and put her head on his shoulder. He traced a line along her cheek.

'When did you sleep?'

She shrugged. 'It is not important.'

'You were here all along?'

She nodded, her almond eyes deep and dark.

'Did I talk?'

'Sometimes. Some things you said were strange. About America.'

He felt his stomach tighten, wondering who else had heard. 'Any people?'

She looked sad. 'A woman. Paula. You spoke her name many times when it was bad.'

'Anyone else?'

She frowned, recalling the name. 'A man. He had a funny name.' She smiled at the memory. 'You did not like him. Bastard, you said. Max, you bastard.'

He lay back and closed his eyes, speaking softly, without emotion. 'They were private things, Tim. Can you forget they were said?'

Her lips brushed his cheek. 'They are forgotten. For always.'

'Even if someone should ask?'

He looked at her, watching the disquiet rise in her eyes. She nodded, knowing it was a serious matter. 'They are gone.'

The relief was washing through him when she frowned and added: 'Should I tell Sioo also?'

'Sioo?'

'She heard you speak last night. She was surprised that you talk in American.'

He closed his eyes and tried to work it out. If he had said anything damaging he would know by now. Sioo was shrewd, she would expect him to speak his native language in delirium. He felt a chill of apprehension. If their suspicions were aroused it could tip the delicate balance of trust against him. A small hand stroked his brow and he glanced at Tim, forcing a casual smile.

'Did Sioo ask you any questions?'

'She say you are strange man, to tell her if you say things that are strange. I tell her that you speak in so many languages that it is impossible for one to understand.'

Lee looked at her blankly. 'You said *what*?'

She grinned mischievously. 'Sioo is also strange. Sometimes she make me do things that are bad – not Buddha's way – so I stay way from her. If she think I cannot understand what you say . . . she not bother me. You will not tell her I lie?'

He gazed at her solemnly and shook his head, 'No Tim, I won't breathe a word.'

He awoke sometime after midnight and found her slender body wrapped around his. She was instantly awake, as though an alarm had sounded. They made love in the stillness of the night, each aware of the other's need and closer because of it. Afterwards she slept contentedly in the fold of his arm, her breath whispering softly as dawn dusted the sky.

Corey spent the following morning going over the details of the operation with Chung. The meeting took place in his private suite above the main hall, a series of spacious rooms connected by sliding panels of mahogany inlaid with traditional patterns in gold and silver. The room which served as a study looked out across the grounds to the river, perched high beneath the central pagoda to give a breathtaking view of the river and the glittering spires of the Temple of Dawn. It was the first time he had seen the famous temple which was inlaid with Chinese porcelain so that the sunlight burnished the terraces and spires from dawn to dusk.

The room itself was an imposing blend of Chinese and Thai art. The walls were hung with scrolls and ink drawings, many of them in the calligraphic style of Tao Ch'i, although Lee's sparse knowledge of Chinese art made it impossible to judge their authenticity. An alcove at one end of the room contained a gilded spirit house, whilst ponderous Yak figures stood in each corner, a mosaic of colour, their grotesque features grinning at each other. The furniture was carved from teak, inlaid with mother of pearl and ivory, and the only note of discord in the Oriental furnishings was a modern telephone which buzzed softly from time to time as they spoke. Chung would murmur an apology then speak rapidly into the telephone in Chinese. The conversations never lasted more than a minute, in itself an indication of the power and importance of the Chinaman.

The attack on the harbour at Vung Tau was scheduled to take place in four nights' time when there would be no moon and they could approach the harbour without detection. The captured American submarines were on the north side of the harbour, moored at a quay used by the naval gunboat that patrolled the coastline. Provided they could reach the subs before the alarm was sounded, they would only have to deal with the night pickets who were there to discourage looters. The main guard quarters were located on the south docks where the freight ships unloaded. The two areas were joined by a series of wooden quays, unsuitable for military vehicles. These would have to use the wide boulevard which curved round the harbour, a relic of the days when the French regarded Vung Tau as a weekend retreat from Saigon, some hundred kilometres to the north.

'It should be possible to seize the submarine before your presence is detected,' Chung said. 'But how long you can maintain that state of affairs depends on the other vessels in the harbour.'

'It could take an hour to get the engines started,' Lee pointed out. 'It depends on how recently the batteries were charged.'

'We understand that one of the submarines is used regularly

for training,' the Chinaman told him. 'It is likely that it will be fully charged.'

'It'll still have to be trimmed, the ballast tanks and fuel checked out.'

'Agreed. Benny and his men will deploy along the quay and on the boulevard above. It will be their job to give you as much time as possible.'

'How good are they?'

Chung allowed himself a contented smile, then opened a drawer in his desk and removed a squat, blunt-nosed weapon which he placed in front of the American. Lee picked it up, noting the cylindrical silencer and folding stock. It was the latest Ingram MAC 11 machine-pistol, regarded by many as the deadliest hand weapon in the world. The gun was capable of firing 9-millimetre short-calibre ammunition at the rate of 1200 a minute, each stick magazine holding thirty-two rounds with a quick change mechanism. In the hands of an expert the small machine-pistol could sweep a wide area, each magazine taking only one and a half seconds to empty, a new one requiring only one second to fit.

'How the hell did you get hold of these?' he asked.

Chung's face was inscrutable. 'Our resources are considerable when our need is great. There are always ways, even for a weapon such as this. It means that a dozen or so of Dang's men should be sufficient, each armed with one of these and ten magazines.'

'More than enough,' Lee agreed. 'We could have done with those in nineteen seventy-five.'

'Ah yes, Stockholm. It did not go well for your people.'

Lee shrugged. 'We had problems. The Baader Meinhof team were inexperienced and the Swedish police had the place ringed with marksmen.'

Chung nodded sympathetically. 'And so they finally attacked?'

Lee smiled, amused by the Chinaman's subterfuge. The seizure of the German Embassy in Stockholm in 1975 had been fully reported at the time and he was certain that the Scorpion would have refreshed his memory during the past two days.

'No one attacked. The explosives went off by mistake because the idiot Hausner had wired it up wrong. By the time the group had recovered the police were all over them.'

'A pity,' Chung murmured. 'I take it you were not present?'

Lee shook his head. 'I was there two days before, checking the embassy out, but the group was led by Holger Meins.'

Chung nodded and turned again to the map. His inscrutable features reflected neither satisfaction nor disappointment at the information, but Corey knew he would be reassured. The Stockholm raid, planned by Carlos and carried out by the Baader Meinhof, had been one section of Uri's file he had taken pains to memorize.

After finalizing the plan, Lee went out into the grounds where Benny Dang was working hard on a coronary. Facing him were six pairs of Thais, their ankles bound with bandages, heads and groins covered by padded protectors. They were going through a complex series of attacks and counter attacks, using short bamboo clubs coupled with lightning fast kicks to the head or ribs. Each attack was accompanied by a stream of vituperative commands from Benny, his face puffed with fury, his body gleaming with perspiration in the humid air.

'Kon', he screamed, and the attackers smashed knees into their opponents' stomachs. 'Teh', he bellowed, and they replied with swinging kicks to the throat. At regular intervals Benny would call a halt, wave his fists in the air and hurl a barrage of abuse at the expressionless fighters, then he would march along the line, kicking and kneeing with savage contempt until half of them were lying on the ground. After he had returned to his position they would begin again, chopping, kicking, finding locks and executing breakfalls. The men held black belts in Silat, the Malayan martial art where the hands and arms are used for defence and the knees and feet for attack. In spite of their prowess Benny Dang seemed determined to break each man before him.

Jack Masters and the two latest recruits, Pierre Lalonde and Dick Parish, were sitting beneath a frangipani tree watching the exhibition and laying odds on the number of Thais who would survive the training. The Frenchman was a small, wiry man with untidy brown hair and ears that would have looked better on a jug. He had a quiet, unassuming manner and ran a garage in

Bangkok which had built up a considerable reputation over the last decade, but little else. With the shadow of war lengthening across the southern borders, his future was beginning to look depressingly bleak. Jack Masters had offered him the job of Number Two in the engine-room, and he had accepted without hesitation.

The electronics man was Parish, a square-jawed, close-cropped American with eyes that never seemed to focus. He was Chung's choice, a CIA operator who sold out years ago and had been blandly ignoring recall orders ever since. He survived because he knew more about Chinese heroin than any westerner in Thailand, and his occasional reports on traffic patterns and seasonal harvests were received with grudging respect in Washington. Successive directors had officially fired him at least five times, and he hadn't been paid since 1974, but Parish was not unduly concerned. He received a generous income from Chung and various opium producers in the north, and his numbered account in Switzerland was fat enough to guarantee a comfortable retirement. He had decided to call it a day after one more profitable deal, and Chung's proposition had tied it all up nicely.

Lee had objected strenuously on the grounds that having a 'spook' on the team was like putting an ad in the *Washington Post*, but Chung explained patiently that Parish's loyalty was not in doubt. If he ever returned to the United States, which was highly unlikely, it would be with Chung's blessing, or not at all. Although the Chinaman did not enlarge on this, it was obvious that he had enough on the CIA man to hang him higher than the Statue of Liberty.

Nevertheless their first meeting was a nervewracking experience. It was possible that Parish had met him at some time in the past, and if so it was more than likely that he would blow his cover. The fears proved to be groundless, however, as Parish beamed at him with his bifocal eyes and warmly shook his hand. After a few minutes it was clear that Chung had told him no more than he needed to know. As far as he was concerned, Corey was in it for the money like the rest of them.

It was the absence of the Commander, Sam Kitson, which concerned Corey. He was the key to the operation, yet neither

Masters or Parish had seen any sign of him. Over a lunch of grilled sea bass and gargantuan prawns, Lee tackled Chung about it. The Chinaman frowned as though the name was completely new to him, then went back to peeling a prawn.

'I can still call in one of my people,' Lee reminded him.

'It will not be necessary,' Chung murmured, nibbling at the succulent meat without enthusiasm. 'The matter is receiving our attention.'

'What's that supposed to mean?'

'That things are proceeding in a satisfactory manner.'

'I still want to know when he's going to show.'

'You are an impatient man, Mr Corey. It is a quality which leads to a weakening of the heart and a narrowing of the mind.'

'It also prolongs life. My life, Chung, because I don't step into that sub unless I'm sure that the captain can remember how to take it down and bring it up again. For all I know he might be a hop-head with revolving eyeballs who gets the sweats every time the lights go out!'

Chung held up a prawn in the sun, then tore off its head and looked disappointed, as though he expected a scream of protest. Jack Masters, who made no secret of his dislike for the Chinaman, rattled his plate noisily as he pushed it aside. Parish sat at the end of the table, half-turned away, his bulky figure signalling to anyone who cared to look that he was really somewhere else and not the least inclined to be included in any count of heads.

'Commander Kitson has agreed to undergo certain treatment,' the Chinaman said, his voice brittle. 'When that treatment is completed he will no doubt wish to join us.'

'When?'

'Two, perhaps three days.'

Lee gave him a hard, uncompromising look, gauging the metal of the man. If he was to consolidate his position with the Scorpion there might not be a better opportunity. Carlos would never be content to sit back and take orders, and he had already given way on two key issues.

'It's time we got a few things straight, Chung.' he said quietly, including Masters and Lalonde in his glance. 'If I'm leading then I'm choosing. If you want to wait three days for Kitson to show, you do that. But don't plan on anything else happening this week.'

'We have agreed on Friday,' said Chung, his features thin and yellow, like old rice paper. 'To leave it longer will jeopardize the main purpose of our plan.'

'Which is what?' Masters asked sharply.

'To obtain a submarine and navigate it across the Pacific,' Chung replied blandly. 'For that small service you are being paid handsomely.'

'That depends on what we're carrying,' the Englishman said stubbornly.

The Scorpion shook his head and disected another prawn. 'The cargo is not your concern. If you cannot agree to that I suggest you leave now . . . before you learn of things which make you a threat to us all.'

Masters paled with anger. 'You know better than that, Chung. If I pull out, that's the end of it.'

'On the contrary, if you pulled out it would be the beginning of something I could not stop . . . even if I wished to. Once before you showed no compunction in using privileged information to obtain revenge. Why should I believe this time would be any different?'

'Because I'm telling you,' Masters said tightly.

Lee gave the Englishman an exasperated look. 'Jack, what are you trying to prove? You're in, whatever we carry, and you know it. There's only one commodity that would make us go to this kind of trouble – and you knew that right from the start!'

Masters opened his mouth to make an angry retort, then snapped it shut and glared impotently instead. Lee swung round on Chung, his voice brittle with anger. 'I'm starting to get some pretty lousy vibrations, Chung. You better come up with something fast!'

'I have every confidence in a man of your stature,' the Chinaman murmured. 'You are used to working with amateurs, are you not?'

The question hung between them, Chung's eyes small and shrewd, waiting for confirmation. Masters was also waiting, his expression thoughtful as he absorbed the information. At the end of the table Parish changed position, once more part of the group.

'What exactly is your line, Corey?' he asked.

Lee considered them with remote features, aware that Chung had once again evaded the issue by putting him on the defensive. He made a mental note not to play chess with him, then ignored Parish's question and stood up. 'I've got one or two calls to make. If I get the answers I think I'm going to get, you guys can relax and forget all about submarines.'

The Chinaman lifted a translucent hand, his voice, though quiet, etched with menace. 'I think that would be ill advised.'

'The whole deal is ill advised, Chung. I came here with a plan that would work, just once. I had a crew and a way of getting us there, but now it's bad news. You expect me to sit at the bottom of the China Sea while your pals work it all out! No way!'

The voice of Benny Dang had ceased to bellow below them some time ago. Lee felt his presence before he glanced round. The squat Thai was standing three feet away, his thick mouth gaping in an ugly grin. His gaze was fixed on Chung, waiting for the command, convinced that no man could speak to the Scorpion in such terms and live. The surprise and disappointment were almost comical as Chung ignored him and regarded Corey with composed features. Only his voice, thin like a broken reed, showed the depth of his anger.

'You will work with these people or not at all. There are reasons for this which need no explanation. Do not attempt to question my decision again.'

'I'll question it until I'm convinced you're right – and that won't happen until I've seen Kitson.'

Benny was breathing noisily through wide nostrils, his eyes begging Chung for permission to strike.

'You forget where you are,' said the Chinaman. 'In Thailand you are merely a name, not even a face.'

Lee shrugged, covering the alarm he felt at Chung's words. 'So?'

'So you are most convincing as an American, perhaps too convincing. A man who can continue to play a part, even in the depths of delirium, is a most remarkable man.'

A cicada began to rasp its call from a clump of jasmine near by, the sound immediately answered from the lotus pool. The Oriental cricket, as though aware of the tensions around him, increased its tempo, bringing other answers from around the terrace. Chung glanced towards it irritably, as if the interruption was an open act of defiance. Benny Dang, pathetically eager to show his loyalty, moved to the shrub and parted the foliage. His hand moved quickly, reappearing with the cicada. He beamed and squeezed with thumb and forefinger. The sound stopped abruptly.

'I thought Buddha was against that sort of thing?' Lee commented as the Thai guard threw the mangled insect to the ground.

Chung made a small gesture, dismissing the thought. 'Buddha placed tranquillity above all else, therefore it is permissible to remove unwelcome friends from our midst.'

Lee smiled, acknowledging the subtle menace in the words. 'That's quite a handy philosophy. It beats turning the other cheek.'

Jack Masters stirred restlessly, baffled by the stillness between them. 'I wish somebody would tell me what the hell is going on!'

'Not much,' Lee conceded. 'Chung has one philosophy, we have another. Personally I don't give a damn about either of them.'

'Then what do you give a damn about?' asked Parish. 'If I'm going along on this jaunt I'd just as soon know now.'

'Staying alive.' He glanced at the Chinaman. 'And you ought to remember, Chung, that the Koran teaches revenge for the death of a brother.'

A wisp of a smile touched Chung's lips, a shadow of inner laughter, but there was no way of telling whether it was derisive or sincere. Masters was exchanging exasperated looks with Parish and Lalonde, aware that some subtle game was in progress and wondering if he was the only one without a bet.

'I suggest you finalize your preparations, gentlemen,' said Chung, rising from the table. 'If there is anything you require I shall be honoured to assist you.'

He turned to leave, aware of Lee's dissatisfaction. As he

passed him he murmured, too low for the others to hear: 'If you are determined to see Kitson you may ask Sioo to take you to him.'

'Do we have to work it out for ourselves, Corey?' Masters asked after he had gone.

'It's called power sharing,' Lee replied mockingly. 'Chung wants to call the shots while we pull the trigger.'

'I hope you are wrong,' said the Frenchman. 'I'm not getting paid to pull triggers.'

'You think we just walk in and wave to the Vietnamese?' Parish asked sarcastically.

'There won't be time for that,' Masters replied. 'With luck the fighting will be after we're on the sub, and our job will be getting those bloody engines started.'

'He's right,' said Lee. 'Benny will take care of any trouble. His men will be using MAC 11s, and that will give them enough fire power to hold the quay.' He glanced at Masters. 'Just how difficult is it to start up the engines?'

'It all depends on the batteries. If they're holding a full charge we just wind up the diesels then push off. The minute we clear the harbour we cut diesel, switch to batteries and dive.'

'Diesels are noisy. Why not go out on electric?'

'The sub can't reverse on its electric motors, and we'll probably need to back away from the quay. But the main thing is we need the batteries for underwater.'

'And if the batteries are dead?' asked Lee.

Masters grimaced. 'Then we have a new set of problems. We'll need to run a lead from the quay, either a mobile generator or a truck. Then we'll have to run on the surface for at least four hours to get a decent charge in them.'

'Christ,' said the Frenchman, 'I don't like the sound of that.'

They looked at each other, weighing the risks. Parish sucked air through his teeth, his pale, lifeless eyes reflecting nothing at all.

'There's still time to pull out,' he said, as though it was a new idea. 'If the Vietnamese get their hands on us we'll all be up against the nearest wall.'

'I'll bet Chung never thought of that,' Lee answered dryly.

Masters agreed. 'If there weren't any risks he'd be paying us by the hour.'

Parish shrugged, his voice cynical. 'Chung never spent a dollar in his life without spitting on it first. But he's straight once he's made the deal, and that goes right down the line. If he says the sub is being used, you can bet your life on it.'

Masters gave him a disgusted look. 'Isn't that what we *are* doing!'

'It all depends on Kitson,' Lee said, gesturing towards the house. 'We have to be sure of him.'

Parish's laugh was sour, derisive, his eyes focusing somewhere behind Corey's head. 'Right now I'd feel better if I was sure of you. Your ID is about as convincing as a hooker on a honeymoon and if you're going to start pussy-footing around up there in Cong country I'd just as soon leave you back here with the butterflies!'

Lee waited until his laughter had wheezed into an uneasy silence. 'Play it cool, Parish. The last time I went to bed with a spook – I buried him!'

He left him with the thought, enjoying the blend of greed and consternation that washed over his features. He looked like a kleptomaniac at a January sale.

Chapter 14

Samuel Kitson was born in Dodgeville, Wisconsin, in the spring of '51, and studied law in Milwaukee, eventually aiming to join his father's practice in Madison. It all went wrong in the long, hot summer of '69 when a certain Penny Fletsbury said no on their third date beneath an arch of moonlit elms only a stone's throw from the local cemetery. The seventeen-year-old's negative response, albeit a reluctant one, came after two hours of heavy petting and was not greeted with much sympathy and understanding by Samuel. The sight of small, firm breasts with nipples still aroused from his ardent caresses; the slender golden legs and full rounded hips was just too much. So whilst Penny said 'no' with increasing hysteria, Samuel said yes and proceeded to back up words with actions. By the time he had reached his goal she had ceased to struggle, lying in frigid silence until he was through. It was only then, as reality intruded on passion, that he began to realize the full consequences of his actions. A mumbled apology hardly seemed sufficient, particularly as his unwilling partner was stumbling towards Main Street with a pair of tattered briefs in her hand.

It would be no exaggeration to say that Penny Fletsbury was mad as hell at losing her virginity. The gamut of emotions that ran with her through the night had little to do with logic. Like so many girls who grew up in pink bedrooms with fuzzy gonks and china ornaments around the photographs of mom and dad, she had fantasized for years about the momentous occasion. The only consistent feature of those fantasies had been that when it happened it would be with her full approval and assistance – and quite beautiful.

Unfortunately none of these conditions had prevailed and it was, therefore, a betrayal of too many dreams to be forgotten or forgiven. The bittersweet fire of revenge had to be assuaged, and the white-faced mumbling idiot running after her down the street was going to get everything he deserved – if not more. It was to be expected, therefore, that Penny's story had some embellishments, and that her mother, after fainting twice, should embellish it further when recounting it to her husband. Maxwell Fletsbury was not a man to be trifled with, nor was he one to let any grass grow under his feet. Less than an hour later he was thundering on the Kitsons' front door with blood in both eyes. What made it all rather catastrophic was the fact that Maxwell Fletsbury was a judge.

As Counsellor Kitson was to say some months later, when the dust had settled and he was able to utter his son's name without prefacing it with an expletive, if the damned fool had to get his end away he could have done it all over town with a very sizeable proportion of the female population, married and unmarried. But to stick it in the judge's virgin daughter was about as stupid as using it to hold up the local bank.

By this time, however, Samuel Kitson had joined the navy.

He was a tall, gangling figure with brown hair and forgettable grey eyes. In his early twenties, as third officer on a corvette, he affected a drooping moustache that always looked lopsided. His life in the navy was comfortable and uncomplicated, and because of his reserved, almost spartan nature, he made a good officer with a future. That future was realized in 1973 when he transferred to the submarine service and quickly became first officer on a Guppy operating out of Pearl Harbor. He took part in various attacks on shipping in the Gulf of Haiphong, hitting at the Hanoi supply lines. But as the war in Vietnam went into its final phase, and Congress began to admit, with increasing fervour, that three million bucks a day was too much to pay for anybody's freedom, least of all a bunch of pot-smoking Asians, Kitson found himself with his first command based at Vung Tau.

The harbour was small and crowded with junks, coastal freighters and barges loading up with the never-ending tide of refugees fleeing from all points north of Saigon. There was so much traffic off the coast that sailing a dinghy was a hazardous operation – navigating a fat-bellied Guppy was pure lunacy. Yet the squadron of submarines based at Vung Tau was under orders to patrol the coast and harass enemy supply ships and gunboats. It was not an ideal situation for a new commander, but Samuel Kitson had long since ceased to wonder at the fickleness of fate. For some years he had been tempering the harsh reality of war with the soporific influence of pot. He had never been a drinking man, and although there were occasional women in his life, he had never quite got over the traumatic experience of Penny Fletsbury. Marijuana brought escape and a loosening of the soul, at first with an occasional cigarette on shore leave, but gradually in long, mind-blowing sessions with water pipes when hashish was laced with increasing quantities of opium.

He got his first 'buzz' with a blend of Thai stick and opium and the euphoria lasted an entire afternoon. His first 'flash' was achieved by sniffing heroin whilst smoking a mixture of hash and opium, but he resisted injecting H into his system largely because the presence of needle marks would be evidence enough to lose him his command. Like so many servicemen in Vietnam, he felt that pot, opium, H and morphine were all part of the local colour to be used as an antidote to fear, depression and sheer boredom. His dependence on the drugs was never apparent until things really got bad at Vung Tau.

Saigon, sixty miles to the north, was about to fall and in Washington Congress was mouthing fresh platitudes about limited commitments and a phased withdrawal. In real terms, this meant a river of humanity stumbling along the main highway to Vung Tau, dull-eyed men, women and children clutching at the last hope of escape. Some days the Vortiko missiles were hitting the highway at five minute intervals, so regular you could set your watch by them, and the wind blew off the paddy fields acrid with the stench of war. Yet the refugees never slackened their remorseless trek to the sea, their minds numbed by the horrors that erupted around them in flame, blood and agony.

Watching them grow into an ever widening sea around the port, Kitson was filled with wonder and enormous guilt. The barges and ships loading each day at the quay could take only a fraction of the vast throng of desperate people, many of them unable to pay the exorbitant fee charged by some of the captains for the brief voyage to Thailand or Cambodia. Any vessel able to float was being put into commission, the harbour and sea beyond choked with ancient junks and sluggish barges. Taking a submarine through them was a nightmare, yet orders were to continue patrolling the coast as far as Da Nang. Of the squadron of four Guppies, one was already out of commission and waiting for replacement parts, another on long-range surveillance off Haiphong. Kitson alternated with their sister sub, spending three days out and three days in.

It was the days in that began to corrode the mind. By the beginning of April more than a hundred thousand Vietnamese were camped around the port. Military Police tried to hold back the majority of them from the docks, but each day it became more difficult. Those who could not walk on to the barges and freighters tried rafts, sampans, even swimming out to clutch at fenders. Each morning there were more dark bundles floating in the oily water like strange sea carrion. After a while no one bothered to remove the bodies any more. They rose and fell throughout the day, a tide of flotsam that had become the ultimate debris of war.

Kitson watched it happen with a black despair. Half the

complement of his submarine now had to protect it from stowaways in the night. They still managed to reach the steel decks, only to be thrown back into the harbour, sometimes with a broken skull. Coming to terms with that, with the ocean of hopeless faces, required assistance. Some chose the bottle, others the eager supply of women who saw the servicemen as another way of getting out. Of the remainder, a considerable proportion chose the euphoria of marijuana, hash, opium and H. By mid-April Kitson was starting each day with a cocktail of amphetamine and barbiturate tablets, followed by a pipe of hashish and opium. The 'buzz' this produced would build to a series of 'flashes' as he sniffed pure Chinese heroin, enabling him to drift in and out of the dream state for the rest of the day. Each mixture was chosen with care, the amounts of opium determined by his mood and schedule for the day. His supplies of hashish ranged from Thai to Turkey and he prided himself on his ability to identify each type. Facing the harsh realities of the world outside became a quite simple formula – a gram or two of hash, a few chips of opium with perhaps just a pinch of morphine. Laid out beside a long-stemmed pipe with the correct level of water in its bowl, would be pure H, barbiturates and amphetamines – the uppers and downers that would counteract the less pleasant side effects of the hard drugs.

It came as no surprise at all to Commander Kitson that he should run his submarine into the side of a 100-ton barge. He had been predicting as much for weeks and, in a blissfully euphoric mood, he confided to his Number One that it was better late than never, and at least they wouldn't have to worry about getting in and out of the fucking harbour any more.

They limped back into Vung Tau with a caved in bow, minus a forward fin and with a jammed main valve. It was 29 April, less than six hours to the fall of Saigon. The sky was agog with giant metal butterflies beating their way out to the carriers waiting off shore, and what few senior officers were left had already begun shredding their files. When Kitson was subsequently relieved of his command and told to prepare himself for a court martial, some fifteen minutes after a medical officer had verified that he was higher than the proverbial kite, the documents accompanying the order were also shredded within the hour. Vung Tau was being hit around the clock by Vortiko rocket batteries surrounding the town, and the remains of the Marine Division were fighting in the suburbs. The latest word from Saigon was that the Chinooks were evacuating the embassy and army HQ, and that Vietcong guerrillas were already attacking the airport.

Kitson, waiting miserably for orders to proceed to the 7th Fleet, some ten miles off the coast, watched his men board a naval gunboat. He was to have the dubious privilege of being flown out by Air America, the CIA's private airline, but the distinctive silver helicopters which were running a shuttle service between the port and the fleet, seemed to have a busy schedule which didn't include disgraced commanders.

By noon most of the small craft, including a fleet of fishing boats and the remaining barges, had put to sea crammed with refugees. Reports were circulating that a Vietnamese armoured column was advancing on the town and that the marines were falling back on the port. Kitson desperately needed to score, but his main supplies were in his quarters a mile up the road, and from the steady thump of rockets and rattle of machine-guns it was not the best time to go. A silver helicopter clattered over his head, hovering, then touching down on the emergency landing pad beside the fuel terminal. He watched lethargically as a bright-faced lieutenant jumped out and dashed over to the marine evacuation marshal. A moment later he saw them looking towards him, then the lieutenant started briskly across. The only emotion he felt was regret that he had not gone into town to get his supplies.

The lieutenant, after a snappy salute, informed him that they couldn't expect to hold Vung Tau for more than a few hours. Kitson gave him a pitying look. Just about anybody at the port could have told him that. He picked up his briefcase, expecting to be taken to the helicopter. Instead the lieutenant, in an apologetic tone, revealed that it had just occurred to the high command that three Guppies were being left to the enemy. They had to be scuttled, and he was the only naval man around who knew how to operate the destruct systems. He looked relieved when the Commander agreed to carry it out, then dashed back to the helicopter, promising to pick him up on his next trip.

Samuel Kitson was already on his way, having just remembered that in his cabin, taped beneath the bunk, was a tin containing his favourite blend of hash and opium.

Reality returned some time after dark as the dream-laden world retreated to the sound of distant explosions. He pulled himself off the bunk and made his way up through the conning tower, the euphoria still clouding his mind so that he was serenely indifferent to the scene which confronted him. The harbour was in flames, the fuel tanks on the north pier cascading rivers of fire into the sea. An assault craft was burning on a slipway less than a hundred yards from the submarine and the night was reverberating with the thud of exploding ammunition from the blazing supply depot. Kitson surveyed it coolly, noting that the tanks moving into the harbour from the boulevard above were Russian. Beyond them the sky was a crimson flower, pulsing with the glow of fires in the town. It had its own macabre beauty, but although he wanted to savour the moment he decided reluctantly to forgo the pleasure.

Moving calmly, without haste, he went along the deck to the forward hatch and dragged out the emergency tender. Activating the twin air cylinders, he let the craft inflate whilst going below to collect the small outboard and fuel tank. Heavy smoke was rolling across the harbour from the burning fuel depot, effectively concealing him from the Vietnamese as they moved along the quays. Kitson gave them no thought, taking his time mounting the outboard, then slipping the tender into the water and sliding down after it. The outboard started immediately, which pleased him, and without a backward glance he chugged out across the harbour, peering through the oily smoke, towards the open sea.

By the time dawn tinted the sky he was two miles off-shore, heading south-west for the headland of Mui Bai Bung. The South China Sea remained calm all day and he was only mildly grateful when a freighter on its way from Manilla picked him up off the headland. Two days later he was in Bangkok and heading for the nearest opium house.

Lee Corey found him curled up on a cot in a room that reeked with odours of vomit and urine. Sioo stood by the door, her nose pinched against the stench. The former submarine commander was skeleton thin, his chest, arms and legs red from the constant scratching as he fought the worst of the withdrawal symptoms, the unbearable itching that felt like an army of ants marching beneath the skin. His eyes were narrow slits of agony, his nose running incessantly, his breath wheezing from tormented lungs. When the American tried to turn him on to his back he whimpered like a wounded animal, covering his eyes with shaking hands.

'It is the worst day,' Sioo said, without compassion.

'And you think he's going to be capable of commanding a sub?' Corey demanded bitterly. 'He couldn't even walk to the door!'

'I know about drugs and people who use them,' she said simply. 'He has not used the needle, so the symptoms are bad but not hopeless. By tomorrow he will be able to take food, the day after the worst effects will go.'

'In case Chung hasn't told you, we're supposed to leave the day after tomorrow.'

She nodded, unperturbed. 'It is no problem. When he has taken food, I will give him methadone in linctus form. It will bring him back very quickly, you will see.'

'I can see now and no way do I submerge with a junkie!'

She smiled patiently. 'It will be all right. Methadone will be very good for him. He will be very sharp, in complete control. I am never wrong about such things.'

Lee gave her a doubtful look and went back towards the house. Dani was waiting for him, her teeth gleaming as he approached.

'Hi, honey, how's the head?'

'Fragile.'

'Maybe we should go into town tonight?'

He gave her a crooked grin. 'You're a glutton for punishment.'

The garuki winked and nodded towards the gardens. They went down past the lotus pool, where Benny's men were sitting in groups taking MAC 11s apart, to the lower terraces that made a wild profusion of colour against the backdrop of the river. A guard was patrolling the wall, but paid them no attention as Dani glanced casually around then sat beneath a palm tree, patting the ground beside her.

Lee sat down, raising an eyebrow. 'If we keep meeting like

this, people will talk.'

Her laughter was soft and full of mirth. 'Not around here, American.'

'So what's on your mind?'

'Boka.'

Lee glanced at her sharply. 'I thought we'd settled that?'

'Maybe. Silva did some checking around the bars last night, looking for reasons why he should stick his nose in. The word is he's going to wait eight days then hang you out to dry.'

'You told Chung yet?'

Dani was uncertain, squinting at the sun. 'He has other things to arrange. You are my problem, so I ask you – why eight days?'

Lee thought about it, waving a hand to discourage a jumbo-sized dragon-fly that was getting aggressive. 'If it's what I think it is, then he's in touch with somebody here.'

Dani beamed at him. 'Hey, for a Yank you're really on the ball. Any idea who?'

'Why don't you do some of the work?'

'Okay. You hit the sub on Friday, get back on Sunday. Two days later we start taking delivery of the cargo. That's eight days.'

'When Boka plans his hit.'

'Right, but only Chung, Sioo, my girls and Benny know that much.'

'You're sure about that?'

Dani steepled hands and gave him a mocking bow. 'I'm sure. It was too soon for Masters and the others to have known. Did you tell anyone?'

He shook his head. 'I hadn't even worked out the timetable. What about Parish, he's used to putting things together?'

'Maybe. I prefer Benny. He's such a stupid shit he would think he could get away with it.'

'That could be tricky. Time to tell Chung.'

Dani plucked a jasmine blossom and proceeded to disect it, not looking at Lee. 'There's the girl, of course. She could have heard things when you were sick.'

'Tim? No way.'

'Sioo suspects her.'

Lee's mouth tightened, his gaze boring into the garuki. 'Then Sioo's full of crap. Tell her that.'

'You don't tell Sioo such things,' Dani murmured quietly. 'Not if you want to keep all your marbles.'

'I get the feeling she's handy with drugs.'

'All kinds. Some lift you, turn you on, others take you so far out you never come back. Everyone is very careful with Sioo.'

'I'll keep it in mind.'

'Do that.' Dani considered him, her mouth small and worried. 'Sioo uses Benny, me, many others. If she thinks Chung is in danger then she will strike first.'

'What's she protecting? A pension?'

Dani's voice dropped to a whisper. 'Sioo is Chung's daughter. There is nothing she will not do to protect him. Even though you are Carlos, it will not stop her.'

Lee shrugged, hiding his surprise at the garuki's casual reference to Carlos. 'We're in this for the same reasons. She knows that.'

Dani was dubious. 'She asks a lot of questions. I think soon she will screw you.'

'Where I come from they wait to be asked,' he said, grinning.

'Sioo will not wait,' Dani replied with conviction. 'She has her own ways.'

With that the garuki rose, smiled briefly and strolled away through the grounds. Lee remained beside the palm and put it all together. Sioo was obviously asking questions about him, but this could be due to her natural caution. His only mistake so far had been during the fever. With a grimace he realized how easy it would be for someone fluent in Russian to trap him. It was the kind of situation that Max Weller liked to describe as – one of those moments when it's wise to check which trouser leg it's hanging down.

He would have been even more concerned if he had known that Chung and Sioo were discussing the possibility of his duplicity that very moment, high above him in the study beneath the ornate pagoda tower.

'He is an intelligent man with the ability to weigh risks and evaluate his chances of deceiving us. He would know that the odds are against such a deception.'

Sioo turned from the narrow window from where she had been watching Corey strolling through the grounds. 'I know he seems to be everything he claims, and yet I feel that he is not. All that we could know about Carlos he would also know, so it tells us nothing.'

'There are the surgical scars.'

'Of course, but again they are not conclusive. He is not as heavy as I expected. Carlos always carried excess fat.'

'Which is an admirable reason to lose it,' Chung murmured, sipping tea from a fragile bowl which he held daintily between the fingers of both hands. 'It would not be a difficult task.'

'I still believe we should contact Black September in Kuwait and have them confirm.'

'You suggest too many impossibilities. In the first instance he would have to be aware of our desire to leave this country, that we have made contact with Palestinians, that they have obtained the list from Farazzi. Such a formidable task would be beyond the bounds of reason.'

'But if it was not,' Sioo said in a brittle-thin voice, 'you would not survive the consequences. Even if you did not lose everything, you would lose face with the warlords and the Triads.'

'What you say is true, yet barely worthy of serious consideration.'

'But tomorrow you make a pact with the warlords. From that moment you are committed to taking all supplies of heroin. You are committed to giving them every dollar you possess – more. To purchase all their stock is beyond us . . . you know it.'

Chung smiled an inscrutable smile and sipped his tea. Sioo considered him with eyes that looked behind the impassive features. After a moment she sighed and sank to her knees before him. 'It is as I feared. You do not intend to pay.'

The Chinaman's voice was barely audible, as though even he did not wish to hear the words. 'I have done business with four generations of warlords, they know me like the Mon and the Meo. If I say the money comes from Kuwait, then they will believe it.'

'And then?'

He gazed around the room, as though committing it to memory for the last time. 'It will be my last transaction. Within hours we will leave Thailand for ever.'

'But they will not allow you to leave.'

Chung looked down at her with a mild surprise. 'Of course not. Therefore they must all die.'

Sioo shuddered, then rose to her feet, taking the bowl from him. She swirled the remains of the tea, allowing the liquid to spill over the sides. She did it three times, then upturned the bowl with an abrupt movement. When she turned it upright again it contained a mosaic of tea leaves. She gazed at them for a time, her eyes small and still. Chung waited patiently for the answer.

'It is a strange path, a tortuous one.'

'But one we must take.'

'Only if the omens are good.' She turned the bowl towards him. 'An eagle watches.'

He nodded. 'Carlos.'

'Perhaps. There are also others. A dog, a jackal perhaps.'

'Again, Carlos.'

She shook her head, her eyes troubled. 'No. It is not the same sign. And there is death. There is much death.'

'Ours?'

'I do not know. Perhaps it is not yet ordained.'

'Then we must tread most carefully,' Chung said, an edge of mockery in his voice. 'We must watch that we do not step into the wrong shadows.'

'We can do that by sending a message to Kuwait.'

The Chinaman hesitated, then nodded. 'Very well, but I do not expect a useful response. If you have to pursue this, you must do it here, with the object of your suspicions.'

Sioo moved back to the window, searching for Corey, finding him on the upper lawn talking to the slender figure of Tim. She smiled, eyes glowing as images surfaced in her mind. When she turned back to Chung he read the naked hunger on her face.

'He must not be harmed, nor alienated.'

'I understand that,' she answered, her voice sharp with reproof. 'It will be a most pleasant experience.'

Chapter 15

Dani's prophecy came true sooner than Lee had expected.

Throughout the rest of the day he relaxed in the luxuriant gardens, content to watch Benny's rigorous training programme. Masters and Lalonde retired to their room to study a detailed plan of the Guppy's engines, and Parish went to sleep on the terrace with a glass of beer at his elbow. In the evening Chung joined them for dinner in the dining-room off the main gallery and the conversation grew increasingly good natured as each course appeared.

They began with Kangtom Yum, a spicy soup containing shrimp and chicken, and flavoured with lemon grass. This was followed by Hor Mok, a large fish of the bass family smothered in hot chili sauce that succeeded in bringing tears to Corey's eyes, to everyone's amusement. There was also Nua Pat Kling, a beef and ginger dish, and a crispy Peking Duck. Sioo supervised the serving of the food by two young Thai girls, paying Lee more attention than usual. She was wearing a colourful sarong which enhanced her pale skin, the flawless contours of a face that glowed like delicate porcelain. Even when she was away from the table, hovering in the shadows along the teak-lined room, Lee was conscious of her gaze. When their eyes met she made no attempt to conceal the heat that lurked there, although he was cynically aware that it was about as genuine as the smile that accompanied all her actions.

Parish, who had lost his earlier antagonism and was clearly making an effort to repair the damage, gave Corey a knowing wink and gestured towards the girl. 'Looks as though you're getting the VIP treatment.'

Lee gave him a nonchalant grin. 'It's just my natural charm.'

'It's not your charm I'm worried about.' He glanced towards Chung who was in conversation with Jack Masters, dropping his voice. 'It's your stamina!'

'I knew I should have brought the Phyllosan!'

Parish chuckled. 'Listen, buddy, that chick has got more potions than Burroughs Wellcome.'

'Anything special I should ask for?'

'Yeah – time off for good behaviour!'

Parish began to shake with laughter, then tried to stifle it as Sioo moved up to them with bowls of tea. Her eyes rested briefly on the CIA man, conveying a chilling warning that choked the laughter in his throat and left him gazing self-consciously at his hands. Sioo smiled mockingly at Lee and went round the table to serve the others.

The incident was further proof, if any had been needed, of the power the woman commanded. Parish was subdued for the remainder of the meal and refused to be drawn on the subject, except to advise him to go along with whatever she had in mind and just hope that it was pleasant.

It was a hope that Lee fervently shared, but when he returned to his room Tim was there as usual and not Sioo, as he had half expected.

'Everything okay?' he asked casually.

She nodded and kissed him lightly on the cheek. 'The minutes are long without you.'

'You're playing hard to get again.'

Her mouth had lines of worry around it, like broken cobwebs. She crossed to a bottle of wine already open on the table beside the bed, pouring a glass and bringing it back to him. He accepted it, watching her and feeling the beginnings of tension.

'You have some too.'

'Later.'

He smelled the wine. It was sweet and full of treachery, and her eyes were windows to sadness. He put it down and folded his arms around her. She was like a spring wound up too tightly.

'You want me to drink it?'

She nodded, not breathing. 'It is a good wine.'

'Chosen by Sioo?'

She flinched as though he had struck her. 'How you know?'

'She's been thinking about it all day.' He picked up the glass of wine and took it into the bathroom, pouring it down the washbasin. She watched worriedly. 'Now what do we do?'

'I must go.' She started for the door, showing little enthusiasm when he pulled her back.

'Tim, it's not that easy. I want answers.'

The fear that warped her mouth made her voice shrill. 'You make it very bad for me. Sioo will say I tell you about the wine. She will send me away.'

He shook his head. 'Not as long as I'm here. All you have to do is say I drank it.'

She considered the idea, at first with hope, and then with dismay. 'She would know. Sioo always knows, so then she send me to Benny.' The brown eyes were huge and sad. 'I no want to go to Benny.'

Lee nodded, not finding it difficult to agree with her. He pulled her to the bed, sitting down. 'Okay. If I take the stuff, what happens?'

She was uncertain. 'She use so many things. Maybe for you it is not so bad.' Her eyes searched his. 'Maybe something you like very much.'

'Do you know why she's doing it?'

Tim nodded, pleased that she had the answer. 'She says you are big mystery man. Sioo wants to know all about you.'

'I'll bet she does,' Lee said tersely, picking up the bottle of wine and sniffing at it. The smell told him nothing at all. He poured some into the glass, tasting it. It was sweet, spicy, like most of the Thai wines.

Tim was beginning to look worried again, glancing at her watch, at the door. Sioo would expect her to call soon. He weighed the odds, not liking the alternatives. If he refused to play by her rules it would be taken as proof that he had something to hide. Chung had too much to lose to take any chances, so his only alternative would be a forced interrogation, probably with drugs. It was a chilling thought.

'What do you think she uses?' he asked Tim.

'Thai stick, opium, pure H and maybe coke too.'

'That's a hell of a cocktail.'

'It is only small amounts. Sioo knows which to use, how to make them . . .' she brought her small hands together, 'become one. People say she also uses Ghost Oil.'

'What the hell is that?'

Tim glanced around the room as though the ghosts were

present. 'It is a voodoo thing. It comes from the dead body of a woman with child.'

'I had a feeling I shouldn't have asked.'

Tim took the glass of wine from him. 'It is very potent, but I do not think she would harm you.' She gave him a nervous smile and swallowed the contents of the glass before he could prevent her. 'Now you can be sure.'

The mixture of drugs took effect almost immediately. Her pupils dilated, her breathing becoming faster as her features relaxed, darkening. She leaned towards him, the movement turning into a slow motion collapse on to the bed, but her eyes were warm and alive, never leaving his face as though half afraid it would disappear.

'You are gold, like Buddha,' she said, a note of awe in her voice. 'You look just like my Buddha.'

'What else do you feel?'

'Things move. The light moves. I feel very good.' She tried to sit up, but it didn't work out and she rolled on to her back, laughing softly. 'I feel so good.'

'You can think straight?'

She rolled her eyes at him, waving a hand that seemed to float in the air with a mind of its own. 'Sure I can think straight. I think about the butterflies and the birds, they are everywhere I want them to be. I think about you too.' She turned on her side, her eyes deep, beating at him. 'I think I want to make love.'

'I wonder what gave you that idea,' Lee said dryly, reaching for the bottle.

There had been a whisper of sound outside the door and he didn't have to be Sherlock Holmes to deduce the cause. He poured half a glass of wine, then carried the bottle into the bathroom and emptied most of the contents down the drain. Returning to the bedroom he put the bottle on the bureau, crossed his fingers and drank the wine. He got as far as the bed before the 'buzz' came and the room began to glow with a golden light. Lying down seemed to be quite a sensible idea, and then as the slim figure of Tim moved against him he began to appreciate the subtleties of Sioo's potion. All his senses were being stimulated, but his tactile sensitivity was phenomenal, enabling him to be totally aware of her entire body from the lightest touch.

A warm wind blew across the room, twisting the ribbons of light, plucking at the corners of his mind so that he seemed to sway with them. He turned and found Sioo beside him, her eyes probing, her hands touching him like silken leaves. Her full mouth curved into a smile, and it was as though he knew what she had said before the words were spoken.

'You gave Tim some wine?'

'I never drink alone.'

'Then she will have to stay.'

'Damned right she will. This could be a very heavy night.'

Sioo's laughter vibrated in the air long after her mouth had closed. She stood looking down at him, then did something with a cord at her neck and the sarong seemed to revolve around her until it was a flimsy puddle on the floor. He gazed at her slim, naked figure and felt a searing need that was blinding in its intensity, but she was gone before his hands could reach her, moving round the bed to Tim who lay on her back with a dreamy expression. Sioo undressed her, straddling her with slender legs, turning to watch his reaction as her hands moved intimately over Tim's breasts. The girl gasped, then as the hands moved down, to slip between her thighs she began to moan, her voice rising to a thin, shuddering cry as Sioo expertly caressed her. When her body finally arched up off the bed she plunged rigid fingers into her and Tim howled again and again, each cry pulsing with the intensity of her orgasm.

Throughout the calculated seduction of the girl, Sioo's eyes had been on Lee, watching each flicker of movement. It was as though she was reading both thought and emotion, sensing his hunger and weighing it against other disciplines that held back the primitive urges in him. He let his mouth and eyes mirror the more basic emotions, reaching for her as she moved away from Tim.

'You trying to prove something?' he asked.

'Only what I already know. You have a taste for decadence, Carlos.'

He pulled her roughly against him, feeling sensations exploding in his brain, forcing a corner of his mind to stay cool and sharp. Her hands plucked at his clothes. Warm air washed against his skin like dry surf.

'It is time we learned about each other,' she whispered. 'I want you to tell me the images that come into your mind.'

'Right now there's only one,' he said, sliding his hands around her waist, moving them to warm, slender legs.

She pushed him gently away. 'Images of home, your mother.'

The buzzing in his head was like friendly bees, rising and falling to the surge of blood in his veins. Her hands stroked him, increasing the tempo, but he clung to her words, pushing the vivid images away and substituting pictures from a file marked Sanchez. 'Dona, tall, dark and beautiful. The best years were in Mexico, then Jamaica. Just the three of us.'

'You and your parents.'

Lee gave her an owlish look and made circles around her nipple. 'No. There had been many rows, so we went away. Father stayed in San Cristobal, we went with mother. Vladimir was born in Mexico, then we all went to live in Jamaica. A big old house looking down on the sea.'

He stared beyond her, as though he was there now. She watched him intently, her eyes like ebony beads. Waves of sound and colour were beating at him, threatening to break down the fragile wall he had erected in his mind. From the increasing tempo he knew he was building to a high and the moment he freaked out the last control would be gone. He could say anything. Destroy his cover, discuss C2, anything. Perspiration burst from the pores of his skin and he was aware of each drop, its consistency, temperature and weight. He felt them beginning to slide down his face, merging together, becoming cool rivers rushing across epidermal plains. Her mouth opened to speak, her eyes already telegraphing the awareness of his struggle. Somewhere in inner space a gigantic clock had been ticking, but now each beat was stretching into a reverberating chime.

He did the only thing he could do that would stifle her questions. Even as she uttered the first word he was reaching out, turning her as she tried to pull away, parting silk-smooth thighs beneath him and plunging into her as the last chime became a ringing bell. He was only dimly aware of her voice, soft and persuasive, trying to bring him back. Instead he concentrated on the focal point of his lust, driving into her with a relentless rhythm until the voice stopped and hands were clutching at him, urging him on. Her first gasping cry was the howl of distant wind, twisting the shimmering room as it built into a frenzy of sound. Arms pulled at him, turning him round, then Tim was thrusting at him, her mouth searching for his, her body shuddering with the intensity of her need.

His first climax was a shattering explosion that sent the mind soaring away from the figures on the bed, and he watched with mild astonishment as the assault continued. After a while it became impossible to differentiate between the two women. At times all three were locked in bizarre triangles, each thrusting at the other, the room a chorus of gasping echoes that built to a single piercing cry. There was no way of telling how long it lasted, how many peaks of sensuality they reached.

The only person who might have known was Sioo, but at some time she had also drunk the wine. Whether out of envy or despair it was impossible to say.

He woke in sunlight to find them both curled around him. His mouth tasted like the bottom of a very busy bird-cage and he felt as though he'd done fifteen rounds with a gorilla. Extricating himself from the girls, he went into the bathroom and stood under the shower. After a few minutes he plucked up the courage to turn it on, groaning under the weight of the jets.

When he returned to the bedroom Sioo was wrapping a towel around herself. She smiled briefly, then went to her handbag and took out a bottle of pills. Shaking two into her hand, she gave him one and swallowed the other. He gazed at it dubiously.

'It will help,' she assured him. 'Tim will need one also.'

He took the pill and sat on the bed, resisting the temptation to crawl under the sheet. Tim showed no signs of surfacing, but if she felt only half as bad as he did it was just as well. Sioo came out of the bathroom and began putting on the flimsy sarong. Her slender legs and flaring buttocks were a reminder of the night. She sensed the thought, turning to him with eyes hollowed by the memories.

'It was . . . interesting?'

He grimaced. 'All of that. What the hell was in that concoction?'

'Things you would know, and things you would not. But no dirt. Nothing to warp the mind.'

'You'd better be right.'

Her lips brushed his cheek. 'You are important to us, Carlos. I doubt if you know just how important.'

'But you still find time to play games,' he said dryly.

She smiled, glancing at Tim on the bed. 'It was a pleasant game, one we must play again.' She leaned against him, her hips moving boldly. 'What a pity you will not be here tonight.'

He pushed her carefully away. 'You mean there's a change of plan?'

She shrugged, as though all plans are subject to change.

'We're not supposed to leave for two days,' he reminded her.

'You leave in three hours,' she said firmly. 'There is a junk sailing on the evening tide. Chung has arranged for you to join it off the Islands of Cholburi. That way you can all go aboard without being seen.'

'And Kitson?' he said sharply.

'He will be ready. I go to him now.'

'He'd better be.'

Her smile was gently mocking. 'I was more concerned about you, Carlos, than Commander Kitson.'

After she had left he sat and smoked a cigarette, the tensions easing from him as he went over her words. There was little doubt that he had removed her suspicions, but he still had to prove that the operation could succeed. He winced at the thought. When the plan had been formulated in Paris it had hinged on his being able to use a fully trained crew who would also back him up if anything went wrong. Instead he was crawling out on the proverbial limb with some very unpleasant people.

There was a groan beside him and he looked down into Tim's tormented eyes. 'How do you feel?'

'I die soon,' she croaked.

He gave her the pill Sioo had left, filling a glass with water. She took it without protest, then as it began to take effect memories of the night came flooding back. Her features went pale, then dark as blood rushed to her cheeks. She glanced around the room, finally at Corey.

'Sioo?'

'She just left.'

'Then she . . . we . . . I?'

Lee nodded. She groaned and vanished under the sheet. He waited until an eye appeared and regarded him curiously.

'Now you think I am very bad.'

He kept his face expressionless and thought about it until she began to gnaw at her lower lip. 'No, I wouldn't say you were very bad. In fact, once or twice you came close to being fantastic!'

She glared at him. 'That wasn't what I meant!'

He grinned. 'Would you believe . . . there were times when I just couldn't have done without you!'

He ducked the first swing and caught her wrist on the second. She was speaking rapidly in Thai, eyes blazing. He had the feeling that much of its flavour would be lost in translation.

Chapter 16

A crimson sun was turning the South China Sea into a lake of fire, smouldering with a humid heat, lapping along the hull of the junk before gurgling into a blazing wake. The rough-hewn decks were still hot from the day, the ragged bands of sail clattering now and then on bamboo hoops. There was a hint of wind in the west, a spiralling of cirrus in the burning sky so that layers upon vivid layers competed with the surrealist sea below. Twenty miles to the north the jungle-clad hills of Vietnam made a v-shaped marker on the horizon, the mouth of the Mekong Delta, then rose steadily to the east above Vung Tau.

'We go in at 2300 hours,' Corey said quietly, surveying the twenty men who sat before him on the fore-deck. 'The submarine pen is at the end of the north quay with a gunboat moored in between. We rendezvous at midnight on the slipway here.'

He tapped a map of Vung Tau harbour, indicating a point mid-way along the north quay. 'There'll be guards in that area, certainly by the fuel depot, and they have to be taken quietly.'

Benny Dang's eyes gleamed and he made a chopping motion

with his hand. 'They are already dead.'

Lee gave him a long hard look. 'I don't want to know about your crystal ball, Benny. I just want those guards taken without a hassle. If they aren't we'll never reach the sub.'

Kitson's gaunt features leaned out of the shadows. 'You could use the sea wall. Go in that way, up to the boulevard and round to the slip road. You'll bypass the fuel depot and the gunboat.'

Lee nodded. 'We did consider that, Commander, but using the boulevard creates an additional risk.' He tapped a shaded building on the map. 'This is the old Grand Hotel which dominates the harbour road. Since the North Vietnamese took over it has become the military headquarters for the region.'

'Jesus!' Parish said softly. 'You forgot to mention that little number back in Bangkok.'

Lee gave him a mirthless smile. 'It must have slipped my mind.'

'Quite understandable,' murmured Masters, 'but while you're on the subject . . . did you forget anything else?'

'Yeah, but it's a small thing.'

'How small?' asked Masters.

'We may have to sink the gunboat as well.'

They looked at him with frozen features, their mouths thin, their heads cocked at odd angles, as though they didn't want to believe the evidence of their ears. Lee gave them a laconic grin, which was a long way from his own reaction when he had received the radio call from Chung that afternoon.

'You're a laugh a minute, pal,' said Parish harshly. 'Just what the fuck do you think we are? Marine commandos?'

'I thought the CIA were experts in that sort of thing,' Lee murmured dryly.

'The CIA are experts on staying alive, buddy! That means we have a list of things not to do. Right at the top of that list, next to the bit about not bugging political campaign offices, is an instruction not to attempt to sink enemy gunboats.'

'It must be a comfort to you on those long dark nights,' Lee said sympathetically. 'At least it removes the temptation.'

Masters gurgled like a drain, Lalonde shaking silently beside him. Benny and his men sat with inscrutable features, trying to work it out. Lee tapped the map, his gaze hard and uncompromising.

'The latest intelligence we have is that one of the gunboats is out on patrol, the other is in for a refit. It's unlikely there'll be any crew on board, at the worst a handful of men, but it carries a lot of fire power. Fixed machine-guns, heavy cannon and a forward turret gun. If anyone gets to them it could be bad news.'

Kitson nodded grimly. 'We'd have to move right past it.'

'Right, so the moment anyone blows the whistle on us, it'll have to go,' Lee said briskly, lifting an incendiary grenade. 'One of these in the right place is all it needs.'

'Forward hatch should put it pretty close to the ammo,' Masters said casually. 'The rear deck fuel valve is another cunning little ploy.'

'Listen, stupid,' Parish snarled. 'It only takes one Cong with a machine-gun and nobody, but nobody, is getting within fifty feet of the fucking gunboat!'

Benny was looking alarmed, his stained-glass eyes flicking at Corey, then Parish. Watching him, Lee was reminded of Dani's suspicions. His concern went deeper than dedication, his ugly features were contorting into something close to terror at the possibility of their not going ahead. The Thai moved to the map, forcing a grotesque smile that attempted to exude confidence.

'My men will deal with the boat,' he said. 'It is no problem.'

'Whatever it is, Benny, it's not your problem,' Lee said sharply. 'Your problem is sealing off both ends of that quay and holding the boulevard above. You got that?'

Benny opened his mouth to argue, then thought better of it and turned back to his men. Lee considered the circle of Thai fighters, impressed with the blandly indifferent expressions that gazed back at him.

'You take and hold the quay,' he said slowly. 'You hold the harbour road until you see a white flare and then run like hell for the sub. The men holding the quay withdraw on the red flare.'

'There's still the gunboat,' rasped Parish.

'I'll handle it,' Lee told him quietly. 'Masters and Lalonde will be needed with the engines, you'll be busy with the control panel.'

Parish gazed at him for a long moment in which no one spoke, then he spat derisively on the deck. 'You'll never make it on your own.'

'You worry about the Guppy, Parish.'

'Jesus!' he snarled. 'I don't know why I put up with you guys!'

'Maybe it's something to do with a quarter of a million dollars,' Masters said dryly, 'or am I being cynical.'

'When I want a fucking accountant I'll call you.'

'You in or out?' Lee asked him coldly.

Parish glared at the crimson sky, the light putting ruddy planes to his face, like a primitive mask. When he finally nodded his voice was flat, empty of all emotion.

'I'm in, which means I'm also in on your gunboat gig. Kitson doesn't need me until he's got the diesels firing . . . and you've gotta have a back-up.'

Lee glanced at the Commander who nodded. 'Okay, you're invited.' He looked at his watch. 'We've got three hours. I suggest you eat, check your equipment, then get the dinghies ready.'

The group broke up, the Thais moving to the fore-deck with Benny where the MAC 11s gleamed in the fading light. There were twenty-four of the machine-pistols, each with ten magazines which the Thais had been laboriously loading throughout the day. The captain and crew of the junk had kept well away from Benny's men during the three days at sea, but as the hills of Vung Tau crawled over the horizon they were becoming noticeably more cheerful. One of the crew, a wizened Chinaman, even offered to help with the inflatables, but Benny waved him away. There was little doubt that they would be glad to see the last of them.

Kitson was a shadow hunched over the stern when Lee found him. He leaned beside him, watching the light go out of the sea as the day suddenly died.

'How do you feel?'

The Commander gave a hollow laugh. 'Ready for a slug of methadone.'

'Later.'

'I've been getting the cramps for the past half-hour. I need twenty mills now.'

'You'll get it before we go.'

Kitson looked at him with plastic features, the sweat a phosphorescent sheen in the half light. In spite of Corey's earlier misgivings, his recovery had been as rapid as Sioo had predicted. By the time they were a day out of Bangkok there was colour in his cheeks, a glint of enthusiasm in his eyes as he discussed the schedule they would follow aboard the submarine. The prospect of returning to Vung Tau did not seem to perturb him at all, nor the attendant dangers of snatching a submarine from the communists. Such actions did tend to bring out the very worst in the Vietnamese. More than once Lee had wondered what inducement Chung had offered the Commander. There were long intervals when he sat in silence, ignoring any attempt at conversation, staring into space with haunted eyes. At such times they learned to leave him alone, talking over and round him until he surfaced. At others, usually morning and evening when he had received his ration of methadone, the synthetic opiate, he would pace up and down the fore-deck, his emaciated frame bouncing with energy, his manner crisp and authoritative as he lectured them on each of their duties on board. It was hard to believe that he had not been near a submarine for three years, even harder to imagine the state he had been in only three days ago.

'You've got plenty of the stuff,' he said finally, in a hollow voice. 'What the hell does it matter?'

Corey was sympathetic, but firm. 'You know the answer to that. Twenty milligrams now will be wearing thin just about the time we're approaching Vung Tau. You'll need more, then maybe you get so high you forget where we are and what you're supposed to be doing.'

'On methadone?' he said cynically. 'You've gotta be kidding. All that stuff does is keep the moths at bay.'

'Moths?'

Kitson nodded, tapping his forehead. 'The ones in here. They flutter about, settle now and then, chewing holes in the brain. They prefer memory cells, you know. God knows how they find them, but each day another memory has gone. Eaten by the moths.'

He said it so calmly that Lee felt a shiver of horror, his nerve ends curling with alarm at the prospect of being in a sub at

Vung Tau with Kitson and all his moths.

'How long's that been going on?' he asked in a carefully neutral voice.

Kitson laughed softly as the night closed in on them, hiding the jerking muscle in his cheek, the beads of sweat on his brow. 'That's the beauty of it, you can never really be sure. But you feel them, the moths I mean. You feel them fluttering about in there, whispering to each other, touching delicate places so that images burst like bubbles.'

He was gazing out to sea, intent on the memory as though that too was about to be eaten. 'Then they begin munching, taking their time of course. A nibble here, a bite there, a gulp and a swallow and the memory's gone. I can always tell,' he paused, gazing intently at Corey. 'You see, the image gets all tattered just before it goes.'

'What the hell made you come on this deal?' Lee asked. 'You ought to be back in . . .' he stopped, grimacing. There was no way he could tell him.

'Bangkok,' supplied Kitson. 'I think I'm better off here, especially if we get my old sub. That way I get to go to the States with Chung, and he'll see I'm all right for things.' He tapped his nose, beaming. 'You know what I mean. Things to keep the moths at bay. If I don't get back, soon, they'll eat it all away. Dodgeville, Wisconsin, even Penny Fletsbury . . .' His voice faded away into despair.

Lee forced an agreeable smile, inwardly cursing Chung's ruthless disregard for the man's condition. All they needed were a couple of moths in the wrong place and he might forget what a submarine looked like. 'Take it easy, Commander. Just concentrate on what we have to do tonight.'

'I'm trying to, but without a score . . .'

'No way. You get it when we leave.'

Kitson pushed a knuckle between his teeth, his eyes fixed hypnotically on Corey. After a moment he spoke round it, his voice beginning to tremble. 'There are worse things than moths, Mr Corey.'

'Yeah,' he acknowledged wearily, 'but don't tell me about them. It just might ruin my day.'

One hour later, an hour earlier than he had promised, he was forcing a spoonful of methadone syrup into the Commander's mouth. It had become necessary when he tried to climb over the side to get away from the spiders. Only Parish witnessed the incident, holding him down until Lee had got the methadone into him.

'What kind of a clown is this?' he demanded harshly. 'He's supposed to be fit, an able-bodied seaman!'

'You heard what I told Chung. Now you know why.'

'Jesus!' Parish snorted. 'We're going down with a fruitcake!'

'He's okay as long as he gets regular doses,' Lee told him. 'At least, that's the theory.'

Parish gazed at Kitson with a sceptical expression. The Commander's white features were beginning to relax, take on colour again. He sat up, managing a shaky laugh.

'I'm obliged, Mr Corey. I shall be all right now.'

'Until you see another fucking spider,' Parish grated.

Kitson gave him an icy look. 'I said I'm all right. My work begins on the submarine. All you need to worry about is that we don't run out of medicine.'

He tapped the bottle of methadone, smiled coolly and walked away along the deck.

'You know what this set-up is beginning to smell like?' Parish said.

'I'm sure you're going to tell me.'

'It's like going on a caper with Peter Pan . . . and any minute the crazy bastard is going to forget how to fly!'

They hit the slipway at precisely one minute after midnight, the four inflatables drifting in with muffled paddles. Benny occupied the lead dinghy, stepping out as lightly as a cat, gesturing to four of his men who ran up the concrete ramp to crouch beside a stack of oil drums on the quay. The men wore black trousers and shirts, their skin stained dark enough to make them invisible at four paces. Their feet were bare, their machine-pistols held in holsters across their chests, leaving hands free and deadly.

Corey moved up the slipway with Benny, ears tuned to the night, analysing the sounds and images around them. The harbour itself was a restless pattern of shapes and noises. Across on the south side a group of sampans clung together, their arched roofs and network of gang-planks creaking rhythmically on the gentle swell. A few lamps still glowed among them, odours of hot fat, garlic and fish drifting over on the warm air. Along the south quay a junk and a battered freighter were moored, both in darkness which suggested their crews were sleeping ashore. A few fishing boats and a rusting dredger were moored beyond the sampans by the sea wall, and along the quay itself the warehouses were dark silhouettes, their corrugated roofs rattling occasionally as a breeze came in off the sea.

The north quay appeared equally deserted at first. The gunboat was moored about a hundred yards from the slipway, but the only sign of life was a security light on the bridge. Beyond it, at the end of the quay behind a wire-mesh fence, the squat conning towers of the submarines could be seen. The fuel depot was close to the slipway, next to a long low warehouse that looked freshly painted, with padlocked doors and red warning signs at each corner.

Parish whispered into Lee's ear, gesturing at the building. 'I'll lay odds they keep ammo and supplies in there.'

'If you're right there'll be guards.'

A truck clattered in the night and they glanced up towards the road that circled the harbour. Headlights swept the sky, the truck grating gears as it changed down to turn the bend that would take it along the wide boulevard before curving back towards the town. No one moved as it passed the closest point where the road jutted out above the harbour, less than a hundred metres from the warehouses.

'Let's hope there aren't many of those,' Lee murmured. 'Make sure your men stay under cover unless things are blown down here.'

Dang nodded, his eyes glinting coldly. 'Like when you take the gunboat.'

Corey gave him an irritable look, not missing the mockery in the Thai's voice. A clicking sound made him turn. One of the men by the oil drums was gesturing towards the warehouse where a match had flared into life. As they watched a soldier stepped out of the shadows, a cigarette in his mouth. Unaware of the eyes upon him, he walked to the centre of the quay and called to someone by the steel fence. A moment later another guard ambled into view, an automatic rifle slung over his shoulder.

Benny clicked his tongue and two of his men rose and ran for the warehouse. Lee watched with a dry mouth. It seemed impossible that they could cover the distance without being seen, but they moved like dancing shadows, flickering from cover to cover, crossing open ground as the two guards stood talking casually. The Vietnamese soldiers had no reason to suspect that this night should be any less boring than the last. They smoked cigarettes, discussing inconsequential things as twin shadows whispered through the dark, rising up behind them, smashing twin blades of bone and muscle into their cervical cartilages, catching their lifeless bodies before they could clatter to the ground.

'Go,' said Corey, and led the dash towards the submarine pen.

Benny's men fanned out behind them, splitting into three teams. Two groups vanished into the shadows at each end of the quay, the third going up the slip road to the boulevard. There was a guard post on the triangle of ground where it joined the main road, the windows brightly lit. Inside four men in dark green uniforms played Won Ton with grains of rice and bottle tops. When the door opened they turned without haste, their expressions mildly curious. The MAC 11 trembled in the hands of the black figure in the doorway, the cylindrical silencer absorbing all sound as the stream of nickel-jacketed bullets swept the group, hurling them back from their chairs, against walls and over tables. When the door closed a wind sighed through the line of ragged holes in the wall. There was no other sound.

They passed the gunboat without incident and broke the padlock on the steel-mesh gate, moving quickly to the three fat submarines that were moored together at the end of the quay. Kitson moved along the bows, checking each one before indicating the last in the line.

'I think we'll take her. The sub in the middle is my old command and I don't know if they've repaired the main ballast tank.'

Masters and Lalonde followed Kitson across the steel deck towards the conning tower. Parish hesitated, looking towards the gunboat.

'Be a pity to wake everybody up just now,' he said.

Lee nodded. 'There's no point unless we have to. All the same, we'd better board it while we can.'

'It's your party.'

They moved back along the quay to the gunboat, senses keyed for the slightest sound or movement as they crossed the gang-plank and made their way to the stern. The decks were cluttered with warps and chains, and from the haphazard way equipment was scattered about the vessel was in the midst of a major refit. They paused at the starboard companionway which was lit by a single courtesy light, listening for a full minute before carrying on to the aft-deck. Parish stopped beside a stack of cans, whistling softly.

'Well how about that? She's getting a coat of paint as well.'

They gazed down at the gallon drums. There were at least fifty of them, stacked neatly in the centre of the deck.

'They must have known we were coming,' Lee murmured. 'That stuff will go up like a volcano.'

'I can hardly wait,' chuckled Parish.

Lee moved around the deck, noting the position of the drums in relation to the twin cannon, the fuel tanks and the ammunition hold.

'This crate is going to last about five minutes.'

'Give or take an explosion or two,' Parish added gleefully. 'Now all we've got to do is wait.'

They settled down in the deepest shadows, checking watches, scanning the quay. There was no sign of any of the Thais, but then they would both have been alarmed if there was. Parish, relaxed and confident now that they were in control of the situation, considered Corey with a shrewd gaze.

'Just who the hell are you?' he asked finally.

'Does it matter?'

'Sure it matters. I like to know who's calling the shots.'

'Lee Corey.'

'Crap. If you were big enough to call the shots with Chung I'd know about you.' Parish sucked air through his teeth, his eyes small, calculating.

'Are you Mafia?'

Lee shook his head. Parish frowned, looking disappointed.

After a moment's deliberation he spoke in a musing tone. 'They say that Joe Farrazi was knocked over a couple of weeks back. The story is that he lost his little black book.'

'Fancy.'

Parish stabbed a finger at him. 'You knocked him over, that's your lever with Chung.'

'You could always ask him.'

'But even if you had the list of dope buyers you couldn't hope to take over,' Parish said, still pursuing his train of thought. 'You'd need a massive organization to do that, but . . .'

He stopped, regarding Corey with surprise, then satisfaction. 'Black September. You're with the kamikaze kooks. You're connected with that Palestinian Chung got hold of weeks ago.'

'I'll bet you believe in Santa Claus too,' Lee said dryly.

Parish grinned. 'Don't snow me, buddy. You're fronting for Arafat's mob, and that means you've got to be high – very high – so you're either Baader Meinhof or . . .' He paused, leaning forward as though he could see Corey's features in the darkness. 'No. No, you couldn't be him.'

'Couldn't be who?' Lee asked quietly, feeling his stomach tighten.

'Carlos Ramirez Sanchez.'

The name hung between them in the night. Parish lit a cigarette, shielding his lighter, his eyes gleaming in the glow.

'I thought this Carlos character was overweight. Anyway his complexion would be darker than mine,' Lee said casually.

'They've got drugs now that can change the pigmentation of the skin, just the way they can lighten hair. Losing weight is easy – providing you don't eat for a month.'

'Who are you trying to convince, Parish?'

'Just working it out, Corey,' he replied cheerfully. 'Either you're German, or you're South American. You tell me.'

'Why should I spoil your fun.'

'Okay, we'll do it the hard way. German you ain't. You don't have their clipped speech. Anyway, a German speaking English sounds like an Englishman. Your accent is soft, east coast, or Latin American.'

'Oh come on, Parish, you know perfectly well that the Latin American accent is nowhere close to an east coast sound.'

Parish grinned and nodded. 'Right. But the fact that you know is enough. You're either Carlos or Bouvier, and I'll put my money on the Jackal.'

'I might take your bet, except that there's no way you could prove it.'

'Crap. Soon as we get back I only need to call the company office and have them run a computer projection on the current whereabouts of Carlos. It'd take maybe five minutes, no more.'

'Do that, Parish, and you're out!' Lee said icily.

His laughter was soft, mocking. 'Okay, okay. I just wanted to know the name of your game.'

'You cause any ripples, Parish, and you'll wish you'd never heard of it.'

'Relax, I don't give a damn who you want to be . . . just so long as your credentials are right.'

Lee smiled in the darkness, wondering with amusement what Parish's reaction would be if he knew the real nature of those credentials.

Chapter 17

The class three Guppy had four diesel engines delivering a total of 6400 horse power into the twin drive shafts. They were located in the after compartment above the main ballast tank which also carried the bulk of the submarine's fuel. The four huge engines, gleaming in the yellow light, ranged on either side of the control stand with its mass of dials, gauges and throttle levers. Directly beneath the steel grill deck were the NLO tanks to lubricate the engines, and beyond them the first of the battery compartments which fed the electric motors on the drive shafts.

Kitson stood beside the open hatch, gazing down at the row of lead-acid cells, each as large as a man. Masters appeared, a smear of grease across his face. His expression was enough. Kitson grimaced and went aft into the engine-room where Lalonde stood by the controls, looking as though he had urgent business elsewhere.

'Try it once more,' said Kitson.

Lalonde closed relay switches that would feed power to the diesel's starter motor. He pressed the starter button for Number One, wincing as the motor grated harshly and turned over once, with agonizing slowness. Kitson stared at the heavy engine as though it had wilfully disobeyed an order.

'Stupid bastard!' he snarled, then turned and marched briskly towards the conning tower.

Lalonde glanced at Masters who had appeared in the doorway. 'He doesn't like our little Guppy?'

The Englishman grinned. 'He's just hard to please.'

When they climbed out of the conning tower Kitson was standing on the aft-deck, glaring at the two sister submarines rising and falling in the gentle swell. Masters went to him and tapped him on the shoulder.

'This isn't the best of places to hang about, Commander. Let's try the next one.'

'There's no point. They'll be the same.'

Masters gave him a quick glance, then smiled patiently and steered him by the elbow off the deck and on to the quay.

'All the same, we'll take a look.'

Kitson followed reluctantly. 'It's a waste of time. Once they get a hold on one sub they infest them all.'

Lalonde, catching up with them, gave the Commander a puzzled glance. 'Infest? What infests what?'

Kitson paused beside the next submarine, considering the Frenchman with a condescending air. 'Bugs. You could hear them. They were all over those batteries, gnawing away. Bastards!'

He stepped on to the deck, moving to the conning tower where he paused, head cocked in a listening attitude.

'*Tabernac*!' Lalonde said softly. 'Now we have the bugs in the bilges!'

'It's just as well we brought our debugging gear with us,' Masters said solemnly. 'We'll clear them out in no time.'

Kitson gave him a pitying look. 'You can't clear out battery bugs. Once they get into that acid they start eating out the plates, the terminals, even the wiring.'

'Depends how soon you get to them,' Masters told him cheerfully. 'Why don't you go down to the con-deck while

Pierre and I take a look. If the engines start, you'll know we've cleared them out. Okay?'

Kitson thought about it until Masters' persuasive smile was developing a geriatric twitch, then he nodded and began climbing the steel rungs up the side of the tower. Lalonde let out a long breath.

'Jacques, maybe this is not such a good idea,' he said miserably. 'If we took to the dinghies we could find the junk, no?'

'From the look on that Chinaman's face he got out of there as soon as we were out of sight. Anyway,' he gestured to headlights that were descending towards the quay. 'I've got a feeling we're about to run out of time.'

Lalonde cursed softly and started up the steel wall of the conning tower.

On the gunboat Parish and Corey watched the truck turn on to the quay and move towards the main warehouse.

'Are you thinking what I'm thinking?' Parish asked, clicking the safety catch off the MAC 11 and resting the squat barrel across his forearm.

'Time to change the guard,' Lee replied. 'Which is a pity.'

'Yeah,' said Parish, squinting along the barrel, 'it's all of that.'

The truck came to a halt in front of the warehouse, the driver flicking his headlights. A deeper shadow moved silently across open ground, freezing as the canvas was pulled aside to enable a soldier to climb out. There was a whisper of sound, the thud of bullets, and the soldier was falling with arms splayed out, his mouth gaping in disbelief. Even as he hit the ground a line of neat holes was pattering across the canvas, stilling the sudden activity inside. More holes appeared, criss-crossing the canvas in the blink of an eye, running across the windscreen in frosted stars with a sound like tearing cloth.

Benny Dang rose to his feet, the MAC 11 in his hand, the smell of cordite rising in blue tendrils from the hot barrel. He went to the truck and looked inside, then round to the cab where he opened the door and switched off the motor and the headlights. He stepped away, gazing at the truck as if he might have forgotten something, then turned and loped off into the darkness.

Corey watched him go with a dry mouth. Beside him Parish

was motionless, his eyes on the silent truck. After a moment he sighed and shook his head.

'How long before the shit hits the fan?'

'Five, maybe ten minutes.'

'Jesus! Why don't those Godamn engines start!'

In the engine-room Masters was screwing the casing back on, glancing over at Lalonde who was studying an amp metre.

'What do you think?'

Lalonde lifted and dropped a shoulder. 'It's low. Maybe ten per cent charge.'

'If it doesn't fire the first time we're going to need a push.'

The Frenchman nodded, the sweat dripping off him as he closed a circuit and put his thumb on the starter button. Masters crouched beside the first engine, wiping a greasy rag over it, gripping the power lead as though it would help.

'Contact.'

Lalonde pressed down. The engine groaned, the flywheel turning slowly, whining, gathering speed. Masters bent over it, talking to it in a tense whisper. The engine coughed, the groan became a grinding rumble. It coughed again.

'Start, sod you!' said Masters.

Lalonde had crossed himself three times with his right hand, his left leaning hard on the button. Suddenly the flywheel was a blur of motion, the casing shuddering and the room filled with a chugging rumble of sound. They beamed happily at each other, then Masters moved to the second diesel.

'Charging?'

Lalonde glanced at the dials, lifted a thumb.

'Contact.'

The Frenchman pressed the button. The second diesel began to turn, coughing and wheezing, but now there was a constant power supply coming from the running engine. After a moment it began to run and Masters moved to the third, checking it, pumping in fuel, then nodding to Lalonde.

On the gunboat Corey had the tab off the grenade, his eyes on Parish who was in the shadows beside the companionway. A light had come on a minute after the submarine's engine had coughed into life. There was the sound of rapid footsteps, then a

Vietnamese appeared, still struggling into his dark blue tunic. Parish hit him behind the ear and swung him over the side in a single movement. He was hitting the water as the second man appeared. Parish tapped him on the nose with the MAC 11 and waved at the water. The sailor was young, but wise. He hardly broke step, just kept right on until he hit the water.

From the boulevard beyond the harbour headlights were approaching. Suddenly the lead vehicle veered off the road, crashing through the low concrete wall and down to the hillside where it burst into flames. A moment later four grenades went off in quick succession and the sky was lit by mushrooms of fire.

Parish had reached the quayside, signalling to Corey. He dropped the grenade in the stack of paint drums, then ran to the side of the deck, leaping for the quay. The blast singed his hair, the paint igniting in a fountain of flame, spraying the entire rear deck so that in seconds it was a raging inferno. Parish tossed a grenade at the bridge, then they ran for the submarine.

A siren began to howl in the night, rising and falling, like an animal in torment. From the boulevard a pistol began to fire, joined almost immediately by the angry snarl of a sub-machine-gun. On the south side of the harbour lights appeared in the Harbour Master's office. Less than a minute later a grenade exploded, blowing out the entire front wall and setting fire to a fuel tender parked beside it.

Benny's men were operating in groups of four, occupying the north and south approaches to the harbour. Moving silently along the hillside beside the boulevard, they swept the road with bursts of gunfire, made all the more deadly by their silence. An open truck roared round the bend, packed with soldiers, slewing round on screaming tyres as the driver saw the blazing vehicles ahead. A grenade detonated beside it, a hail of bullets plucking at the soldiers as they lunged for cover. The petrol tank exploded, throwing a curtain of fire at the sky. Two soldiers scrambled to their feet and ran for the shelter of a building, but long before they reached it bullets were plucking at them, twisting them round until they sprawled with bloody mouths upon the road. In the distance other sirens were waking the town, echoing down to the harbour where the blazing gunboat was blowing itself apart.

In the engine-room Masters was coaxing the last of the diesels into life, perspiration running off him like tropical rain. The engine wheezed and shuddered, but refused to start. He cursed bitterly and gestured to Lalonde, who took his hand off the button.

'Let's get the casing off,' he said, 'it sounds like an airlock.'

Lalonde gazed at him with frightened eyes. The thump of explosions and rattle of gunfire could be heard above the sound of the engines.

'Jacques, an airlock could take a hell of a time to clear.'

'So move, damnit. There's no way we can drive two props with three engines.'

Corey entered as they lifted the steel casing off. He stood behind the Englishman, watching his quick, deft movements. His large hands were fast and sure, yet surprisingly gentle. The wrench closed, twisted, then spun the nuts so fast they seemed to fly apart.

'We going to make it?' Lee asked in a casual voice.

'Ask me tomorrow.'

'I'm asking now.'

Masters glanced up at him with an exasperated expression. 'Maybe. Give me five.'

Lee nodded, turning away. 'That's about all we'll get.'

He ducked through the hatch, moving quickly to the control-deck where Parish was hunched in front of a mass of glowing panels. Kitson was beside the chart table, looking bemused. Lee crossed to him.

'We may be set in five minutes. When do you want me on the helm?'

Kitson made no reply, gazing past Corey towards the stern. He had the eyes of a frightened child.

'Commander, do you want me on the helm?' Lee repeated sharply, forcing the eyes to focus on him.

'Yes,' he muttered. 'Yes, you take the helm.'

He smiled for no reason and started to turn away. Lee pulled him back, his anger spilling over. 'Shape up, Kitson, or we're not going to get out of here. And if that happens I'm going to make sure you go the hard way.'

The Commander nodded solemnly. 'You're absolutely right. But it doesn't matter, we can't get out. The boat's crawling with the most unspeakable things.' He gazed at Lee as though expecting confirmation. 'Haven't you seen them?'

'No,' Lee said tightly, 'but if that's the way you want it I'm tossing this over the side now.'

Lee produced the bottle of methadone, avoiding Kitson's hand as he reached for it frantically.

'Jesus no! Don't you see? That's just what they're waiting for.'

He made another grab for the bottle and Lee slammed him back against the bulkhead, holding it an inch from his nose. 'You better clean those cobwebs out of your skull, Kitson, or I'm going to let this drop.'

Kitson licked dry lips, his eyes small, gleaming like a startled ferret. For a moment it seemed that the fragile forces which held him together would collapse, bringing madness and despair. Instead he took a long, deep breath, shut his eyes tightly, every muscle tense as he fought for control. A shudder ran through his thin frame, then he opened his eyes and Lee knew he had won.

'I'll take the con and run the helm myself from up there,' he said crisply.

'You can manage that?'

'I'll manage. Leave one of the Thais with me. This will keep you free to handle the trim. It could be our biggest problem.'

He took Lee across to a bank of dials and levers, each set of controls numbered. 'I'll play it by ear from the con, telling you which tanks to flood or blow. If we're lucky we'll have her trimmed before we dive.'

'How long will it take to charge the batteries?'

'About four hours. That means we'll still be running on the surface at dawn.'

Kitson moved to Parish who was studying a radar screen. 'You happy with this gear?'

'I'll get by. The sonar seems to have two different systems.'

'That's right. One is the normal array sonar, giving us bearing and distance. The other is dived fire control, which I hope we don't have any use for.'

He turned back to Corey and jerked a thumb up towards the

conning tower. 'I'll get myself trimmed out up top. As soon as you're ready to recall the men, use the forward hatch.' He started to climb the steps, then glanced down, his mouth thin. 'Take care of that bottle, Mr Corey.'

'Aye, aye cap'n,' Lee replied.

From the stern there was a sudden shuddering roar, subsiding almost immediately to blend with the hum of the engines. But now there was a steady throb of power pulsing through the deck. A phone buzzed beside Parish and he picked it up, although they both knew the message before it came.

'We're ready to go when you are,' said Masters in a laconic voice.

The white flare exploded a hundred feet above the boulevard, drifting away towards the town. The road was almost hidden by billowing clouds of smoke from burning vehicles, but now and then a gust of wind made it veer away, revealing the huddled bodies in dark green uniforms scattered along the road.

The main group of Vietnamese troops was advancing behind a small pick-up truck, a young lieutenant deploying his hastily assembled force of thirty men. He knew it would be ten to fifteen minutes before the half-tracks and armoured vehicles arrived, and from the destruction in the harbour below there would be little left by then. The flare above was clearly some kind of signal, so he shouted to his men and began to run, waving a revolver above his head. The acrid smoke clung to the throat and burned the eyes, but beyond the blazing car he could see an open stretch which would give them a commanding position above the harbour.

The smoke billowed around him, then he was stumbling through. Facing him was a man dressed entirely in black, small and still, with bare feet and a strange gun in his hands. The lieutenant stopped and aimed his revolver, gripping it with both hands, as the weapon he'd never seen before began to shimmer, bright flame flickering from it. There was never time to pull the trigger. Bullets took him in the chest, stomach and throat, tossing him back into the arms of his men.

The Thai slipped the empty magazine out, tossing it aside and fitting a new one. Soldiers were racing out of the smoke from a dozen points, dropping to their knees, raising rifles, all of them aimed at him. The first bullet took him through the head and he knew no more.

Along the boulevard two black figures ran for the parapet. The first leapt for the hillside below, the second paused to sweep his gun across the advancing soldiers. There was the rattle of a sub-machine-gun and he shuddered, the MAC 11 dropping from his hands. Then as more shots raked his body he fell back upon the road.

Some twenty Vietnamese under the command of a general who had been working late at the military headquarters had climbed down the hillside to the seawall and made their way along to the south quay. They were now advancing on the north quay where Benny's force controlled the warehouse and access to the slip road.

As the white flare fizzled out in the sky there was another burst of light and a red flare hung above them. Benny grinned and shouted a command to his men, then pulled the tab off an incendiary grenade and tossed it into the fuel depot as the Vietnamese began to appear. He moved back, firing steady bursts, pinning the soldiers down. There was a sheet of flame, then the ground shook and the corrugated-iron building came apart like a house of cards. The grenade had landed beside a five-hundred-gallon tank of fuel and this ignited with an explosion that would be heard five miles away.

The blast threw Benny and most of his men to the ground, but they were far enough away to escape the shower of blazing fuel which sprayed a wide area of the quay, driving the advancing Vietnamese back, some with their clothes in flames so that they were forced to jump into the harbour. The gunboat was still blazing as the Thais raced past it, but the hull was already low in the water and it would not be long before it foundered.

Corey was beside the forward hatch, urging them on. Fourteen men hit the deck and ran for the hatch, then Benny appeared and cast off before boarding the submarine. He moved to Corey, grinning and gesturing towards the crimson sky, the air still shuddering to the sound of exploding fuel and ammunition.

'Good job, eh?'

'I'm sure everybody's very impressed,' Lee said dryly. 'How about the rest of your men?'

Benny shrugged and stepped through the hatch. 'I have no more men.'

The throb of the engines took on a deeper note and the submarine began to slide out of its berth, easing past its sister ship, angling away from the burning gunboat where ammunition was exploding like Chinese crackers. Along the quay figures were appearing, running to the water's edge, kneeling and firing at the disappearing boat. Lee followed Benny through the hatch, closing and locking it as bullets began to glance off the steel hull, ringing an angry tattoo along the decks.

Chapter 18

'Shit,' said Parish. 'I think we've got company.'

The American was hunched over the sonar and radar screens on the control-deck. Lee was at the helm, holding the submarine on a heading of two-four-zero which Kitson had been keeping to for the past hour. A tall, loose-limbed Thai called Matis had been assigned to assist Lee and was clearly itching to take over.

'You understand it?' Lee asked him, indicating the compass.

The Thai nodded vigorously. 'I am boatman. It is no problem.'

'Then she's all yours,' replied Lee, stepping away from the helm.

He crossed the narrow deck which throbbed with the beat of the diesels and stood beside Parish.

'What kind of company?'

Parish pulled off his earphones and pointed to a blip on the radar screen. 'I'm picking something up. It's coming fast, too fast for a freighter and not big enough for any kind of tanker.'

Lee watched the steady sweep of the radar, the phosphorescent glow on the fringe of the scan. Within five sweeps it had come perceptibly closer.

'What do you think?'

Parish wiped perspiration off his forehead and allowed his

eyes to focus briefly on Lee. 'I think we've found the other gunboat.'

'It's a long way off.'

'Twelve miles. It'll be kicking our ass in less than an hour.'

'Or cutting north up the Mekong Delta?'

Parish gave him a disgusted look. 'That's crap and you know it. Whatever's behind us is coming fast on a direct intercept.'

Lee considered the screen for a further five sweeps, then nodded grimly. 'Okay, I'll brief Kitson.'

'Better hold on to him when you do,' Parish said sarcastically. 'He's just as likely to jump over the side.'

Corey found the Commander hunched in a corner of the control tower, his face glistening with perspiration in the cool night air. A steady wind blew up through the hatch, laced with the smell of diesel fumes. The sea around was calm, only a slight swell dipping the blunt bow against the water. It was almost two hours since they had cleared the harbour at Vung Tau and the red glow in the sky had long since vanished to the east.

He stood beside Kitson and lit a cigarette, offering one to him. The Commander shook his head, his lips compressed tightly, as though contemplating pain.

'How long before we can submerge?' Lee asked him casually.

'Two hours minimum.'

'How about thirty minutes?'

Kitson leaned over the edge of the conning tower and watched the bow cleave the sea as though he had never appreciated it before. After a minute Lee stirred restlessly.

'I said thirty minutes.'

'I heard you, Mister, but you obviously didn't hear me. In two hours we will have enough charge in the batteries to dive.'

'We've got company. Parish thinks it's the Vietnamese gunboat.'

'Then it probably is.'

'So what happens if we have to dive?' Lee asked patiently.

Kitson gripped the steel coaming with hands that looked as though they wanted to tear it apart. After a moment he spoke in a voice creaking with despair. 'We would have to surface in an hour or so, otherwise the air would foul and the power would be too low to manoeuvre.'

'One hour? You're certain?'

He made a quick, irritable gesture. 'Maybe ninety minutes. It doesn't matter, the gunboat can hunt us for days – weeks.'

'Unless we dive.'

Kitson's mouth twisted savagely as he turned to him. 'Mister Corey, have you any idea what it is like to be hunted with depth charges? With fully charged batteries it is a nightmare. Without that power we would have to sit on the bottom with the air going stale, unable to manoeuvre, listening to the explosions getting closer and closer . . . watching the water coming in, knowing there is no way out.' He shuddered, his voice no more than a whisper. 'At least up here dying is not an ordeal.'

'Nobody's dying, Captain. Not yet,' Lee said tersely. 'This sub has torpedos, why don't we use them?'

'We don't have the men,' he replied simply. 'Our normal complement is eighty-nine and in a torpedo run we'd need every single man.'

'We've got Benny's men. They can load the forward tubes now. You and Masters can arm them. Parish can fire on your command. At least we'd get one shot.'

'And who mans fire control sonar, array sonar, the ballast tanks, motors, stabilizers, vents and props?' His face was melting with fear so that bones seemed to protrude at ugly angles. 'Have you any idea how complex it is to aim and fire one torpedo? To have any chance of a kill we'd need a spread of four, launched at a precise angle to take the gunboat broadside.'

'So work it out. One shot. If it fails we surface and take our chances.'

'It can't be done.' Kitson's voice cracked and he shut his eyes tightly, his narrow chest heaving.

Lee glanced at his watch, calculating their chances, then wishing he hadn't. Kitson was their only hope. He took the bottle of methadone linctus from his pocket and held it out to the captain.

'How much of this stuff can you take and still think straight?'

A pale tongue moved over dry lips in an unconscious reflex. 'I can handle it,' he said, reaching for the bottle.

Lee allowed him to take it, then as he unscrewed the cap gripped his wrist firmly. 'Make no mistake, Kitson, if you freak out on me I'll lock you in the forward tube and leave you to rot.'

The captain nodded, then swallowed a mouthful. He looked up at the sky, his lined features already beginning to soften. After a moment he gave an audible sigh and lifted the bottle again.

'You better believe me,' Lee warned him.

'I heard you, Mr Corey,' Kitson said, sipping the linctus as though it was a delicate wine. 'But if you want me to behave like a madman and attempt a torpedo run, then first I must loosen the shackles of the mind.'

He laughed and toasted the stars. 'Lovers and madmen have such seething brains, said Shakespeare. He was right. Mine seethes . . . It burns and seethes and aches for solace. Only I think he had a different kind of solace in mind.'

'Keep on like that and I'll loosen your teeth,' Lee said sharply. 'You've got about forty minutes to set it all up.'

Kitson gazed at the bottle for a moment, then screwed on the cap and placed it in his pocket. When he spoke his voice was firm, crackling with authority.

'One try then. Shall we?' he bowed mockingly towards the hatch.

Lee descended the steel rungs into the inner chamber, then through the second hatch to the control-deck. Parish turned from the radar, his expression grim. He didn't need to say the words, the screen said it for him. In the past five minutes the blip had moved an inch, its course aimed directly at the centre.

'So what do we do?' Parish asked cynically. 'Take to the boats or dive?'

'Could it track us on sonar from that distance?'

'If it's got Russian electronics, which I expect it has.'

'Then we'll take it on.'

Parish's bifocal eyes bulged with disbelief. 'Corey, you're out of your tiny mind. We can't even get the bloody Captain to come down and say hello, let alone run a Godamn war.'

'Thank you, Mister Parish. Kill the white, I want station red and silent running!'

Parish swung round to find Kitson already beside the communications panel. Although his eyes were unnaturally bright, his movements were steady and decisive. The perspiration had gone from his face and with it the haunted mask of fear. He waited, cool and composed, until Parish turned the switch to replace white light with the deep red which would enable their eyes to adjust instantaneously to night, or day, either on deck or through the periscope.

A klaxon sounded its harsh ooga ooga throughout the submarine, then Kitson spoke through the intercom. 'This is the Captain speaking. I want every available man in the forward torpedo room on the double. Mister Masters will supervise the loading of tubes two, four, six and eight in that order. From now on we are running silent, which means no man on board will speak above a whisper.'

Kitson replaced the microphone, then crossed to the series of levers controlling the ballast tanks. He beckoned Corey over and indicated those controlling the forward tanks.

'As we load the tubes you'll see the horizontal plane shift about two degrees as we alter our centre of gravity. The moment it starts you gently blow the forward tanks until we level out.' He indicated the dials reading pressure and the large central dial showing their horizontal plane. 'If you overdo it you must close the stern vents and blow to compensate. That clear?'

Lee nodded, then pointed to the next set of controls. 'Will it help to use the stabilizer?'

Kitson shook his head. 'It's a job for the specialist. When we dive I'll take over and you hold the con.'

With a final glance at the radar he moved away through the hatch towards the bow. Parish let him get out of sight, then threw his hands in the air. 'Jesus, Corey,' he whispered furiously, 'he thinks he's Captain Nemo! How much of that stuff did you let him have?'

'All he needs. It was either that or taking to the life rafts.'

'You just answered my second question.'

'Without this sub we're back to square one. We've got to take the chance.'

'Correction. *You've* got to take the chance. One week ago I was all set to spend the rest of my life yodelling across the valley to my bank manager. I don't even know what I'm doing here!'

'Making money, Parish. Your favourite occupation.'

Parish put two fingers in the air and swung back to the radar screen. Lee went to the Thai at the helm and checked the bearing.

Matis grinned broadly. 'Two-four-zero, pappasan.'

Lee nodded and tried to look delighted.

The torpedo room was located in the narrow bow section, the rows of torpedoes chained in stacks of three against the hull. There were four stacks, with an overhead hoist to swing them forward to the tubes. Kitson finished inspecting the blunt-nosed projectile, then closed the panel and moved to Masters who was probing the innards of the motor with a screwdriver.

'What do you think?'

Masters straightened with a grimace. 'They haven't been serviced for two years, but without pulling the motor out and checking the induction chambers I can't tell.'

'There's no time for that.'

Masters gave him a patient smile. 'Yes, Captain, I know. But if you start unloading stationary torpedoes with their detonators primed we could blow ourselves right back to Vung Tau.'

'Or into tomorrow,' Kitson said with a whimsical smile. 'All the way into tomorrow.'

Masters' mouth tightened angrily, but he moved to the front of the torpedo and examined the safety interlocks which would automatically arm the torpedoes in the tubes. Kitson watched him with a serene expression. 'They're very simple mechanisms, Mister Masters. The TDC will soon tell us if they're faulty.'

'The torpedo data computer hasn't been checked out either, Captain, and as far as I know there isn't anyone on board who can do it.'

A muscle twitched in Kitson's face and for a moment the fear showed. 'We have no time for a test run. We'll just have to go for broke.'

Benny had the hoist ready with four of his men and together they swung it into line with the number two tube. Masters eased it gently into the mouth, then signalled for them to slide it forward out of the sling.

When only the stabilizing fins protruded, Kitson adjusted the steering vane to give it a two degree angle to port before closing and locking the tube doors.

'You're going for a salvo,' Masters observed.

'Our only hope. With a spread at one thousand metres we stand a fifty-fifty chance.'

'You'll never get that close. Those gunboats can do about twenty-five knots.'

'You may well be right, Mister Masters.' Kitson cocked his head at an odd angle, as though listening to the rush of water past the hull. 'But the sea is our friend – their enemy.'

He smiled and moved to the next torpedo. Masters resisted the impulse to shake the man by his scrawny neck and gestured to Benny to hoist it out in the sling. The chances were, he decided fatalistically, that the torpedoes would not run, that the gunboat would not be there if they did, and that Kitson would come apart at the seams at the first click of a depth charge.

The gunboat found them fifty miles due south of the Mui Bai Bung, a rocky headland marking the beginning of the Gulf of Siam. Dawn was still an hour away and although both vessels ran in darkness they were fully visible to each other, opposing blips emitting electronic echoes as distinctive as fingerprints. The Vietnamese Commander knew little of the circumstances of the submarine's departure, only that his orders were brief and specific – to locate and destroy.

Kitson watched its approach on the radar screen, measuring its speed and manoeuvrability as they set a zig-zag course. He felt no emotion as the gunboat matched each move in less than a minute, the cloying euphoria of the methadone blunting his ability to be surprised or alarmed by any eventuality short of losing an arm or a leg. The 'buzz' was a constant and beautiful companion, reducing the realities around him to distant echoes – as though he was watching the world through a looking glass, unable to alter its course or destiny.

'Secure all hatches,' he said crisply into the microphone. 'Dive, dive, dive.'

Corey flooded the forward and main tanks, whilst Parish put on the sonar headphones. The constant vibration of the engines ceased as Masters switched to the electric motors. In the aft mess-deck Benny Dang stood clutching a stanchion, his gaze locked on the silent row of men who listened with dry mouths as the sea rushed across the deck above them.

The Captain was beside Lee as they submerged, adjusting trim and operating the diving vanes to increase their angle of descent. At thirty feet he levelled off and checked the dials before crossing to the periscope, pressing the button which slid it smoothly up out of its well.

'Change course to three-two-zero,' he said, gazing through the eyepiece, letting his vision adjust to night before flicking in the infra-red.

The gunboat was a featureless glow, still on the same heading, but even as he checked the range it began to alter course.

'Turning to three-two-zero,' said Parish softly.

'Come to new heading,' murmured Kitson. 'Bring her right round to one-six-zero.'

The deck trembled beneath them as the submarine swung in a wide arc towards the approaching gunboat.

'Sonar contact steady,' said Parish, a stream of perspiration dripping on to the console before him. He glanced quickly at Corey, but he was busy adjusting the delicate trim controls. The deck angled beneath them and Kitson turned from the periscope.

'Hold her steady, Mister Corey. Blow three and one, gently.'

'They're changing course,' said Parish. 'New heading two-eight-five.'

'Range?'

Parish shook perspiration from his eyes and checked the calibrations. 'Five thousand, whatever it is you use.'

'Metres, Mister Parish. Just metres.'

Kitson stared intently through the periscope until the silence around them sounded like breaking glass, then he sank it back into the well and crossed to the command seat behind Corey. He sat down and glanced at his watch, ticking off seconds. They waited, unable to conceal their apprehension.

'Kill sonar, Mister Parish,' the captain said finally. 'Bring us round to two-four-five, Mister . . .' He looked at Matis who bobbed his head and began to spin the helm.

'Why run blind?' Parish asked tersely. 'He could be over us before we know it.'

'Probably,' Kitson agreed. 'But as long as we're transmitting sonar he knows exactly where to find us. This way he's got to use his head as well as his hardware.'

The throb of heavy engines came from ahead, growing rapidly louder as the two vessels approached each other. When it was directly overhead the steel hull seemed to shudder with the sound, and then it was retreating. Parish gripped the control panel, his mouth a white line. Corey hooked his arms under the steel seat, knowing what was coming.

The depth charges were so close they heard the clicks of the detonators, left and right, then the air shimmered and the deck jumped beneath them as the twin explosions shattered the silence. There was a frozen moment directly after the concussions in which no one seemed to breathe or move, and then there was a dull thud, followed almost immediately by two further detonations, all of them well astern.

Kitson sat hunched in his chair, his features contorted into an imbecilic smile, his hands tying knots in themselves. As the explosion faded his right hand, seeming to move by its own volition, reached into his pocket and brought out the bottle of methadone.

'Not now, Kitson,' Lee said sharply.

'There will never be a better time,' he replied, unscrewing the cap and swallowing a mouthful of the linctus. 'If I kill him you can put me to bed. If I fail, he will do it for you.'

'Jesus!' Parish whispered. 'How did I get into this!'

'Ghosts,' said Kitson, and laughed with eyes that burned like rubies in the crimson light. 'Ghosts brought us all, one way or another, and they're with us now.'

He looked beyond them to the vacant seats along the control console, bowing mockingly to the figures that seemed so real, and yet could not possibly exist. Zabrinsky was there, his small eyes gleaming. Ferris was by the helm, Jinx Maddon on fire control. If he looked hard he could see Purvis by the scope, and Dave Simons, his Number One.

'It's been a pleasure men,' he told them. 'Just to have my old crew back on board is all I could ask.'

'Oh, Christ!' said Parish. 'I'm getting out of this now.'

He lunged for the ballast controls, reaching for levers. Corey slammed him back in his seat and stabbed a finger at the sonar. 'You get back on that and call out the bearings.'

'Look at him! He's freaking out!'

'Then get calling before he stops listening.'

Parish glared at him for a moment, then shuddered and

turned back to the sonar, putting on the earphones and beginning to turn the listening dial. Corey crossed to Kitson, watching his eyes, trying to gauge his ability to comprehend. The Commander was smiling and nodding towards the chart table, as though listening to a conversation. Occasionally he swayed, steadying himself against a stanchion, his gaze never moving from a spot three feet above the chart table.

'Captain,' Lee said quietly, 'we have the forward tubes ready.'

'Good man, Simons,' Kitson replied. 'We'll take him on the next run. What's our heading, Ferris?'

The Thai hesitated, but after a bewildered glance at Corey mumbled the course they were on.

'Sonar?' snapped the Captain.

'Turning now on to two-four-zero.'

'Range?'

'Three thousand.'

Kitson smiled and spoke into the intercom. 'All engines stop. Stand by for maximum revs. Trim crew correct for forward roll. Fire control set for salvo on tubes two, four, six and eight on my count. Hold her steady, Zabrinsky, I want a flat deck.'

'Range two thousand,' said Parish.

'Let her come,' murmured Kitson.

They listened, avoiding each other's eyes. The gunboat was at first a whisper, then a dull rumble that echoed along the submarine.

'Depth charges,' said Parish, his voice thin with fear.

Lee watched Kitson, his mouth dry as the Captain swayed to an impossible angle before lurching against a stanchion. His mouth was slack, like a dreaming child, and none of his movements were sure. But as the first depth charge exploded he was gripping steel, checking the second finger of his watch. The second explosion was directly above them, sending the submarine into a rolling plunge. The lights dimmed, then brightened, and from the rear there was the clang of an emergency hatch being closed. No one knew whether it was out of fear or necessity.

Parish sat with the headphones in his lap, clutching the control panel with white features. Two more explosions came in quick succession, reverberating through the submarine so that the ears ached and the very air seemed to shiver. The next one was a distant thump and people began to move again.

'All start,' Kitson said briskly. 'Blow forward tanks, I want periscope depth and new heading three-one-five.'

The electric motors hummed as Lee snapped open the forward vents and blew air into the tanks. The deck rose beneath them and they surged towards the surface.

'Attack sonar, give me a pattern,' called Kitson, already raising the periscope.

'You don't have attack sonar,' snarled Parish. 'I can give you range and heading.'

'Don't argue with me, Parish,' Kitson snapped. 'Switch on TDC and tap it out.'

Parish muttered savagely, but turned to the torpedo data computer and switched it on. Red and green lights flowed. He tapped out two, four, six and eight. Answering panels glowed into life as the tubes charged the induction chambers of the torpedoes with compressed air. He gazed at the lights with a helpless expression.

'Are we charged, Mister?' Kitson asked sharply.

'How the fuck do I know,' Parish replied, the sweat pouring off his pale features. 'I've got a Christmas tree here!'

Kitson glanced quickly at the board, then turned back to the periscope. Lee was watching the depth gauge, reducing the air to the forward tanks and hoping they would level out before they stuck their bow out of the sea.

'Bring her round five degrees starboard, Mr Ferris,' said Kitson.

The Thai shrugged and turned the helm.

Kitson began to laugh softly. Parish groaned, his features like melting wax. Lee was too busy fighting to get them on to an even keel to worry about the cause of the Captain's laughter.

'Stand by to fire all tubes.'

The gunboat was beginning to turn to starboard in preparation for another attack as the periscope cleared. Kitson's mind soared with elation at the sight. A beautiful purple whale browsing in a silver sea, and the sky was the darkest blue he had ever seen. He closed his eyes, pinching them tight, savouring the images.

'Range – mark,' he said, and laughed again. 'Bearing – mark.'

Parish pressed the keys on the TDC and watched lights flicker as bearing, range and deflection were calculated from the periscope plate, fed automatically into the computer.

'Arm,' said Kitson.

Parish stabbed the arming key.

'Set for one thousand, angle on the bow is zero-four-zero.'

Parish typed one thousand, then glanced helplessly at Corey. He didn't know where to begin to compute a bow angle. Corey held up crossed fingers and winced. Parish knew he was going to vomit. He also knew there wouldn't be time. Around him the TDC clicked and whirred, the four panels now glowing an angry red.

Kitson gazed through the periscope, only distantly aware that the images should be dim, etched with crimson. Instead the sea was now molten gold, the gunboat a shimmering bird reaching for the indigo sky. It was the most beautiful sight he had ever seen.

'Fire!' he said with a note of awe in his voice.

Parish groaned and stabbed the fire control button. Four torpedoes leapt from the cluster of tubes in the bow, whining towards the surface on tails of foam. Ahead the gunboat was half-way through its turn when the look-out spotted the diverging lines. An alarm sounded, engines began to race and the bow started an agonizingly slow turn to face the oncoming torpedoes. The range was so short that it had made only ten degrees before the first one hissed past the bow. The second took it amidships even as the third was blowing off the stern.

The captain on the bridge had watched it all with a kind of numbed disbelief. No one had told him that the submarine was armed, much less dangerous. The last image his brain received was of the deck erupting on a fountain of flame.

In the submarine Corey and Parish were gazing at each other in disbelief. The double explosion had been unmistakable and they could hear the cheers from the mess-deck. Kitson stepped away from the periscope and let it sink into its well. Then he moved to the command seat and slowly sat down.

'That was fantastic,' said Lee.

Kitson nodded, his features serene. 'And beautiful,' he said. 'Absolutely beautiful.'

And he began to cry.

Chapter 19

'Bangkok Night' was living up to the rather dubious reputation of being that city's leading showplace of erotic art. Jack Masters had insisted on keeping a promise he made as they stepped into the dinghy off Vung Tau – 'when we get back I'm going to take you to a place that'll make your hair curl!' Watching a slim, olive-skinned girl blow smoke rings with a part of her anatomy never designed for that purpose, Lee Corey was inclined to agree with him. Whilst his hair had not yet gone into peristalsis, there was a distinct prickling at the back of the neck.

They had reached the Gulf of Siam without further incident after the sinking of the gunboat, which had been just as well since Kitson had to be tied to a cot for most of the journey. The massive dose of methadone had quickly sent him plunging into a black world of nightmare fantasy, and if they had not restrained him he would have jumped over the side at the first opportunity. When they submerged for the run to Bangkok his screams of terror had echoed through the submarine, until Benny had him moved to the aft storage hold.

The Thai fighters proved to be able seamen, navigating the submarine along the coast of Cambodia with only occasional checks through the periscope. Masters and Lalonde remained in the engine-room throughout, nursing the batteries during the day until they could surface at night and run on diesel engines. The actual operation of the submarine was left to the two Americans, but as they were cruising at periscope depth in ideal sea conditions, it proved to be far easier than Lee expected. Shortly before dawn on the second day they dropped anchor in a small bay on one of the coral islands of Cholburi, less than a hundred miles from Bangkok. They left six of Benny's men to guard the submarine, although discovery was remote as the island was one of the furthest from the mainland and uninhabited.

Long-tailed boats took them to Pattaya where the Mercedes were waiting to deliver them to Chung. It was almost noon by the time they reached the pagoda-style villa, and without exception they went straight to bed and slept until dark. Chung waited patiently until they assembled that night in the dining-room, then bowed solemnly to each in turn.

'You have accomplished the most difficult task of all, and I congratulate you.'

'So when's the pay-off?' asked Parish.

The Chinaman smiled faintly and considered the golden Buddha at the end of the room. 'In two days we will have left my country for the last time.'

'With Kitson in command?' Lee asked cynically.

A shadow crossed Chung's face. 'The man is a problem, I agree. However, Sioo is with him now and will be during the voyage. His addiction can be contained, and of course there will be far more people on board.' He smiled without warmth. 'No one will be indispensable.'

During the meal Masters announced his intention of having a night on the town, informing Lee that he would accept no excuses. Chung had no objections, insisting only that Dani and one of her assistants accompany them. Lalonde declined, pointing out that he would have to be at the island early next morning to begin supervising the refuelling. A tender manned by Chung's men would be leaving the river at dawn.

Afterwards Chung took Lee into the gardens, following the winding path down to the lotus pool where lanterns hung in the trees, flickering in a gentle breeze. The Chinaman paused beside the pool and contemplated their reflections.

'We are almost there, my friend.'

'There's still the Pacific.'

He dismissed it with a wave of his hand. 'That is merely water to cross. I shall feel more at ease when we have traversed the river.'

'The Kwai?'

Chung nodded, the shadows etching lines deep into his face so that he was like something hewn from old ivory. When he spoke his voice was barely a whisper, his hands still, joined by thumb and forefinger, physically framing the words.

'You know what is happening now in my country?'

'It's not the best of times to buy real estate.'

'No.' The word was tinged with regret. 'The border incidents escalate each month. The government increases its pressure on the left-wing dissidents, the military pretends it has a capability and the people believe that life will go on as it has for a thousand years. They talk of Laos, Vietnam and Cambodia as though they are part of a destiny from which we are excluded. *Mai pen rai*,' he said bitterly. 'A state of mind which bears the seeds of our destruction.'

'You'll be out of it soon enough.'

'Ah yes, but to accomplish that means a course of action which is linked with dishonour and certain death if I fail.'

Lee succeeded in looking vaguely puzzled. Chung's shrewd eyes searched his face, reflecting disappointment at his lack of perception. 'I have known the warlords for most of my life. When I was a rickshaw boy they gave me opium so that I could find them guns. When they grew, so too did I. Throughout the long war I was their eyes and ears, sometimes their hands. I gave them the CIA, the poppy fields, the markets in Taiwan and Hong Kong. They are now most powerful men who control vast areas along the borders of Burma, Thailand and Laos.'

'Why are you telling me all this?'

The Chinaman studied the delicate filigree of the frangipani tree against the night sky. 'I think you know that the vast sum of money required to purchase the total production of heroin is beyond the means of any one man.'

'There are ways,' Lee replied carefully. 'I'm sure you've thought of them.'

'Tell me how Carlos would achieve it?'

'This is not my territory. But you must have their trust, and as you will not be coming back . . .'

'Trust will not be enough. I will need you at the rendezvous to insist that the heroin is sent up the river before you make payment. Their trust will extend to my leaving with the cargo, and your reputation will convince them that I will return.'

'And when you do?'

Chung sighed. 'I do what must be done.'

'Okay, but make sure you don't do it in my direction.'

Chung smiled bleakly. 'The real dangers will be afterwards. To kill a warlord will unleash a hundred assassins. To kill ten . . .' His hand made a short chopping motion as he gazed at the American. 'I give you my life, signor. Never forget that. In return I expect you to fulfill every promise . . . totally.'

There was a chilling warning in the words which left Corey under no illusions as to his own precarious position. Chung was gambling everything on a massive coup which would retain his power and wealth, albeit in another country, long after Thailand had fallen to the communists. If he discovered that the key to his plan was an imposter, his revenge was likely to be swift and savage.

Later, on the drive across the city, Lee assessed the odds against Chung breaking his cover. He had survived the early suspicions and Sioo's inquisition, and it was highly unlikely that the warlords, isolated in their mountain strongholds, would be in any position to challenge his identity. After the rendezvous there would only be the run for the coast and the departure aboard the submarine. Long before they reached San Francisco Max Weller would know they had the Guppy and the heroin.

The girl on the stage had finished smoking her second cigarette and was bowing to scattered applause, ignoring a large cigar which had been thrown by an over-enthusiastic spectator. A bikini-clad waitress was moving around the tables beside the stage with a bowl of ping-pong balls and Masters quickly beckoned her across. With a grin at Parish he took three of the balls and passed them round.

'Now I know we're not going to play ping-pong,' Lee said dryly. 'So just what are we going to play?'

Parish and the Englishman grinned and said nothing. He looked at Dani and Silva, but they were no help either. On the stage the girl returned to her former position, lying on her stomach with her legs brought over her shoulders. The waitress handed her one of the ping-pong balls, then stepped a good ten feet away and held up the bowl. With growing disbelief Lee watched the Thai girl insert the ping-pong ball into what was clearly her most valuable asset. Sighting carefully at the waitress she fired the ball, with an audible 'pop', on a perfect trajectory to land it back in the bowl.

Masters roared with laughter, more amused by the look on

Corey's face. For the next five minutes the male customers were queueing with their ping-pong balls, holding up glasses and ash trays for the girl to hit. She rarely missed, to the delight of the audience, and somehow managed to retain her sang-froid throughout. When it came to Lee's turn he stepped on to the stage and inserted the ball, watching with fascination as powerful muscles contracted and adjusted its position.

'You wanna catch?' she asked him with a mischievous grin.

'I'd rather pull the trigger,' he replied, then pointed to Jack Masters who was about to take a drink. 'You think you can hit that?'

She swivelled her hips, squinting at the Englishman some ten feet from the stage. Her stomach muscles tightened, her thighs jerked and the ball arced through the air to land in Masters' glass.

'Fantastic,' said Lee, as the audience roared with laughter. 'If they ever put this one in the Olympics you'll walk away with the gold.'

He was returning to the table where Jack Masters, to the amusement of everyone near by, was asking the waitress for a fresh drink, when he saw the face. His stomach lurched and for a moment his training was forgotten as he froze in mid-stride and stared at the man in disbelief. He was the last person he expected to meet in Bangkok, and his mere presence meant that he was already in great danger. It was the only reason Uri Lasser would come.

Masters and Parish were still chuckling when he reached them, his brain racing over the chilling possibilities that could have brought the Israeli here. Fortunately the large quantities of drink already consumed, and the boisterous spirits, had prevented any of them from noticing his reaction. He sat down and took a long drink of his bourbon, examining the groups at nearby tables, paying particular attention to those composed entirely of men. The only suspicious group was three young Thai men near the door, but he had already agreed with Dani that they were Boka's men and would be no trouble.

The garuki was explaining that the girls who performed the very unusual feats of dexterity were trained in the art from a very early age. Parish spluttered into his glass, then offered his services as coach. Dani smiled patiently, saying it was all taken very seriously and the girls always received the highest fees at the clubs. She turned to Lee, asking if he was impressed.

'She's a knock out,' he said, grinning. 'How do I get back-stage?'

Dani gave him a quizzical look. 'You're serious?'

He nodded. 'I feel like Henry Ford with a chance to ride in a Rolls.'

Masters and Parish hooted with laughter, then solemnly laid ten dollar bills on the table.

'You get ten minutes to collect.'

Lee stood up and drained his glass. 'Eat your hearts out!'

Walking across to the bar he stopped a waitress and asked if there were any private rooms upstairs. She looked interested and indicated a door at the side of the bar, slipping his ten baht note into her bikini.

'You want me?' she asked hopefully.

He gave her a look dripping with lechery and shook his head. 'Maybe later.'

The waitress lifted a dubious eyebrow, then moved away towards the tables. He strolled to the door, which could not be seen from the main room of the club, and slipped inside. Narrow stairs, reeking of last night's beer, led up to a small landing with four doors leading off. A fat, greasy woman in a voluminous black skirt sat at the head of the stairs.

'Fifty baht,' she said, as though that was the price of the world today.

He gave her the note, glancing towards the doors. 'Which one?'

'Depend what you want. Boy, girl, two girl.'

'Just a room, for five minutes.'

She scratched her head, looking very worried, as though he was some new kind of pervert. He gave her another fifty and watched the worry vanish as she indicated the furthest door from the stairs.

He had been in the small, squalid room for no more than two minutes when there was a discreet tap on the door. He unlocked it and Lasser stepped in, light as a cat, moving to the single stained window that looked out over waste ground to a canal. Lee leaned against the wall, lighting a cigarette to cover the tension that was twisting his stomach into an icy ball.

'Shalom,' said Uri. 'You look well.'

'I felt well until a few moments ago.'

The Israeli sighed and sat on the bed, his features etched with deep lines of exhaustion. 'Carlos left Venezuela twenty-two hours ago.'

'His destination?'

Lasser grimaced. 'Bangkok.'

Lee's mouth dried out, although he had known it had to be something like this. He studied the burning end of his cigarette until the blood stopped pounding. Uri gazed at his hands, waiting.

'So he's here now?'

'I think not. I came as fast as the airlines could take me, direct to Sydney, from there to Singapore, then on to here. It's possible that Carlos travelled via Tokyo. He has friends there.'

'But you're not certain.'

Uri looked apologetic. 'He flew to Honolulu and changed planes. I was sure he was coming here, so went direct to Australia.'

'Who got to him? Do we know?'

'Paris thinks that his people in Kuwait got worried when he failed to report. They probably used embassy couriers, then found he was still in Venezuela. I think we can assume that he doesn't know about you.'

'That's a hell of an assumption. You ought to take up faith healing!'

The Israeli gave him a tired grin. 'Relax, he's not here yet. We'd know.'

'Who's we?'

'Locals. The airport is tabbed.'

'So when?'

'Tomorrow, I think. That would give him a full day in Japan. He'll need disguise and fresh papers. No problem, but it takes time.'

'So then he contacts Chung?'

'Not immediately. He'll establish a base, sniff around the clubs, probably take a look at Chung's place. By tomorrow night he'll be ready to move, which is a pity.'

'Why?'

'It means you have to get out. The first flight tomorrow.'

Lee checked his watch. He'd been in the room for seven minutes. With a grimace he shook his head. 'I'm tied up tomorrow.'

'Don't give me a hard time, Corey,' the Israeli said wearily. 'We're winding it up.'

'No way. We've got the sub and by tomorrow night we'll have more heroin than Bristol Myers.'

'You'll also have the Jackal.'

'Or *we'll* have *him.*'

The Israeli spread his hands with an exasperated expression. 'That is not the assignment. You get out – and that's an order.'

Lee rose to his feet and moved towards the door. When he gazed back at Lasser his eyes were as cold and brittle as his voice. 'You need a good night's sleep. When you've had it, start working out a way to join me at Chung's. We go up the River Kwai at noon.'

'Then you go alone.'

'Suit yourself. But if I pull out now I put nine and a half tonnes of heroin and the means to deliver it right in the lap of Carlos. Think about that.'

The Israeli winced. 'Bastard!'

'See you tomorrow!'

Lee went out of the room, past the woman who was gazing at the opposite wall as though it was playing her favourite movie, and down the stairs into the club. Parish and Masters were enjoying the antics of two girls on the stage who didn't seem able to decide whether they were friends or enemies. As Lee sat down at the table the heavier of the two girls was enthusiastically slapping her slender companion all over the stage, but the stupid girl kept coming back for more.

'How did it go?' grunted Parish, his eyes fixed on the couple on the stage.

'I owe you ten.'

Masters swivelled round long enough to grin. 'She wouldn't play?'

'She never got the chance. Along the way I met the cutest little waitress . . .'

Dani gave him a disapproving look, but Masters was already concentrating on the stage. The girls finally settled their differences and proceeded to demonstrate that fact in various explicit ways. By the time they rose to their feet and bowed to the applause there was little doubt in anyone's mind that the experience had been both satisfying and rewarding.

On the way back to the villa Lee took the opportunity of questioning Dani about Benny Dang. Parish and Masters had long since passed the point of intelligent conversation, the Englishman spending the entire journey crooning his version of 'Strangers in the Night' to the accompaniment of discordant snores from Parish.

'He has been closely watched since you returned,' Dani told him. 'And if he makes an attempt to contact Boka or anyone else then . . .' She drew a finger across her throat with enough satisfaction to suggest that she was not heading the list of Benny's admirers.

'Does he know that we make the pickup tomorrow?'

Dani nodded. 'Sioo told him tonight. He's also on duty until dawn, so there is no reason for him to leave the grounds.'

'He has a problem,' Lee agreed.

'So have you,' she said slowly.

'Anyone I know?'

'Me.'

He waited, knowing she wasn't joking.

'The rooms above the bar are convenient if you want a woman in a hurry, but that's not your style. So I asked which girl, and it turned out to be a man. That isn't your style either.'

Lee covered his tension by lighting a cigarette, blowing smoke at the alert head of Silva who was driving the Mercedes. 'You could have saved yourself a lot of trouble by asking.'

'It was no trouble . . . then. Now I must tell Chung.'

'That's okay with me.'

Dani's wide brown eyes searched the American, knowing it was not 'okay', and concerned about the extent of his deception. The silence grew between them, building walls.

'As a matter of fact,' Lee said finally. 'He's coming out to the villa tomorrow. If I'm going up the Kwai with Chung I want someone along I can trust.'

'You mean he's one of your people?'

'You must have known I'd have someone?'

'We searched, of course.'

'He's here, and tomorrow I tell Chung I want him along.'

Dani smiled with relief. 'For a while there you had me worried.'

Parish leered at them from the front seat. 'What are you two getting so friendly about back there?' he sniggered and gestured at Dani's low cut blouse. 'Don't let those tits fool you, pal. Underneath it all she's just one of the guys.'

Dani's eyes glittered as she leaned forward, patting the American's cheek. 'Don't get bitchy, Parish, or I just might forget that I'm supposed to be a lady.'

Parish tried to focus whilst searching for a suitable retort, but had to settle for a lopsided grin that didn't really come off.

The headlights of the car swept across the gates to the villa, holding on a Thai guard who waved them through with a Skorpion machine-pistol. Lee watched the lush vegetation sweep along their tunnel of light, knowing that other guards would be watching, checking the occupants. He felt his stomach tighten as they stopped outside the villa. In spite of Uri's assurance, it was possible that Carlos had arrived. In which case they would probably let him get about three feet from the car.

No one was waiting, but he did not begin to relax until he was in the house. Tim was awake, her eyes deep as she watched him move around the room. He showered, then stretched out on the bed beside her, lighting a cigarette, watching the smoke curl in the moonlight. Only then, as the stillness hollowed the mind, was he able fully to assess the situation. The appearance of Carlos, anywhere in Bangkok, would be known by Chung in a matter of hours. He would react immediately, holding them both until he knew which one to kill. Everything hinged on when the Jackal arrived, and how skilful was his disguise. By noon they would be leaving for the Kwai, fully committed to seizing the heroin and running for the submarine. If Carlos stayed out of sight until then they could be at sea before he tried to contact Chung.

Tim's lips brushed his cheek. 'Why you worry?'

He reached for her, feeling the slim, warm body curl around him. 'Tomorrow is a busy day.'

'You win,' she said confidently. 'I see it in the cards. You win all time.'

He grinned. 'Don't you people ever make a move without dealing a deck of cards?'

'The cards always know. Sometimes those who read make mistakes, but not the cards. They say strange things about you.'

'How strange?'

She hesitated, letting her lips trace a line across his chest. After a moment she turned on to her back and spoke softly in the darkness.

'Cards say you are lion in strange land. They say you walk with many shadows, and there is one who follows. He dangerous man, but there is much water between you.'

'You got that from cards?' he said, astounded by her perception.

She nodded. 'You must walk with care.'

'And you? What do they say about you?'

She gave a small shrug. 'I go with you to America, but not for long. *Mai pen rai.*'

'Maybe you should stay. You must have friends here?'

'It would not be allowed. Chung no let his people go way. Not now.'

'You could run?'

'No,' she said sadly. 'If I leave I die, but that is nothing. My father, he die. My mother, she die. Her children, my sisters, they die . . . or worse. It will happen if I run. It is the way with Chung.'

The anger coursed through him at her words, but there was nothing he could say. Neither she nor Chung could know that he was about to shuffle the cards, and the chances were that Carlos would be there to cut the deck.

Chapter 20

In the few weeks that Lee Corey had known Uri Lasser he had developed both a liking and a respect for the man. He had more than his fair share of virility and aggression, but then this was true of so many Israelis. He had courage and determination, each tempered with a calmness of spirit which showed in the stillness of eyes and mouth. But the most impressive quality was his style. If there were two ways of doing a thing, Lasser found a third.

This was never more evident than when he made his appearance the following morning.

They had risen late, collecting on the terrace where a table was laid with an array of fresh fruits and crusty rolls. The sky hung low, a burnished bronze, and the air was thick, humid enough to melt the nerve ends. Parish looked as though he was two steps from the embalming table, his tormented eyes sunk deep in burning sockets. Even Jack Masters, unable to suppress a hoot of laughter, took pity and mixed vodka, cayenne and tomato juice in what appeared to be equal proportions. He watched with satisfaction as the American choked, heaved, then gasped in anguish.

'Do you the world of good,' said Masters cheerfully.

Parish was beyond speaking. On the lawn below them Benny Dang was putting a dozen of his men through the early morning workout, his grating commands ruining what was already a depressing morning. Chung joined them with a rare display of amusement, then revealed that Sioo had already left with Kitson and Lalonde for the island.

Watching the Chinaman, Lee could detect no coolness in his manner, although Dani must have reported the previous night's incident. He was about to bring up the subject when he caught a flicker of movement from the corner of his eye. He turned just in time to see the Israeli step out of a clump of fronded palms at the corner of the villa. He was less than twenty feet from the group at the table, moving towards them in such a casual way that no one even noticed his presence until he sat down and calmly helped himself to a slice of pineapple.

'I thought this place as supposed to be guarded,' he said, and sucked noisily on the fruit.

Parish and Masters gave him an astonished look, then the Englishman shook with laughter, gazing at Chung who sat like stone at the head of the table. Not a muscle moved in his face until Masters's laughter had ceased. The Israeli finished the pineapple and looked pointedly at the coffee. Chung gave a barely perceptible nod, then turned to Corev.

'I take it this is the man you met last night?'

'We thought it was time,' Lee replied coolly, wishing he knew what name Uri was using.

'The name is Haj Hagir,' said Uri, his eyes flicking at Corey as though he had read the thought. 'Can we talk openly here?'

Chung gazed at his fingers, ignored the question to pose one of his own. 'Getting in is not impossible, Mister Hagir, but getting out is a matter of some delicacy.' He offered a wisp of a smile. 'If not danger.'

Uri nodded thoughtfully, pouring coffee. 'For some it might be. But in my case I'm staying as long as my commander instructs me to.' He paused and let his eyes dwell coldly on the Chinaman. 'That is understood.'

Chung became very still, as though all breath had left him, then lifted a hand and snapped two bony fingers. On the lawn below one of the housegirls murmured quickly to Benny Dang. The Thai turned from his men, glancing up at the terrace. The stunned amazement that contorted his features was almost comical. Even as he started towards them at a shambling run, Lee was speaking rapidly to the Chinaman.

'Hagir is with me on the Kwai, Chung, or we're going to have to change our plans.'

'It is too late for any change.'

'I don't go into situations unless the odds are on my side. That's how I've survived. That's why they call me "The Jackal".'

Masters's head came up sharply, his features reflecting surprise, then disappointment. There was no time for comment because Benny Dang arrived at the table, legs straddled, gun held low. Lasser glanced at him briefly, then reached for more pineapple.

'On your feet!' snarled Benny.

'Up your arse!' replied the Israeli.

The Thai's ugly features became positively grotesque, but before he could translate his fury into action Chung was holding out his hand in an imperative gesture, speaking coldly in Thai. Reluctantly Benny handed him the Colt Commander, the bulk of the heavy weapon incongruous in the delicate porcelain hand. The Chinaman considered the automatic with a vague distaste, then swung the barrel in the direction of Lasser. The Israeli froze, gazing over the piece of fruit in his hands. There was no emotion in his face, only an awareness that a split second separated him from oblivion. Lee opened his mouth to utter a sharp warning, but Chung spoke first.

'You are clearly a man with special talents. Perhaps you would be kind enough to place your gun on the table.'

'No gun,' said Lasser, beginning to relax again. 'With the kind of guards you have it hardly seemed necessary.'

Benny's breath hissed between rusted teeth. Chung nodded, placing the gun on the table and covering it with a napkin as though its presence offended him. He turned back to the Thai, his mouth tightening with contempt.

'You will explain to me how this man came to be here?'

Benny grunted, shifted his feet, twisted his hands together and mumbled something in Thai. Chung allowed his lips to curl with scorn, then stabbed a finger at the men below.

'Whilst you bellow at your men like a bull, the cat is playing beneath your nose.'

'It will not happen again,' Benny said thickly, his small eyes fixed on the Israeli.

'That is true,' Chung answered. 'Not only have you earned my displeasure . . . you have also earned my distrust.'

The Thai went very still, his eyes going dull, as though a light had gone out somewhere. After a long moment, in which everyone around the table watched the doubts and fears come and go, he said: 'There is no one more loyal than I.'

'Last night you met a man at the gate in the river wall. You spoke to him for ten minutes, then returned to your post. The man has been persuaded to repeat that conversation to me.'

Perspiration was erupting from the Thai's pock-marked skin, running down the frozen features like a veil of tears. 'I know nothing of this,' he croaked.

Chung turned to Lasser. 'Can you kill, Mr Hagir?'

Lasser nodded, his gaze flicking at Benny, then to Lee.

'Then kill Benny. His presence no longer pleases me.'

Breath rattled from Benny's throat and he stepped back, hands raised more in supplication than defence. Chung ignored him, reaching for the coffee as though the matter was already closed.

'I didn't come here to do your dirty work, Chung.'

The Chinaman's eyes glittered and he tapped the gun on the table. 'Travel carefully, Haj Hagir. I am still deciding whether you can be trusted on the Kwai. If you cannot, then perhaps Benny should kill you.' He glanced towards the Thai with a thoughtful expression. 'It could be that Benny, in ridding me of one problem, could persuade me to postpone the other.'

Benny's face lit up like a Hallowe'en mask and he began to measure the Israeli with growing confidence. Lee started to get to his feet, but Lasser's warning glance was quick and final. The Israeli stepped away from the table, crossing the terrace and descending to the open lawn below. The guards stood around with expressions of studied disinterest, but as Lasser slipped off his sandals and turned to meet Benny, there were looks of approval coupled with a glimmer of hope on more than one face. The Israeli moved with deceptive speed, his hands held loosely at waist level, his weight evenly balanced so that either foot was free to attack or defend.

Benny's mouth gaped in a malevolent grin and he began to shuffle forward, his stubby legs flexing to the traditional rhythm of Thai boxing. It was as though he was hearing the pipes and drums. One step, sway, two short steps, then back, sway, sway, and begin it all again. He took his first kick on the third round of the dance, a high, swinging 'Teh' to the head. Uri bobbed lightly aside, then kicked for the knee. It connected, but Benny only grunted and came on. There was a flurry of holds, blows, kicks and feints, and then they were circling again with Benny falling back into his rhythmic dance.

The Israeli was studying Benny's pattern of movements, aware that the strength of his adversary would give him an increasing advantage the longer the fight lasted. He needed to get close enough to use his hands, but the wide, swinging kicks made it virtually impossible. Benny moved forward again, jabbing with stiff fingers, kicking for the head. Uri jumped back, stumbled and allowed himself to fall, but instantly rolled and came up on one knee. The Thai was lunging for him, moving with remarkable speed for such a squat, bulky man. The watching Thais were hissing in expectation of the kick, their faces frozen in grimaces of disappointment that it would end so soon. The foot lashed at the Israeli's head with lethal force, but in the blink of an eye the head was gone and an iron grip had replaced it. Uri rose to his feet, heaving and twisting in a single motion, then as the Thai was catapulted away he sprang after him and struck three sickening blows that brought agonized gasps from Benny's gaping mouth.

The first was a right hand, palm up and stiff, that slammed into the Thai's kidney. The second was an elbow, delivered with every ounce of his strength, that smashed into the base of his spine. The third was a chopping blow with the edge of the palm, the hard ridge of muscle and bone driving into the bulging neck with enough force to kill a lesser man. Benny Dang stumbled away, eyes glazed with pain, breathing in desperate gasps. His balance had gone and his right shoulder was now lower than his left, suggesting the collar bone had snapped.

The Israeli lunged after him, striking at forearms, kicking his legs from under him when he tried to slam a knee into his groin. The Thai smothered most of the blows, but he was weakening and knew it. As Uri went into a crouch, hands poised to launch a fresh attack, the Thai suddenly turned and hurled himself at the group of watching guards. Before they had time to think about his purpose, Benny had hit the nearest man, seizing the pistol from his belt as he spun away.

Lasser froze, his eyes fixed on the gun as Benny brought it round. The move had been so sudden that before they had even absorbed the fact Benny was flicking off the safety catch and pressing the trigger. The Israeli flung himself desperately to one side, the bullets cracking the air. He rolled as Benny tracked and held him, then began to squeeze the trigger. The shots that came had a different sound, popping thinly in the humid air. Benny staggered, tried to turn, was hit again in the side. He gazed at the gun clenched in his hands, then slowly forced himself round to face the new attack. Dani stood in the shade of a clump of jasmine, the 7·65 Beretta smoking in her hand. As Benny desperately tried to press the trigger it fired again to place a small black hole in the centre of his forehead.

Even as the body of the Thai was sprawling in a lifeless heap, Chung was rising to his feet and speaking briskly to the group at the table. 'We will leave at noon. Some of you will join Sioo and the Commander at Cholburi, others will remain with me. Our final rendezvous will be with the submarine at midnight tonight.'

'And when do we see some money?' Masters asked quietly.

'San Francisco. I shall require your services in the engine-room all the way, Mister Masters. But I think you will agree that it is a small price to pay for a vessel of your own.'

'That would be true,' said the Englishman, gazing steadily at Chung. 'If your word was more important than your life?'

The Oriental's face tightened, then his eyes fell and he sighed, not without sadness. 'You are right to ask. Let us say that I do what I must to prolong a life which dwindles here in Thailand. In San Francisco your fee will be an insignificant price to pay. You will have your vessel. That is my word.'

When he had gone Parish said: 'If you're thinking of getting out, Jack, you can forget it. That Oriental bastard is leaving a dozen of his best men behind just to take care of loose ends.'

'The thought never crossed my mind. As long as he doesn't try a double-cross I can live with the rest of it.' His pale grey eyes rested on Corey with a chilling hostility. 'Even the dregs of this world who kill to get a few miserable headlines in the morning papers!'

Lee gave him a mocking grin. 'Everything is relative. You're selling out for a ship, Chung for a country.'

'And you?' Parish asked bleakly.

'I sold out a long time ago for a free state of Palestine. It's a dream that has already cost the lives of thousands, but if that sub reaches the States it will be closer than any time since 1949.'

'So that's it,' said Parish slowly. 'Another Arab-Israeli war? And you're crazy enough to think you'd win.'

'I didn't say that,' Lee said calmly. 'Even if we won the West Bank there would still be a hell of a lot of very unfriendly Jews creeping around. No, Chung has a much better plan. We're going to hit a country that doesn't even know how to hit back.'

Parish nodded coldly and pushed back his chair. 'You're doing a hell of a lot of talking for a man with so much to lose. If it's all the same to you, I don't want to hear any more.'

Masters joined him, his mouth curling as he turned away. The Israeli, who had overheard the conversation, sat down and regarded Corey with a puzzled expression. 'What the hell did you do that for? We need them as badly as Chung.'

'Sure we do, but just suppose things go wrong today and Carlos manages to get on top. At least they'll know the score, and it's a long way to San Francisco.'

'And if they let Chung know you've been talking?'

Lee grinned ruefully. 'I never said I was perfect.'

Chapter 21

A fleet of three Mercedes and two mini-buses took them north from Bangkok to Kanchanaburi and the River Kwai. From here the roads narrowed to dusty tracks that eventually dwindled to village trails through dense jungle. Further north were hills that rose in ragged tiers into Burma and to the east, Laos. Principal industries were teak and bamboo, but the further north one travelled the less economical it was to produce either. Instead the mountain people harvested opium, bringing the blocks of sticky poppy tar down the mountains to hand over to a local warlord for a hundred dollars a kilo. The warlords processed it in long corrugated-iron shacks where it was boiled over wood fires, then mixed with quicklime to precipitate it into base elements of codeine and morphine. After straining away the impurities, and adding a small amount of ammonium chloride, it was allowed to dry into blocks of pale chocolate-coloured crystals which was morphine base. This, in turn, was taken to one of four secret jungle camps where the heroin laboratories were located. Teams of skilled Thai women operated the massive stills where the morphine base and acetic acid were heated to exactly eighty-five degrees centigrade for some six hours, and then distilled in much the same way as the German firm of Bayer first did in 1898.

The only difference was that now each kilo was worth a million dollars – in the right market.

The boat station at Kanchanaburi consisted of a jumbled mass of rafts and floating houses connected by sagging planks which disappeared beneath the muddy water when supporting anyone over one hundred pounds. Moored along the rafts were the long-tailed boats, the narrow, flat-bottomed craft that could carry up to twenty people at remarkably high speeds. They got their name from the propeller shafts which extended some ten feet behind the stern, driven by converted eight-cylinder automobile engines, most of them polished with loving care by their owners. By using the weight of the engine as a counter-balance, the boatman could pivot the shaft from side to side, or hold it just below the surface in the shallowest of water. The result was a boat with great speed and manoeuvrability.

Chung led them to six boats tied up at the furthest jetty from the shore. He occupied the first with his four personal guards who made no attempt to conceal the machine-pistols they were carrying. Various steel boxes were loaded into the boats, some of them heavy enough to require two of the strongest men to carry them. Others were placed in the bow of the remaining boats, together with long wooden boxes which could only contain weapons.

Dani, Silva and two other garukis joined Lee and Uri in the second craft, but after talking briefly about the kind of weather they could expect at the head of the Kwai, they moved up into the bow. It took almost half an hour to load the boats, the midday heat oppressive beneath the canvas awnings, but finally they were ready and Chung nodded to the boatmen who cast off and drifted out into the mainstream. The engines started up with crackling roars, picking up speed until they began to plane, throwing a curtain of spray over their wake.

The river was thick, muddy with rain from the hills, and after the first mile it narrowed to some twenty metres, the velvet jungle rising up from the banks on either side to fade into purple mist on distant hills. The boatmen sat low in the sterns, riding the boats like flying spears through narrow passes enclosed by mountains, over rapids that plunged through warm rain to emerge on wide, oily reaches where oxen gazed from sandbars with sad eyes. At times the river twisted so sharply that all the boats were lost from each other, at others they were a procession of noise, skimming across still water and throwing wavelets at shelving banks of sand.

As they went deeper into the hills the floating houses of the

Mon people began to appear. Built on a framework of bamboo, with woven reed panels for walls and thatched reeds for the roofs, they floated on rafts of bamboo the ends of which had been plugged with cement. Along the Kwai and its tributaries more than ten thousand Mon lived out their lives on the water, killing the cobras which swam out at night with no more concern than city dwellers despatched mice.

They were a pleasant, hardy people who knew the river in all its moods, and the jungle in all its majesty. Many of them, together with the Meo mountain tribes, spent the summers high up on misty plateaus, burning off sections of jungle to plant poppy. In the autumn, after the harvest, they would descend to the valleys and rivers to hunt and browse the rainy season away.

It took four hours to reach the head of the Kwai, the last thirty minutes at a far slower pace as they negotiated shallows and narrow channels. They finally emerged in a valley dominated by a spectacular waterfall which plunged over a cliff a hundred feet above the river. Below the falls, nestled against a golden beach, was a collection of floating houses joined by a network of gangways and steps. The legendary 'Floating House on the River Kwai' had been built in 1975 by a French bamboo merchant and boasted the only rooms with toilet and shower this side of the Andaman Sea. On this occasion the owner was absent, but the Mon family looking after the hotel quickly produced dishes of rice, fish and spicy curry.

Chung informed them that the boats would remain at the Floating House whilst they completed the journey on foot. They ate quickly, then crossed a narrow gangway to the bank and set off through dense bamboo jungle for the border of Burma, some ten kilometres west of the river. Chung took the lead, a thin, diminutive figure in black flanked by his quartet of guards who rarely spoke, and then only in monosyllables. The remainder of the Thai guards remained at the boats, but the garukis joined Corey and Lasser, chattering cheerfully as they walked through the steaming heat. Above them the bamboo, interwoven by trailing vines, closed out much of the light so that they walked in a hot, twilight world in which all sense of direction was soon lost.

The jungle was alive with sounds, from the chattering cries of monkeys overhead to the distant, but unmistakable snarl of a tiger. At one point they passed carefully beneath a huge python, at least twenty feet in length, wound along the branch of a tree.

They had been walking for the best part of an hour when they were stopped by a distant shout from the rear. They waited until one of the Thais they had left at the river trotted into view. He was panting for breath, soaked in perspiration, his eyes glazed with exhaustion as he reached Chung and gasped out a message in Thai. The Chinaman gazed back along the trail with a grim expression, then asked a series of rapid questions. The answers did nothing to cheer him up and when he started off down the winding path his pace was noticeably faster.

Dani dropped back to Corey and the Israeli to tell them that the Thai had brought news of another boat which had followed them up the river from Kanchanaburi. According to the Mon people who had seen it pass, the boat had been carrying four men, one of whom had been Boka.

'And the others?' Lee asked her quietly.

Dani shrugged. 'We don't know, except that one of them was a long nose.'

'A what?'

She grinned and tapped his nose. 'You are a long nose.'

'Are you thinking what I'm thinking?' Uri asked after Dani had moved up to rejoin the other garukis.

'I'm trying not to.'

'It has to be our South American friend.'

'Why do you have to look on the black side? It could be anyone.'

Uri gave him a pained look.

Lee said: 'There's the CIA?'

'Sure there is, but not behind us with Boka. It has to be Carlos. What we've got to worry about is how much he knows.'

'So I'm worrying.'

They walked in silence for some minutes, then Lasser paused at a fork in the trail. Chung and the Thais were already moving down the left-hand path.

'If he's working with Boka then they could know where the rendezvous is, and that could put us both right in it.'

'You're reading my mind.'

'So do we pull out, or play Russian roulette?'

Lee gazed down the dim trail to their right. 'Pull out where? Right now I don't even know which country I'm in.'

A shrill whistle echoed through the jungle. The Israeli grimaced. 'They've just made up our minds for us.'

They took the left fork, rounding a bend to find Dani and Silva waitıng for them. The garuki's face cleared when she saw them. 'It's not far now.'

'Great,' said Corey, without enthusiasm. 'Let's hope they're home today.'

General Twan Chi Sen had built his camp on the brow of a hill that dominated a long narrow valley intersecting the border of Burma and Thailand. Jungle-clad ridges rose in tiers to the north and south making the valley a natural route for anyone crossing between the two countries. The trail that wound through the valley was not exactly the M1, but the traffic was sufficient to keep the general well supplied with whisky, tobacco and Amarit beer – the price of safe passage through his region.

General Twan was a short, barrel-chested bull of a man with eyes of cut glass and the mouth of a sadist. He had fled into Burma with the remnants of Chiang Kai-shek's Kuomintang army in 1949 and struggled across fifty miles of hostile jungle before finding an ageing local chieftain who was ripe for overthrowing. With fifty of his men, plus two hundred locals, he set about pillaging the adjacent villages. By the mid-fifties he was the acknowledged warlord for the region, but it wasn't until Chung introduced him to a young, clean-cut American with a disarming grin, that fortune smiled on the general. The American was a member of the Central Intelligence Agency and he was prepared to supply weapons and ammunition if the general would patrol the border region and prevent communist infiltration. Twan had long since developed a simple philosophy in life to excuse the trail of death and destruction he had left over the years. Anyone he didn't like was bound to be a communist.

The American's proposition was, therefore, attractive at any level. It became even more attractive when Chung, acting as negotiator for a dozen warlords, suggested that in return for this dangerous duty the CIA should assist them in the irksome task of smuggling opium to the coast from where it was shipped to Taiwan or Hong Kong. Such a service, Chung pointed out, would release many hundreds of men to fight the common enemy in the north. The CIA, after weeks of haggling, finally agreed and Air Opium was formed to fly everything direct to Taiwan. For twenty years the warlords grew and prospered, as did many politicians, Taiwanese, and members of the American high command in Vietnam, until the service was abruptly terminated in 1976 when the United States finally withdrew its forces from South-East Asia.

Over those years General Twan had consolidated his position, eliminating any who were foolish enough to doubt his wisdom. At the age of sixty-two he was a man to be feared, rather than respected; flattered, rather than provoked; and at all times obeyed without question. The only man that Twan would listen to was Chung Li, and if the Chinaman had found a new market for the heroin that was all the general needed to know.

When they reached the village of Tha Pha Yang they were greeted enthusiastically by two hundred armed soldiers who proceeded to discharge a considerable quantity of ammunition into the air. The rattle of gunfire that rolled out across the valley was the most unwelcome sound that Lee Corey could have wished to have heard. It would travel for miles, alerting anyone with a suspicious mind to the possibility that the mountain village was welcoming either friends or enemies.

The village consisted of a collection of reed and bamboo huts, a few corrugated-iron shacks, and a palatial residence that sprawled across the summit of the hill. General Twan waited for them on the veranda, which extended along the front of the building, flanked by six warlords wearing a variety of combat uniforms festooned with insignia, medals, and ammunition pouches. These men effectively controlled the infamous Golden Triangle, the trails that led out of it, and a significant number of politicians, police chiefs and military officers. They could also raise an army of ten thousand fighting men at the drop of any of their hats.

After the traditional greetings, during which they sipped jasmine tea and ate rice cakes, Chung retired into the house with the warlords and the remainder of the party were left to roam the only street in the village. Along it were stacks of polythene-wrapped bundles, ten in all, and squatting around each were groups of wary-eyed soldiers who gestured fiercely at anyone who came within spitting distance of the bundles.

'Do you think they have any idea how much that lot is worth?' Uri said softly as they passed the last of the stacks.

'No way. Twan probably tells them it'll get them through the winter with enough left over to buy next year's opium crop.'

'I counted a hundred and fifty bundles in that last stack, and they probably run to five kilos a bundle.'

'Which is about ten tonnes of Chinese pure,' Lee murmured, smiling at the nearest guard. 'That's Chung's ten billion dollar nest egg.'

'In San Francisco. Here and now it's worth what he pays for it.'

'Or doesn't.'

Uri nodded. They turned and strolled back along the street. Dani and Silva were sitting with a group of soldiers, their laughter tinkling in the hot air. Either the soldiers hadn't yet discovered they were garukis, or they didn't care. Chung's guards lounged outside the house, looking like cats who knew where the mouse was, and beyond it was the jungle, swaying now and then as guards circled the village.

'If we had incendiary grenades we could save everyone a hell of a lot of trouble,' Uri commented.

'If we had webbed feet we could quack!'

The Israeli grinned. 'All the same, keep your eyes open for grenades. I'm not mad about the submarine bit.'

'But it was your idea.'

'Sure it was, but how was I to know I'd end up going with you!'

They came for him after half an hour, two grim-faced soldiers who informed Corey that General Twan required his presence. He gave Uri a casual wave and went up to the house, but his mouth dried out when he stepped into the long, teak-walled room and saw the faces of the warlords. They looked like the 'Four Just Men' who had come face-to-face with Jack the Ripper. Sitting beside Twan was Chung, his inscrutable features giving no hint of the power game that had raged in this room, but his eyes were hollowed. There was no triumph, only apprehension.

'It is said you are Carlos, The Jackal,' said Twan, his voice grating unpleasantly on the ear. 'And that you are the man who will arrange our payment.'

'That's true,' Lee acknowledged, his eyes fixed on Chung. 'But I have left all negotiations to Chung Li.'

'They are completed,' said Twan. 'The price is fifty million dollars, in gold.'

There was a flicker of warning in Chung's eyes. Corey gazed around the faces at the table, then made an abrupt gesture with his hand and turned to leave. 'Then I have wasted a journey.'

'I did not say you can leave,' snarled Twan.

Two soldiers stepped in front of Corey, their mouths as cold and hard as the barrels of the A-18s they pointed at him. He shrugged and went back to the table.

'What kind of a rip-off is this? You guys get a thousand bucks a kilo in Taiwan, seven fifty in Bangkok.'

'That's morphine base,' said a thin, grizzled general. 'Since Taiwan is no longer operating we have our own conversion plants and what you will get is Number Two heroin.'

'I have conversion plants of my own,' Corey said sharply. 'If that's the deal I'll take morphine base at seven fifty.'

Chung was leaning back in his chair, inspecting the tips of his fingers. Twan looked as though he wanted to go outside and kick somebody.

'You take what we have,' he grated. 'We have spent a month bringing it here at great danger. We have promised payment to the Mon, the Meo, the Lahu and the Shan tribes. For the total harvest you must pay fifty million dollars.'

Chung sighed and rose to his feet, smiling a distant smile as he crossed to the door. No one stopped him, although a vein was tying itself in knots across Twan's temple. Chung stood in the doorway and beckoned to one of his guards A moment later the man appeared, carrying something heavy wrapped in hessian. Chung spoke briefly and he took it to the table, placing it in front of Twan. Chung returned and delicately unfolded the hessian to reveal a bar of gold.

'This weighs ten kilos. It is worth fifty-seven thousand two hundred dollars anywhere in the world, more in some places as you know. We have brought one hundred of them to a place along the river.'

'Then you are not the wise man I have known all these years, Chung,' Twan said coldly. 'All you will take from here is one tonne.'

'Then we take nothing,' Corey replied. 'My people need the total amount. It is the only way we can become the suppliers in the West. It is our only guarantee that we do not find ourselves unable to sell because you have supplied our competitors.'

'It is as I told you, Twan,' said Chung. 'These people are the new force in the world of narcotics. They must control that world, or they will fail.'

'It is not enough,' Twan said sullenly. 'The lowest price we will accept is . . .' He looked at the grim faces around the table. 'The very best you will get is two thousand dollars a kilo. You know what it is worth in America.'

'We are a long way from the street traders of New York and Los Angeles,' Lee pointed out. 'There are many risks we must take.'

'One thousand a kilo,' said Chung. 'The gold today, the rest in dollars within a week. You have my word on that.'

Twan looked unhappy. The setting sun burnished the bar of gold on the table before them, drawing their eyes. After a moment the general muttered something in Chinese. The heads nodded one by one. He glanced at Corey.

'It is agreed. One hundred kilos of gold today, four million in dollars next week.'

Corey nodded, watching the gleam of triumph light up Chung's face. 'Your men will deliver to the boats and then withdraw.'

Twan's mouth tightened, but he agreed. The warlords had cheated enough in the past to respect the man who used caution. He turned to Chung. 'We will make the exchange at the Floating House.'

Chung steepled his fingers and gazed through them at the warlords. When he spoke his voice was soft, apologetic.

'This transaction is the largest we have ever made, and Carlos has travelled a long way with many eyes upon him in his own country. We have no wish to offend the warlords or your armies, but Carlos insists that the boats leave first with the heroin. When they pass a given point, this will be the signal for the boat to bring the gold.'

There was an angry murmur around the table, then a rapid exchange in Chinese. Lee tried to look unconcerned, but ice was forming in the pit of his stomach. This was the crunch. If they bought it he had still to find a way out. If they refused, Chung's grand design would be in tatters.

'It is not necessary,' Twan began coldly. 'You have our word that your boats will leave the moment we have the gold.'

'You have my word that the gold will be delivered as soon as the boats are on their way,' Chung replied smoothly.

The faces glowered across the table, then Twan stabbed a finger at the American. 'Then you will remain here until we return with the gold.'

Corey took a deep breath and nodded. Chung rose to his feet and bowed solemnly to each warlord. As he turned towards the door his eyes locked with Corey's and for a brief moment he allowed the jubilation to show.

'I will see you tonight,' he said solemnly. 'I'm sure our friends will not detain you for long.'

Chapter 22

It took most of Twan's garrison of soldiers and fifty pack horses to move the heroin and by the time they had left the village the sun was low over the ridge of hills to the west. Twan had made no objection to Lasser remaining with Corey, nor the two garukis whom, Chung had pointed out, would be needed as guides and interpreters. The four of them gathered in the house together with four guards. The general had the grace to apologize for the inconvenience, his early suspicions beginning to mellow at the prospect of a hundred kilos of gold. Corey solemnly shook his hand and forgave him.

They played with a dog-eared pack of cards that reeked of

curry, then Silva told their fortunes. The predictions were, without exception, predictable. The guards, unable to resist the national pastime, gathered around the table to watch. As Silva elaborated unashamedly on the queen of hearts, Dani rose to her feet and strolled to the window. The light was fading and most of the villagers had gone indoors for the evening meal. Silva gathered up the cards and turned to one of the guards, asking him to shuffle and cut the pack, Dani began to drift back, her eyes bright as she glanced at Corey. He nodded and nudged Lasser beneath the table. Silva dealt the cards face up, the four guards completely absorbed as she spoke rapidly in Thai, tapping first one card, then another.

The Israeli leaned over the table, as though equally fascinated, but he was now within reach of the guard facing him. His hand spread flat, stillness descending over him like a shroud. Silva's glance flicked at Corey. He nodded, then stepped clear of his chair. Silva stabbed a finger at one of the cards, then as the Thai leaned forward swept the stiffened hand up into his throat. His choking gurgle was the signal for the others. Dani had positioned herself behind the guard furthest from the table and in three seconds she delivered three slashing blows, the last across the carotid artery. The man slumped to the floor like a sack of rice, even as Lasser was slamming a fist behind the ear of the astonished guard he was holding by the hair. Corey was waiting for the fourth Thai as he lurched away from the table, fumbling for the rifle he had slung over his shoulder. A stiff hand in the stomach bent him forward to receive a chopping blow across the neck that ended his interest in the proceedings.

They stood beside the unconscious guards, listening. After a moment Dani moved to the window and looked out.

'Everything okay,' the garuki said. 'Now we go.'

They bound the guards with their belts and webbing before leaving from the rear of the house, running for the jungle at the edge of the plateau. There were no cries of alarm, no shots cracking the air around them, and once in the jungle Dani quickly led them around the village and down to the main trail in the valley below. A full moon gave them sufficient light to make good time until they reached the denser bamboo jungle a mile from the village. From here they moved in single file, Dani leading with

Silva in the rear. For Corey and Lasser it was like a game of 'blind man's buff', the impenetrable darkness making any kind of orderly progress impossible. The jungle was alive with the sound of animals, some distant, others close enough to make the stomach lurch. Corey tried not to think of the cobras, or the equally deadly tigers that roamed the darkness. At one point Dani stopped them with a sharp exclamation, waiting until some unidentifiable beast had snarled a warning before moving away.

'Any idea what that was?' Uri asked as they started forward again.

'Cheetah, maybe leopard,' Silva replied.

'Thanks a lot,' said Lee. 'I'd just convinced myself it was a Siamese cat with laryngitis!'

A few minutes later they left the tunnel of bamboo to emerge on open, rocky ground. Dani stopped, listening to the night. The landscape seemed an alien world in the harsh moonlight, the encircling jungle looming like some dark, primeval force.

'How far do you reckon we've come?' Lasser asked softly.

Dani made no reply, sniffing the air with wide nostrils, like a dog scenting water – only the garuki was scenting danger. Even as Corey felt the prickling along his scalp, the sudden awareness that the night was too still, the dark shapes rose around them. Silva gave a sharp hiss of warning, the safety catch clicking off her automatic. It was instantly answered by the snarl of a machine-pistol and the garuki spun round, mouth gaping, the cry a choking gurgle of anger and pain. Then she collapsed without a further sound.

Lee dropped into a crouch, turning to face a whisper of movement behind him. There was a heavy thud as the Israeli sprawled to the ground, and then the cold barrel of a gun stroked Corey's neck. Dani had dropped to the ground with the first burst of shots and now, rising to her feet, began a run for the jungle. Flashes of light stabbed out from four points, bullets cracking the air, but the garuki was moving with the speed and agility of a cat. She was almost into the jungle when a burst of shots swung her round, sent her staggering back. Somehow the garuki kept her feet, bent low and dived into the wall of bamboo. The firing continued for a full minute as the shadowy figures raked the undergrowth, then silence descended once more.

Corey could only wait, the gun boring into his neck at any sign of movement. Figures moved across the grey landscape, pausing beside the body of Silva, then Lasser. Someone knelt beside the Israeli and grunted something in Thai. The shadows rose and advanced on Corey, squat shapes who materialized into Thais. They considered him with hooded eyes, the machine-pistols in their hands like fingers of doom. One of the men stepped closer and with a sense of bitter defeat he recognized the ugly features of Boka. That left the man who had been behind him throughout. As though reading his mind the pressure of the gun vanished. A moment later its owner appeared.

He was slightly shorter and stockier than Corey, and a beard obscured most of his lower features, but the eyes were wide, mocking, and the voice was unmistakable. Assured to the point of arrogance, slightly clipped with the merest suggestion of a latin 'r', he had to be Carlos.

'So you are the one who claims to be Carlos,' he said softly. 'How amusing.'

'So laugh a little.'

He smiled. 'Later, when I hand you over to Chung and the warlords.'

One of Boka's men tied his hands behind his back, another looped a rope around his neck, pulling it brutally tight. They dragged Lasser to his feet, slapping his face until he regained consciousness, then bound him. The Thais set off along the jungle trail at a loping run, pulling them by the ropes around their necks and kicking them savagely whenever they fell, which was often. Boka had a powerful flashlight which lit up the trail ahead and in less than an hour they had reached the banks of the river. Using the flashlight to signal the Floating House, Boka stepped out on to the bank and bellowed across the water. After a moment someone shouted back. Boka put his gun on the ground and moved forward on to the gangway leading to the first of the rafts. Carlos followed, the Thais dragging Corey and Lasser in the rear.

General Twan was waiting for them in the largest of the rooms on the centre raft, the remainder of the warlords sitting in the shadows with impassive features. Only Twan showed emotion, and this quickly grew into rage as Boka began to speak. At one point he beckoned to Carlos, who stepped forward and produced papers which Twan studied before passing them to the other warlords.

Lee was studying the room and the open veranda beyond, which extended the length of the raft. There seemed to be no more than a dozen guards, which explained the glow of camp fires they had seen further up the river as they crossed to the Floating House. General Twan had been true to his word and put the majority of his men on neutral ground, though this was not likely to last for long now that Boka was opening the biggest can of beans the warlords were ever likely to find. Twan's eyes were already glittering with an evil menace every time they rested on the American. Corey resisted the impulse to look at his watch, wishing he knew how long it had been since Chung left with the heroin.

Twan and his generals were asking more questions and Boka was doing most of the answering, but the information was not doing much for the warlords' peace of mind. Uri was giving him pointed looks, his eyes flicking to the window and the river. He gazed back without enthusiasm. The chances of them hitting the water with less than a dozen holes in them were so small he would need a calculator to work it out.

Their only hope lay with Chung. Whatever it was he planned to do to solve his pressing financial problem, it was likely to be quick and final. He edged closer to the Israeli, gazed at him intently, then said: 'My call.'

Carlos's eyes flicked at him, narrowing suspiciously. The Thai behind him yanked on the rope, effectively cutting off further conversation. Boka had stopped speaking and there was silence in the room, then Twan stepped forward and tapped the American on the chest.

'You in big fucking trouble, long nose.'

Lee managed a politely bored expression, nodding towards Boka. 'You don't believe that piece of shit, do you?'

Twan blinked, momentarily thrown off balance. 'What you mean?'

'I mean he's been trying to screw up Chung's deal for weeks. He was forced to hand me back a few days ago. Ask him.'

Carlos stepped up to him, his lips curling in an icy smile. 'Try telling *me* who you are?'

'The Jackal.'

Carlos hit him hard in the groin, watching him fold up into a gasping heap on the floor. The Thai jerked the rope, pulling him over backwards until Twan lifted his hand, speaking sharply. Corey took his time getting up, his eyes boring into the South American.

'I ask you once more?' he said.

'You know who I am. It's you everyone ought to be worrying about.'

'Later!' Twan said as Carlos moved to strike him. 'Chung will come soon.'

'You think so?' Carlos replied sceptically. 'You've seen the last you'll see of Chung.'

Twan's face darkened with anger. 'You talk of man of honour. I know Chung thirty years. He know me. If he no pay money he dead a thousand times.'

'Only if you find him,' said Carlos. 'Right now he's got the biggest reason a man ever had for disappearing.'

Twan gazed at them both with a baffled expression. The other generals were beginning to talk to each other in worried tones. Twan glanced at them irritably, trying not to show his own growing apprehension.

'All you have to do is wait,' Lee said calmly. 'When he shows, he'll sort out Boka's garbage, and this character he's got with him.'

Carlos's face tightened, but he was wise enough to understand the general's dilemma. 'That's okay with me. But how long?'

Twan scratched his chin, grappling with the baffling situation of having two men claiming they were one and the same. 'He late now,' he said finally. 'We wait five minutes, then my men begin to get at truth.' He gazed at them both. 'They are very good at finding truth.'

Corey nodded, trying to exude confidence whilst his stomach was going into free fall. 'Can we do without these,' he said, indicating the bound hands.

Twan started to say no but Boka spoke first, protesting in a harsh, imperative voice. The general glanced at him angrily, then waved to the Thais. 'Untie hands. Keep ropes round their necks.'

Boka glared at them sullenly, but refrained from further protest. Carlos glanced pointedly at his watch, then went to stand against the wall, his eyes fixed on Corey as though trying to read his thoughts.

Lee stood in the hot, humid night, feeling the perspiration running down his face, measuring seconds. Not for the first time he found himself wondering at the ease with which he had come to accept the risks. In many ways he was a cautious man, but behind that caution lay a deep sense of purpose together with an assurance that over-rode all logic in moments of danger. It was as though a syringe was poised in some corner of the brain, ready to inject the required amount of adrenalin that would get him through. The fact that one day adrenalin would not be sufficient, that instinct, training, split-second reactions would fail to stop the last bullet, had never before been a reason to turn back.

Facing it now he perceived, with a rare insight, that part of the magic, part of the thrill, was in knowing that each time the odds were greater than the last. The laws of probability would ultimately strike him down, but when? How?

With a wry amusement he realized that he was as much an addict as Kitson, only his monkey was adrenalin. When it poured through the blood, when the gut lurched and the mind went into overdrive, he was riding a high that combined fear with equal amounts of audacity. And if it had to end, better here with a purpose than in some dismal room, ravaged by alcohol and worry; better now, with the light going out in a blinding flash – not a flicker.

When the distant roar of a long-tailed boat echoed down the river, rising in a crescendo of noise between the hills, a guard appeared at the window and spoke in Thai to Twan. He nodded, glancing at Carlos and Boka with narrow eyes.

'Chung comes,' he said. 'He comes with this man's gold.'

Carlos glanced quickly at Corey, realizing immediately that there could be no gold. The roar of the powerful engine was beating at them, filling the night so that he had to shout above it.

'Then it's a trick.'

Twan's lips curled with contempt and he walked towards the window. The Israeli was watching Corey, noting how intently he was listening to the approaching boat, gauging its arrival to the second. Carlos was also aware, his dark eyes gleaming as he started towards the American.

'It is a trick!' he shouted.

'Now!' Corey said, and tore the rope from the Thai's hands, plunging to the floor.

Lasser was a split second later, kicking the Thai in the kneecap, then diving forward. Boka screamed a warning, clawing at the pistol in his waistband. Even as he brought it up to fire the air shimmered and the room seemed to explode around them as a hail of bullets ripped through the bamboo walls. Twan, at the window, was lifted off his feet and thrown across the room, his body jerking this way and that as bullets slammed into him. Other bullets tore into Boka as he pressed the trigger, turning him round so that he fired a burst of shots into the wall before falling to the floor. The warlords had no time to cry out, no time even to comprehend the extent of Chung's treachery. The fusillade of bullets bent them down like broken reeds, their eyes vacant with death even as their bodies twitched and writhed in the last agony. The first withering bursts from a dozen silent MAC 11s swept the room and veranda, killing the soldiers and the warlords where they stood. The boat then made a tight turn in the centre of the river as Chung's gunmen reloaded, coming back along the Floating House to sweep all the rooms and the entire length of the veranda with murderous bursts. As it accelerated away down the river with a crackling roar of power, the clouds of splintered bamboo were still hanging in the air, falling gently on the bloody, broken bodies below.

Corey lifted his head, gulping air. Around him the bodies were sprawled in lifeless attitudes, the only sound the rattle of death from a man in the corner. He looked for Uri and found him already on his knees, inspecting the carnage with grim features. He crawled towards him, jerking a thumb at the tattered rear wall where bullets had torn out entire sections.

'Carlos went through there on the first burst.'

'Was he hit?'

'If he wasn't he's used up the rest of his nine lives. He hit the water clean.'

'Then let's get out of here. If he gets hold of a gun we've got problems.'

Uri nodded and they rose to their feet, moving quickly out of the room and along the veranda. Two long-tailed boats were moored beside the last raft which housed the Mon families who worked at the hotel. As they checked the boats they saw pale, shocked faces in the doorway. Lee went to them, advising the family to get into the jungle before Twan's soldiers arrived. There were already shouts and sounds of activity beyond the waterfall, but it would take them some time to work their way along the bank.

Lasser started the engine of one of the boats, throttling it back, then checking the fuel level. Lee stepped in beside him, casting off as the Israeli put it into gear and moved them out into mid-stream.

'How are we fixed?' Lee asked, pointing at the fuel tank.

'It's full, but I don't know how far that takes us.'

Lee glanced at his watch and made a quick calculation. By leaving the boat at Kanchanaburi they would make better time to Bangkok, but it would be midnight before they reached the boat station and getting transportation might prove difficult. He had no way of knowing what arrangements Chung had made, for they and the garukis had planned to rendezvous down river. Chung would have waited for as long as he dared, but by now must have assumed the worst.

'We'll try to take it all the way. The river comes out into the Bay of Bangkok at Samut Songkhram and from there we can cut across to the islands.'

'How long?' Uri shouted above the roar of the engine as he gave it full throttle.

'Four hours to Songkhram, another two to the islands. With luck we'll make it by dawn.'

Uri grinned and gestured at the sky. 'God is with us tonight, my friend.'

Lee nodded, thinking cynically that Chung was probably saying the same thing. The brilliant moon bathed the river ahead in a silver glow, making it possible to travel at full speed for most of the time except when they entered one of the narrow passes where cliffs drew in above the water, dropping a curtain of impenetrable gloom. On those occasions Uri would let the engine idle, allowing the current to take them through. They were negotiating one such stretch of the river when Corey heard the boat for the first time.

It was far behind, perhaps half a mile, but the snarl of its engine was unmistakable. The sound whispered through the night, rising and falling, then fading altogether as they swept round a bend into the depths of the pass.

'Twan's men?' said the Israeli, without conviction.

'No way. They'll have had their hands full counting bodies. That boat must have left right after us.'

'We should have put a hole in it.'

Lee nodded. Neither of them mentioned Carlos. It wasn't necessary. If there was a boat close behind it had to be the South American.

The next time they had to slow down to negotiate rapids it was there again, a distant roar that assumed menacing proportions as they drifted silently through the darkness.

'He's closer,' Uri commented.

'Taking chances,' Lee agreed. 'With luck he'll take one too many and rip the bottom out of his boat.'

During the next three hours there were many opportunities to establish that he was gradually gaining. Once, as they drifted into a narrow, rocky channel, they saw the boat sweep into view on a long stretch of river. In the pale, misty light it had a ghostly quality, the plume of spray hanging behind it like a silver shroud. A moment later it vanished as cliffs closed in around them.

'Either he's a damn good boatman or he's got the luck of the devil,' commented Lasser.

'We're his only lead and there's no way he's going to lose us.'

'Unless we settle it now?'

Lee weighed the advantages against the loss of time and the risks involved. They had brought a pistol with them, but this would be useless if Carlos had picked up an automatic rifle or sub-machine-gun. Reluctantly he shook his head. 'He's as sharp as a fox. We might waste half an hour running him down, and then lose out. If we don't get to Cholburi by dawn Chung is going to pull up the gang-plank and push off without us.'

'Okay,' Uri said philosophically, although he was clearly disappointed. 'I'll try to lose him before we get to the sea.'

They roared past the floating boat station at Kanchanaburi shortly after midnight, their wake washing through the mass of rafts, causing the irate occupants to bellow curses at their vanishing stern. Exactly forty-five seconds later they had the opportunity to repeat the exercise as a second boat howled by, rocking the creaking rafts so badly that the owner of the general store was heard to utter the *kaeu kong*, calling on the *Nagas* to devour them before dawn.

In spite of the powerful exhortation, the snakes and dragons of the nether regions were otherwise engaged that night. An hour later they had entered the River Klong and were heading for the coastal port of Songkhram. Occasionally, in the distance, they picked out the fleeting shadow of the pursuing boat, but once they were into the harbour it became lost in the traffic of rice barges and coastal freighters that moved in and out of the waterway every hour of every day.

They wasted valuable minutes at the mouth of the harbour checking their remaining fuel. There was less than two gallons in the tank, but providing the sea was calm it would be sufficient. They were drifting in deep shadows beside a derelict wharf when the long-tailed boat came into view around the stern of an anchored barge. In the gloom it was impossible to identify the figure at the helm, but as the boat droned in widening circles it became clear that the occupant was searching.

'How the hell does he know?' Uri asked bitterly. 'We could have headed straight out.'

'He's playing hunches,' Lee replied. 'That's all he's got left.'

The boat had turned and was coming towards the wharf. They crouched down, the Israeli clicking the safety catch off his pistol. Lee glanced at his watch, knowing that time was running out. The boat suddenly began to accelerate, the engine roaring as it went into a sweeping turn and headed out of the harbour into open sea.

'Give him one minute,' Lee said quietly, 'then go like hell. With luck he'll be heading along the coast for the Chao Phya and Bangkok.'

They listened to the sound of the boat's engine fade into the night. A tug hooted across the harbour, answered almost immediately by the deeper call of a barge. Lasser pulled the starting cord and the engine roared into life. They surged out of the shadows, sweeping around the end of the wharf and out into the Bay of Bangkok. In the east the sky was beginning to lighten with the first hint of dawn. The Israeli aimed the bow at it and opened the throttle wide.

The first bullet cracked the air above their heads, taking them completely by surprise. Lasser cursed and pulled on the engine, swinging them left and right as more bullets whined through the gloom, ripping holes in the canopy, splintering a ragged line across the bow.

'The bastard's telepathic,' shouted Uri.

'And he's got an Armalite,' Lee replied, gazing back along the foaming wake. 'But he can't shoot and drive.'

As if in confirmation the firing ceased and a moment later he saw the slim shape of the long-tailed boat swinging out from the shore to fall in behind them. It was less than a thousand metres away, but they had already begun to plane across the choppy waves and during the next two minutes doubled the distance, losing the boat in the darkness.

Corey shouted into the Israeli's ear: 'We can't lose him until we reach the islands. It's going to be close.'

Lasser grimaced. 'It's been close since he showed his face in the jungle. You think he knows where we're heading?'

Lee nodded. 'We're pointing straight at them. He knows.'

By the time a crimson sun had tipped the horizon, painting rivulets of red and gold across the sea, the dark cones of the islands were silhouetted against the sky. They swept past the first ten minutes later, swinging round it to block out the pursuing boat. There were three small islands ahead, rising up like stubby fingers. Lasser sent them skimming past a rocky headland, arcing around it and across a narrow stretch of water to the third island. They rounded it before the pursuing boat had cleared the first, then Lee pointed to a distant hump. 'That's where it is, if

Chung hasn't pulled out by now.'

The long-tailed boat arrowed across the still water that was turning a brilliant blue beneath them as the sun changed from red to gold. Ahead they could see features on the island, pick out the golden beaches and the dark green fronds of the palms. There was still no sign of Carlos as they howled across a sheltered bay, rounded a promontory of sand to see the gaunt grey outline of the Guppy before them. As they approached they could see activity on the deck, the shimmer of diesel fumes from the stern. The unmistakable figure of Chung stood at the bow as they approached and grabbed a rope one of the Thai crew tossed to them. They climbed up to the steel deck, glancing back towards the promontory. Nothing moved and the sea was silent.

'You never cease to surprise me, Mister Corey,' Chung said in a voice that was totally unsurprised. 'Another minute or two and we should have had to manage without you.'

'Hard to believe,' Lee replied cheerfully, casting off the long-tailed boat. 'Without me you'd have no place to go.'

Chung inclined his head, allowing himself a wisp of a smile and led the way to the conning tower, speaking sharply to the two Thais on deck. They ran ahead, scrambling up the steel rungs and disappearing into the submarine. Even as they climbed after them the throb of the engines took on a deeper note and they began to move away from the shelving beach of the island. The Chinaman entered first, climbing gingerly through the hatch. Lee followed, glancing up at Lasser who was framed against the sky, looking west. He dropped down beside him, jerking a thumb over his shoulder. 'And not a moment too soon,' he said softly.

'All part of the rich tapestry of life,' Lee murmured. 'But any minute now it's going to get a little tattered for our persistent friend.'

They climbed down to the command deck as the klaxon sounded throughout the submarine, immediately followed by the voice of the Captain. 'Stand by to dive. Secure all hatches.'

Corey and Lasser exchanged grins and locked the hatch above them. Kitson was at the ballast controls, watching the dials intently as he began to flood the forward tanks and trim the diving vanes. Parish was beside him, lifting a questioning eyebrow as they crossed the deck.

'You cut things pretty fine.'

'We hate to hang about,' Lee told him dryly. 'And then there were these two girls . . .'

Parish chuckled. 'I'll bet.'

Kitson, looking drawn, gestured to the periscope. 'Take the con, Mister Corey. I shall be trimming ballast.'

Lee nodded, moving to the periscope well and pulling the lever which slid it smoothly up to eye level. Opening the hand grips he stared through the eyepiece, slowly turning it 180 degrees until he was gazing back along their wake. The rear-deck was already awash, which was just as well. Beyond it, less than five hundred metres, was a long-tailed boat approaching at full speed. He watched, his stomach tightening, as it swallowed the distance between them. The deck vanished beneath the sea, but it came on, surging over their wake as though determined to ram the conning tower. He felt the deck tilt beneath his feet and then they were submerging at a sharp angle into deep water. The last image he had, before the sea closed over the lens, was of Carlos standing in the boat with contorted features, firing with futile rage at the disappearing periscope.

He closed the handles and let the periscope sink into its well. The Israeli was waiting, the tension beginning to drain from his face.

'How was the view?' he asked.

'Very moving,' Lee replied. 'It almost brought tears to my eyes.'

Chapter 23

The majority of the Thais were gathered on the central mess-deck, sitting nervously at the long steel tables as the submarine hummed and vibrated around them. As far as they could tell there were at least fifty members of Chung's personal guard, some of whom had been on the journey up the Kwai. With them were a few women who would operate the galley during the voyage, among them Tim who ran to Corey with radiant features until she remembered the formalities and quickly bowed her head, speaking humbly. 'It gives this unworthy person much pleasure that you are well and with us.'

He grinned and touched her hand. 'Let's hope we all stay that way.'

She lifted her head, eyes glowing. 'I know you would come. I have found a house for us, in the front part where the roof comes down and there are many ovens.'

He looked baffled. 'Ovens?'

She nodded, holding up six fingers. 'Six of them. I can cook for us.'

'Not in those,' Lee said with a laugh. 'They're torpedo tubes. What you put in goes out the other end.'

Lasser joined them, pointing down at stacks of boxes and bundles that filled every spare corner of the lower-deck. 'Looks as though Chung moved house.'

'We bring many things,' Tim agreed, then lowered her voice to a whisper. 'But things not good here. Much bad talk about you since Chung and his men come back.'

'From Chung?' Lee asked, exchanging a look with the Israeli.

She frowned, uncertain. 'Not Chung, his men. When they came during the night there was talk. Your name. His.' She pointed to Uri. 'I do not know why, only that Sioo was very angry.'

They had been moving along the deck towards the bow as they spoke, passing into the forward compartment which included the galley and a second mess-deck with a dozen folding bunks against the walls. A few Thais were sitting in a corner playing cards, paying them no attention. They paused in a casual group at the far end beside the companionway leading to the storage hold.

'Where is Sioo now?' Lee asked.

Tim waved a hand towards the stern. 'She with Dani.'

The words startled them both, but explained many things which had been bothering Corey since he came aboard. Chung, though polite, had been distant, nor had he shown any curiosity about the missing garukis. The fact that Dani had made it back was disturbing. It meant she could have seen the confrontation with Carlos.

'You saw Dani?' Uri asked quietly, still unable to believe it.

Tim nodded, sensing the tension in them and puzzled by it. 'They carry him to hospital in back. Dani hurt bad. Bullet in stomach,' she pulled a face. 'Maybe no get well.'

'Jesus!' Uri said quietly. 'Where the hell does that put us?'

'Next question,' Corey said dryly, then seeing the concern on Tim's face he gave her a reassuring grin and told her to carry on down to their new 'home'. 'I'll join you later. First I must talk to Dani.'

He headed back down the submarine with Uri, appearing not to notice the Thai gunman who lounged beside the companionway. It was one of the men who had been waiting on the deck with Chung, the man who had been on the control-deck when he took over the periscope. He watched them pass with impassive features, but before they had reached the hatch leading to the control-deck he was moving again, drifting casually behind.

'I feel like a mouse in a room full of cats,' the Israeli commented as they walked briskly through the radio room.

'You ought to watch more Tom and Jerry,' Lee replied cheerfully. 'The mouse always wins.'

Uri grunted something unintelligible as they entered the control-deck. Chung was with Kitson at the chart table. Parish was leaning back in his chair, looking relaxed. Corey moved up to the Chinaman, speaking coldly and sharply.

'You didn't mention that Dani got back. Why?'

Chung took his time looking up from a chart, his inscrutable features giving no hint of the thoughts that lay behind them. 'There was much to do, and if the matter had concerned you greatly then you would have asked.'

'The last time I saw Dani was when Boka and his men took us. I thought that both the garukis had been killed.'

Chung inclined his head. 'You were fortunate that Boka spared you. He is a man of very base instincts. When faced with an enemy he will kill first and debate the wisdom of his actions later.'

'He won't any more,' Lee said tersely. 'Your men blew him apart on the Floating House.'

'Indeed,' said Chung, as though the news was only of passing interest. 'No doubt it was a fitting place to meet his destiny.'

'He had a theory that you wouldn't be back.'

'Ah,' said Chung, and turned back to the chart.

The Thai gunman was browsing among the rows of dials on the control panels, trying to look as though they made sense. Kitson began to indicate the course pencilled in on the chart, informing Chung that it would take fifteen days if they ran on the surface by night.

'Where is Dani?' Lee asked, making no attempt to conceal his anger.

The Chinaman turned with a vaguely surprised expression, then waved a hand towards the stern. 'In the sick-bay, of course.'

'Thanks,' said Lee curtly and began moving towards it.

'Without your gun,' Chung murmured, gazing at the chart. 'Weapons are no longer necessary now we are out of danger.'

Lee hesitated for a fraction of a second and in that time the Thai gunman had turned from the control panel, his right hand splayed across his shirt front, close to the holster that bulged beneath his armpit. The American shrugged and took the automatic from his waistband, placing it on the chart table. Chung glanced at Lasser for the first time, waiting. The Israeli held out empty hands.

'We travel light.'

'And fast,' Chung observed, with a vestige of a smile. 'It is a prerequisite of those who survive.'

When they had left the control room Chung placed a finger on the chart, sweeping it up the coast of the United States to Canada.

'I want a new course set for Vancouver, but no one else is to know.'

Kitson looked alarmed. 'Vancouver? That means I would have to negotiate the Juan de Fuca Straits without detailed charts. All my preparation is for San Francisco.'

'You will have the charts, and three weeks in which to prepare.'

Kitson's face had grown gaunt and pale, perspiration polishing it in the harsh light. When he spoke his voice was thin, plaintive, as though apologizing for his own fallibility. 'If we are detected in those straits we will have no chance. They can block us in, force us to surface. It's . . . it's madness.'

'They won't detect us. Those who would be interested in our

cargo already believe our destination is San Francisco. Such knowledge breeds arrogance, and arrogance carries with it the seeds of failure.'

'You mean they know of the submarine? Your plan?' Kitson asked in a horrified voice.

Chung nodded imperturbably. 'That is our secret, Captain. From now on you will keep a chart which shows the course and destination to be San Francisco, but you will operate from another which will place us here, in Vancouver,' he stabbed the chart, 'at precisely the same time.'

The sick-bay was a narrow cubicle between the crew's quarters and the engine-room. Two hinged bunks folded out from the grey metal walls leaving barely enough space for one person to stand beside them. Sioo occupied the cramped area, checking a saline drip that hung above Dani. She turned as Lee entered, greeting him with a cool nod before bending over the garuki.

'How bad is it?'

She lifted her head, the full mouth set hard against her teeth. 'There is nothing more to be done.'

Recognition flickered in Dani's eyes and she tried to raise a hand. Sioo stepped away from the bunk, squeezing past Corey so that he could move closer.

'You . . . got . . . way,' Dani whispered.

'We were lucky. They took us to the Floating House.'

The garuki nodded, her eyes going to Sioo in the doorway. When she spoke her voice was barely audible. Lee bent down, trying to pick out the words that came in painful gasps.

'You . . . bastard,' she said, then grinned. 'You tricky bastard.'

Lee managed a casual smile. Sioo spoke from the doorway, her voice sharpened by the frustration of being unable to hear the garuki's words.

'It is bad for Dani to talk. It would be better if you leave.'

The American nodded. 'Okay. Just give me a minute.'

Sioo seemed about to argue, but the garuki lifted a hand, waving it weakly at the door. She turned abruptly and left them.

'What did you hear?' Lee asked her quietly.

Dani was fighting for breath, her face a deathly pallor. 'All . . . I understand . . . then.' A fit of coughing wracked her slim figure and a bloody froth appeared in her mouth.

'Don't talk,' Lee said. 'Just nod. Have you told Chung?'

Dani tried to speak, summoning all her strength, but another violent fit of coughing left her gasping weakly, eyes narrow slits of pain. The single sheet on the bunk had slipped down to reveal that the bandages around the garuki were stained with fresh blood. Lee started to rise to his feet, intent on summoning Sioo, but Dani reached out and clung to his hand. He leaned close as she strove to speak.

'Why you do it, long nose? Why you do this crazy thing?'

Lee smiled tiredly. 'It seemed a good idea at the time . . . and I needed the holiday!'

Dani's eyes widened, then her mouth gaped in a wheezing laugh that shook the length of her body. It ended suddenly, in a small sigh, and the hand gripping his wrist slipped away to fall limply towards the floor. Lee gazed at the slack features, the eyes now vacant in death. He could only guess at the courage and determination that had enabled the garuki to drag herself to the river, to make the rendezvous with Chung. In spite of the strange role that Dani had chosen to play in life, she had never lost a sense of humour that had laughed at herself as much as those around her. Sadly he drew the sheet over the still features and left the room.

Outside Sioo was waiting beside the hatch to the crew's quarters. She started towards the sick-bay as he appeared, then stopped as she saw his expression.

'You brought her all the way down the river like that?' he asked.

Sioo shrugged, displaying no emotion. 'It was the only thing we could do.'

'Crap!' Lee replied sharply. 'You could have left her with the Mon, or at a village, or even had someone take her to Bangkok.'

'It was the only thing we could do,' Sioo repeated coldly, then pushed past him into the sick-bay.

He ducked through the hatch into the crew's quarters, ignoring the curious glances from a dozen Thais. Uri was waiting for him at the hatch to a short passageway leading to the control room. Two doors opened off the passage, one to the Captain's cabin, the other to the radio room. Uri opened the latter and slipped inside, Lee following and closing the door.

'So how deep are we?' the Israeli asked.

'I don't know. Dani just died, but I couldn't work out how much Chung was told.'

'Nobody's taken a shot at us yet.'

'Maybe they're saving us for a rainy day.'

Uri chuckled. 'I suppose it beats tombola.'

He moved to the communications equipment and began to inspect it, flicking switches and watching dials come alive, announcing after a while that both transmitters were in working order.

'I can't see Chung letting anyone in here once we get close to the States,' Lee observed. 'Not unless we can work out some kind of diversion.'

'Maybe it won't be necessary. Max will have the naval listening stations on the look-out once he realizes we've left.'

'I hope it's enough. We won't be making much noise, not compared with the heavy shipping they've got moving up and down that coastline.'

'They'd find us. A sub has got a pretty distinctive sound, and as long as they know our course and heading we should be picked up at least two days out.'

They stepped away from the transmitters as footsteps approached the door. A moment later it opened and Chung entered, bowing formally before waving a hand at the transmitters. 'We are fortunate that the equipment is functioning, but sadly my men have little understanding of such sophisticated transmitters.'

'I'm sure Mister Parish can handle it,' Lee said.

Chung nodded. 'Indeed, but he will be fully occupied with radar and the sonar devices.' He turned to Lasser. 'It would be too much to hope that you have knowledge of radio transmitters?'

Uri grinned broadly. 'You're in luck, Chung. There isn't much I don't know about them.'

The Chinaman's thin mouth curved into a satisfied smile. 'Splendid. I trust you will agree to act as communications officer for the duration of the voyage?'

The Israeli nodded, waiting until Chung had left before cursing softly in Hebrew. 'That bastard is trickier than a left-handed monkey,' he said finally. 'This is the last place he should want us.'

'We go along while it suits us,' Lee decided. 'But don't think they call him the Scorpion because he's born in November!'

Chapter 24

The vast watery desert of the Pacific opened up beyond the Philippines, enabling the inky shape of the Guppy to slip undetected through the night. From Guam to Midway they saw nothing, not even a plume of smoke on the horizon, and after ten days Parish had logged no more than a dozen ships within listening range of the submarine.

For the majority of those on board it was a period of unutterable boredom, each day spent in a hot, steel cave that throbbed and rolled to the swell of the ocean, the air going staler by the hour. Only the nights offered any form of recreation, the submarine surfacing as darkness fell to run on diesel engines and recharge the batteries. With the aft and forward hatches open, together with the bridge-deck, the interior of the submarine became bearable once more and spirits would rise. The main meal of the day would be served at this time, the majority of the Thais eating on the ridged steel deck, oblivious to the spray that frequently rose up from the plunging bow.

Chung had appointed a man called Jaras as his chief guard and it was largely due to his insistence on regular exercise for everyone on board that discipline was maintained during the long, claustrophobic hours beneath the waves.

He was a tall, angular man with heavy brows and a wide mouth. His manner was in complete contrast to his predecessor, Benny Dang, being without arrogance or malice. Throughout the day he would move along the submarine, joking with the women, watching the interminable card games, assuring everyone that they were making good time.

He kept well clear of Corey and Lasser, treating them with a wary respect. Only Masters seemed to develop any kind of relationship with him, but this was almost certainly due to the Englishman's frequent requests for men in the engine-room. The huge diesels were in constant need of attention, having to be oiled and cleaned during the day, then watched and regularly oiled as they thundered through the night. Lalonde and Masters took turns supervising the work and there were never less than four Thais in the engine-room, glistening with oil and sweat, but eager to find any task that would break the monotony.

Navigation was left to the Captain who spent many hours at the chart table, then on the bridge at night taking bearings on Rigel and Antares. In spite of Lee's misgivings, Kitson appeared to be coping well with the voyage, although it was obvious on occasions that he was surviving with the help of methadone. The paranoia was gone, as was the uncertainty and fear he had displayed in Vietnam. And yet, as Corey studied him on the bridge on their fifteenth day at sea, he suspected that Kitson's composure was only skin deep. Whilst things were going smoothly he could function, but at the first sign of stress he began to come apart.

This had been demonstrated only the previous night when the look-outs, perched high up on the cross tree between the twin periscopes, had sighted the lights of a supertanker on a course that would intersect their own. Parish, on radar, should have alerted them long before it was within visual range, but he had taken a leisurely meal on the cigarette-deck. The sea was quiet, a velvet carpet, and in the warm night air some fifty Thais were relaxing on the forward-deck. Kitson had stood in the conning tower, gazing towards the lights he could not yet see, his face ghostly pale in the glow from the bridge below. For a full minute they waited for his order to clear the decks, but it never came. Above him both the look-outs were staring down in bewilderment. One of them shouted again, but Kitson stood and fumbled nervously with his binoculars.

Lee climbed up from the cigarette-deck, where he had been talking to Parish, and stood beside the Captain. He was whispering something, too low to make out, and his eyes were bright beads of fear. It was as though the cry of the look-outs had triggered some mental image he was not prepared to face. He had clearly forgotten what to do.

'Hadn't we better submerge, Captain?' Lee asked him mildly. 'If that gets much closer they could have us on their radar.'

'Yes,' he said slowly, without conviction. 'We should submerge.'

And still he did nothing. Parish appeared, gave him a disgusted look and leaned across, pressing the dive alarm. The klaxon sounded, sending the Thais scurrying for the hatches. Two minutes later they slid softly beneath the velvet waves, Kitson once more in command, checking the ballast tanks and trim.

But it had been an illuminating display. The Captain, for all his brisk authority, was stumbling through the labyrinth of his own private hell . . . and any crisis could open all the wrong doors.

Watching him now checking the calibrations on his sextant, Lee could detect the effects of a recent dose of methadone. No one on board ever saw him receive the synthetic opiate, but rarely an hour went by without Sioo appearing for a brief word with the Captain. Occasionally they would go into his cabin and when he reappeared there would be colour in his cheeks, an unnatural sparkle in his eyes. It was that way now – flamboyance to his movements, an inner glow that added a subtle exaggeration to each action, as though it was all part of a private charade.

'He's on the juice again,' observed Lasser.

'Which means he'll be coming down about dawn.'

The Israeli nodded. It was shortly after midnight. 'She times it well. I wonder what would happen if she got her sums wrong?'

Lee winced. 'He freaked out after we sank the gunboat. We had to tie him to a bunk for two days.'

Lasser studied the Captain with a thoughtful expression. They were beside the rail of the cigarette-deck, directly below the conning tower. On the forward-deck Jaras had the full complement of Thais going through a complex series of exercises as the boat rose and fell on a gentle swell. Above them the Milky Way was a blaze of light, almost blinding in its brilliance.

'Maybe that's the answer,' Uri said slowly. 'If we could do something about Sioo's supply it could keep Chung and his boys off our backs long enough to send a signal.'

'It might work,' Lee agreed, 'but then it could give Chung the lead he's waiting for. All he has to do is alter course and everything's screwed up.'

'I need five minutes in that radio room tomorrow night when everyone else is busy.'

'Will you settle for one minute?'

Uri shook his head. 'I'll have to raise the naval base at Frisco, clear the recognition code, then give them our ETA.'

They sat and thought about it until Parish came up on deck and joined them, lighting a cigarette and sniffing the air.

'Jesus, that smells good. The diesel stinks up that sub enough to make you puke.'

'Anything on radar?' Lee asked.

'Nothing we need bother about. A couple of biggies to the south, probably on a line for Venezuela.'

He lapsed into silence, leaning on the rail and watching the dark shadows of the Thais snapping arms and legs into rigid profiles accompanied by the commands of Jaras.

'Hell of an ocean,' Lasser said some time later. 'Makes you wonder why we bothered to take a sub.'

'Small sky,' Parish replied. 'In daylight there are regular flights by the met boys, plus naval reccies and satellite surveillance. They'd peg us cold on the surface.'

'Still could,' Lee mused. 'The satellites have infra-red tracers.'

Parish gave him an odd look, causing Corey to regret the words. Carlos was unlikely to know much about satellite technology.

'Where do you get that from?' Lasser asked, his eyes signalling alarm. 'Moscow?'

'That's right,' Lee agreed. 'They filled us in on the hardware.'

Parish relaxed, moving back up to the conning tower a moment later where he paused to complain about the air-conditioning before dropping through the hatch to the bridge-deck.

'Okay, I was careless,' Lee said as the Israeli gazed at him accusingly. 'But Parish is already working out his pension plan. Three more days and he gets the golden handshake.'

'How about Masters and the Frenchman?' Uri asked. 'Could we expect any help there?'

'Jack hasn't spoken a dozen words to me in a week. He keeps to himself and his engines, and I expect that's the way he'll keep it to the end.'

'And Tim?'

Lee's mouth tightened and he gave the Israeli a hard look. 'As far as I'm concerned she's an innocent bystander, Uri. She doesn't get involved.'

Lasser shrugged. 'Okay, but when the shit hits the fan I hope she's got an umbrella.'

Later, in the forward storage room which Tim had turned into their private stateroom, he lay beside her and tried to explain the dilemma which had haunted him during the past two weeks. She watched him with dark, unfathomable eyes, only the tension at the corners of her mouth indicating her apprehension. He told her that in three days the voyage would be over, that things might not be the way she would want. That perhaps things would happen which would confuse her.

'You go way without Tim?' she asked finally. 'You not free to stay?'

He sighed and shook his head. In spite of her oriental acceptance of whatever role fate decreed, she was no different from any other woman in that she was incapable of thinking objectively. Everything had to be related to her, created for her or against her.

'This has nothing to do with you, or us,' he said. 'It is something I cannot involve you in, not without placing you in great danger.'

She shrugged and would have said *mai pen rai* if he hadn't covered her mouth with his. She nestled against him, immediately content.

'I don't want you to get involved,' Lee told her. 'No matter what happens you know nothing, you do nothing.'

She gazed at him with a worried frown, then sat up on the mattress and gazed around the small steel room with its drab grey paint and rows of boxes containing spares and tools. Her few belongings were packed in two canvas bags, a small spirit house in red, blue and gold occupying the only uncluttered corner in the room. A faded blue flower wilted at its base.

'I have been very happy here,' she said haltingly. 'We have been together all time, and no one else come here. It will make me sad to leave. It will make me sad if you go way without me.'

Lee gazed at the almond eyes in exasperation. The fact that she had spent two weeks cooped in a hot metal cell, vibrating constantly as the sea rushed over the hull, did not concern her at all. The menace of Chung, of the Thai gunmen, of their cargo, was of no consequence. She was happy, and that in itself was sufficient.

'I know,' he said gently. 'For me too. But if something bad happens you will do nothing.'

She smiled and ran a delicate finger along his cheek, pausing in the centre of his lower lip. 'You waste both our time, pappasan. What happen to you, happen to me. That cannot change.'

'Christ,' he murmured, 'you're not even listening.'

He turned on to his back and tried to think of another approach. Her lips moved across his chest, her hands fluttered around him like warm silk before tightening triumphantly. He glared at her, but she knew him too well. With an impish grin she straddled him, letting her long black hair flow down, cool and scented, like a summer's night.

'We were having a serious conversation,' he reminded her.

'I know,' she replied, still smiling. 'But now it is time for our bodies to talk and for us to listen.'

The radio room was separated from the control room by a single bulkhead, flanked on the other side by the Captain's cabin which Chung had occupied since he came on board. Kitson had moved in with Parish into what was once the officers' quarters. Throughout the day there was frequent movement between the two areas and, as Chung was rarely less than six feet from the radio cabin, the opportunities to get a message out were severely limited.

It was midnight of the following night, after Corey and Lasser had discussed every conceivable way of diverting attention for some fifteen minutes, when Chung astonished them by providing the perfect opportunity. He found them on the conning tower bridge and brusquely informed Lasser that he would be using the transmitter. Together they went down into the submarine where Chung ordered everyone, including Parish, up on to the deck. Only when the control room was deserted did Chung follow Lasser into the radio cabin.

'You will tune to this frequency,' he told him, handing him a piece of paper.

Lasser nodded and set the dial, rewarded immediately by a

voice speaking rapidly in Chinese. Chung took the microphone and switched to transmit, speaking briefly. A moment later the voice replied. Chung took a sheet of paper from his pocket, referring to it as he spoke. The conversation, entirely in Chinese, lasted ten minutes. At the end of it Chung handed the microphone to Lasser and told him to listen on the frequency for the next thirty minutes. If there was any further transmission he was to call him on the bridge.

The Chinaman left, closing the door, and Lasser beamed at the transmitter, then quickly reset the frequency for the FBI station at San Jose.

'Eagle calling Charlie One. Eagle calling Charlie One. Come in.'

The static crackled and he turned the dial a fraction, then repeated the call. A moment later a laconic voice replied: 'This is Charlie One to Eagle. We have you at level three.'

'Okay Charlie One, this is Blue Index, rush for C2 nix all stations. Repeat, Blue Index for C2, nix all stations.'

'Reading you, Eagle. Nix all stations. Standing by to tape.'

Lasser glanced at the door, cupping his hand around the transmitter. He had memorized the chart position less than an hour ago, together with their heading and ETA off the Golden Gate.

'Position twenty-three-hundred hours was latitude one-five-zero. Repeat, one-five-zero. Longitude three-seven degrees. Repeat, three-seven degrees. Confirm.'

The voice repeated the position, then Lasser gave the speed, course and ETA at San Francisco. A thin film of perspiration covered his forehead as he watched the minutes crawl by whilst the operator at San Jose read the figures back.

'Surface speed is twenty knots, dived is fifteen. Total complement is sixty-nine.'

'Understood, Eagle.'

'We are carrying approximately ten tonnes of heroin. Repeat, ten tonnes.'

'Charlie One to Eagle. Can we have that again?'

The thousand miles separating them could not disguise the total disbelief. Lasser grimaced, looking at the clock again.

'The figure is one-zero-tonnes.'

'Okay, Eagle, we had it the first time.'

'Message ends. Eagle out.'

With a sigh of relief Lasser switched off and reset the dial to the frequency Chung had given him. The transmission had taken slightly more than ten minutes, but it would already be on the way to Max Weller who would have them fixed on sonar and radar before dawn. There was no further transmission on Chung's mysterious frequency, so after switching off the receiver, Lasser made his way through the deserted control room and climbed up into the bridge. As his head came through the hatch he sensed movement behind him, but even as he started to turn he was aware of the still figure of Corey beside the periscope tube. The cold muzzle of a pistol touched the side of his neck and he froze.

'An interesting experiment,' said Chung, stepping forward into the harsh red light. 'Although we never doubted that you would accept my invitation.'

'What the hell are you talking about?' Lasser asked, climbing carefully up into the bridge, noting that the gun was held with convincing assurance by Jaras.

'Save it, Uri,' Lee said in a flat voice. 'They had the transmitter wired into a speaker here. They heard it all.'

Chung allowed himself a brittle smile. 'We have known, of course, since Dani revealed the confrontation between Boka's companion and your partner.'

'Then why let me transmit?' Lasser asked, already knowing the answer. 'I just gave away your position.'

Chung laughed softly. 'Our true position is a thousand miles from the co-ordinates you gave. No doubt they will become increasingly baffled by our elusiveness, but by the time they show their hand with a sea search we will be approaching our true destination.'

'Vancouver.' Lee said bitterly. 'It's the only place left for you to operate.'

'Not the only one,' Chung disagreed. 'But the Triads there have been growing in strength since the European purge. During the next few days others will be arriving, from San Francisco, London and Amsterdam. Long before I unload our cargo I will have a thousand men at my command.'

'You'll need them,' Uri said quietly. 'Every last one.'

There were footsteps in the conning tower above, then Kitson appeared in the hatch, clambering down the companionway into the bridge. His pale eyes moved nervously around the room, pausing on Lasser, then the gun in Jaras's hand.

'You have a problem, Mister Chung?' he asked in a clipped voice.

'Nothing which need concern you, Captain,' the Chinaman replied smoothly.

For a moment Kitson seemed inclined to argue, but instead he went to the helm and checked the bearing. Gazing studiously at the compass he spoke in an empty voice.

'I suggest you move these people off my bridge, Mister Chung.'

Chung nodded to Jaras who waved Lasser and Corey towards the hatch. They moved casually towards it, exchanging the briefest of glances. Uri dropped through first, Corey taking his time in following. There was a metallic tap from below and he glanced down to find a Thai guard beside the Israeli, smiling without humour as he rapped the barrel of his Skorpion against the ladder. With sinking spirits he climbed down into the control room where they waited for Chung and Jaras. Sioo appeared, her doll-like features ice cold as she led the way aft to the sick-bay. Jaras pushed them in, indicating the two bunks which were now equipped with twin sets of manacles.

'Looks as though you're expecting someone,' Lee observed dryly.

'I've been looking forward to it,' Sioo replied in a voice that made his stomach lurch.

They put them into the bunks, manacling a hand and a foot to the stanchions. Chung entered and inspected them, gesturing for Jaras to leave once he was satisfied. Sioo closed the door and then they stood, contemplating them in silence.

'I cannot decide whether your actions are an insult to my intelligence or your own,' Chung said finally.

'Think about it,' Lee said coolly. 'You're here with ten tonnes of heroin and a price on your head. The minute you start to market that stuff you're dead.'

'You underestimate me, Mister Corey. I have considerable funds on board, in gold and precious stones, enough to buy all the time and protection I need. Furthermore I have the organization to approach anyone I choose, whether it is the Mafia or those you claimed to represent.' He paused, only his eyes conveying the bitter anger he felt. 'Yet it would be foolish of me to pretend that your deception has not severely damaged my plans. For that you will both pay with your lives, but not before you have told us everything you know about the Farrazi list and the real Carlos.'

'Unless my watch is wrong,' Uri said, 'you've only got a day and a half. It takes me longer than that to remember my birthday.'

Sioo leaned over him and patted his cheek, her full mouth dilating into a cruel smile. 'In less time than that you will tell me anything I want to know – in exchange for death.'

Uri nodded grimly, looking deep into her. 'Yes. You'll enjoy it. You will be a bad one.'

Sioo straightened, her eyes glowing. 'Then let us start.'

Chung watched the two men as she opened a medicine cabinet and took out a syringe and a tray of small phials. Neither showed emotion. His mouth wrinkled with distaste and he touched the woman's arm.

'There will be time for that. We have things to do.'

She looked disappointed. 'I thought that was not until tomorrow night.'

'No. By then we will be too close to the coast. I have looked at the charts and find that the tides could be a problem.'

She accepted it, though her glance at the two men was full of regret. 'We must wait a while,' she said softly. 'Time for you to contemplate your destiny.'

They left, closing and locking the door. Corey let out a long breath, glancing at the Israeli with a grimace. 'We should have guessed the radio was a set-up.'

'Maybe,' Uri admitted. 'But the Oriental bastard gave us a long rope. If he was going to act it should have been two weeks ago.'

'Now we've got Max searching the wrong piece of ocean. He's going to be convinced we're coming into Frisco.'

'Friend, right now that is the least of our problems.'

Lee winced and nodded. 'You don't happen to have a bent pin?'

'I naturally thought you'd be carrying a set of keys.'

They looked around the narrow room, but the bleak furnishings had nothing to offer. In her haste Sioo had left the tray on the table at the end of the room, but apart from the phials and syringe there were no instruments. Lee began to edge himself to the furthest corner of the bunk, stretching out his left hand. He was two inches short. Uri was facing the opposite way, his feet pointing at the table.

'If you're thinking about the syringe needle forget it.'

'I already did,' Lee said, pulling hard until the steel bracelet was biting deep into his wrist. 'I'm trying to even the odds a bit. One of those bottles has got Kitson's methadone in it.'

'I like it,' Uri said, lifting himself on an elbow, watching as he strained to reach the tray. 'You got maybe an inch to find. Go flat on your back, I'll call it.'

Lee lay on the edge of the bunk, gazing at the grey ceiling, took a deep breath and stretched out. His right wrist bent back, the steel biting in until the skin parted and blood flowed.

'Left. Just a fraction.'

He moved his left hand, felt the tips of his fingers brush the tray, then made a supreme effort and hooked one nail against the wood, pulling it slowly towards the edge of the table. With a groan he relaxed, turned his head and saw that it was close enough to lift. A moment later it was on the bunk and he was examining the phials and bottles. All were marked in Chinese characters which told him nothing, but the methadone was the largest of the bottles and unmistakable. It was half full.

'What do you think?' he asked, holding it up. 'If we smash it she could have more?'

'Probably,' Uri agreed. 'What else is there?'

Lee pulled corks out with his teeth, sniffing at contents. Two made him wince, another was almost certainly morphine. A small phial contained a clear, odourless liquid that had a syrupy texture.

'I'd say this was acid.'

'Then that's the one. Lace his medicine with LSD and we're minus a Captain.'

Lee hesitated, remembering Kitson's agony on the way back from Vietnam. Uri watched, a tautness coming into his face as he recognized the repugnance.

'For Christ's sake, Corey, we're running out of chances. You saw what he was like. He'd burn his mother for a fix!'

Lee nodded and poured about a gram of LSD into the methadone, replacing the corks before returning the tray to the table, giving it a sharp push so that it slid beyond his reach. He lay back and gazed at the ceiling, trying not to think of Sioo's next visit.

At that moment Sioo was in the forward torpedo room, closing and locking the hatch to the deck above. She moved back through the submarine, past the sick-bay and the officers' mess-deck, climbing down into the pump room to see if any of the Thais were on duty. It was deserted, the massive twin pumps gleaming in the yellow light. Returning to the main-deck she closed and dogged the hatch before moving along the companionway into the main control room. Chung was there with Jaras, his eyes resting briefly on her, then he reached for the intercom microphone and handed it to the Thai. Parish lounged in his chair beside the sonar, watching curiously as Jaras spoke into the microphone, his voice echoing throughout the submarine.

Chung stood beside him, his face inscrutable, as Jaras told the Thais in the submarine that they should all go up on deck as this would be their last opportunity. The following night, he explained, they would be too close to land to risk surfacing for more than a few minutes at a time. The majority of people were already on the decks, but the remainder lost no time in making their way up through the conning tower or the after hatch. In less than five minutes the submarine was deserted. Chung nodded to Jaras, advising him to make the exercises particularly strenuous. Jaras beamed and turned towards the ladder. Almost as an afterthought, Chung asked him for the machine-pistol, saying that he would feel safer with a weapon now that they were carrying prisoners. Jaras immediately offered to remain with the Chinaman, or at least place one of his men below. Chung smiled and shook his head, telling him that the weapon was merely a whim, no more.

As soon as Jaras had disappeared into the darkness above,

Chung turned briskly to Parish. 'You will remain on duty here, Mister Parish.'

The American grimaced. 'I could do with some fresh air.'

'Not now, please.'

Parish shrugged, wondering at the tension in the pair. He assumed it was to do with Corey and his partner who had not been seen for the past hour. As Chung and Sioo moved away towards the rear of the submarine he wondered idly what Corey had done to incur the Scorpion's displeasure. Whatever it was, he decided, they had better not try to involve him.

In the engine-room Masters paused to wipe perspiration from his brow, leaving a black streak of diesel in its place. Lalonde was on the engine platform, checking the dials. Beneath them the deck vibrated to the steady roar of the four engines, the air heavy with fumes being sucked up into the ventilation ducts to be blown out with the exhaust gases through vents in the hull. Chung appeared with the Thai woman, moving carefully between the engines, then shouting into his ear. The voice was reed-thin, but authoritative.

'Do you have any of the Thai men down here, Mister Masters?'

The engineer stabbed a finger upwards. 'They're taking a break on deck.'

Chung nodded, his eyes moving to the hatch, then to Sioo. She smiled and gave a small shrug. The Chinaman nodded and turned back.

'You will receive an order to switch to batteries in a few minutes. You will do so.'

Masters frowned. The question came out as a command. He scratched his head, gazing thoughtfully at the pair. 'Why batteries? We don't submerge for two hours yet.'

Chung's mouth went thin, but he remembered to bow politely before turning away. Sioo went into the rear torpedo room, ignoring the Englishman's puzzled glance. A moment later they heard the clang of the hatch and the rush of air stopped. Chung had begun to move back towards the crew's mess as Sioo re-appeared.

'It gets pretty foul in here with that hatch closed,' Masters told her irritably. 'What the hell is going on?'

'It will not be for long,' she said smoothly and followed Chung out of the engine-room. Lalonde rolled his eyes and shook his hand as though letting go of something hot.

'She is a barracuda, that one,' he said. 'You could lose your harpoon just thinking about it.'

'You lost your harpoon years ago,' grinned Masters. 'And she knows it.'

Tim had descended through the conning tower to the bridge, having failed to find any trace of Lee or Uri on the decks. Kitson was beside the helmsman, studying the compass, as she lightly crossed the bridge and dropped through the hatch to the control room. The only person she saw was Parish, but he was leaning back in his chair with his feet up on the console. For a moment she considered asking him where Lee was, but decided against it and made for the rear of the boat. She was about to step into the crew's quarters when she saw Sioo and Chung approaching. They were absorbed in conversation and, unaccountably, she found herself stepping back out of sight into the galley. In the shadows of the narrow room she tried to analyse her subterfuge, aware only of a strange premonition that made her feel afraid. The fear coalesced into terror as she heard Sioo say casually to Chung: 'There is no time for subtlety with Corey. He knows he's going to die, so pain is my only form of persuasion.'

They moved past her as Chung said: 'I need to know if the authorities have the list. If that is so then at least we do not waste our time searching for a network that is obsolete.'

'He will tell us,' she promised as they passed out of earshot.

Tim stood in the shadows of the galley with fear clutching her throat. It was a full minute before she could begin to think again, and then it was with utter despair as she realized the enormity of the situation. There was nothing she could possibly do, and yet to do nothing was to sacrifice the man she had come to love. The conflict made her feel sick, put a weakness in her legs which made her clutch at the steel counter for support. Around her the submarine throbbed and swayed, the steady roar of the engines a constant intrusion. She took a deep breath and tried to think, pressing her clenched hands over her ears to shut out the sound.

She remembered Lee's words the previous night, his insistence that sne do nothing. The memory brought an icy shock. He must have known, even then. But even as the thought astounded her she was recalling her own words – '*what happens to you, happens to me also*'.

The inescapable truth in the words brought a strange calm. Leaving the galley she moved swiftly through the mess, down the corridor past the radio cabin to the entrance to the control room. Chung was beside the chart table with Sioo, talking quietly to her. Tim watched them, knowing that Lee must be at the front of the submarine. She remembered the sick-bay where Sioo kept her drugs. It was the only place where anyone could be held in secret.

Chung looked at his watch, then pointed towards the bridge. Sioo nodded and they crossed the room, climbing up the ladder and through the hatch. Tim felt the blood hammering in her chest. There was only Parish and he had his back to her. She held her breath and ran, flitting lightly across the room, pausing by the chart table, then the periscope. Parish stirred and yawned, glancing towards the chart table as though sensing movement. Tim froze behind the periscope well, a crimson shadow in the deep red light. Parish turned back and bent over the radar screen, yawning as he studied the scan. There was movement above, sending her flying for the passage into the officers' mess. By the time Sioo had descended into the control room, Tim was out of sight.

'Will you signal the engine-room to stop our engines,' Sioo asked Parish.

The American turned from the radar with a frown. 'Doesn't the Captain do that?'

'He's busy,' she said with a cool smile. 'You do it.'

Parish considered her with a bored expression, then rose to his feet and crossed to the helmsman's seat. The Thai in charge of the helm was using the bridge wheel at present, which made it all the more confusing. They could just as easily ring the engine-room from there. He moved the lever forward, then back to stop, and blew into the voice tube.

'All stop,' he said shortly.

'All stop,' replied a voice he recognized as Lalonde's.

A moment later the muted roar of the diesels cut out and as silence descended the submarine began to wallow in the choppy sea. Parish remained by the helm, watching the woman, becoming uncomfortably aware of tension in her. The flawless features had grown hard, like an alabaster mask. There was a clatter from above, the clang of the conning tower hatch as it was closed. With a sudden chill of horror he knew what they intended to do.

Sioo was watching him intently and even as the awareness came she lifted her hand from a fold in her skirt and he saw the stubby Beretta.

'Jesus,' he said hoarsely. 'You're not . . .'

'It is better that you take no interest in what must now happen,' she said calmly. 'Instruct the engine-room to go to batteries.'

He licked lips that were suddenly dry and cold. The Thai helmsman was sliding down the ladder, his face pale and beaded with perspiration. He stood to one side, hypnotized by fear, his arms held stiffly at odd angles. Kitson followed, crossing to the command seat with haunted eyes, waiting for Chung to appear and close the connecting hatch to the bridge before sitting down.

'There are more than sixty people up there,' Parish said quietly, astonished at the matter-of-fact way he said it. 'You can't let them drown.'

Kitson didn't even look at him. He just placed his hands on the console, letting them lay beside the ballast-tank levers.

'Batteries, Mister Parish,' Sioo said sharply.

He pushed the lever forward, then all the way back to batteries. It was answered immediately by the whine of the twin electric motors on the prop shafts.

'All ahead one third,' said Kitson, looking at his hands.

'Oh Jesus!' said Parish.

Sioo stepped forward and pushed the lever to one third, her black eyes glittering with contempt. Kitson began pulling levers, flooding the forward tanks, opening the main vents and extending the diving vanes. The deck sloped beneath them, and then they heard the screams of terror from above. There was a rush of feet on the deck, hoarse shouts and a banging on the hull. No one moved. In the conning tower above their heads fists pounded on the steel hatch with futile rage, and as the water rushed across the decks the cries became shrill, plaintive, before being swallowed by the ocean above.

They heard Masters coming all the way from the engine-room. Chung waited with a kind of fatalistic calm, the heavy Skorpion hanging limply in his hand. The Englishman pounded into the control room and stood, braced against the periscope, his eyes burning into Chung.

'You unutterable filthy bastard!' he said, and there were tears on his cheeks.

'It was not possible to take them further,' Chung said without a trace of emotion. 'Nor was it possible to send them back.'

'You're a fucking liar!' snarled Masters. 'You could have left them in Thailand, put them in dinghies, let them find their own way ashore. But not this. Only a vicious Oriental bastard who clawed his way out of the gutters of Bangkok could think of this one.'

Chung made a small gesture, dismissing the insult. 'We can no longer go to San Francisco. For the past week we have been on a course for Vancouver, and our plans now mean that I could not risk landing sixty people without papers.'

Masters snorted in disgust. Kitson had levelled out, reporting in an empty voice that they were at two hundred feet.

'You are not stupid, Mister Masters,' Chung continued in a calm voice. 'You know what it would mean if the authorities became aware of the illegal entry of those people. They would be questioned, information would be exchanged with the United States, and within hours someone would have revealed the existence of the submarine and our cargo.'

'Then why the hell did you bring them?'

'Because I did not know that Lee Corey was an agent of the United States. I had papers, money, and safe houses to go to in San Francisco. In Vancouver none of that exists.'

Masters and Parish stared at the Chinaman in stunned amazement.

'Corey?'

'We became certain tonight.'

'You still didn't need to kill them,' said Masters savagely. 'I'd have got them back. Somehow.'

Chung shook his head. 'No. My new plan means that we must leave the submarine in deep water off Vancouver Island. It will remain there, with its cargo, until I have established new distribution markets in North America. Only six people will know of its location. Three I can trust,' he said, including Kitson in his glance. 'The other three must be bought.'

'Or killed,' Masters said cynically.

Chung looked genuinely troubled. 'I hope not. I believe that if the three of you accept my price, then you also accept what has been done tonight. In fact,' he smiled without warmth, 'if you did break your word I would implicate you all.'

He lapsed into silence, his gaze wandering to the frightened mask of the Thai at the helm. He lifted a delicate hand. 'You need have no fear. You will serve me and will be well paid.'

The man gulped and tried a grin that emerged as a grotesque spasm of relief. Chung turned back to the Englishman. He was gazing at him with bitter defeat. 'How much?' he asked tonelessly.

'One million, each. You will receive it tonight in diamonds, sapphires and emeralds. Once you leave the submarine our association is ended.'

Parish sucked air between his teeth, his bifocal eyes shuttling from Masters to Chung. In a strangled voice he said: 'I'm in.'

'Well, Masters?' Sioo asked softly, speaking for the first time.

The Englishman looked at her with undisguised contempt, then nodded abruptly and started towards the hatch.

'All right, Chung,' he said bitterly. 'You've found my price. Now do me a favour. Stay out of my engine-room!'

With that he left them, surrounded by the hum of the motors and the gentle hiss of water on the other side of the hull. Kitson rose from his seat and went to Sioo, bending so that he could whisper in her ear. She touched his arm sympathetically and shook her head. Her mouth formed the word '*later*' and Kitson's shoulders sagged. He went to the periscope and stood looking at it, as though he wasn't quite sure what it was for.

The grim significance of the sudden dive beneath the surface was not lost on Corey or Lasser, nor the frantic scrambling over the deck above them. With the realization of what Chung had done came rage, despair, and for Corey a deep sense of loss as he accepted the inevitable conclusion that one of the people struggling in the sea would be Tim. Savage emotions coursed through him and he tore at the manacles, oblivious to pain, consumed by a blazing pillar of fury that shook his body as he cursed the Chinaman. When the door to the sick-bay slid open he went very still, steeling himself for one desperate lunge. But the face that moved into his line of vision was the last he expected and a great relief washed the anger away.

'He has killed everyone,' Tim said in a bewildered voice. 'He let them all drown.'

'Does he know you're on board?' Uri asked her urgently.

She shook her head, her eyes still glazed with horror. 'He think I drown also.'

She sat on the bunk beside Lee, reaching for his hand. She was like a lost child, seeking reassurance.

'Below decks,' the Israeli said quickly. 'It's her only chance.'

Lee nodded, gripping her hand tightly, forcing her to look at him. 'There isn't much time. Go into the mess to the hatch against the port side. Lift it up and you will see a ladder going down to the hold. There are batteries there, lots of them. You must hide among them.'

'I want to stay with you,' she said firmly. 'When Sioo come I kill her. I kill Chung, Sioo, all of them.'

'You don't kill anyone,' Lee said harshly. 'You do what I say. Go down to the batteries, then wait.'

She began to cry. Lasser cursed softly and swung his hand awkwardly, catching her across the shoulder. 'Listen, will you. If they don't know you're on board there's a chance for us. You must hide, then some time during the day you will hear things go wrong.'

'Wrong? How wrong?'

'The Captain,' Lee told her. 'He's going to go crazy.'

'He already crazy,' she said positively.

'Jesus!' said Lasser, 'Will you shut up and listen. When it happens there'll be panic. You do two things. Get to the control room and wait until they have left, then go to the sonar equipment. You know where it is?'

She shook her head.

Lee explained patiently. 'It is where Parish sits. There is a screen and some switches, and he has earphones that are connected to the panel which hold those switches.'

Her face brightened and she nodded. 'I know. He let me listen.'

'Right. One of those switches has the word "*transmit*". Just that. "*Transmit*".' She nodded. 'You put that switch on, then go back to the batteries.'

'I come set you free.'

'No!' Lasser said savagely. 'You just do that.'

She gazed at them stubbornly. They were both conscious of minutes ticking away. That any moment Sioo could arrive.

'All right,' Lee said tersely. 'After you have switched to transmit, you come to us. But only if it is safe.'

Her eyes glowed and she stood up. 'I will do what pappasan say.'

She kissed him, then went to the door. As she prepared to step out Lee spoke quietly without emotion.

'You do nothing until the Captain breaks, Tim. No matter what happens in here. If you act too soon we are all dead. You understand? You may hear things, but you must take no notice.'

She shivered, understanding what he meant. He gazed steadily at her, watching the gentle eyes fill with tears. And then she had gone, closing the door behind her.

They lay in silence for a long time, dreading the shout that would mean she had been discovered. But after five minutes there had been no alarm and they began to believe there was a chance.

'She'll use the drugs,' Uri said calmly. 'That means we have to find something to screw it all up.'

'It's a great thought,' Lee said dryly. 'But can you be more specific?'

The Israeli glanced across at him, his face a granite mask. 'You ever had a bad trip?'

'This one gets my vote,' Lee replied, then shook his head, knowing what he meant.

'When you start going up and the buzz is clear, set your mind on something ugly. Build yourself a nightmare – and you'll just freak out. There'll be nothing she can do until you come down.'

'If I come down,' Lee said.

Uri gave him a bleak smile. 'You'll be back. Just don't be too quick about it!'

Chapter 25

The long night ended with the submarine cruising at a depth of fifty feet, some four hundred miles off the Queen Charlotte Straits. They had surfaced for two periods of one hour, submerging just before dawn with batteries fully charged and an empty ocean in front of them. The coastal shipping lanes were less frequently used north of Vancouver Island, with only the main Alaska route presenting any kind of regular activity. The yachts, day boats and coastal freighters using Vancouver harbour and the Straits would be no danger in the early hours of dawn when Chung planned to make his approach to Hope Island.

'We will approach it from Queen Charlotte Sound,' he told Parish and Kitson, tapping the chart. 'Arriving between Hope and Nigei islands just before dawn. Masters and Lalonde will prepare the dinghy on the aft-deck whilst we bring up the things I will want to take with us.

'You, Mister Parish, will use the sonar to establish that we are over the deepest water in the area. According to the chart it should be twenty-five fathoms.'

Parish nodded, studying the chart. He took calipers and measured the distance from Hope Island. 'It's about a quarter of a mile out.'

'Indeed,' said Chung. 'We will use the outboard motor and should reach the island in half an hour.'

'Leaving the submarine sitting there like a lame duck,' Kitson murmured.

Chung gazed at him with polite despair. 'No, Captain. You will flood all ballast chambers, then get out through the conning tower, locking the hatch. You will need to be quick, but I have every confidence in you. The submarine will sink to the ocean floor, leaving no trace.'

'With the heroin?' Parish asked.

'Of course. Later, when it is required, my people will reach the submarine with aqualungs.'

'Neat,' Parish conceded. 'In that depth of water it should be safe enough. But we've still got to get off Hope Island.'

'That has already been arranged. People will arrive later tomorrow morning.' He looked from Kitson to Parish, dismissing them brusquely. 'I suggest you both sleep for most of the day. I shall wake you if it becomes necessary.'

'Suits me,' said Parish and moved towards his quarters.

Kitson hung back, waiting as Chung crossed to the helmsman and told him to take the auxiliary helm on the bridge. The Thai seemed happy to comply. Sioo was sitting beside the trim controls, knowing what he wanted. He went over to her, saying nothing, his hands twisting and turning around each other.

'You want sleep, Captain,' she said, and held out a small blue capsule. 'This will help.'

'I need more. You've given me nothing since last night. I can't . . . can't put things together.'

'You don't need to,' she said coldly. 'Not until tonight.'

Reluctantly he took the capsule, gazing at her bitterly as he swallowed it. She smiled then and patted his arm. 'That's better. Now sleep.'

In the engine-room Lalonde stretched out on his bunk and drifted into a fitful sleep. Masters oiled and cleaned the silent engines without even being consciously aware of his actions. His mind was fully occupied with utter self-contempt.

Somehow, somewhere along the way, he had lost the things he held most sacred. Integrity, compassion, the will to play the game, those things he had cherished as a young man and kept at the forefront of his ambitions during the bad times and the good.

The years in Asia had gone so quickly, like the long procession of women gasping in the night, remembered fleetingly for the degree of passion their bodies evoked. Never for their minds, their conversation or even their love. He had never been sure whether they had corrupted him, or he them, just as he would never know if the good years running his own ship had blunted his ability to survive. All he did know was that after the *Leonora* sank and it was impossible to find a new ship, he had become afraid.

The old image of Jack Masters still dominated his actions, made decisions and faced the world. The style was there, the mocking smile and cool grey eyes that could open doors – and people. But at night the façade collapsed beneath the weight of uncertainty and despair. At thirty, tomorrow had been an adventure unfulfilled; at forty, it was fraught with peril, faced with defiance instead of hope. And somehow the days seemed longer, filled with fragments of fear. It was inevitable that he should accept Chung's offer, swallow his pride and embark on a voyage which was a betrayal of everything he respected in himself. At last he knew his price, and with that knowledge came the realization that there had always been a price.

When the screams started he climbed up on the engine platform and slammed a fist into the rail. A moment later he quietly closed the hatch, but he could still hear it, like the mindless howl of an animal in pain. A feeling of nausea came and went, then a numbing lethargy which dulled the anger but failed to quench the fear. He wondered if Parish had heard it, if he too would do nothing.

Corey had watched the woman work on the Israeli with horror. She prepared the mixture of drugs whilst Chung stood in the doorway with a gun aimed steadily at them. When she injected it into the artery in his left arm, Chung had left. Sioo stood between the bunks, the Beretta in her hand, inviting Corey to make a move. He turned away from her, knowing that a bullet now would destroy all their chances. He heard her whispering and was revolted by the blend of lust and cruelty in her voice. And then Uri had screamed.

He tried to hit her with his free arm but she chopped it viciously with the barrel of the gun and then, as he flailed weakly, pinned it to the bunk and stabbed the syringe into a vein.

'Sometime today I will kill you,' she said coolly. 'But how long that will be depends on your own stupidity. All you have to do is tell me who has Farazzi's list and which department you work for.'

'Go to hell,' said Corey.

She smiled. 'In a few minutes I will be the centre of your universe. You will have no other thought, no greater desire, than to possess me.'

Even though the room had begun to flow into liquid shapes that seemed to shimmer on the fringes of his vision, he managed to underline each word with contempt. 'You may be right, but in case you are I think you ought to find a brown paper bag.' She looked puzzled, so he spelled it out. 'If I screw you again I'm really going to have to throw up!'

Blood darkened her cheeks and her eyes went ugly. Her hand reached out and hovered over him, but she changed her mind and turned back to the Israeli. What shocked Corey more than anything else was that she did so little. Her hands moved over him, touching, pressing, building sensitivity until he no longer had any control, and then she squeezed and he arched up off the bunk, screaming in a thin, anguished voice long after she had stopped.

'The Farrazi list?' she whispered. 'Who has it?'

Lasser turned his head, speaking awkwardly, as though he had forgotten the word. 'Shit,' he said.

When she squeezed again he passed out.

In the darkness of the hold Tim crouched between the rows of battery cells, each lead-acid unit almost as large as a man. They hummed softly around her, smelling of ozone, the heavy-duty cables snaking away into the darkness towards a massive junction box. She had been covering her ears for almost an hour, praying to Buddha, asking for guidance when she knew that this in itself was an admission of weakness. '*Death is merely a transition, pain is only a test.*' She remembered the words of the monk who taught her in the village when she was a child. '*All things have beauty, all life has purpose,*' he had told her. But there was no purpose here, she whispered. There was no beauty in this alien world, only evil and pain that echoed along the hold, threatening her sanity, twisting her mind. She wondered if she was capable of killing, tried to assess degrees of hate and then imagine herself in the room with Sioo. It accomplished nothing, only increased her terror and despair.

At last she crawled along the hold to the hatch, climbed the ladder up into the brightly-lit room. She paused there, white and shaking, her heart thudding against her ribs so hard that each breath was an effort. The sick-bay was no more than twenty feet away, the mess-deck deserted. She crawled out, then crouched in a corner and searched for a weapon. The cries that came from the room were different now, no longer coherent, no longer born of pain. She cocked her head, concentrating on the sounds. Someone was shouting, a long stream of obscenity, and then a cry of fear. It was the other man, not Lee, she decided. A moment later she heard his voice, strangely remote, like someone talking in a dream.

The door slid open with a clang and Sioo stepped out, gazing back into the room with tight, angry features, before walking rapidly away towards the control room. Tim crouched beside the bulkhead, listening to the crazy voices, realizing with a sad relief that both Lee and his friend were beyond help. She had seen a man in that condition once before. He had been an Arab Sioo kept locked in a room at Chung's villa. She didn't want to see Lee like that.

The loneliness and despair welled up inside her, and as a shrill shout of fear came from the sick-bay she went back to the hold and curled up between the batteries, listening to the submarine, wondering if the Captain really would go crazy.

The North American continent crept over the horizon as the sun began to fall into the ocean behind the submarine. The first sighting was a ragged white line of cloud which gradually solidified into the snow-capped peaks of the Rockies, but within an hour the dark mass of Vancouver Island appeared, dead ahead and less than an hour away.

Chung turned the periscope to full magnification, picking out distant yachts and motor cruisers. The sea was rising as the wind strengthened and by nightfall he knew that conditions would be perfect for their approach to the northern tip of the island. To the south was Cape Flattery, marking the entrance to the Straits of Juan de Fuca. He studied it for a long time, knowing that along the straits was Port Angeles where the US Coastguard maintained a base equipped with launches and a high-endurance cutter. If anything was going to detect their presence in these waters it would be the US Coastguard cutters.

'Our voyage is almost over,' he told Sioo, sliding the periscope down into its well. 'I think it is time the Captain was roused.'

'He will need methadone,' she said.

Chung shrugged. The matter did not concern him. She got to her feet, picking up the pistol, toying with it. 'There will be no more time to question Corey.'

'There are some hours yet. Surely their condition will not last all night?'

Her mouth tightened, the frustrated anger flaring again at the humiliation they had caused. Chung had made no criticism, had indeed showed sympathy, but she knew that behind the impassive features there was disappointment and surprise. She had never failed before.

'I cannot tell how long it will take,' she admitted. 'The recovery will be slow for they have retreated into their own worlds. It could become a permanent state.'

'Ah,' said Chung, frowning at the prospect. 'That would indeed be a pity. It is unlike you to be over-zealous in these matters.'

She flushed at the gentle reproof. 'It happened. I think they knew enough to choose the way themselves.'

Chung went very still. 'If that were true there would seem to be no purpose to it.'

'I could kill them?' she offered.

Chung considered the tips of his fingers, then placed them carefully together and shook his head. 'Not yet. There may still be time to learn something of value.'

Sioo nodded and placed the gun on the chart table. When she left Chung closed his eyes and thought about the American. If his daughter was right then he must have had a motive. But what? There was no way he could pose any further threat to them. Chung sighed. Perhaps it was nothing more than Sioo's refusal to admit that she had erred.

Sioo collected the methadone from the sick-bay, inspecting Corey and Lasser to find, with some relief, that they were both now much calmer with pulses back to normal. She checked their pupils and found them still dilated, but they were clearly recovering.

She went through to the forward quarters and woke Kitson, using a barbiturate to counter the effects of the heavy sedative she had given him earlier. He swallowed the capsule with a shudder, his face chalk white.

'It is time,' she said, putting warmth into her smile. 'The last watch.'

He nodded jerkily, his watery eyes drawn to the methadone. A spasm shook his thin frame and for a moment she thought he was going to vomit, but he recovered and rose unsteadily to his feet. He was frail, almost too weak to stand, and the running nose and watering eyes were obvious symptoms of withdrawal. With a twinge of annoyance she realized that the usual dose would not be sufficient.

'I think we will main-line tonight,' she said, filling a syringe from the bottle.

Kitson was pathetically eager, rolling up his sleeve and holding out his arm. She injected the methadone quickly, watching the effects take hold, never failing to be surprised at the speed of an intravenous fix. In ten seconds the colour was coming back into his cheeks, his eyes were beginning to glow and the frail, stooped body was straightening with renewed strength and assurance. For Samuel Kitson it was a magical elixir. She turned away, satisfied, and began putting the bottle of methadone and syringe into her bag. It wasn't until she turned back and saw his eyes that she knew something had gone wrong. Badly wrong.

'They've come back,' he whispered.

She covered her fear and forced a smile. His eyes were hypnotic, the muscles of his face rippling, his left cheek already in spasm. Even as she watched waves of raw emotion rolled across his features, melting one expression into another.

'Who are back, Captain?' she asked tensely.

'The dead,' he answered. 'All those people we killed last night. They've come back.'

She shook her head, stepping carefully away from him. 'No. That's impossible. They can't come back.'

His head was moving from side to side, his gaze flicking from one corner of the room to another. He didn't seem to be listening, but she knew he was. He would be acutely aware of everything in the room. He would know when she moved, almost before she had done so, and he would know each conscious decision she made. Already he would be smelling the fear in her.

'Captain,' she murmured, 'you must trust me now and come with me. The things you are seeing are not real. Only I can take them away.'

She read the decision in his eyes, but could do nothing. The fist hurtled at her, smashing lips and teeth, knocking her the length of the room. She lay on the floor, tasting blood, and then she began to scream.

Tim heard the scream and felt an enormous relief. She scrambled up the ladder on to the mess-deck, hurrying towards the control room. When she reached it Chung had already left and she could hear Parish shouting. The sonar glowed in the red light and she ran to it, her hands fluttering nervously over the panel. There was a switch on the right with a single word above it. 'Transmit'. She flicked it on, watching a small green light begin to glow. From the headphones on the chair came a faint but steady ping.

Sioo had crawled into the corridor beside the pump room, holding her battered mouth. Chung and Parish reached her as Kitson, shouting curses, hurled a chair at the bulkhead and ran into the forward torpedo room.

'What the hell went wrong?' Parish snarled.

'The methadone,' she said, wincing with pain. 'I don't understand. It shouldn't have had that effect.'

'Can you correct it?' asked Chung.

She pulled a broken tooth from her mouth, feeling waves of pain beginning to rise from her lower jaw. She stifled a sob and fumbled in her bag for a pain killer. Chung stopped her, gripping her wrist in a rare display of anger. She shook her head.

'I don't know. He's undergone some sort of personality change. His eyes . . . it's as though . . .' She stopped suddenly, the blood draining from her cheeks.

'As though what?' snapped Chung.

'Acid,' she said bitterly. 'Someone put acid in the methadone.'

'Oh Christ!' said Parish. 'That tears it. That really fucking tears it!'

From the forward torpedo room there was a clang of metal, then a crash. Parish gazed towards the sound, wincing as they heard another.

'He's in with the torpedoes for Christ's sake!'

'Kill him,' said Sioo, her mouth twisting viciously.

'No,' said Chung. 'Without Kitson we cannot navigate this submarine, or find our way to the island. He must be restrained, and then we must wait until you can bring him to his senses.'

'You're out of your tiny mind,' Parish said. 'He's going to kill anyone who goes near him.'

'You go,' said Chung, lifting the Skorpion. 'That is an order.'

Parish stared at the gun, cursed softly and walked across the sleeping quarters, looking back once before ducking through the hatch into the torpedo room. Kitson was crouching beside the tubes, snarling at the opposite bulkhead. A torpedo lay on the deck, rolling with the motion of the boat. It came up against the starboard torpedo rack with a clang that made him cringe.

'Captain Kitson, you're wanted on the bridge,' Parish croaked, stepping carefully to one side.

Kitson came at him like a mad dog, eyes bulging, mouth gaping with a moan of rage that made his blood run cold. He ducked the lunge, chopped hard for the throat but caught the shoulder instead. Kitson turned, swung a wild punch, then kicked him viciously in the groin. Parish gasped and went to his knees, trying to fend off the Captain as he grabbed at his throat and swung him half-way across the room. There was a heavy steel locking pin beside the torpedo hoist and Kitson wrenched it free, lifting it high above his head. Parish watched with frozen horror as he prepared to smash it down, but before he could start the downward swing Chung had stepped up behind him and rapped the barrel of the machine-pistol across the back of his head. Kitson collapsed without a sound.

'Get him to the control room,' Chung told him sharply. 'We have less than an hour.'

'He won't be thinking straight for a week,' Parish said savagely. 'You've both blown it!'

'Do what I say,' said Chung in a brittle voice.

With some assistance from Sioo he dragged and carried the limp body of the Captain to the control room, putting him in a chair. The woman bent over him, checking his pulse and pupils. Her mouth was small, angry, and when she spoke it was to ask Parish to get her bag which she had dropped when Kitson attacked her.

'You must find a way,' Chung urged after the American had left.

'I will have to use Naloxone,' she said, referring to the narcotic antagonist drug used to counter the effects of opiates. 'But it will be dangerous.'

'No matter. We need him for a few hours, that's all.'

She nodded, checking his pulse again. The anger and humiliation in her was so great she had difficulty keeping her voice steady.

'This must have been done by Corey. I want to kill him. Now.'

'There will be time for that,' Chung assured her. 'Let us first undo the damage.'

Sioo bit her lip, but nodded. Parish arrived with her bag and she quickly found a phial of Naloxone, drawing a small amount into the syringe and injecting it into his arm.

'If he's on acid and methadone there's not a damned thing you can do,' Parish observed tightly.

'You know nothing of these things,' she snapped. 'This drug will dull the effects.'

'Of methadone, maybe. Not acid.'

Kitson groaned and opened his eyes. They were vacant, lifeless. Parish turned away, cursing softly.

'He must be ready in an hour,' Chung said quietly.

'Look at him,' snarled Parish. 'He couldn't navigate a fucking dinghy!'

Chung's control almost snapped. He swung round, the machine-pistol quivering in his bony hand. 'Silence,' he said in a shrill voice. 'You will do as you are told!'

Parish gazed at the gun, then turned his back on them and went to sit beside the sonar.

Corey emerged from a dark fog in which alien voices echoed down impossible corridors, grating on the consciousness. As the fog cleared he found a grotesque face filling his vision, elongated so that the forehead seemed to soar away into a bright light. The eyes, however, were gentle and drew him to her. The voice became clear, and then the room snapped into focus and he saw that Tim was bending over him.

'You must help us, Lee,' she was saying urgently. 'There is little time.'

He sat up, finding that his wrist was free. Uri sat on the opposite bunk, taking long, deep breaths, his shoulders hunched. Tim had a pair of heavy cutting pliers in her hand and began to worry at the manacle on his ankle. He leaned forward unsteadily and took over, snapping through the steel.

The Israeli lifted his head and regarded him with bloodshot eyes. He looked as though he would be more comfortable in a mortuary. 'We're going to have to move.'

Lee nodded, then wished he hadn't. He turned to Tim who was beginning to look relieved. 'Did you get to the sonar?'

'Yes. It is working.'

'How long ago?' croaked Lasser.

She frowned, counting minutes. They waited, swaying with waves of nausea, watching the room bend and shimmer with the fading effects of the powerful hallucinogens.

'Ten, maybe fifteen minutes,' she decided.

Lasser lurched to his feet, holding out a hand for Corey. 'Think you can make it?'

Lee swayed and clutched at a shelf. 'Just as long as I don't pass any mirrors – if I look half as bad as you I'll get hysterical.'

Parish had been sitting beside the sonar equipment for a full minute before the faint ping from the headphones intruded. He turned towards the control panel, suddenly alert to the possibility that someone was looking for them.

'Oh Jesus!' he exclaimed, gazing at the transmit light in disbelief. 'Who the hell switched that on?'

Sioo ignored him, working on Kitson with feverish haste. She was rubbing his hands, massaging his neck and shoulders, speaking softly in a soothing voice. Chung turned towards Parish as he switched off the sonar signal. He showed no concern.

'You don't understand, do you?' Parish asked him bitterly. 'We're finished. Done for. The whole thing is a total fuck up!'

'I am rapidly losing patience with you, Mister Parish. The equipment is your responsibility.'

'But it was switched on!'

Chung shrugged, turning back to Kitson. 'So now it is off. We have more pressing problems.'

'Listen to me, you stupid bastard!' Parish yelled, his face crimson with fury. 'They know where we are. That signal can be picked up five hundred miles away. It's been on long enough to give them a fix and a full identikit of this sub.'

Chung and Sioo stared at him in disbelief. He groaned and switched on the speakers, turning up the volume until the ocean was a dull roar around them. Almost immediately they heard a steady ping coming at one-second intervals.

'You know what that is?' Parish asked them contemptuously. 'It's a US Coastguard cutter, probably out of Seattle. It's homing in on us, on its way here at full speed.'

He turned the listening dial, watching the read-out, then flicked in filters and increased the volume. The ping was loud, but also they could hear the rhythmic rumble of engines.

'That's the cutter all right. I make it two miles off and closing fast.'

Chung moved to the equipment, his disbelief turning to rage. The impassive features twisted, his eyes blazing as he lifted the gun, wanting to strike the American down. 'How?' he asked.

'I don't know. It doesn't matter. They've got a fix on us and that's it.'

Chung went quickly to the periscope and pulled the lever that raised it up out of its well. He pressed his eye against it, swinging it round. Even as he found what he was looking for they heard a second ping echo over the first. Parish turned the dial, locating it, then sat back with a grimace.

'That's another cutter, probably the sister ship.'

'They still can't touch us,' Sioo said nervously. 'Not Coastguard vessels.'

Chung was turning back from the periscope with white, contorted features. Parish moved to the ballast controls.

'Those cutters have got anti-submarine equipment, including depth charges and homing torpedoes. We haven't got a hope in hell.'

He reached for the levers, but Chung's sharp command stopped him.

'I give the orders here,' he said. 'We must go deeper.'

'We can't,' Parish told him patiently. 'Only Kitson knows how to adjust the trim. Anyway, that won't stop them.'

'I think you did this,' said Sioo, her voice shrill and afraid. 'You're the only one who could have.'

Parish gave her a disgusted look, about to make a seething retort. He was stopped by the voice of Lee Corey. They turned towards it in disbelief.

'It's over, Chung,' he said calmly, standing in the crimson shadows by the aft hatch. 'You put the gun down and let Parish surface.'

Chung's thin mouth twisted, his gaze malevolent as he stared across the room. Lasser stepped through the hatch beside Corey.

'I should have killed you both when you first came on board,' he said bitterly.

'We all make mistakes,' Lasser replied laconically. 'Yours was in thinking you really could take it with you.'

Chung nodded, his features hardening into a mask of self-control. He glanced at Parish as the rumble of engines through the speakers rose to a steady roar.

'Flood all tanks, Mister Parish.'

Parish swallowed, his eyes wide and frightened. 'You're crazy,' he said hoarsely. 'We won't stand a chance.'

'Flood them!' he ordered.

'Like hell,' Parish replied and reached for the levers.

The sound of the machine-pistol was shattering in the steel room. The bullets smashed into Parish's chest, killing him instantly. Even as he began to fall limply to the floor Chung was swinging the Skorpion, searching for Corey and Lasser. He fired a burst towards the hatch, but they had already dived through into the passage beyond.

The deafening gunshots penetrated the drugged mind of Kitson and he rose to his feet, gazing first at the bloody figure of Parish, then at the woman beside him. He could smell the fear on her, taste the death and evil in the room. Around him the air vibrated with the ping of sonar and the roar of heavy engines overhead. He turned and walked towards the ladder leading up to the bridge in the conning tower.

'Where are you going?' asked Sioo, running after him.

'Out,' he said calmly. 'I am going out.'

She shook her head, clutching at him. 'No, Kitson. That's impossible.'

He took hold of her with both hands and pushed, propelling her back against the periscope so that her feet caught the rim of the well, throwing her off balance. She stumbled, grabbed for the periscope and missed, plunging into the well, crying out in agony as she slammed down into the base of the tube, an ankle breaking with the impact. Kitson ignored her cries and began climbing up into the bridge.

Chung had run to the hatch, firing another burst at the disappearing figure of Corey. He was about to follow when he heard Sioo's cry, turning back with reluctance. He was just in time to see Kitson disappear through the hatch.

The frightened helmsman on the bridge watched Kitson cross the steel deck and climb the rungs up to the conning tower hatch. Only as he reached for the locking bar did he realize what the Captain intended to do. Lunging from his seat he ran towards him, his shrill scream of warning dying in his throat as Kitson pulled the bar over. The water came down like a battering ram, smashing the Captain and the Thai into the deck.

Below them, Chung was kneeling beside the periscope well, reaching for the terrified woman who was frantically pointing up at the bridge.

'Kitson!' she screamed. 'He's getting out!'

Chung started to shake his head, then stopped, realizing that common sense did not apply to Kitson. He rose to his feet, looking up through the hatch. In the dim red light above he saw the Captain reaching for the locking bar. Even as he raised his gun in desperation, he saw the helmsman lunge towards him, then the wall of water coming down. Sioo's piercing scream was lost in the roar of sound. Chung, thrown back by the force of the torrent, grabbed for the periscope. His frantic hand caught hold of a lever and he grabbed it, feeling it give, then turn down. With horrified eyes he watched the heavy periscope slide smoothly into the well, crushing the helpless figure of his daughter. He staggered back, his cry of agony cut off even as it began by the torrent of water that knocked him to the deck, then propelled him like a piece of straw to slam him into the bulkhead with bone-breaking force.

Corey and Lasser had been moving across the mess-deck when they heard Sioo's scream, followed by the unmistakable sound of a hundred tonnes of water hitting the control-room deck. Tim was waiting by the sick-bay, her face still taut with concern for their safety. They began to run, shouting to her. With wide, unbelieving eyes, she watched a wall of water erupt through the hatch behind them. It came like a white, seething demon from hell, roaring around the walls, boiling towards them as her mouth opened to scream.

'Run!' shouted Lee, but she heard nothing but the noise of rushing water. A hand grabbed her arm, pulling her violently along the passage into the engine-room. She staggered in, seeing the grim features of Masters as he let go of her arm and lunged for the hatch.

'No!' she screamed.

He glanced back, grimacing at her terror. A split second later Lasser dived through the hatch, followed by Corey. Masters slammed the steel door, spinning the wheel to lock it even as the sea hit the other side.

Tim clung to Lee, sobbing hysterically. The deck sloped beneath their feet and Masters shouted to Lalonde to kill the motors. They stood and waited, holding on to struts as the angle increased.

'You any idea how deep this area is?' Masters asked.

Corey shook his head. 'I forgot to ask.'

It seemed an age before the submarine hit the bottom, the force knocking them all to the deck and filling the air with the groaning of tortured steel. The lights had cut out as water shorted out circuits in the control room, but within minutes Lalonde had rigged an emergency circuit from the batteries. In the dim glow they walked back past the engines to the aft torpedo room.

'We're sitting tail up on the bottom,' said Masters quietly. 'And with luck we're no more than one hundred and fifty feet down.'

'You mean it matters?' Lasser asked dryly.

'Damned right it does,' Masters replied. 'These subs were used for laying mines as well as torpedoes. You can vary the air charge in the tubes.'

'So?' Lee asked, looking puzzled.

'So you can get out.'

They looked at him in astonishment. Crossing to the four stern tubes he opened the doors on each.

'I can fire you out on low pressure and you'll head for the surface fast. If we're around one hundred and fifty feet you should make it on one very deep breath.'

'And if we're deeper?' Lee asked.

'Then you'll turn into a fish!'

They stood beside the tubes and considered it. Lasser indicated the firing buttons, posing the question in everyone's mind.

'Who lets you out?'

Masters gazed silently at the Israeli. Lalonde started to say something, but Masters gave him a sharp look and he bit off the words.

'What's the alternative?' Lee asked.

'Chlorine gas. The sea water will be in the batteries now, producing gas that will be working its way up towards us. If you're going to go it has to be now.'

'We'll get a diver down to you,' Lee said quietly.

Masters nodded, then moved briskly to the fire controls. Lee helped Tim into the first tube, squeezing her hand, telling her what she must do. She nodded, her eyes big and trusting. He turned away from her quickly in case she saw the doubt.

He was the last to climb into a tube, gazing back at the Englishman. Masters gave him a crooked grin.

'It's a hell of a way to make a living, Corey.'

Lee grimaced. 'You're reading my mind.'

Masters closed the door and locked it, then went to the controls and pressurized the tubes. After checking the dials, he opened the outer doors and stabbed the buttons in quick succession. The only sound was a hiss of air, but the four of them were on their way to the surface.

Leaving the torpedo room, he went back to the engines and sat on the edge of the platform. It was very still, but peaceful, he decided. Picking up a wad of cotton he began to polish the number one engine. A thick green mist had begun to seep up through the metal grille. He ignored it, continuing to polish. After a while he began to whistle.